Also by Christina Hopkinson

Cyber Cinderella

The Pile of Stuff
at the Bottom of the Stairs

The Pile of Stuff
at the Bottom
of the Stairs

CHRISTINA HOPKINSON

GRAND CENTRAL
PUBLISHING

NEW YORK   BOSTON

Grand Central Publishing
Hachette Book Group
237 Park Avenue
New York, NY 10017

www.HachetteBookGroup.com

Printed in the United States of America

First U.S. Edition: April 2011
10 9 8 7 6 5 4 3 2 1

First published in Great Britain in 2011 by Hodder & Stoughton,
an Hachette UK Company.

Grand Central Publishing is a division of Hachette Book Group, Inc.
The Grand Central Publishing name and logo is a trademark of
Hachette Book Group, Inc.

The publisher is not responsible for websites (or their content)
that are not owned by the publisher.

Library of Congress Control Number: 2010937506
ISBN: 978-0-446-57318-4

To Alex—you constantly inspire me but you are *not* the inspiration for the story of a grumpy woman married to an untidy man.

The Pile of Stuff
at the Bottom of the Stairs

I

The Pile of Stuff

The solitary jigsaw piece sits in the corner of the living room,
daring me to ignore it. It is a battle of wills between me and it. I
try to stare it out, but the corner section of a 32-piece puzzle of a
dog flying an airplane wins, of course.

"What are you doing?" asks Joel, who is setting up our latest DVD box set, a classy American import with impenetrable
dialogue.

I'm rifling through the shelves to find the puzzle that it belongs
to. "I can't watch TV knowing there's a stray jigsaw piece. Think
how annoying it will be next time we do the jigsaw and the last
bit is missing."

"Chillax, Mary."

"Chillax? What are you? Twelve? Don't you think that vam-
pires are, like, the coolest things?"

He laughs and gets on with his episode selection.

The world divides between those who can watch television
knowing there's an isolated jigsaw fragment lying on the floor
and those who can't. While I'm down there I look under the sofa
to see if there are any of its colleagues and I see something else:
a cup. I look inside it and realize that it's been buried there for
weeks, but the tide has finally washed it ashore. I think it once
had coffee in it, but it's hard to tell now that a mold lathers up

its sides like a green-tinged cappuccino froth. Since I drink only expensive soy lattes, I know it belongs to my husband.

"Look at this," I say as I thrust it in his face.

He doesn't recoil, but peers at it with interest. "Don't you think it looks like one of those foams that they put around food in fashionable restaurants? I don't know, hand-stacked quail confit with spume of snail extract." He looks closer. "We should show it to Rufus. He'd be really interested to see how spores form."

"Are you going to take it to the kitchen?"

"How do you know it's mine?"

"Because this is the mug you always use because it's so big, which is great because it means you can always leave some at the bottom for someone to spill." He shrugs and presses play on the DVD. "Well, aren't you?" One, two, three, I count slowly, just as I learned in an article I read recently about anger management.

"Laters."

"When later?"

He turns the sound up on the TV. I increase the volume of my sigh and stare at him hard. I crack first, I always do, and take the mug to the kitchen. I tip its contents down the sink and manually squish the bits of mold through the sieve that guards the plughole. My husband's cup overflows with fungi. Mine with fury and irritation.

"Joel," I shout on my return, having dispensed with both the mug and any attempts to avoid being angry. "I'm fed up with living in this squalor." No response. "If you just tidied up as you went along..."

He's entered that trance that our sons do when placed in front of a TV. I half expect him to go and sit with his face six inches from the screen. I try again, this time actually stamping my feet like Rumpelstiltskin. "You never do a thing around here, you're worse than a child; my life would be so much easier if I had only

2

two boys to contend with. You, you," I splutter, groping for the best example to illustrate his total blindness to the quantities of detritus that I sweep away for him, "you don't see how much I do. And how little you do."

"Like what?" he says, finally.

"I don't know, it's not like I keep a list," I said.

"Maybe you should."

"Maybe I will."

A list, I think the next day, maybe I should keep a list. One with all the things he does or doesn't do around the house. I can't see any other way of making him understand the state we're in. What would I do with this list? Is making a list yet another thing that falls onto my plate, while the only thing on his is large hunks of meat?

I'm distracted by Gabe, who has retreated to the corner of the kitchen with the look of a mathematician thinking about the world's largest prime number.

"Gabe, what are you doing? Wait, don't do it, wait, wait, wait, let me get the potty. Here it is." His trousers are whipped off and his bottom planted just in time to catch the daily event around which my life seems to revolve. "Well done," I exclaim brightly, though in reality it's more my triumph than his. "You are such a clever boy." I hug him, which is ill-advised as I haven't yet done a thorough wipe. "And clever boys get stickers."

I go to the chart on the fridge door that proclaims to the world all of my second born's successful encounters with the potty. There are not very many of them. "Here we are, football or dinosaur?"

We've had four months of more poo than a pig farm but we finally seem to be getting somewhere. I've always been skeptical about star charts, but our newly instituted one appears to be effective. He gets a sticker or a star for every potty success, every painless exit from the house to get Rufus to school and every prompt bedtime. There are no black marks for misdemeanors, not because Gabe is the sort of child who is free from sin, far from it, but because we're the sort of craven parents who can't bear to tell our children off. (And when we do dare to give them the meat of criticism, we have to douse it in the ketchup of endearments. "I'm not sure everyone else in the restaurant wants to hear you make farty noises, *darling*," "*Sweetheart*, Mommy doesn't like it when you hit her.")

"Superstar Gabe, you are well on your way to getting that Thomas the Tank Engine Aquadraw Deluxe set." If only Joel were so easy to train.

And that's when it hits me. Of course: that's what I can do with the list of everything he does to annoy me. I will make the spousal equivalent of a star chart. Except because he's 38, not two and a half, he won't get a star for every good thing that he does, but a black mark for every bad one.

I shall compile a list of all that he does to irritate me and then I'll note how often he commits one of these sins. It will be an accurate account of every balled-up tissue left on the side, every empty carton of milk put back in the fridge, every pile of laundry ignored, every time I've had to put my hand in the kitchen sink to pull out those grotty bits of yuk he never seems to notice. It will be a spreadsheet detailing all misbehavior over a period of, let's say, six months.

I haven't felt such excitement in years. It reminds me of how I used to feel when in the early stages of developing a new format at work. Everything is falling into place. It is brilliant. I am brilliant.

My list will be a thing of beauty and efficiency, a work of art of Excel and observation. If it were published, it would be admired, but I'm not going to stick it up in the kitchen like Gabe's star chart, amid the party invitations, school dates and shopping lists. Joel's not a potty-training toddler, but a grown man with more than a fortnight to prove himself. And he won't be getting a Thomas the Tank Engine branded treat as a reward, no he won't.

If my list, his star chart, proves him to be an asset in this house then he gets to stay in it. If it doesn't, well, I suppose that means he doesn't and we will have to rethink everything we've ever believed about this marriage.

So here's the thing, Joel: all you have to do is avoid making me angry.

The problem is, I'm angry most of the time. I'm so permanently irritated that I feel that my life is narrated in CAPITAL LETTERS.

I know I'm not supposed to be angry. I am supposed to be able to "manage" that emotion, just as I manage people and budgets at work. Anger is not fashionable or righteous anymore; we are not storming barricades and taking pride in it. It is an "inappropriate" emotion.

It's not as if I'm entirely one-dimensional; my moods are nuanced. I can range from mildly irked right through to incandescent fury, but anger is the umbrella emotion under which these gradations shelter from many things that provoke them.

Things that make me angry include: the phrases "too posh to push," "methinks she doth protest too much," "reader, I married him" and "it is a truth universally acknowledged"; baby girls with slutty whores' names like Lola, Delilah, Jezebel, Lulu and Scarlett; any use of the word "mummy" unless uttered by a child to its mother (yummy mummy, mummy tummy, slummy mummy); people talking about size zero and middle youth.

I'm angry that I work; I'd be even angrier if I didn't.

Most of all I'm angry at you, Joel. And if I could distill this anger to its purest essence, it would consist of some bracken dishwater with floating bits of lamb chop grease in it to represent your total inability to help around the house. So not very pure at all; in fact, not so much an essential oil as an oil slick of filth polluting my hearth and heart.

It's not my fault I'm angry. I was always destined to be so. My parents used to tell me that I was born during the Winter of Discontent, which I believed and I think they did too. I grew up with tales of how my parents had battled through streets stacked high with uncollected rubbish and stench to a power-cut hospital unmanned by striking midwives. Then I read that the Winter of Discontent actually occurred some years later and I had merely been born during a freakish cold snap and it was snow rather than rubbish that was piled high. But the myth was there, that I had been born during a national strop, a collective temper tantrum. "You're just like a union leader," my parents used to tell me, "always whining." They'd snap "Life isn't" at me, whenever I uttered the phrase "It's not fair."

How much sunnier I would have been, went the family joke, had I been born during the Summer of Love instead.

And just to compound matters, my parents named me Mary. As in quite contrary, which my mother tells me I was from a preternaturally early age. Even in the womb, I reacted furiously to any food other than white bread and water, giving my mother violent morning sickness morning, noon and night for the full nine months of pregnancy. Once born, I refused to drink the cheapest brand of formula. I refused to be laid down on my front, as was prescribed in those medically incorrect times, but screamed and screamed until put on my back. I frowned until furrows lined my face, but failed to smile until almost three months old. I scratched myself so much I was forced to wear tight mittens all the time. My colicky crying time was not limited to early evenings, but lasted all day and much of the night. My bottom, my mother tells me, was an angry red too—so bad was my diaper rash that it bled. (Looking back, it seems evident that I was suffering from an extreme dairy intolerance that would have been easily rectified had I been breastfed by a mother prepared not to drink cow's milk herself, and, yes, I am a bit angry about that too.)

These facts alone were enough to ensure my choleric temperament, but then my newborn head's colorless fuzz soon gave way to bright red hair. Not auburn, nor titian, nor merely "warm," but proper red. Otherwise referred to by well-meaning folk as "At least it's not ginger," a shade of hair color also known as "Well, it's OK on a *girl*" (this latter frequently said in the presence of my similarly flame-haired firstborn boy child). Red hair, like big boobs and poker-straight tresses, is one of those things that people strive to achieve through artifice but decry if natural. Think of all those millions spent on henna and hair dye and yet when you've got it naturally you just get "Well, at least it's not ginger." And when the child with red hair first throws the standard toddler temper tantrum that all do some time after the age of one, everybody says, "Ooh, isn't she fiery?" instead of "Look at that toddler throwing a tantrum as toddlers are wont to do." To this day, I'm not allowed to show the slightest ill temper without someone referring to my hair color. I'm a "feisty redhead" if liked and a "ginger whinger" if not.

So, you see, it really isn't my fault I'm so angry. I was born this way.

I'm 35, though not for much longer. Thirty-five: the age at which fertility falls off a cliff, apparently, and so looms large in the forward planning of any early thirtysomething. It's the age that we women must skirt and plot around. Thirty-five, the midpoint of your thirties, the decade in which you must both churn out children and soar in your chosen career. The crucial decade when lawyers become partners, journalists become editors, doctors become consultants and teachers become heads and deputy heads. One small decade, only ten years, just like the rest of them. What bad luck for women that these biological and professional imperatives should coincide and collide so exactly. This coincidence double-glazes the glass ceiling.

The thirties are also a woman's peak time for death in mysterious circumstances. Sylvia Plath, Princess Diana, Marilyn Monroe, Paula Yates, Jill Dando, Anna Nicole Smith. It's a wonder that any of us make it through alive.

Actually, I'm not sure there is any mystery to Sylvia Plath's death. She hadn't really set out to kill herself, she'd just been examining the inside of the oven to see whether it needed cleaning or not and on finding it quite so filthy with the fat spat from the sausages that Ted Hughes had cooked before dumping her for another woman, she decided to switch it on and keep her head in there.

I'd never kill myself. Though I might kill Joel. The list is my attempt to avoid blighting my sons' lives with a dead father and a mother locked up for his murder.

At least Christmas is now over. I don't know why they said that the First World War would be over by Christmas when there's no time of the year more likely to spark battles and hatred. A dozen explosions and skirmishes daily over the festivities: me buying all the presents for your numerous godchildren; the fact that you don't "believe" in Christmas cards so I have to do them all as well as sit over Rufus as he labors over one for each of his classmates; your mother sitting on her ample behind telling me how lucky I am that she brought up her son to be such a hands-on father and fabulous cook. "Yes," I spit, "he's so *wonderful*, I'm so *lucky*."

No turkey could have been stuffed as full as this house was by discarded wrapping paper and toys with itty-bitty constituent parts. Each time a present was opened, which was approximately every three seconds, I'd wince at the challenge of finding somewhere to put the vast plastic monstrosity or cringe at the tiny, easily lost parts that spilled out. I tried to feel happy as my children squealed with delight, but instead I'd be filled with dread. Each time we played with one of these new games, I'd interrupt with "Don't lose that counter, darling, it won't work without it," "No, you're not allowed a hotel until you've put up three blocks," "Gabe, if you choke on that I'm not going to be the one to take you to the hospital."

I've got three weeks to go until my birthday, which falls on the last day of January. See what I mean about my life being destined to complaint? Fancy having a birthday at the exact point in the year when everyone feels most depressed. When half the people at your so-called birthday celebrations are on the wagon or detoxing.

For my birthday, I'd like teeth-whitening, a week off from bottom-wiping both real and metaphorical and a subscription to *Interiors*. For my birthday, I'll get a homemade card, a croissant in bed and a "kiss that money can't buy." My first words on turning 36 will be "Don't get crumbs on the bed."

For these three weeks I shall be thinking of every irritating thing that Joel does and compiling them into a list. I will then organize these misdemeanors into logical sections on a spreadsheet. After my birthday, from February onward, the six-month trial period will start as I mark his behavior against the debits outlined in the document. The system will be rigorous and able to withstand scrutiny should I ever show it to Joel, which I might if he needs to see proof. It has to be as perfect as our home and marriage is imperfect. It shall be a feat of Excel formatting and punchy punctuation. It will be definitive. It will be scrupulously fair even if, so I'm told, life isn't.

Let the list-making begin.

Here is my dream of a perfect Saturday. The boys are such champion sleepers that I have to wake them at nine, whereupon they wolf down their quinoa porridge before settling down to some educative but tidy art activities. A shadowy employee with wet wipes for hands hovers in the background, cleaning away, freeing me to engage fully with Rufus and Gabe, who greet all my suggestions with enthusiasm and don't get cross when I try to make their abstract daubs "look more like something." We join our good-looking friends and their good-looking offspring for a jolly brunch and afterward our children are whisked away by the delightful and loving nanny-housekeeper figure long enough for me to enjoy my freedom from them, but not so long that I miss them too much. Perhaps a shopping expedition to pick up a party frock for the evening's event. A little trip to the cinema. To the hairdressers for what Americans call a "blow out." An hour spent getting ready, moisturizer, primer, foundation, highlighter and blusher; three different sorts of eyeshadow; lip liner, lipstick and gloss. The party—tinkling laughter, champagne, cocktails, tipsy not drunk. Home at midnight, safe in the knowledge that my darling boys will not wake until late on Sunday, when the four of us will lie together in our vast, specially designed bed before having a playful fight with our pillows covered in 1,000-thread-count Egyptian cotton cases.

Or, welcome to the reality of my Saturday.

Having played our usual game of nocturnal musical beds, Joel is on the floor in the boys' room, while Gabe has taken his place in the marital bed. Except he's cunningly expanded his tiny two-and-a-half-year-old body to ensure that at least two of my limbs overhang the edge. I look at the clock and at least the time begins with a six, though only just. The street light pours through the bit where the curtains fail to meet and shows me more of my surroundings than I want to see.

Our bedroom looks like a terrorist attack in the Gap.

1) *Leaves clothes anywhere but the laundry basket. Or, rather, either of the two laundry baskets that I introduced for a new system of separating whites from coloreds. When I explained the new system, he said he wasn't going to practice laundry apartheid and then went off giggling at his wit. He made a similar comment about repatriation of socks and the extraordinary rendition of his last remaining clean underpants that I held hostage in a bid to get him to contribute help as well as clothes to the laundry. He keeps claiming amnesty from the totalitarian regime of my impotent laundry systems.*

   Though I suppose I should be glad that he's consistent in dropping his clothes on the floor, in a little crumpled ring at his feet. My friend Jill's husband puts things in the laundry basket on the days they're both working, but on the one day she works from home and at weekends, he leaves them on the floor, like then it's her "job" to pick them up.

It's symbolic that Gabe has taken Joel's place in my bed because in many ways he's also annexed the place in my heart that contains what's left of my patience, generosity and indulgence. Gabe and I are always going off on old-fashioned dates, sharing a decaf latte in the café and splodging the frothy soy milk onto one another's noses, wandering around farmers' markets and playing hide-and-seek in museums, before settling down to share a bed for the night. He's currently sprawled on top of me and any sensual urge I may have for physical contact from Joel is sated by Gabe. Joel once said he felt like he'd been superseded by a younger and cuter version of himself.

An odor winds its way up to my nose. This younger and cuter version of Joel is also incontinent. I've been sharing my bed with a male packing a full, oh let's see, actually overflowing, excrement-filled diaper. "Sweetheart, can't you tell me when you've done a poo and I'll change you, or even better let's go to the potty. You know you get a sticker if you do that." He gives a look of satisfaction, akin to that of a ten-year-old who's just done a "silent-but-deadly" fart over his little sister's face. He's supposed to be potty trained, night as well as day. Mitzi's kids are always dry through the night by this age. "And hasn't anybody told you it's the weekend?" I mutter to him. He continues to bounce on the bed, shaking that perilous diaper as he does so. "That hurts. Mommy doesn't like it when you jump on her, please, sweetheart."

"Breakfast, breakfast, breakfast," he sings to an indeterminate nursery rhyme tune. They're kind of all the same, like hymns.

I've drawn the short straw today with this boy child, since he wakes up a full hour before Joel's charge.

"Good afternoon," I say, when he and Rufus eventually come down to breakfast.

"I know, the decadence of it, quarter past seven."

"Still, an extra hour."

"Sleeping on the bottom bunk of a bed made for dwarves. Every time I sit up I get my hair caught in the springs above me."

I watch him get breakfast for Rufus. He rips the packet like he's wearing gardening gloves and a blindfold.

2) *Sprays cereal around the kitchen as if he's turned on a leaf blower near an open packet of Special K.*

3) *Puts used tea bags in the sink. Why do people do this? Sometimes they have little bowls for them instead, which is marginally less annoying, but still, why not just put them straight in the bin—or, if you're being environmentally sound (which of course you should be and everything, but sometimes I just can't be bothered to go to the recycling box and I love my tumble dryer, I really do, I shall definitely be getting custody of that in the divorce), in the compost container?*

4) *Puts used tea bag in the sink after making a cup of tea for himself without offering to make me one.*

5) *Can't remember how I have my tea. Soy milk, no sugar. Not that difficult, is it?*

6) *Calls herbal tea "boiled pants" because that's what he says it tastes like. Better than one bloke I went out with who consistently referred to it as "lesbian tea."*

"I don't like the tiny bits of Shreddies," says Rufus.

Gabe shares this opinion but expresses it by coughing the crumbs up onto the table.

"That's disgusting," observes Rufus, correctly.

"You make them better," says Gabe, pointing at me. "You make them big. Make them big again. I want big Shreddies."

"There's a word missing, Gabe? I want big Shreddies..."

"NOW!" he screams.

"No, that's not the answer I was looking for. I want big Shreddies..."

13

"HERE!"

"No, 'please'—'please' was the word I was looking for. You've had two pieces of toast already, do you really want cereal too?"

"We're running out of Shreddies, by the way," says Joel.

7) *Tells me stuff is running out in a really accusatory way. After it's already run out. And won't chalk it up onto the shopping list on the section of kitchen wall painted in blackboard paint, something I copied off the interiors magazines I can't stop myself from buying. Except in the magazines someone has always scrawled "I* ♥ *you" in those pictures, alongside a shopping list that includes Goji berries and champagne.*

"I'll nip down to the shop to get some more," I say.

"No, I'll do it."

"No, really, I'll go."

"No, I insist."

We look at each other. "First to the door," he shouts and being a man, he already has his wallet in his pocket, good to go, and beats me to it.

I'm left to deal with the ongoing tantrum of our second child, the dauphin, whom our lives revolve around. When I have calmed his fury over the tiny bits of Shreddies and distracted him with alternative sustenance, he demands that I get the yogurt out of his stomach and back into the pot. I am then admonished for having got the spoon out of the drawer for him. I put it back and invite him to get it out. It's too late then, of course, I've already ruined everything. He has turned me into some sort of Arthurian knight who is set a series of impossible challenges in order to win his hand. I am asked to rid sausages of the brown bits, make fruit slices drier, reattach clipped fingernails, make rainy days

14

sunny and change the colors of the clothes in his picture books. In our house, the devil wears Primark boys' combat trousers in a 2–3 and a secondhand stripy T-shirt from Baby Gap.

Calm has been restored when Joel returns with the new packet of un-crumbled Shreddies.

"What are we doing today?" he asks—because I'm his PA, obviously.

"Rufus's swimming lesson. You take him every week."

"Oh, right. Where's his stuff?"

"In the bag in the cupboard by the door." Where it always is. "And then it's Mahalia's party in the afternoon. Have you got her a present?"

He looks very confused. "Mahalia? Remind me."

"Mitzi's second kid, bit younger than Rufus."

"I can't keep track of them."

"Molyneux, he's six or seven, Mahalia, then the twins, Merle and the boy one. What is his name? Begins with an M."

"Obviously."

"I was joking about the present; don't worry about it, I think there's something in the present drawer." Present drawer. I have a present drawer. When did I get to be the sort of person who has a present drawer? "Milburn, that's the boy twin's name, Milburn."

8) *Puts milk bottles and cartons back in the fridge if they're empty. That's not fair mostly he makes sure there's a couple of drops left in them to save them from unequivocal emptiness. But weirdly, he will always leave the bottles with lots of milk in them out on the counter in order that they go sour.*

9) *Takes the stickers off bananas and apples and sticks them on the kitchen table.*

I whirl around the kitchen picking up, wiping, depositing and washing as I go. I make sure Rufus's swimming stuff, coat and outdoor shoes are ready at the door while trying to phone Mitzi to check what time the party is.

"Have you seen the car keys?" Joel asks me. Most of the sentences we utter to one another start with the word "where" or some such variant.

10) *Asks me questions when I'm talking to someone else on the phone.*

"Sorry, Mitzi, I'm being summoned. Aren't they on the hook in the kitchen where they're supposed to be kept?"

"No, that's why I'm asking."

"Well, I always put them back there. You must have left them somewhere else."

"I haven't used the car in ages."

This is true. I scurry into the kitchen, hoping that I'll find them on the hook where they're supposed to be. Which they are, although partially obscured by a mug.

11) *Asks me where something is and I tell him and he doesn't look properly so I have to go and find it for him myself. If I say something's in the fridge, he won't see it unless it's in the front of the fridge, as if it's too much effort to move the jar of chutney that's permanently rooted to a piece of prime fridge real estate.*

"Oh, look, on the kitchen hook, where I said they were." I hand them to him and make a dash for the safety of the sitting room, doing what he's usually better at doing than I am—leaving the children and assuming that someone else (me) will look after them. I sort out the time of Mahalia's party and then start hunting around.

"Joel!" No answer. "Joe-WELL! Which one of these effing cables is for the laptop?"

"The black one," he shouts back, eventually. I look down at the nest of vipers at my feet, a coiling mass of unmarked and mostly black cables. These phone, camera and computer chargers have joined old keys as things we can no longer throw away for fear that the moment we do so, we'll discover both what they are for and a need to use them.

"I told you to mark any new ones with a label and then put them all back in their original boxes together with their electronic husband."

"Oh well," he says. "Looks like they're getting a divorce."

You may joke, I think, with a strange jolt of satisfaction at hearing him say the word out loud. "I know it sounds like I'm being anal, but I say it for a reason. Now I can't find the laptop charger and it looks exactly the same as the one for the camcorder and we've got five different mobile chargers and I can't work out which one is for the old phone. And what's this?" I pick up a lonely white cable.

"For your old toothbrush?"

I stomp off, though he doesn't notice as he's become engrossed in playing back some footage on the camcorder that he shot of the boys on holiday. "Bugger," I hear him shout. "The battery's gone. Where have you put the charger?"

12) *The way he leaves all the phone chargers and cables out so that I can never work out which electronic item they belong to.*

My path away from him is impeded by a blockade of shoes, buggies, scooters, bikes, helmets, the recycling box and the disgorging contents of a mini packet of raisins that I manage to further squash into our neutral-colored and, in retrospect, far too pale sisal carpeting.

The stairs provide a new hurdle. At the bottom of each flight and half-flight in our house are small foothills of debris: slippers, books and clean clothes on their way up; old newspapers, empty glasses mottled with evaporated wine and dirty clothes on their way down. They say that the peak of Everest has become strewn with rubbish. I bet it looks like the landings of our house.

13) *The way he can ignore the pile of stuff at the bottom of the stairs.*

Like a driver reversing his 4×4, Joel has a dangerous blind spot when it comes to the stairs that allows him to trot past these stations without ever thinking that perhaps he should pick this stuff up; an ignorance of the fact that humans are the conveyor belt that will carry it home. I once decided to let it all pile up to show him how much I was frantically shoveling to keep this house clear. Gradually the possessions silted up our stairs until they formed barricades. Still he managed to ignore them, actually vaulting over to reach his destination. Then, one day, poor Rufus slipped on an empty packet of Kettle Chips and hit his head against the balustrade and we ended up in the ER. I felt guilty, of course, but it was Joel's fault.

I lock myself in the bathroom, hunch over the laptop with its fast-fading battery and click on a document called "House admin" (it's a safe bet that Joel will never open that one). I type furiously in all senses of the word, finishing off with a last flourish:

14) *Never hangs up the swimming stuff but leaves it in the bag to go moldy.*

I'm obsessed with cleaning and housework, but my house doesn't appear to reflect my pathology. If I described someone as being obsessed with cleaning, you'd assume their house to be spotless with vacuumed upholstery and cupboards filled with alpha-betized Tupperware for their extensive rice collection. No, I'm obsessed with cleaning and yet live in a filthy home, which is a raw deal, much like it is for my friend Daisy, who complains that she was built with the ample curves of an opera singer, but with a voice so bad that she has to mime "Happy Birthday" so as not to ruin anybody's party.

Nobody talks about cleaning. Why would they? It's bloody boring to do and even more boring to talk about, but it's there. It's a dirty secret that we don't want to admit to. Well, I'm going to come clean. I spend more time on sweeping, tidying, home management and wiping than on anything else in my life. It's my hated hobby, my pastime. Now that I've gone part-time in the office, I think I may actually spend more time on housework than paid work. You'd never know the extent of my cleaning load by my conversations with others or by my outward appear-ance, and least of all by the outward appearance of my house. Nobody ever talks about cleaning or seems to show that they do much, yet they live in spotless, ordered houses. It's as if their houses are cleaned by osmosis, or fairies that come in the night, or mute Brazilians on £7 an hour.

Everybody bangs on about sex, but I spend many more min-utes cleaning, doing laundry, tidying and bill-paying than I ever will having sex. It's very likely that I spend more time thinking about it too.

Nobody talks about cleaning except my mother, and lord how

my sister and I despised her for it. Jemima and I didn't do cleaning, you see, because we were feminists. The funny thing about feminism is that it hasn't actually decreased the amount of washing to be done and surfaces to be wiped, nor does it seem to have increased the amount of time men spend doing it, either.

Where do other people put their phone chargers? Where do they lurk? I don't understand other people's houses. Where are the odd socks and junk mail? Where have they secreted the broken toys, incomplete jigsaw puzzles and spare coats? Other people's homes look as if they are on permanent standby for estate agents and buyers' viewings when they are not even on the market. If we ever wanted to sell our place, then we'd have to hire another house just to hide all our clutter.

Perhaps that's the secret. That the owners of all these inexplicably perfect homes have another place down the road that's a moldering mess of outgrown baby clothes, broken toys, unopened mail, half-filled handbags and muddy shoes. It's the house equivalent of the picture of Dorian Gray, allowing their owners to present their perfect lives while hiding their increasingly squalid parallel home.

When I talk about perfect houses, I suppose I'm really thinking about Mitzi's. In Mitzi's house, there's a place for everything except unsightly door knobs. Instead, kitchen doors just ping open at your touch to reveal a bespoke compost repository or a recycling area pre-divided into cans, papers and bottles. Since marrying into money, Mitzi has come to believe that windows are the windows of the soul, especially when they are draped with curtains made from reclaimed Welsh farmhouse bedspreads.

Mitzi's house has hallways off hallways and a separate utility room with space to hang up clothes to dry and so avoid using the tumble dryer, thus offsetting the carbon used on all those skiing trips and half-term jaunts.

Rich people turn left to first class when they get on a plane. When you go to houses like Mitzi's you don't just walk into the kitchen, but are automatically spirited upward to begin the tour of the house and to admire its latest incarnation, which either involves stripping back or reinstating the original fittings, depending on the year. There is no interiors trend too fleeting to have not been embraced by Mitzi. One wall covered in ornate Timorous Beasties wallpaper at a hundred pounds a roll—check; reinforced glass balcony—check; oddly sized black-and-white photos of her children gliding up the staircase—check. Then there are the quirky individual touches that the rest of us swoon over, which usually testify still further to the perfection of her life and love. The coffee table papered with an antique map of Sicily, where she and Michael spent their honeymoon. The subtle pattern below the cornicing in the hall that is made up of a series of interlocking Ms. The wallpaper in the downstairs loo that is their wedding invitation blown up to a hundred times its original size. The same room's industrial concrete floor with each member of the family's footprints immortalized, including the tiny ones of whichever of the brood was newly born at that time (these redecorations tend to coincide with the arrival of a new baby, but then, as Mitzi has had four of them over three pregnancies, most things do).

Mitzi's current project involves the greenification of her 4,000-square-foot house with wind turbines and solar panels, rather than just ugly old loft insulation like the rest of us. Her new-found mania for all things environmental has opened up whole avenues of consumerism that she is enthusiastically motoring down in her brand-new Lexus hybrid.

I like to go to Mitzi's house and sneak upstairs while the other women are having handcrafted organic flapjacks in the kitchen and peer into all the bedrooms, half hoping to find them a shambles, just this once. I always offer to help make the tea as an excuse to thrust open the cupboards and admire the way that her foodstuffs are arranged in the larder (a larder! Just imagine), with flour that comes dressed in old-fashioned sackcloth and jars filled with exotic dried beans.

Later in my Saturday I cook lunch. Or lunches, since every member of the house has a different food issue. Rufus at a ridiculously young age has decided he doesn't eat anything with a face (bless him for his emotional intelligence but curse him for the hassle); Joel doesn't eat anything without one. Gabe won't eat anything at all, really; he has the dietary habits of a Hollywood starlet, all uncooked frozen peas and rice cakes. I have whatever anybody else leaves over. Unless of course it's dairy, because I've got a proper intolerance to that rather than all these made-up allergies that the males in my family claim to suffer from.

"Joel, can you clear up a bit so we can actually eat?"

15) *Puts wet tea towels back in the clean tea-towel drawer. When something does spill on the floor, he uses a tea towel to dry it up rather than the mop.*

16) *Goes on about how he does all the cooking, which he doesn't. He does all the grandstanding, while I do all the boring everyday stuff—the reheating, rehashing, pureeing. When he does cook, he expects me to be some sort of sous chef to him, fetching, carrying, chopping and washing up his saucepans as he goes along. When I cook, I cook alone.*

17) *Calls saucepans and pots "the scary ones" and doesn't touch them when it's his turn to do the washing-up.*

"How was swimming?"

"Good, thank you," says Rufus. I have a suspicion that Gabe

will remain in touch with his inner tantruming two-year-old for the rest of his life, but Rufus can sometimes sound as if he's channeling the spirit of a taciturn octogenarian. He is like everybody's favorite granddad and I adore him for it (though wish at the same time that he might tell me just a little bit more about his day at school).

"Who was there?"

"Nobody."

"What, not even the teacher?"

Rufus rolls his eyes. "The teacher was there, silly."

"And about six other kids," adds Joel. "The mother with the string bikini."

"And the heeled flip-flops?" I add. "And the extraordinary abs?"

"That's the one. And the really fat woman with the bleached hair."

"And the inexplicably hot black partner? I don't get that one at all."

"Actually, can I say something?" asks Rufus. "It's not appropriate"—he pronounces the word as if it's filled with "b"s—"to talk about the way people look. Even if they are a fat pig. Why are you squeezing me, Mommy?"

"Because you are so sweet and serious."

He wriggles away from me. "It is serious. We're not allowed to say nasty words."

"Like what?"

"Oh my god," he whispers.

"Is that what they teach you at school these days?" asks Joel. "Of course, they're completely right." I catch Joel's eye and we both stifle smirks before I'm distracted by a pile of unscraped and unwashed plates piled precariously on the worktop.

"Can't you put these in the dishwasher?"

"Nah, it's already full."

18) *Dishwasher—never empties it, although he has been known to take out a couple of clean items should he need them. Or sometimes he just takes a few things out in order to put some dirty things in amid the clean ones. Or just leaves those dirty ones on top of the counter with the words "the dishwasher's full." Or, on the rare occasions he does empty, he just puts the clean things on the side in piles for me to put into the cupboards properly. And if he should deign to put something in, stacks from the front so I have to reorder everything.*

Any feeling of closeness to Joel evaporates and I feel exhaustion wash over me. "If I take the boys to Mahalia's party and give you a break then, can I go and have a nap now?" Of such horse-trading parents' weekends are made.

"Sure."

"Me sleep with Mommy," says Gabe. "Please, Mommy. Me a little bit tired." Oh, the unfairness, I think—first, that both his childcare stints today will consist of pushover Rufus, and that even while napping I will not be spared the demands of our second born. What I lose in sleep, however, I will gain in the human hot-water bottle warmth that my chubby cherub provides.

19) *Tells me it's bad to let our sons watch too much TV (of course, his mother, Ursula, didn't even have one in the house when he was a boy, and he would go and stand outside the TV rentals shop for hours to stare at the magic moving images. Which is probably why he's ended up making*

programs to go on it as a grown-up) and yet when he's on duty, it's permanently switched to CBeebies.

"Fine, but if you come into Mommy's bed you have to sleep, OK? No mucking around. Really, I mean it."

Some time and no sleep later, I am trudging to Mitzi's house. While pushing a buggy, you always trudge, never trot. It's not far away geographically, but light-years away socially.

I almost expect a maid to let me in, given the house's imposing double doors, but this type of rich person tends to keep her servants a secret. That's not to say she doesn't have any. Mitzi has such a large retinue that running her house is like managing a small corporation. She occasionally complains in hushed tones about one or other of her staff—the nanny, the au pair, the masseur, the cleaner, the acupuncturist, the guy who does the lawn—and I try to feel sorry for her, but it's really hard to sound like a nice person when one is talking of the modern servant problem.

Michael opens the door. I wish I could say that he's short, bald and fat, but he combines money with height and dark hair that's graying at the temples in the way that Hollywood make-up artists apply fake white to denote age and distinction. I think he's what you'd call a silver fox.

"Good to see you," he says. I can't tell if he means this. Some of my friends' husbands have never morphed into the mates category. He retains all of the scary elusiveness that schoolfriends' dads used to when we were children. Without even asking, you know he's going to have a special kitchen chair with arms that nobody else is allowed to sit in and might get grumpy if you mess up the newspaper before he's read it.

Mitzi doesn't have to relocate her children's parties to the local church hall, so cavernous is her kitchen-dining-family-whatever room. When Mitzi invites you to a dinner party, she always says it's "just a kitchen supper." Which is like calling her kitchen "just a kitchen" when it is in fact a 40-by-20-foot glass-cased temple to food, families and the good life. It's got the same stuff in it as our kitchen, what they refer to in department stores as white goods—except of course in Mitzi's they're not white, they are galvanized steel, and everything is twice the usual size: a double oven, a two-doored fridge, a reclaimed medieval refectory table that comfortably seats 20, a separate utility room. We're all about eating at home these days, but filling our kitchens with industrial catering equipment.

People seem to be breeding a need for more space in their house, don't they? Children don't share bedrooms. Their rooms must double up as sort of kiddie offices cum leisure centers with a desk and a computer, a TV and a DVD player. We need enormous rooms to do everything in as a family, but then we realize how grim it is to do everything as a family, so we yearn for all these private anterooms: the home cinema, the library, the gym. Except Mitzi doesn't yearn—she has.

20) ~~Doesn't earn shedloads of money in the City so that I can have a vast number of rooms that somebody else cleans for me.~~

I scratch that one from my mind and vow not to include it on the list, feeling a blast of shame. I'd hate to have one of those big money banker type husbands. It's not as if money buys everything. Though it does buy quite a lot of handstitched soft furnishings, I can't help but notice.

Michael ushers me into the kitchen palace where women who

look too skinny to menstruate let alone give birth sit sipping champagne (champagne! Not just sparkling or cava), while children dressed in exquisite clothes frolic. I recognize a few faces from the book group I go to and from all the birthday parties and christenings and celebrations of Mitzi and Michael's fecundity that have been held over the years. We friends of Mitzi are like readers of a celebrity magazine, invited regularly into her lovely home to coo at newborns and new extensions.

Mitzi canters over to me. "Mary! How brilliant to see you." She manages to make it seem like she really, really means it. That's the thing—I want to mock Mitzi, but then she's like this, so effortlessly disarming. She's doing casual but is glammed up by her trademark vermilion lipstick. Everything is trademark in Mitzi's world. It's like the way she doesn't buy things, she "sources" them.

"And vice versa. Have you bought another new car?" I hate myself for having noticed the G-Wiz parked next to the Lexus. I hate that I care what car they have parked on their off-street parking. I hate that I care that they have off-street parking.

"Dear, isn't it? It's so miniature, the kids love it. And so environmentally sound. I don't have to pay the congestion charge and I can practically park it anywhere. Now we've got the Lexus hybrid and this one so we're really cutting down our emissions."

"Gosh, two environmentally friendly cars. I guess that makes you twice as green as us with our crappy old petrol-using estate."

"Actually, since you don't have even one green car, that makes us infinitely greener than you, if my math serves me correctly?" She grins and I think she's being ironic. I'm trying to remember exactly how it was that Joel had told me it's better to drive an old car, however rubbish its engine is. Something about carbon costs of production, but Mitzi's in full flow. "To be honest, we're trying to save money as much as the planet at the moment, so it's a bonus that there's no car tax or congestion charge on it."

"I don't think of you as being on an economy drive."

"Every little bit helps," she says. "Austerity Britain and all that."

"And there was I imagining that you thought austerity Britain was just a vogue for expensively home-produced veg and lovely Second World War light fittings."

"Indeed, one must keep calm and carry on."

"Carry on spending," I say, "apparently, to help the economy."

"I like to do my bit," she says and laughs.

Gabe is clinging to my leg like some sort of rutting terrier, while Rufus, too, remains connected by an invisible umbilical cord. I try to shake them off, literally in Gabe's case, but they hover.

I look around at the dozen or so children. "It's so great that you don't feel you have to invite Mahalia's whole class from school."

"But I have," Mitzi says brightly.

"Blimey, those private school class sizes really are a lot smaller, aren't they? Worth paying ten grand a year just to avoid having to have thirty kids at your birthday parties."

"No, silly," she says. "Mahalia's having two birthdays."

"Like the Queen?" Well, she is a bit of a princess.

"I suppose." Mitzi makes as if to frown, but her brow remains remarkably unlined. I have a permanent frown mark etched on my face now. "I'm having a separate party for all Mahalia's schoolfriends. I thought it would be a bit hectic if I had all her home friends and her schoolfriends in one bash. Are there really thirty kids in Rufus's class? There are fifteen in Mahalia's. And two teaching assistants. And it costs more than ten grand, what with all the extras. Over twelve."

Twelve times four children out of taxed income. My very-gifted-at-numeracy elder son would be able to make that calculation in a trice, but I settle at the vague answer A Lot Of Money. A lot of money that everyone else at the party is happy to pay, it seems. I wonder, as ever, what it is other parents know that I don't which means Rufus going to the local state primary condemns him to a life of crack addiction and a career in armed robbery. I worry that he can't write out his birthday cards in the medieval-monk-of-Lindisfarne perfect illuminated script that Mahalia's privately educated friends have written out hers ("Have a delightful birthday" one reads. Delightful?).

21) *Doesn't worry enough. I have to do all the worrying for our children's future while Joel just says that they will probably turn out fine and there's not a lot we can do about it anyway.*

I regret wishing that Gabe would detach himself from my leg now that he has and is approaching the art cupboard with dangerous intent.

"He's very boisterous, isn't he?" says Jennifer, whose child appears to be on Mogadon. "Have you thought of getting him tested?"

"For what? He'll do enough tests when he has to start going to school."

"Attention deficit disorder," she says. "I know a great educational psychologist."

"We had to see one of those for Oliver—you know, because of the gifted and talented thing," says Alison.

"Well, he can't get his hyperactivity from his father," says Mitzi. "He's so laid back he's upside down." Everyone laughs. Hang on, I think, you're not allowed to slag off my husband.

Or my son, who is not hyperactive, he's spirited. "Have you met Joel?" she continues. "He's this totally adorable slob."

Less of the slob. And less of the adorable, while you're at it. "Actually," I say, a word I've caught off Rufus, "Joel's a very successful executive TV producer-director."

"I know he is, darling. And you know how much I love him." Again, she turns to her audience to explain, "Joel and I have a special relationship."

That's what I can never work out. Whether the sniping between Mitzi and Joel is born of antipathy or some sort of heat between them, like they're characters in a 1930s screwball comedy. Joel had the choice between us when we met all those years ago. Does he ever regret his choice? Looking around the vast acreage of the house and garden, I'm sure Mitzi doesn't regret hers.

At last it is time to go. Rufus and Gabe get a goody bag made out of actual cloth to take away, while my own leaving present is the familiar sense of both inadequacy and disdain. This particular cocktail of emotions is fed further by the discovery that one of the myriad gifts in the goody sack is the book that we've just given Mahalia as her birthday present. Except ours was wrapped in newspaper as we'd run out of wrapping paper, while this one is in beautiful handmade and recycled paper with perfect hospital corners and a ribbon. "Horrible materialism," I say to Joel later. "Horrible material," he says, pointing to the patchwork of silk remnants that makes up the party bag.

I'm thinking about Mitzi's larder later that evening, as I sit in bed flicking through the latest Lakeland Plastics catalog. Just looking at its storage solutions section offers me the promise of a well-ordered home and I turn down the pages of color-coded

Tupperware that will revolutionize my cupboards. Family life is a constant storage challenge in search of a solution.

22) *Has a constantly growing collection of glasses by his bed. Each has a different level of water left to stagnate within and it looks like he's trying to get enough to be able to do that music hall turn of rubbing the rims to make different notes.*

I stare at Joel. Even in bed, he's untidy, flinging his limbs across it, mummifying himself in the duvet and throwing off pillows. His face is sandpapered with stubble. His face is crumpled in a frown.

23) *Checks his BlackBerry in bed. Is important enough at work to be given a BlackBerry, while since my part-time down-shifting career choice, I don't even get given a company mobile.*

He senses that I'm looking at him. He mistakes my disgust for lust and leans over to me.

24) *Checks his BlackBerry in bed and then expects me to have sex with him when he puts it down.*
25) *Checks his BlackBerry while having sex with me, on occasion.*

"Piss off, J." He looks wounded. "I'm tired and you can't just switch me on like a BlackBerry."
     "It's work."
     "It's Saturday night."

"Exactly."

"It's just not that sexy to use your BlackBerry in bed."

"But reading about Tupperware is the height of eroticism, I suppose," he says, gesturing at my catalog.

"It's work, too. The difference is that it's work I have to do when I get home from my job." I roll away from him, feeling so angry that my skin tingles with it. I'm not quite sure why I do or where it comes from.

My life is going down the drain, and it's a drain clogged with swollen Shreddies, solidified globules of grease and a dried-up piece of Play-Doh.

2

He Takes the Rubbish Out

On my way to work, I pretend that I'm a single glamorous woman, soy latte in one hand, expensive buckle-laden statement handbag in the other (only one part of this image is factually correct and it's the one that cost £1.90 from the café).

My office is some sublet space in a large industrial warehouse. Our floor is shared between other two-bit/four-people television production companies fermenting in the media brewery and we feel like the tent-city of offices: displaced, floating, chaotic. The other areas of the building are used by a very cutting-edge advertising agency and some vague "media consultants." The reception area is most unreceptive, all unpainted concrete and ironic retro office furniture, while the still-remaining Christmas tree, which is black and decorated with white cube-shaped baubles, only serves to make it more so.

I get into the lift with one of the advertising girls, who wears clothes that I think are described in fashion-speak as "directional."

"Which floor?" she sneers. I am just about to answer, when she looks me up and down then presses three, correctly, for me and the panoramic penthouse for herself.

"Thanks," I mutter. For what? Judging that my mom uniform of smocky top and not-that-skinny jeans could have only belonged to what's known as the dowdy floor in this building.

I arrive at the sanctuary of the dowdy floor and plonk myself down next to Lily with some relief, even if she is the most fashionable and youthful beacon in this area of the building. She even has the name of a coltish young supermodel (or a toddler—a florist couldn't have as many Lilies, Irises and Poppies as Rufus's class at school). Advertising shrew would never have guessed that Lily works on this floor. She wears clothes that are so directional as to have performed a 180-degree turn and become the sort of things that my senile great-aunt would wear on escaping from the care home. There's no trend too ugly for her to embrace. She even went through a self-harming phase as she'd been told everyone was doing it, though she cheerfully admitted that she hadn't actually managed to pierce the skin on her arms with a biro, just to make it look like she was trying to do her own tattoos.

"Do you know what?" I say to her. "Some stupid cow from the advertising agency just assumed I worked on this floor."

"Well, you do," Lily observes, while performing a good-tempered version of the up-and-down look that I got in the lift.

"True. Good Christmas?" I ask.

"Eggs-hausting," she replies in exhausted fashion. I stop myself from telling her she doesn't know exhausting until she's had children. Much of my conversation with Lily consists of me trying to stop myself from explaining to her that it won't necessarily be easy for her to have "twins, a boy one and a girl one" by IVF at a moment convenient to her, once she's won an Oscar and written a best-selling novel, or "move to a big house in the country and start a really successful Internet business with a really gorgeous husband" at some point in her thirties. She's always telling me that she doesn't understand why I work part-time—"Like, why don't you just get more babysitting?"—which is also her answer to any complaints about not being able to get out much these days.

When I first met Joel, I was an assistant producer and he was a researcher, having frittered away most of his twenties on his band, or "the band" as it's always referred to, like it produced a few seminal albums. I had clawed my way to that position by the time-honored, by women at least, route of starting as a secretary at minimum wage, having written to every production company in London with my CV. He got his first position in telly via a phone call from his mother to an old friend who'd done a documentary with her in the seventies. Within six months of him starting, he was a producer too, though I consoled myself that I was still senior to him and whatever happened I'd always have better A-level grades. Soon we were competing to be the first to get a producer-director credit, that sweet mix of the practical and the creative. We spent our days making reality shows and our nights planning the world-changing documentaries we were going to make together.

And now he's an executive producer and I'm a...a what? A sort of production managers' manager? Development slash coordination slash human resources? When we've got a program to work on, which we don't at the moment, hence the tiny corner of sublet office space, I'm the last staging post on a production line of whining—the whinge sponge, if you like. Production managers are kind of like mothers in that they tidy up, budget for and chase after creative, tantrum-throwing types. I'm the person that even the production managers complain to and demand that I find order in their chaos. Professionally speaking, I'm the mother of all mothers.

I used to be one of the creative ones, I used to have ideas. Now I'm a backroom girl. I'm like one of those women in World War II films who push airplanes around maps, allowing the pilots to soar off on their adventures. Opportunities for part-timers, mothers and over 35s are limited in the *Logan's Run* world that is television.

"Is no one else in today?" I ask Lily.

"Nah. Do you want to see my new Facebook page?"

"I thought you did MySpace."

"Yu-huh. I've got both." She looks at me like I look at my mother, like my children look at me.

"Perhaps I'll get myself one of these Facebook thingies one of these days," I tell her.

"Yeah, you should. There are loads of old people on it these days."

"Yes, I believe that Saga has even set up a social networking site for us."

She gives me the "whatevs" face and we settle down to work. A new production starts in a few weeks and I busy myself with color-coded schedules and timetables, trying to slot together the incoming hordes and marshal the troops, much as I do at home for the three males. Time flies by in a way that it didn't when I was ensconced in the bosom of my family for that eternal Christmas break, and before long it is midday.

It's traditional to dread Mondays. I yearn for them. Especially every other one, when I get to have lunch with my friend Becky. A proper lunch break out of the office was one of the things (along with status, salary and prospects) that got reduced once I went part-time. Workload wasn't.

Our lunch venue is not exactly The Ivy; we're balanced on uncomfortable stools eating sandwiches at a bar, looking out on the street through a fogged-up window. We swap Christmases, hers an enviable-sounding one of much "mooching around" London interspersed with occasional bouts of family. For the childless, family is something you get to dip in and out of.

"Seeing you twice in one week," says Becky. "That's a rare treat."

"Oh, yes, Friday," I say as if I've only just remembered the invitation to Cara's party, the date of which is inscribed in both my diary and my head. As if I'd forget, as if I get invited to lots of smart parties in flats that look like they belong on the set of a film about glamorous women. "What's it in aid of?"

"It's not for charity," she says.

"No, I mean, is it someone's birthday? Your anniversary? Ooh, are you making an announcement? Is there a civil partnership looming?"

"Jeez, why is everyone on at us about that? Bloody civil partnerships. Do you know what nobody seems to have twigged about them? In terms of acrimonious splits and their financial repercussions, they're just as bad as any marriage. I don't know why everyone's so celebratory about them, the only people who should really be celebrating are us lawyers. Ya-hey." She makes a champagne toast with an imaginary glass. Becky is a family lawyer, which is more commonly and less euphemistically known as a divorce lawyer. The word "family" is often used as a euphemism, I find—family fun, family film, family day out. Just an adjective meaning "crap," usually—though that's certainly not the case with Becky, whom I'm told is quietly brilliant at her job.

"Still, it's great for me," I say, "since now you can be as bugged by annoying questions as Joel and I were before we finally caved in and got married. I wonder if you'll get spared the ones about children along with crude remarks about your ovaries."

Becky looks terse at this point and I wonder if I have said something wrong. "It's just a party, Mary. If anything it's a professional thing for Cara's clients, drum up some business. Not the best time to be in financial PR."

"It probably is quite literally easier to sell snow to Eskimos than to get good press for bankers. Still, if anyone can do it, Cara can. I expect she can persuade anybody of anything." I use the pause that follows to dive into what's been preoccupying me all the while. "In your professional opinion..." I begin to ask.

She sighs. "A lot of my friends' sentences begin that way these days. Something to do with forty a-beckoning."

"Sorry," I continue. "In your experience, what's the most common reason people give for wanting to get a divorce?"

"Obviously, there's the usual—infidelity, money problems, domestic and verbal abuse. Often, it's not so much what someone has done as what they've failed to do. Neglect, lack of respect, nothing in common. You can't really generalize."

"What about housework?" I ask, concentrating on drawing a series of stacking cubes onto the window's condensation.

"What about it?"

"Do people get divorced because their houses are a mess?"

Becky laughs. "No, not generally. I suppose if it were symptomatic of some sort of wider malaise. What's this about?"

"A program we might be doing, a bit like *Wife Swap*," I say.

"I knew you weren't talking about you and Joel. Your house is always immaculate."

"Yeah, right," I say. "It's a disaster." But I feel a burst of womanly pride that somebody has been fooled by the brief frenzy of tidying that goes on before we have visitors. "You only say that because you're like my mother-in-law in your belief that cleanliness is next to gormlessness."

"Ursula is a marvelous woman," Becky says with a frown. "I wish I lived with her instead of Cara."

"How's that going?"

"Fine. Sort of. She's just so anal. Everything's just so and tasteful and perfect. Everything has to be *exquisite*, do you know what I mean? She has a DustBuster—you know, one of those mini vacuum cleaner things and she uses it around my chair before I've even finished eating."

"I do that a bit, with the children."

"Exactly. With. The. Children. And that's not all. It's a bloody Philippe Starck DustBuster. All polished chrome. Even the bloody DustBuster has to be the world's most tasteful Dust-Buster. I'm only allowed to put my stuff, you know all my vases, ornaments, presents that people have given me, things that mean something to me, in the spare room. She has a computer pro-gram for working out which art should go on which wall space. She's a gay man trapped in a lesbian's body." She frowns some more and then contradicts herself. "Except she doesn't have a lesbian's body as it's far too gym-toned and hairless. It's a gay man's body."

"Right, a gay man trapped in a gay man's body?"

"Who fancies women," corrects Becky.

"So a straight man, then," I say. "Except she fancies lesbians."

"Not strictly true," Becky says. "Cara's always had a thing for turning straight women gay. Especially the married ones."

"Really?" I feel a surprising charge.

"Yes. Haven't you noticed how much more femme I've got over the last year?"

True, ish, I thought; Becky had become a little less Weimar Republic lesbian of late and now made the occasional uncom-fortable foray into dresses.

"So Cara's a gay man trapped in a gay man's body, but with boobs and stuff, but who's like a straight man as she fancies straight women..."

"I think this analogy's run its course," Becky says with a full stop.

"Indeed. You were telling me, about divorce and housework, is there a link?"

"Not unless it's a reflection of something else. A deep inequality in the relationship, I suppose. Are they really doing a program about housework?"

"No," I say mournfully. "It's Joel. He's driving me mad."

"So you're going to divorce him." Becky laughs.

"I'm serious."

She looks at me. "Oh my god, don't you think you're over-reacting?"

I shake my head. "No. It would be an over-reaction to kill him. Which I have thought of doing."

"Come on, Mary. It's not like he hits you or anything."

"Every time he leaves the sodding milk out, or his bloody socks on the floor, or drops his coat as he comes in, or a tea bag in the sink," I say, "it feels like a little blow to my head. A small, well-aimed punch in my stomach."

"Really worth divorcing him over, then. Perhaps you and I should do a wife swap: you come and live at our palace of clean and I can go and luxuriate with Joel in the warm gunk of your place. Joel is wonderful. You're so lucky."

I look over to the corner of the café, where three women, as pregnant as each other, are sitting and having a no doubt decaffeinated coffee together. Everything about them says first-time mothers. They wear gorgeous box-fresh maternity clothes and give off a throb of excitement and hope. Children are still a potentially chic accessory and how you give birth is something you dictate in a plan. They still live in this edgy, urban area, but they'll move soon, you know, they'll say—the schools in the inner city . . . so many kids with English as a second language . . . besides, we wanted a garden and a proper high street.

I've never felt such optimism as I did when I was pregnant with Rufus. Joel used to stroke my belly and talk to it, telling it funny stories and singing his favorite songs. We knew we weren't the only ones in the world to be having a baby, one trip to the nursery section of a department store put paid to that, but that didn't stop us feeling like we were. We wallowed in every cliché, believing that somehow we were the first people in history to be going through them.

My preparation consisted of reading Internet message boards discussing perineal massage and wincing, while Joel's was creating the perfect birth playlist.

"Do you want songs that are about children or is that a bit literal?" he asked me as I lay eight months pregnant with Rufus on the sofa. He was rifling through CDs with an energy that I no longer see from him. He was keen to play lots of them to the bump, in the manner of someone who thinks fetuses become cleverer if they listen to Mozart.

"I don't know. Does it matter?"

"This is our progeny's introduction to the world of music so, yes, it does matter. Bob Dylan's 'Forever Young' as an opener, yes, perfect. Throw in a few love songs, 'At Last' by Etta James, and Primal Scream, but which one? I know, 'I'll Be There for You.' Bowie's 'Kooks' is about kids, though it's not such a great song, is it? What other songs are there about children?"

" 'Thank Heaven for Little Girls,' " I suggested. I was enjoying his seriousness.

"Always good to have a song with a whiff, or should I say *soupçon*, of pedophilia. Shall I add Serge Gainsbourg's loving duet with his daughter, 'Lemon Incest,' while I'm at it?"

"Can't think of any other ones about kids. Sorry."

"Nor can I. Except Brotherhood of Man's 'Save All Your Kisses for Me.'"

"Never too young to be introduced to the delights of the Eurovision Song Contest." Six years ago my knowledge of pop trivia rivaled his.

"Very true." Joel's love of music was as wide as it was deep. He loved genres that others dismissed, Broadway musicals, 1930s folk and 80s pop. "Do you know what? I'm going to start by concentrating on upbeat but not pappy numbers. 'Hallelujah,' 'Mr. E's Beautiful Blues'..."

"You who?" OK, maybe he always knew more about music than I did.

"The Eels. 'Perfect Day,' of course—wouldn't everybody's life be better if they came into the world listening to a bit of Lou Reed?"

"Isn't it about heroin?"

"The baby's not going to know that."

"The baby's not going to know about much, really."

"Our baby will be born a genius." He kissed me. "With your brains. And my, no, your looks too."

"No, your charm. And your looks too." At this point, I still felt that he was too good-looking for me, that strangers would point at us and wonder what this god was doing with someone so ordinary.

"No, please no. Not my girth." He slapped the then small overhang above his belt.

"I love your girth." I giggled at the other interpretation of this statement and somehow we maneuvered both our growing bellies onto the sofa and celebrated our hope and love to some of the tracks we later chose for Rufus's birth album (but never actually played, what with the panic over his heart rate, the forceps and all those worried-looking doctors).

"Mary," says Becky, interrupting my thoughts. "Joel's wonderful, isn't he? You do know that?"

"Yes, of course he is," I say. "He's wonderful. I'm so lucky."

I can almost hear the tracks running in my head all these years later as I pass the pregnant women in the café when we get up to go. There are three of them. One of those will split up with the father of their child, statistically, and another will feel as full of irritation toward their partner as I do toward Joel. I do a little eeny-meeny-miny-mo and pick on the woman in designer glasses as the only one who'll still be happy in five years' time.

I get home before Joel, despite having to get some shopping on the way back. Each working day, I'm a Cinderella who must get to the child minder's in time to pick up the kids. As I run through the streets from the station, I feel as if when the clock strikes 6:30, Deena will spontaneously combust, leaving nothing in her wake but two abandoned children and a pair of inappropriately high shoes. Childcare runs on a strict meter: I shove the coins in to cover just the amount of time I need, to the last minute, not wanting to pay anything more than I might possibly want.

26) *The fact that childcare is paid for out of my salary. As if paying someone else allows me to work whereas it actually allows both or either of us to work, doesn't it? Which means I have less money than Joel does. Of course, it's both our money, or more accurately both our debts, but I can never buy clothes for myself without clearing it with him first as there's never any money in my account, while Joel is always downloading music that he'll never listen to. If he were a woman and those tracks were shoes, he'd be hiding them in a cupboard and saying, "These old things, I've had them for years."*

27) *That whenever I complain that it's me who has to rush back to pick up the kids, Joel says, "Just pay Deena for extra hours, then."*

28) *Similarly, when I complain about the house being a mess, he says, "Just pay someone to clean, then." I remind him that*

we do, for a few hours a week, to which he just says, "Pay her some more, then." But we'd need a cleaner to work full-time, to follow him about picking up the trail of clothes, food and half-empty glasses that he leaves in his wake. Is the cleaner going to be there last thing at night when he drops all his clothes on the floor? Will she be there every time he eats? Is she going to flush the loo for him? I don't want to pay for a cleaner, I just want him to be cleaner.

My most frequent nightmare used to be the one about discovering that you hadn't in fact finished your exams at school, but had to do one more paper that you hadn't done any revision for. Now, my recurring one is that I've left the house, arrived at my destination and suddenly realized that I've forgotten to arrange for someone to look after the kids and they've been left at home on their own. I'm rushing to get back, frantically phoning neighbors, but things keep stopping me from getting there.

"Hello, Deena, sorry I'm a couple of minutes late," I say breathlessly. I run not only because I don't want to be late, but also because I long to see the boys again, like a girl on her way to a first date.

"Don't you worry about it, we've been having a grand time, haven't we?" Deena beams, balancing her latest grandchild on her hip. I look past the door to the sitting room to see Rufus and Gabe's ketchup-smeared, television-glazed faces and don't doubt it. Deena is, as ever, looking as if she is about to enter a glamorous granny competition, with stacked heels, makeup applied with a paint-sprayer, and a magnificent embonpoint. After the patchwork of disastrous childcare arrangements that we've had over the years, I'm craven in her presence. I want to say something about the television, the nuggets, and the fact that the squash she gives my kids is not butternut but additive-filled drinks, but am worried that whatever I say will have an invisible subtitle ticking along below it, reading: "Can you just be a little more middle class, you know, like us?" And it's unfair, really, given how much she reads to them and properly plays with them and how much better her own children have turned out than the offspring of some of my friends.

Gabe is sitting on Rufus's lap while they read a book together. Rufus is ignoring the text and making up a story that involves the little girl in the pictures, but rather than being afraid of shadows in the night, in his story she is attacking them with invisible swords made out of thoughts. They look up and see me.

"Mommy," says Rufus. "Do you know? I missed you."

"And I missed you both, so much." For this brief moment everything is perfect.

"Don't want to go in buggy. My want to walk," Gabe begins.

"I don't have time for this," I reply as I karate chop him into the stroller.

"You're always saying that," says Rufus. "You say it ten million times a day."

"I say it because it's true, now come on. How was school?"

"You're always saying that, too," Rufus says.

"About ten million times a day?"

"No, not that much."

"So how was it?"

"All right."

"Who did you talk to?"

"No one."

"Did you eat anything?"

He shakes his head. I give up. I briefly entertain a fantasy about my unborn girl child, Willa or Aphra or Eudora is her name, who'd giggle and share secrets with me of who her best friend is as we sit on the bed looking at books with a reading age of at least five years in advance. Mothers of girls are always telling me how amazing their daughters' reading and handwriting is, while I vainly try to counter with the fact that Gabe can divide up vehicles into those with caterpillar wheels and those without. If you're a mother of girls, these women tell me with indulgent pride and barely hidden pity, you get to choose Disney Princess duvet covers together, and have the chance to buy patterned tights and to dress your daughter in a sticky-out pink tutu. We poor mothers of boys instead merely learn ace new skills, like a bicycle kick, as we burn off calories with our adrenalin-pumping games of football in the park. We replace our single women's knowledge of star signs with hard facts about the order of the solar system and the size of the planets. We enjoy their wondrous otherness and melt at the sight of their tiny, unthreatening willies.

I banish all thoughts of Eudora/Aphra/Willa. I love being the mother of boys, however much those with girls find it hard to believe. When I think about Rufus and Gabe, how could I ever want them to be anyone other than themselves?

An hour after I return home, Joel gets back.

29) *Times his return to the exact moment when he's too late to help with bath- and bedtime, but not late enough to allow me to eat my unmessy toast for supper and watch what I want on TV, which is usually property shows.*

30) *Scoffs at property shows and says they're part of a horrible Little Englander conspiracy to coerce us into an obsession with house prices. Usually starts frothing about "Thatch" and the 1980s while he's at it. Generally we fight along male and female lines over the remote control. I concede that he is a rare man who doesn't like watching football (I gave up my own, rather transparent, interest in it when we*

got together), but he is following classic middle-aged male precedents by getting into military history and so watching endless documentaries about Nazis. All men do this, don't they? Reach a certain age and begin to obsess over military history. Antony Beevor's Stalingrad *is their gateway drug and, whoosh, before you know it they're reading books filled with maps showing fronts and pushes. That and suddenly deciding that £5 bottles of wine are no longer good enough for them—those are the male symbols of being over your prime. For women, it's the development of an interest in interior design. I plead guilty. Men begin to read the business supplement that comes with the Sunday papers, women the travel and gardening ones.*

As he comes in, I realize that he's not alone.

"Ursula, what a surprise," I say on seeing my mother-in-law, resplendent in full-length velvet skirt, floral turban and dangling parrot earrings. Ursula is a 1980s Posy Simmonds cartoon made flesh, but doesn't seem to have any awareness of the fact that she dresses like a feminist in panto. I kiss her cheeks, which smell and feel like Vaseline Intensive Care and turn to Joel. "You never told me that your mother was coming over tonight."

"Didn't I? I thought I had."

31) *Never writes anything on the family calendar that I designed and printed out myself on the computer at work and that now hangs prominently in the kitchen.*

"Sorry, Ursula." I gesture down at her ugly-but-not-in-a-fashionable-way boots, but her feet are staying firmly shod.

She looks quizzical, so I nod my head toward my discarded shoes and my own socked feet.

"Oh yes, of course, you make people take their shoes off before they're allowed into your house. I always forget that. Do you know what Geoffrey Manley says?" she asks Joel. "He says that if you go to a house where you have to check in your shoes at the door, you'll need to check in your intelligence at the same time. Isn't that just too true?"

"Actually," I say, "I think it's a sign of intelligence to take your shoes off inside as that way you're avoiding dirtying the carpet and having to vacuum it later on. I mean, would you call the Japanese stupid?"

"Here you are, Urse," Joel says, while waving my new sheepskin slippers and rolling his eyes to communicate that the "no shoes inside" rule is nothing to do with him.

"Are you staying for supper, Ursula?" I ask. "I'm afraid I didn't buy quite enough for three."

"Chill," says Joel. "We'll just get a takeaway."

32) *When it's his turn to cook anything less fancy than the complete works of Escoffier, gets a takeaway and thinks it counts.*

Ursula clasps her hands together in excitement. "What a treat!" Ursula regards using taxis and going to restaurants as decadent luxuries, while living alone in a five-bedroom, albeit rapidly deteriorating, house in one of London's more expensive areas is frugality itself.

"You haven't tasted it yet," I say. "I wish I'd known and I'd have cooked us something more wholesome."

"Darling, don't waste your time. I'd much prefer a takeaway."

She clasps her hands with slightly less excitement to say, "Now, where are my gorgeous grandsons?"

"In bed. Sorry, if I'd known . . ."

"It's not even eight o'clock," she says. "I love the idea of little children running around until midnight like they do in Italy and Spain. So wonderful. Why don't you ever eat with them? Sometimes I wonder whether you really like them."

"I love them." As I say this I am momentarily tempted to wake them to show them that I do with my kisses. Much as I long for them to go to sleep, I long for them when they're gone from me and sometimes gladden when one of them has a nightmare and needs comfort. But I won't wake them now because we're a house with evening stories and regular bedtimes. "Children need their sleep. Poor Rufus is tired enough as it is with all this school stuff without having his night interrupted. There have been studies showing that they get ill and it damages their brains and they become obese if they don't get twelve full hours every night."

"Nonsense," says Ursula. "When Joel was a baby, he'd stay up and join in with all our discussions. I can't tell you the number of times he'd curl up and fall asleep in a pile of Afghans—coats, I mean, obviously not people from Afghanistan, though we did have quite a few of those too. My darling boy has been to more consciousness-raising meetings than any other man has ever been allowed. Of course, some of the sisters used to say, 'No one with a penis,' but I told them not to be so ridiculous—my scion is hardly the enemy, is he? Quite the contrary, and anyway his penis is so tiny you can barely see it. I'm sure imbibing all that marvelous thought is why he's so enlightened today. You ought to think about the women who might end up with Rufus and Gabe, I'm sure they'd benefit from all we'll have to talk about tonight."

"Let's go and wake them to find out, shall we?" I say.

"We could do," says Joel. "I didn't get a chance to see them tonight. You can be a bit of a routine Nazi about bedtimes."

33) *Takes his mother's side over mine, every time.*

"No, we can't. I'm not having them woken. They need their sleep and it wouldn't be fair on anybody." I pour myself some more wine to make myself clear.

"Maybe next time, Mother," says Joel.

Ursula gives me a look that says: what a shame you hate your children so. It's the look she gives me every time we've gone on holiday to a place with a kids' club.

"Seriously," I say, "please can we just leave them be? They've had a tiring day. And more to the point, I've had a really tiring day." She snorts. "Sorry, Ursula, what was that?"

"You've hardly been down the mines, have you? Or raised a family of four children single-handedly like some of my friends? Honestly, you lot don't know you're born." Joel retreats from the kitchen. "You young women seem so angry."

Oh no, here we go again. The "you young women have never had it so good speech" and "you can never thank me enough." "More wine, Ursula?"

She is not so easily deflected. "Angry all the time when you haven't really got anything to be angry about, have you?"

Except being lectured by you every time you come over and get a couple of glasses of Pinot Noir down you. "Well..." I begin, but she's off.

"You've got it all: the right to have interesting yet flexible jobs and still see your children; to wear what you want, even if it is most dreadfully whorish in the name of so-called empowerment; wonderful husbands who work so hard and still do all the housework—not that there is any these days, what with all your dishwashing machines and microwave cookers. You're so lucky. Maybe you're angry that you haven't got more to be angry about." She chortles, a particularly irritating chortle that her son has inherited from her.

"I don't know where to start," I say truthfully. "You're right that feminism has brought us many benefits..."

"Thank you," she says, as if it were she that powered the revolution single-handedly.

"It's great that we can work—great, really. But it's as if the outside world has moved at one pace and the inside one, what goes on here," I jab my finger, "at home, has gone at another, much slower one. There's like this disconnect..."

"Disconnect? What a horrid piece of management speak."

"Looking after the house and the children, it hasn't caught up," I continue, gabbling my words to stop her interrupting me again. "No, that's wrong. It's like women's development has moved on one track and men's on another. We've had the revolution for women, but we didn't realize that of course it wouldn't work unless men had a revolution too."

"Some men have, haven't they? Just look at Joel," says Ursula.

I try to follow her command, but Joel is nowhere to be seen—as is always the case when Ursula and I do battle.

"Joel is wonderful. You're so lucky," she continues.

"Yes, obviously I'm really lucky. But even someone as wonderful as he is, is not quite 50–50 when it comes to the dirty washing and the worry and the shoe-buying and the thank-you letter writing and the organizing of playdates..."

"Playdates?" she exclaims.

"It's like when you arrange to meet another parent so that—"

"Yes, I know what it is. But my dear, what a ghastly Americanism. It's like all these people saying 'hey' instead of 'hello.' Don't you think it's dreadful, Joel, the word 'playdate'?" He reappears on cue in a way that he never does for me.

"Yes," he agrees, of course. "It sounds like something you might have with a Playboy bunny in the Playboy mansion.

Involving two of them wearing something pink and fluffy and grappling each other in a softplay zone."

Ursula and I uncharacteristically unite to throw him a despairing glance. He sometimes adopts this irksome men's magazine persona when his mother's around. He disappears into the back garden for some unfathomable reason. I think about the first time that Ursula lectured me. I agreed with everything she said and felt giddy with flattery that she should think me worthy of her energies.

"Seriously, Ursula..." I'm wondering whether to go into the fact that part-time work is a con. That shared parenting is a myth. That her feminism has got me the work outside the home but hasn't rid me of the work inside it. That her son is a disgusting slob who's been brought up with unhygienic levels of tolerance of squalor. By her. "The battle's not been won. Men aren't doing much more at home."

"I think you'll find that statistics show they're doing a lot more childcare."

"Childcare, yes, maybe. The fun bits of childcare, certainly— the trips to the zoo and the panto, and the organized stuff. But not the boring bit, the daily grind..." At that moment, Joel chooses to walk past us, straining under the weight of our overfilled rubbish bag.

"I thought I'd do this now," he says to no one in particular. "In case it's forgotten about later."

Ursula looks at him the way I do Gabe when he gets a poo in the potty—bursting with maternal pride.

34) *He takes the rubbish out. That sounds like a good thing, doesn't it? But it isn't, not when it's seen as the domestic equivalent to doing the laundry. Four people's dirty clothes every day—the washing, the sock-ball rolling, the pant*

folding—versus taking the rubbish out once a week. Hmm, like that's fair. When I think about it, all his domestic chores are the one-offs, the once-a-weeks, like rubbish bags, or the annual jobs like the car's MOT, the insurance. While mine are the ones without end or beginning, the ones that can never be ticked off. The wiping down of one surface while another is being smeared. The putting clothes in drawers while the laundry bag fills. I get all the modern Herculean labors.

Though I can only remember one of Hercules' labors now that I think about it, and it's the one about the stable where as fast as he clears the hay, more dirt just keeps appearing—there's a river running through it, carrying a perpetual tide of filth. There's one streaming through here too.

"Shit," I hear him shout, followed by the sound of objects being picked up, accompanied by an exaggerated gagging sound.

35) *Insists that we only fill one rubbish bag a week. I try, I really do, with the compost and the recycling and, for a very brief time, the reusable diapers, but Joel is going to have to accept that we are profligate landfill site contributors and that's just tough.*

"Yes, it's great that Joel does the rubbish." I'm distracted by the little trail of non-specific rubbish bag juice that's zigzagging across our kitchen floor and is now no doubt variegating our oatmeal-colored carpet in the hall. "But there's those daily, endless, non-tickable-offable"—Ursula raises her eyebrows at my poor use of English—"bits and pieces that only women seem to do. Just ask anyone. Any woman."

"I do hope our conversation isn't going to just end up being a discussion of who does the washing-up," she says. "In the old days, when we were having a barnstorm about gender wars, we'd joke to one another, 'this isn't going to end up as an argument about who does the washing-up.' Sadly, it too often did. Don't you think you're worrying too much about petty domestic tasks when there are more important issues like the global levels of female circumcision or the lack of financial equality at work?"

I'm on my knees, physically and probably metaphorically, as I wipe the floor of the bag's dribble. "But don't you see, there will never be equality anywhere until there is at home?"

"Equality begins at home?" she chuckles.

"Exactly," I say.

"Really, dear, you're far too concerned with the outward appearance of your house." She glances at me and the carpet cleaner gun I'm wielding as I plan to do battle in the hall. "You all are, your lot. Obsessed with shiny new kitchens and bathrooms that look like they belong in a hotel. Do you know, it would no sooner have occurred to us to replace a kitchen that hadn't completely collapsed than it would have to replace our own bodies with bits of plastic. Then again, your lot do quite a bit of that too."

"I don't see what's wrong with trying to make your house hygienic..."

"Don't think we didn't talk about all this. We had 'wages for women' campaigns and housework strikes and we did all this to death. But I think we've moved on, don't you?"

She has certainly moved on, from me to the living room to squeal delightedly over the takeaway menu that Joel's pulled out for her to have a look at, grinding in some of the rubbish bag's juices along the way. She strokes his cheek in a frankly revolting way.

"Can we have Thai, rather than Indian? You know all that

ghee is a nightmare for me," I ask as they excitedly pick out their choices.

"Yes, remember that Mary's intolerant," says Joel, giving a fine example of the aforementioned chortle.

"Dairy intolerant," I correct.

"Yeah, intolerant," he says.

"I don't know," says Ursula. "Nobody was ever allergic to this and intolerant to that when I was young. I think we were too busy fighting the state to fight the plate." I can see her mentally note the phrase down for her next book.

"I get all wheezy," I protest. "My nose streams for weeks if I dare have a non–soy milk latte. Isn't that true, Joel?"

He shrugs his shoulders, allowing Ursula to continue to expound her latest theory.

"I notice that a lot of young women seem to be vegetarian without actually caring about animals, and intolerant to—what a coincidence—anything that might be considered fattening."

"Joel's the one who used to be a vegetarian. Hard to believe now..."

"Yes, but he was a vegetarian for ethical rather than aesthetic reasons, wasn't he? Isn't it all a socially acceptable way of controlling your food? By banning whole food groups, you can essentially eat less, can't you? But it's all food disorderly conduct."

"I haven't got a food disorder," I say.

"Well, you did have that phase when you were a teenager, didn't you, with your sister?" says Joel.

Crime number 33 over and over again.

"Jemima and me got into a bit of competitive dieting, that's all. It's completely normal." Of course, Jemima won that little bout, by only going and getting herself full-blown anorexia complete with protruding ribs, a brief stay in the hospital and traumatic parental self-recrimination.

"For your generation, yes," says Ursula. She turns to Joel. "They're a generation of control freaks, aren't they?"

"Too right."

Did she just call me a control freak? Preceded by a general accusation of being a lazy, silicone-filled, hygiene-obsessed ingrate. I have to get out of here. "Excuse me, I think I just heard Gabe." I run out.

I sit on the marital bed. What will it be called after the divorce, I wonder? The ex-marital bed, I suppose. I tell you what, though, I'm definitely getting it in the settlement, for the dozen times you just agreed with your mother over me. I look down at my chest and wonder whether I might as well get myself some plastic surgery, since Ursula seems so convinced that everyone of my generation is at it.

When Ursula was my boyfriend's mother, there was no one I liked and admired more in the world. I think I fell in love with her as much as with Joel. To have a famous feminist for a mother seemed to me to be the most glamorous background in the world, added to which she was not only right-on, she was also from a rich and aristocratic family. The fact that she was a single mother, too, just made her impossibly exotic. And her house! Book-filled and decrepit, ancient furniture stained by Isaiah Berlin's gin and tonics, an old-fashioned drinks trolley sticky with liqueurs that she'd picked up from speaking engagements in far-flung places. It was just the sort of life I dreamed of as a teenager, the kind I read about in novels by Margaret Drabble and Iris Murdoch. I'd even read her seminal work, *Cleopatra's Needle Wasn't Used for Darning* (followed up, with diminishing returns, both intellectual and financial, by *Ophelia Should Have Learned to Swim, Joan of Arc's Inflammable Tunic* etc., etc.) and had vowed to live my life by such creeds.

My boyfriend's mother was the person I most admired, yet

my mother-in-law is the one I most resent. Some sort of reverse alchemy takes place on marriage and having children, where all the things that I most loved about Joel became the things I now most hate.

By pretending that Gabe has woken up, it seems I've caused him to do so in reality and I hear him wailing in his bedroom. Joel and Ursula go in and begin reading to him.

"Thomas is all covered in mud," I hear Joel saying. "Really useful engines must be clean. He needs a bath." Short "a."

36) *Does really irritating Northern accent for the Fat Controller in the Thomas the Tank Engine books. I suspect he bases his characterization on my dad. I can't stand Thomas the Tank Engine and his endless friends. I'm sure my unborn daughter Eudora/Willa/Aphra wouldn't want to read them. She'd probably be on C. S. Lewis by the age of three.*

I update The List and feel a lot better.

When did everything that I love about Joel turn into everything that makes me want to wax his chest, not because I like hairless torsos, but in order to cause him pain? The way we met and got together was a chick-lit novel made real, role reversed with Joel taking the part of the ditzy protagonist, forever losing things and arriving late, while I was the haughty Mr. Darcy figure. Our romance came complete with a full complement of misunderstandings and wrong impressions, the victory over the heroine's more attractive friend, and the culmination in a love and sex fest of a few years' duration. I used to stare at him and wonder how on earth I'd ever got so lucky. I used to think, "I don't deserve you." Now I think, "I don't deserve *this*."

The rot sets in as the placenta comes out, when we had our first child. Looking back, there had probably been intimations of how life was going to be when we moved in together, and a few more when we got married, but I ignored them. Maternity leave was when our roles got stuck in aspic. When I became sitcom woman—shrewish, nagging, worrying about getting my whites whiter—and he became sitcom man, avoiding The Wife by hiding with a can of cold lager, and later, making up for not being there all the time with the children by being the "fun one" when he was.

It's ironic that we should have turned into Man and Woman, because when we met, I loved all that was feminine about Joel. I can cry tears of frustration and anger, but rarely ones of happiness or melancholy. Joel, on the other hand, wells up at the mention of Joe Strummer or when Leonard Cohen sings "So Long, Marianne." He notices sunsets and will call purple "lilac," "indigo" or "mauve." He was, is, an amazing cook and will want to discuss whether it's dill or chives in the side dish that we're eating at a beachside café on holiday. He spent his teenage years experimenting with eyeliner and even kissed a few equally hairy-faced men. He has a penchant for exquisite socks and likes to smell nice. I took all this as proof that Ursula had done her job and that here was a truly emancipated man, one who was in touch with his feminine side. In short, a man as different as could be from my father, who has to have a week's worth of meals labeled and put in the freezer when my mother escapes him to go on a work conference.

And Joel loved all that was masculine about me. I could read maps and put up shelves. He used to beg me to get naked but for my tool kit, said that me wielding a power drill was as sexy as it got, while at the same time useful as I did all the DIY at his place. I knew more about football and could beat him at table tennis. He loved that, and I loved that he did—unlike previous boyfriends, he never felt threatened by my competitiveness and joy in winning.

Then Rufus came. I, much to Joel's initial envy, got the maternity leave. He expressed jealousy at this fact and said that he was sad he'd never know what it would be like to grow a living creature in his stomach, while never offering to give up alcohol and soft cheese in sympathy. He said he wished he could feel the closeness of a breastfeeding mother to her child, but never bothered to help me arrange the bank of cushions necessary for this unromantic maneuver, or think to get me a glass of water once Rufus had finally, painfully, become plugged in.

He had a fortnight's paternity leave, which he kept on referring to as "holiday" and treated it as such. "What are we going to do today?" he'd ask each morning. "Who's coming to visit?" I could only sit on an undignified inflatable ring due to the macramé performed on my nether regions, while Rufus seemed to be feeding constantly and yet not putting on the requisite weight. I'd listen to Joel telling the world how much he'd never known that such a tiny creature could inspire so much love, while I was thinking about how I'd never known that such a tiny creature could create so much laundry. As Joel would proclaim how much he loved being a father, I'd think, yes, a father, I'd love being a father. He'd never known love like it and I, too, was oozing love, except mine was overwhelming me. Joel's love for Rufus seemed fun, like a summer affair, all giddy and euphoric. Mine was anxious and exhausting, as my head filled with calculations about feed times and terrifying visions of the accidents that could happen to my darling vulnerable boy. Joel would laugh when I tried to tell him how frightening I sometimes found it to carry Rufus up and down stairs. "What if I trip and fall?" Or worse, unspoken, that some malevolent spirit would cause me to throw him. "What if someone steals him in the buggy when I turn to reach something down from the supermarket shelves?" I asked. I didn't understand how it could not have occurred to Joel that a baby of Rufus's evidently exceptional beauty and intelligence was a magnet for child snatchers.

Once we had a baby, I used to wonder what I had ever found to worry or argue about before then. Having a baby had opened up huge over-stuffed cupboards of fights to be had. All the love I had felt for Joel seemed to have been transferred to this tiny creature with his little cap of already red hair. The more enchanting I found Rufus, the more irritating I found my husband. He who I'd loved so unreservedly, I loathed. I loathed the way he put on diapers, the way he wouldn't bother to do up all the snaps on a babygro, the way he'd throw Rufus at me the minute he started crying with the words "I think he needs feeding again."

If paternity leave was bad, life got worse when he went back to work. He was at work, I was at home and without it ever being said out loud, this meant that I was responsible for all things to do with the house. He stopped being able to wash his own shirts or go to the supermarket—after all, what else did I have to do all day? I was lucky enough to have this holiday, this protracted honeymoon of baby bonding, and so I had no right to complain about a few extra chores.

I envied him going to work, but when the time came for me to do so, I was horrified at the prospect. Only a combination of Mary Poppins and Mother Courage could be trusted with my golden child. Since she didn't exist I put him into a nursery, which might as well have been a Romanian orphanage for the cruelty I felt in doing so. I went back part-time, because the law said it was my right. Mitzi had said she didn't know why people had babies if they weren't going to be with them, though she managed to have as much childcare as I did, despite not having a job to go to. Twenty percent less money and one more day with Rufus had seemed like a favorable exchange rate, but I hadn't realized that it represented about 100 percent of the money I had to spend on anything other than mortgage and food. Somehow, too, the fifth of the job that got reduced was all the bits that I had liked best about it and none of the boring grind I'd gladly have eschewed.

Part-time work had seemed to be the perfect solution and everyone told me how lucky I was. But it only further calcified the roles that had begun to form on maternity leave. I'm home, he's work. Part-time work for me didn't translate into part-time home for him, and my longed-for weekday with Rufus was quickly filled with fixing the washing machine and standing in the line at the post office clutching passport applications. The legislation that gives the right to part-time work for mothers is cited as a great victory for women, but I felt like I no longer fit in at the office, nor did I fit in with those mothers who didn't have a job. I needed to be amphibious, but instead I was a fish out of water. I ruminated on going full-time or giving it all up. I'm not sure it would have made much difference if I'd gone back full-time, since Joel's level of housework would not have risen as much as my resentment; while if I'd given up, I'd have been buried in even more dirty laundry than I already was, not to mention the disastrous effect on our finances.

So here we are. I'm not quite sure how we got here, though I suppose I must have done my fair share of the driving.

The next day over breakfast, I ask Joel, "Can you remember any of the labors of Hercules?"

"Hmm," he answers, not at all surprised that I am asking him this random question, but eagerly searching for some trivia. "There was the lion, wasn't there? The one whose skin was impervious to arrows or daggers. Ursula had a brilliant illustrated book of the myths of Greece and Rome. What was its name?"

I shrug and he continues: "The best one was that he had to capture the Hound of Hades—he had three dog heads. Did that involve Medusa? I wonder if I could find my old copy. We should get a Greek myths book for Rufus, shouldn't we?"

"Yes, that's what I was thinking," I say. "Just what I was thinking."

3

Wet Towels on the Bed

Friday comes and I throw off the shackles of domesticity to prepare for the party. The party in a fancy flat with architectural details and skylights and industrial concrete floors and child-unfriendly sculptures. Cara's party.

Cara and her flat deserve an unusual amount of care with my appearance. I put on a new dress, a claret-colored chiffon affair, which shimmies over my Spanx pants (these serve the dual purpose of squidging in my post-partum belly and being sexually repulsive to Joel. Result). The dress also requires that I plump up my cleavage, which, with the help of an extra-strength shove-up bra, can go from *National Geographic* to *Sports Illustrated* in seconds. I've just lost the last of those remaining pregnancy pounds and if I squint at the mirror I feel really quite pleased with the result. I don't know if I'm the old me, the pre-children one, or a very new me, some post-breeding upgrade, but I feel good.

My makeup bag is ringed with stains, like the trunk of a tree telling of past eras. To look through its wares is to look through my history: the set of brushes I bought after a terrifying makeover in a Manhattan department store, which I went to on a trip with a previous boyfriend; the ancient lip gloss I wore on my first date with Joel in an attempt to make my thin smackers look sensual and gooey, but which instead seemed to trap locks of my hair and then later in the evening, mission accomplished, some of his; the full eyeshadow palette that I got for my wedding day makeup, only one color of which I've ever used. Each item tells of a previous life of vanity. I miss my vanity, which abandoned me the day that Rufus was born. I feel like narcissism was one of those school friends you'd had since your teens, who you both loved and loathed in equal measure and long wished to be rid of, but then when she was gone you missed dreadfully. Looking in the mirror so much reminded me that I was there. Now I don't even know that I have a reflection—I might be like a vampire and when I look, there'll be nothing. The only time I see myself in a mirror, it feels like, is to hold up a baby to show them their reflection, providing a mocking contrast between their pudgy, non-sundamaged skin and mine.

I emerge, as glamorous as it gets, to the bathroom, where I am greeted by a husband and two wailing children, the older of whom has recently become self-conscious about nudity. They both stand up, shivering, in the bath, with Rufus cupping himself like a footballer about to defend a free kick.

37) *Never pulls the plug on the boys' bath water, leaving me to do it later, which involves me being elbow-deep in tepid water and ensures that the stain of grime around the edge has calcified.*

38) *Bathroom floor is always soaked whenever he's been in there. Doesn't matter if he's had a bath or not. It's like he's got some sort of unique ecosystem running in there, with permanently rising sea levels.*

39) *Ignores the towels hanging on the boys' pegs and instead takes out some fresh, fluffy, special occasion towels out of what I like to refer to as the "airing cupboard," aka one shelf squeezed above the immersion tank.*

40) *Leaves used bath towels to marinate in said pools of water.*
41) *Or throws them on the bed.*

Joel does a proper builder's whistle. It was one of the talents that really impressed me when we first got together. "Nice dress. Nice body, too."

Rufus will soon reach the age where he'll gag at this sort of remark, but instead adds, "You look really pretty, Mommy," and I feel a flush of love along with a fearful acknowledgment that it won't be long now before he decides that he doesn't want to marry me after all.

"Is it chiffon?" asks Joel. "It's gorgeously floaty."

"Thanks." In the litany of Joel's faults, I cannot add a failure to notice a new haircut or outfit. He's frighteningly in touch with that bit of his feminine side, the bit that appraises a wardrobe rather than ever tidies it. "You look smart too." He's put on a suit in the manner of a man who doesn't have to wear one for work so it's quite fun to dress up at weekends.

We make our journey to Cara's flat, which is in an old factory in an area of town once colonized by young artists, but now populated by estate agents advertising "live-work spaces." I know it well since it's also infested with small television production companies, including mine.

A couple clutching a gift buzz on Cara's entryphone system before us and we slip in with them and have one of those embarrassing "I guess you're going where we're going" conversations, where you hope you get to the flat quickly enough to avoid the "So how do you know Cara?" next stage. Should I have bought a present? What would I bring Cara? Some sort of bespoke olive oil?

Becky opens the door to the flat and the couple smile politely and give her their coats while waltzing past.

"God, who are they?" I whisper to Becky.

"I don't know them and they evidently don't know me. Do I look like the hired help?"

"Totally," I say, checking out her ill-advised attempt at cocktail chic, which does nothing to flatter her rangy figure and generous boobs, the ones she's always talking about getting reduced.

"I'm so glad you're here," says Becky and I realize she's slightly drunk already, an impression not dispelled by the way she grabs a flute of champagne from a passing woman—one who is, in fact, the real hired help, brought in for the evening. "It's full of Cara's work contacts. You asked me what this was in aid of, and I can tell you: fattening Cara's client list. So many boring financial journalists and businessy people, you wouldn't believe it. You've got to come to the lav with me."

I leave Joel, who shrugs and goes in search of a stranger to talk to with confidence, and follow Becky into the loo.

"What's up?"

"I had an ultrasound scan yesterday."

"Oh?" She's pregnant? Or, oh my god, cancer?

"I was referred by my doctor. They wanted to see if I've got polycystic ovaries."

I compute this. "Oh, that—thank god. I thought you were going to say polycystic fibrosis. That's the one with the lungs, isn't it? The one you've got is the one with the ovaries?"

"No shit, Sherlock."

I dredged through a mental file index of health pages in glossy magazines. "Polycystic ovarian syndrome, isn't it? It affects your fertility." What else? "Is it the one where you put on weight and become hairier?" How awful would that be?

"That's the one. Hairiness is one possible symptom, yes. Book that session at the beauticians, why don't you—PCOS *and* I'm a lesbian. Hairlessness was never an option."

"Becks, I'm sorry." And I am because she doesn't deserve any pain, ever. "What does it mean, in practical terms?" I hate not being near the Internet when faced with any medical diagnosis. My fingers itch for a consultation with Dr. Google.

"Getting pregnant might be more difficult or impossible. I don't ovulate every month, you see. And I just thought I was lucky to have such light and irregular periods." She gives a rueful little laugh. "It means I ought to get going on it."

"On what?"

"Trying for a baby."

"I never knew you wanted children. It's not something we've ever talked about."

"So if we don't talk about something, it means I'm not allowed to think it? Or is it that I'm not allowed children, is that what you think?"

"God, no, that's not what I meant. I just didn't know, that's all. You'd be a brilliant mother." Would it be crass to ask who would be the father? "So you'd do it, like, on your own? Proverbial turkey basters and stuff?"

"Ideally not." She sighs. "I don't know what to do about Cara. It's only been a year, so it seems too soon to be discussing children, but at the same time I don't feel I can hang around waiting."

"Do you need her permission? Can't you just go ahead and get the sperm or whatever and go for it?"

"On my own? Is that what you'd do, if you hadn't met Joel, at our age?"

"I don't know. I think I've always seen children in the context of a relationship..."

"And what makes you think I'd be any different?" Becky snaps. "Why would I not want my children born in the context of a loving relationship?"

"I didn't mean that." Though I suppose I did. I meant she was going to have to acquire the sperm anyway, so I wasn't quite sure how Cara's role was as central as that of Joel. "What does Cara think about children generally?"

"She doesn't think about them much at all." I look around at the bathroom with clear-glass double hers-and-hers sinks and open shelves that looks like a branch of a chic apothecary. "Though she once said," Becky continues, "that she doesn't know anyone who's been improved by having children. That was her word, *improved*."

"Ouch. What could she mean?"

"I think I want a child. I don't know. Let's say I want one and I want her. Except it'll probably turn out that I can't have them anyway so I'll risk driving her away for nothing. I've got to get on with trying but at the same time I'm scared of trying, as then I'll find out that I can't, so it's just easier not to do anything at all. But then I'll resent Cara for making me not try when maybe she'd be happy for me to try anyway. What am I going to do?"

"We could write a list. Of all the different options. Let's have a think, I'll help you. We can work it out together. I'll write it up for you, make it all clear, then everything else will follow. Decision one: have a baby or not have one. Two: what health questions need sorting. Three: when. Four: Cara or not. Five: who's the father. Honestly, there's nothing in life that can't be helped with the aid of a good list."

Becky snorted. "You and your lists. I've kept the one you did for me when I was trying to decide whether I should come out. Do you have your highlighter pens at the ready?"

"I do my lists on a computer these days. You may mock, but it will really help you. At least we can get things straight in your mind so that you can speak to Cara. You need to talk to her as soon as you know what you need to say."

"You're one to talk. Or not, as the case may be."

"What do you mean?"

"You were telling me the other day that you're going to divorce Joel because he doesn't disinfect his socks."

"No, I wasn't. I just feel there's quite a lot of things he does that piss me off. I'm writing a list."

"I know you are, all about whether I should have a baby or not."

"Yes, that one, but another one too. I'm writing one about Joel." Becky seems drunk enough for me to be able to begin explaining The List to her. I have to confide in someone. "A list of all the things he does that are really thoughtless, and after six months I'll go over it and this way I'll know my criticism of him is fair. He does quite a lot of things that make me unhappy."

"And he does a lot to make you happy." Becky is now on the loo, poking at her stomach. "Stupid crusty ovaries. Name me one thing that Joel does to annoy you."

"I don't know . . ." I pretend to be vague but I'm actually working out which of the transgressions I've noted so far is the most illustrative. "He leaves shit-filled diapers on the floor." Take that—sure to freak out a childless person.

"Having changed the diaper in the first place. Lots of men don't ever change diapers. Does he get a point for that, then? A plus point for being the sort of man to change a diaper?"

"What? Why should he get a medal for changing a diaper? I change a hundred bloody diapers for every one of his. It goes without saying that he should change a diaper."

"Yes, but you can't just count up the negative bits of a relationship without thinking of the good bits, can you? God knows what Cara would come up with against me if she did that."

There is a banging at the door. Becky covers up her stomach and opens the door.

"Cara," she says. "How long have you been there?"

"Long enough to know."

"Know what?"

"That whoever was in here was not merely evacuating."

I think Cara has the most beautiful clothes of anyone I know. If Armani had made clothes in a 1940s world with no rationing, this is what they'd look like. "I had assumed it was that ghastly man doing his drugs, so I'm rather relieved to find that it's you two, holed up cozily together." She raises a single eyebrow. I wish I could do that.

Becky is grappling with her pants. Cara's eyebrow goes up still further. "What are you two up to? Should I be jealous?"

"God, no," I stammer. I always stammer and blush and fumble around Cara.

"I was only teasing," she laughs. Of course—nobody would ever transgress if they were lucky enough to be with Cara.

"We were just talking," says Becky, grumpily. "What, like there's a law against it?"

"You're drunk."

"Am not."

"I think you'll find that you are."

"Am not, am not, am not."

If Becky goes on behaving in this way, then they're really not going to need any children, since the household already contains one ready-made teenager.

"Sorry, Cara," I mumble. "We'll get out of the loo now."

"Don't worry about it. I love your dress," she says and strokes my arm while looking me up and down. Thanks to the control pants and my weight loss I sense that I might make the grade. "What a lovely froth it is."

I'm sure I feel a spark, but that may just be the static created by her rubbing the, in fact, rather cheap viscose of my high-street purchase. She leans over and whispers in my ear. Her breath is actually cool; it feels as if it would smell like she'd just had a scrape and polish with a dental hygienist.

"Can you look after her?" she says. "She seems to have hit the champagne a bit early."

I nod.

"Thank you," she says, giving my arm another stroke. As if I had any choice in the matter. I can't imagine anybody refusing Cara anything.

I drag Becky off in search of Joel, who is chatting to a girl who's running her fingers through her hair and who quickly recedes on being introduced to the wife.

42) ~~Is weirdly attractive to other women. It's his disheveled charm, I guess—though I should know, I fell for it myself.~~

All right, all right. It's not as if he can help it. Though I'm not sure he needs to listen quite so intently to what strange women have got to say to him. "You're great, Joel," Becky begins to say to him. "Really great. I hope Mary appreciates you."

"I'm sure she does," he says. "In a secret, special way."

"Just tell her to remember all the good things, too, not just the bad ones."

"I do," I interrupt. "Really I do, Becky."

"Promise me, Mary. Give credits as well as debits."

"What are you talking about?" asks Joel.

"Nothing. I promise, Becky." I look around, frantic for distraction. "I didn't know you'd invited Mitzi."

"I didn't. Cara did. Cara thinks Mitzi's one of the few acceptable people she's met through me. Wasn't really through me anyway, was it? It was through you two. They've really taken to each other. Ring each other up and stuff."

"They would, wouldn't they?" I say. Cut by a tailor—no, costumier—from the same expensive cloth made by "an amazing collective in India, they're artists, really": blonde Mitzi and dark Cara, Rose White and Rose Red, like two sisters in a children's story. Cara greets Mitzi with an extravagant enthusiasm, which is followed by them standing a foot apart, still clutching each other's hands, swapping compliments.

I feel a pang of jealousy. It's always unnerving to see two people who only know each other through me become friends in their own right. When they finish admiring each other's shoes, Mitzi comes over to join us.

"All right, Mitzi," says Joel. "How have you been?"

"Well. Busy, frantic."

"Really?" he says. "Doing what?"

"Raising four children in a complicated world, Joel, to begin with."

"Yeah, but when are you going to go back to work?"

43) *Insistence that "work" is something only done in an office, factory or building site.*

"Because working in TV is such a valuable contribution to society, isn't it?" says Mitzi, giving him that pouty smile of hers.

"Better than shopping."

"I don't do much of that."

"Really?" he says.

"No, I never buy anything any longer. I make and knit everything these days."

"Mary showed me your goody bags. Quite the Maria Von Trapp with the sewing machine, aren't you?"

"I like to think I have the spirit of Maria trapped in the body of the Baroness." Mitzi smoothes her dress over her hips as she says this. Her body is very toned, I observe. I notice Joel is looking too, which was the aim, I suppose.

"And the mind of the Hitler Youth post boy," he adds.

"You're so funny." Their exchange finishes with a look that I've seen between them before, one that suggests they know something the rest of us don't.

"So, what have you been so busy with?" I say to change the subject. Joel wanders off, perhaps to find the flicky-hair girl again.

"The house in Norfolk." Ah yes, the house in Norfolk. "It's a nightmare. We've got a brilliant architect, quite brilliant, you'll be hearing so much about him in the future. But not everyone understands our vision, which is amazing and unprecedented and probably going to be the blueprint for all future conversions. The magazines are already ringing us about it. The local authorities are having ten types of hissy fit about the wind turbine. You'd think they'd want us to help the environment, since Norfolk will be the first one under water come the floods."

"What's their problem?"

"Something about the original flint and brick not being obscured is the official line. I think it's more likely to be resentment at second homers."

"They've got a point, I suppose." Second-home ownership is something on my long list of Things That Make Me Angry and I'm not even a poor, priced-out-of-the-market local.

"You think? Oh well, then, that means you'll be turning down our invitation for you all to stay to christen it for the half-term week at the end of May. To celebrate the building work being done." There is a steely edge to her voice that suggests she will be brooking no more delays from pesky bureaucrats or the builders. "It will have been a year since it began."

"Sorry, was that an invitation?"

"Well, if you can find it in your heart to forgive those who own a second home, then Michael and I would love to have you to stay," she says.

"Yes please. I'd love to see it. I think second homes are marvelous things, so long as they are shared with pauper friends."

"Of course. It's so beautiful, really it is. We can see right out over the marshes to the sea and the children can do all sorts of lovely old-fashioned things like cover themselves in mud and learn to sail and go crabbing." It sounds like an upmarket children's clothes catalog made flesh. I can see it now: "Molyneux, 6, likes dune jumping and crab sandwiches, wears Sloppy Joe in Teal."

"We'd love to."

"And just think, no horrid flights to get there either."

"Enough, enough. You had me at 'free holiday with friends.' Thank you so much." We look around the room. "I gather that you're bezzie mates with Cara these days."

"She's great, isn't she? I do hope your friend Becky doesn't screw this one up." We watch as Becky gesticulates wildly in conversation with one of Cara's clients.

"Or vice versa."

"I don't think Cara screws anything up," she says.

I'm woken at 3 a.m. by the smell of bacon and then can't get back to sleep.

44) *Gets up in the middle of the night when drunk to make carnivorous snacks for himself. Not just toast or biscuits like a normal person.*

45) *Obviously doesn't wash greasy meat-produce-smeared pans or surfaces after these midnight feasts.*

My mind is whirring with the combination of a couple of glasses of champagne, envy and the smell of pork products. I keep going over my conversation with Becky in the loo. So stupid of me not to think that she might want to have children. She'd be such a brilliant mother, firm but fair, involved without interfering. She's generous, too, and has more love to give than perhaps cool Cara is able to absorb. In the early stages of a hangover, I let myself think about not having children, but since I do have them, this can only happen in the event of a terrible accident or the courts ruling that I am an unfit mother. Perhaps I am. I feel sick at the thought of either of these occurrences and know that I will not sleep until I've gone to their room and checked that they are breathing.

I open the door and stare at them, enjoying my children at their most angelic, asleep. Gabe has a permanent cold and his tiny body gives out improbably loud snores. Rufus has pressed his whole body against the wall with the residual fear that he might fall from the top bunk, his thinking through of the consequences of "what if" remaining strong throughout the night. They are my life. Today, I think, I'll tell them that, instead of merely telling them off. I wish I loved being with them as much as I love them, but it's so hard in the bad and boring bits of the day.

Looking at them, I know that Becky should have children. She'd be all the love but none of the ill-temper. She'd work in the office efficiently and guiltlessly and then come home to love instead of to hector. She wouldn't have a problem with the mess of it. I should tell her to go for it, whatever Cara says. But then if I tell her how brilliant it is to have them, what if it turns out she can't after all? I'd be making it so much worse. How insensitive of me to even think it. Should I tell her how awful children are to make her feel better if she can't have them? But then that might sound ungrateful coming from someone who's been blessed.

I give up and think about what she had to say about the other list, my list. Maybe she was right in her drunken way, maybe I do need to outline Joel's plus points too. I'm sure it won't take long. It would be the first thing he'd complain about if I showed him The List—he's always telling me how I don't appreciate all that he does for me. I suppose The List could work like a bank account, with credits and debits—or, if it were like kids' charts, with smiley and unsmiley stickers. I start drawing up The List in my mind; how many columns, how many points, how does it work? It must be scrupulously fair, of course.

I wake, or am woken, in the morning, take a deep breath and vow to only see goodness for this one day. Joel is groaning and I hear the familiar crackle of a couple of ibuprofen extra strength being popped out of their foil. Abstention is a habit that I never quite got out of after the eighteen months of my two pregnancies, coupled with the fact that my hangovers are now more murderous than ever, and children and a hangover is the most toxic combination nature has invented. I thus rarely drink but try not to be smug about it.

"Don't give me that smug look," says Joel.

"I wasn't. It was a look of fondness."

"Yeah, right. Don't say anything."

"I won't." And I shan't. Not about the fact that he leaves unused analgesics lying around at child height, and worse, puts the empty foils back in the drawer so I can never find any pills when I've got a toothache. I shall not mention the disgusting phlegmy sounds he makes in the loo when he's got a hangover, nor that last night's clothes form a trail from the bathroom. God, his hangovers bug me. You know how men upgrade a cold to flu? It's the same with bloody hangovers. According to him, it's a pain akin to childbirth which he is most stoical to endure, rather than a self-inflicted inconvenience. I mean, if it's so terrible, why doesn't he just not drink?

"Poor you," I say, stroking his clammy forehead. "Is there anything I can get you?"

He doesn't look shocked by this uncharacteristic response, just relieved that I should finally be giving him the tenderness he deserves. "Can of Coke, please," he croaks. If I am to get anything positive down on The List this weekend, I'm going to have to get him in recovery, and fast.

In an act of extraordinary self-sacrifice I take the boys down with me, negotiate the bacon-greasy pan and loaf of bread left out in the night so the surface has gone stale, and scuttle back with the Coke, which he accepts weakly.

46) *Gets time off when he's ill. Only men and child minders are allowed to be ill. Mothers just have to get on with it.*

Sorry, today was supposed to be the positive day, wasn't it? I am about to throw the empty can of Coke into the bin, when I think of Joel and go the extra (carbon-free) mile to put it in the recycling.

1. **Is trying to do his bit for the environment. He bikes to work, turns the dregs of the veg box into soups that he eats when the rest of us refuse to, and gets up to turn the TV off at night rather than just leave it on standby. Is critical of Mitzi's eco efforts, though, as he says that being green should be about *not* doing stuff—flying, driving, buying—rather than doing all the expensive things that she's into: the new cars, the solar panels, the ethical clothing, etc. He maintains, for example, that she should just buy fewer clothes, instead of spending even more money on articles from pricey ethical fashion lines.**

I pass the bathroom, which fairly hums with the stench of urine, throwing me back to having to walk past the men's urinals in the park. I breathe out to evade its tendrils and to calm myself.

2. **Is so solicitous about the world's resources and our children's future that he has inaugurated an "If it's yellow, let it mellow; if it's brown, flush it down" policy on household flushing, thus saving, ooh, enough water each year to fill, a bath/swimming pool/pond/lake/an area the size of Wales.**

Oh, god, it's revolting. I spend my life flushing and flipping down toilet seats. It's so embarrassing when someone comes round and is faced with the Lucozade-like viscous goo. All pretty counterproductive, too, since the stains left behind force me to use ever more virulent chemical cleaners.

47) *Doesn't flush the loo. There, it's both a plus and a minus point.*

And, while we're on the subject...

48) *Believes that his quarter of an hour straining on the loo each morning is sacrosanct, that he is allowed time off from the breakfast frenzy to do his business, while I just have to fit my efforts in when I can, and as a consequence they take minutes—seconds, even—rather than this prolonged sitting at the throne of his daily bowel movement.*

It's the death of romance, isn't it, the fact that married people insult each other like siblings about their bodily functions? Joel and I spend an unhealthy amount of time discussing shit of the literal kind. "Big as a baby's arm," he'll say proudly, or "Could have sunk the *Belgrano*." "You're disgusting," I'll reply, in what he considers to be my bourgeois manner, to which he'll rejoin, "Well, at least my shit doesn't float." "That's the sign of a healthy digestive system," I'll insist, desperately trying to flush it down by dousing it in bleach. "Your digestive system is costing the earth," he'll point out. "Put down the gun," he'll gesture at the lime-scale remover. That's before we've even got onto the wonder that we express over the abnormal-colored sludge studded with undi-gested Lego that makes up the content of Gabe's diapers.

I remember Mitzi telling me once that Michael had never seen her go to the loo. "Not even a wee?" I asked and she shook her head. "What about farts?" "I'm not sure I've ever consciously done that," she said, and I thought of all those times that Joel had said, "Better an empty house than an ugly tenant" on letting out a particularly malodorous one, or I'd blamed Rufus for any smell coming from my direction.

He stumbles down half an hour later, by which time the boys' shrieking is making me feel as though I might as well have a hangover. He kisses me with beery breath.

"You look great," he says. "How come you look so lovely and I feel so lousy? You've stolen my youth and bottled and drunk it."

"I think it's what you may have drunk from a bottle that explains it, my darling."

3. **Compliments me. Not so extravagantly as he did in the beginning, but even now, he manages to find ways of telling me that I am nice to look at.**

"What are we doing today?"

Here we go. "Swimming and then trying to get through, I guess. It looks pretty grim outside and we haven't got any kids'

parties or anything. Maybe one party a weekend is enough for
you?"

He's slumped over a second can of Coke.

49) *Drinks fizzy stuff and eats crisps in front of the boys. Usually just before mealtimes. I always decant my Diet Coke
into a mug and hide in a cupboard to eat chocolate, in the
manner of a bulimic.*

I know, I know. Positive day and all that. It's just so bloody hard
when he does things like this.

"No, Rufus, you can't have any Coke."

"But..."

"I know Daddy's having some, but he's not feeling very well.
You're feeling fine." I turn to Joel. "Did you have a good time
last night?"

"It was all right. I don't really get the point of these stand up
and chat parties."

"As opposed to what, lie down in silence parties?"

"You know what I mean."

"Who did you talk to?" God, I speak to him in exactly the
same way as I do the boys. Is he going to mumble "no one" and
"nothing" at me?

"Becky..."

"A bit drunk."

"No, she was just having a laugh. She's great."

"She's your number one fan."

"Well, someone has to be."

"Who else?"

"Michael, though we run out of things to say to one another
once we've done the Premiership."

"You don't even like football."

"I don't even know that he does. And all I want to ask him is how come he's still so rich."

"Can't see any evidence to suggest he's not."

"More's the pity."

"Mitzi's looking good, isn't she?"

"Urgh, no, something weird's happened to her face. She's definitely had some work done."

"What?"

"Botox, obviously."

"Do you know, I think you might be right. That's why she has that shiny forehead that actresses have. I just thought they must all use the same moisturizer."

"And she's way too scrawny."

4. **Is good at saying other women are unattractively thin. I'm not sure I believe him, but well done him for trying. It is of particular importance to me that he should say this of Mitzi because of what happened when we met, back when the three of us worked together.**

"By the way," I say, "Mitzi's invited us to stay over the half term, you know, the summer one, at their new place in Norfolk."

"Did you manage to think of a good enough excuse?"

"No, of course not. Didn't even try. It will be great to have something to do then. Everywhere's so expensive over half term and it will be fantastic for the boys. Apparently, it's like *Swallows and Amazons*, all sailboats and buckets and spades and identifying the different species of seagulls."

Joel snorts. The whole of Britain outside London is a flyover state to him. Ursula would take him, occasionally, to the family cottage in the West Country, but most of the time they'd find themselves abroad doing a term's sabbatical in San Francisco, Hong Kong or Rome.

"Well, I'm going," I say. "You can stay here if you want and find another way to amuse two feral children for free in overcrowded museums for a week."

"What makes you think staying with Mitzi and Michael is free? At the very least, we'll have to pay for it by being entertaining. That is what we're there for, isn't it, to entertain all their boring banker friends?"

"Well, it's lucky that you don't find it an effort to be entertaining then, isn't it?" It's true. I feel that I work really hard to cultivate friends, while Joel does so effortlessly. Yet another thing I found attractive about him that is now irksome.

"I think there's something weird about Michael."

"I know you don't like him. You're always going on about how much you don't like him, to such an extent that you're the one who's being a bit weird. I don't know why, he's not that bad."

"He is. There's definitely something a bit evil about him."

"Like what?" I ask.

"I don't know. I don't know him well enough, but he's a bit Stepford. He's such an alpha male, with the City swinging-dick job and the kite surfing and the extreme sports, but I've never actually seen him behave in a recognizably human manner."

"Maybe Mitzi got him made in a lab to order. He's just what she always said she was going to end up with. Do you remember how she used to say that you don't love money, you just love where the money is?"

"Horrible bars in the City, as it turned out."

I shiver. "Do you remember that silver place with all the Russian girls? It was so blatant."

"But were they any more whorish than Mitzi is?"

I blanch, which Rufus takes as a sign that something is wrong. "Has Daddy said a rude word?"

"A bit, yes."

"Which one?"

"I'm not telling you."

"I wouldn't use it anyway. Some boys at school say 'fuck' and I think it's really silly of them to."

"Good for you, darling." I turn to Joel. "Why don't you look at the half term in May as an opportunity to stake out Michael? An interesting bit of fieldwork."

5. **Is very perceptive about people. Likes to observe then share his observations, and I find them endlessly interesting, except I wish he'd lay off Michael. This isn't really working, is it? It's not really the moral equivalent to leaving a tea bag out. His good points are too amorphous and vague, his bad points all too specific. Am I going wrong with The List or is he going wrong with his behavior? The latter, I'm sure. He doesn't do enough specifically good things. And that is why he drives me mad and why we'll end up divorced.**

I yawn. Then I yawn again in case he didn't notice. Please, I say to myself, I'll call off The List, I'll never nag again, just turn to me and say, "Darling, you look a bit tired, why don't you go back to bed and I'll take Gabe along when I take Rufus swimming?" I watch him in anticipation.

"I suppose you want me to take Rufus swimming," he says, instead.

I shrug, unable to speak.

"It's just that I think the chlorine will make me feel sick. You know how sensitive my stomach is."

"OK, I'll take him."

"Do you mind taking Gabe with you?"

The List is back on.

I continue making pacts with myself at the swimming pool. If he hasn't done anything to tidy up the breakfast stuff by the time I get back then I'm not even bothering with The List and six months' grace. It's over—right here, right now. And even if he's tidied up, if I discover that he's read all the sections of the paper already, and done that thing where it looks like he's spread them across the bed and rolled over them, then I'm certainly not going to bother with writing down his paltry collection of good points.

"Can't you even pull up your own trousers, Rufus? You're five years old."

"But Mom, I'm sick of doing everything. Gabe does nothing."

"Gabe's younger." And incompetent. But possessed of more natural charm than his elder brother. "I'm sick of doing everything, too."

Rufus gives me a look. It's a look that isn't even to say, "But that's your job." It's a look that says, "You? You have feelings?"

"Come on," I chivvy. "Let's get going. I don't have time for this."

I walk home with almost a thrill of anticipation. Decisions about our marriage don't need to wait six months; let's make them now. Let's make them on the toss of a domestic coin; say, whether he's put the cereal away.

I come back to find the kitchen clean, ish. It's not to my standards, he never wipes surfaces, but the breakfast things have been put away and a path burrowed through the felt-tips and Play-Doh tubs scattered across the floor.

6. **Is good at doing the occasional manic tidy. He argues that he does just as much tidying as me, which isn't true anyway,**

but even if it were, it doesn't take into account that I'm much better at avoiding creating a need for tidying up—the washing of pans as I go along, the feed-wipe routines, the one toy in, one toy out policy. But when he does tidy, I admit, he does so with some efficiency. Until he finds something, a newspaper or an old toy, that sets him off on some reverie. It doesn't matter if something is left half tidied, you see, because someone will be along later to finish the job. The transparent cleaner-mother-wife person who Rufus looked at so oddly when she dared to express some dissatisfaction.

"Thanks for tidying," I say and then kick myself. Why do I say thank you for tidying, when it would never occur to him to say thanks to me? All I do is perpetuate the idea that it is my job to clean and anything he does is a gift to me.

"Pleasure," he says. "Well, not really. Cleaning is bloody boring, isn't it?"

"Yes, it is."

"We ought to get a cleaner."

"We've got one."

"Not you. I mean a proper one."

"We have. Kasia. She comes on Tuesdays for three hours. I get in a paddy about how messy the house is, you tell me not to be so suburban, cleaning the house for the cleaner, we argue about what she's there for, and you complain as she puts your flowery shirts in my cupboard as she evidently can't countenance a man wearing such fripperies."

"Oh yes, her. Well we ought to get her more often, then. Although are we exploiting a woman from a poorer nation so that we don't have to do our own manual labor? Can it ever be right to have someone else get on their hands and knees in your own house?"

"There *is* something very, I don't know, supplicating, about cleaning floors and toilets, I agree." I stop myself from pointing out that the only time he gets on all fours is to amuse the boys by pretending to be a hippo. I spot a half-eaten biscuit on the floor and immediately get down to pick it up. While there, I start trying to pick out debris from under the fridge.

"Kasia's the one who's always throwing paper into the rubbish bin instead of the recycling, isn't she?" he says.

"And cleaning the house with paper towels and vacuuming the kitchen floor instead of wiping it and asking for powerful chemical detergents and putting the washing machine on with just a couple of dish towels inside."

"Really? Why didn't you ever tell me?" he asks.

I shrug. "I've never met an environmentally conscious cleaner."

"That's a bit rubbish of her. Have you had a word with her?"

"No, god, no, I'd never do that. If we're so awful that we need someone else to clean our toilets for us, then the last thing I'd do is give her strictures on how to do it."

"It is pretty awful that we have a cleaner, isn't it? I mean, we're young and healthy, perhaps we should do it ourselves."

"Why is it that it's socially acceptable to subcontract traditionally male jobs, like painting the house or clearing out the garden, but somehow I should feel ashamed about the fact that we have a cleaner for three hours a week? Ursula never felt guilty, did she?"

"True," he says. "And we always had a daily, so called because she came in every day."

"Not that it did much good."

"True. OK, so we have a cleaner, but couldn't we find someone a bit more environmentally sound? Is there no agency for green cleaners? Greeners, maybe?" He chortles.

"Like I say, I don't think those that clean can ever have the luxury of being green."

"Being green is not a luxury, it's a—"

"Leave it out, Joel. Save it for Mitzi, you and her have so much in common these days."

In a bid to get the number of positive points for my list up to a nice round dozen, I let Joel dictate the day's events. Which in reality means having to draw up a menu of suggested activities for him to choose from and then do all the prep to facilitate them.

50) *Uses me like some sort of parental PA. Typical weekend conversation runs like this:*

Him: "What are we doing today?"

Me: Respond with a detailed itinerary or, when I'm feeling up to it: "I don't know, what do you think we should do?"

Him: "I don't mind."

Me: "Well, we could go to the Science Museum to see the Heath Robinson exhibition, or we could go to the woods, it's supposed to be nice weather."

Him: "I don't mind."

Me: "OK, we'll go to the museum."

Whereupon if the excursion is a disaster, it's all my fault.

As if he were a child, I give him three choices, and, like a child, he inevitably opts for the last one presented to him: baking. I suppress the urge to suggest an alternative, since this activity inevitably leads to flour covering the kitchen like cocaine in a rock star's dressing room.

"Put in about four tablespoons of sugar, Gabe; one—that's

right, more or less—two, keep going," he orders gently and I watch as our second born treats the mixing bowl like a sand pit, completely failing to get the requisite spoonfuls of sugar into the mix.

7. **Bakes with the boys.** If there's one activity that seems to be the distillation of all that we hold dear in modern parenting, it's baking with the kids. It's as if the amount of time you spend baking is the simplest measure of How Good A Mother You Are. Baking combines our mania for home-cooked, unprocessed food and quality, old-fashioned activities with the children. It's a recipe for parental smugness. The mothers I know will never have a baking session without making sure that the activity is broadcast to the world. "Sweetheart, let's go home now and make that cake"; "Here, we brought you some alphabet biscuits—we made them ourselves, didn't we, Felix? Yes, that's right, it's a 'wuh' for Waitrose"; "We're a bit tired, I'm afraid, as we've been stirring the Christmas cake mix."

Joel is different, though. He doesn't make a big deal of his cooking or announce it to the world. He just does it and gives every impression of enjoying it.

I sort of like baking, too, but never so much as I think I should. I find myself not letting the children do the measuring out and spooning in for fear that the proportions will not be recipe-exact. I don't like them licking the bowl because the mix is full of raw eggs, which pregnancy has taught me is A Bad Thing. Joel lets them do what they like with the ingredients and yet somehow the results always seem to taste better than mine.

I feel an unexpected burst of love that is directed at Joel as much as at Rufus and Gabe. They look like an ad for the perfect father and sons, doing cute things with icing sugar on noses and learning about weights and measures in the process.

"Do you want to do the coloring, Rufus?" Joel asks. "You're mixing red and green. Interesting. What happens when we mix red and green?"

"It looks like poo poo," says Rufus, peering at the icing.

"It makes brown, yes. Shall we make poo biscuits?" He takes a small disc of mixture and rolls it into a sausage. Rufus and Gabe fall about laughing and enthusiastically copy him. "We'll put this lovely poo-colored icing on it when they come out, shall we?"

8. **Makes our children laugh. Is the funny one. I'm the boring one, the Wise to his Morecambe, the Dean Martin to his Jerry Lewis.**

A man as big as Joel can't help but look incongruously gorgeous while sporting oven gloves and putting a tray of poo-shaped biscuits in to bake. Bless, I think. Curses, I think as he then leaves the room with the boys trailing in his wake as if he's the Pied bloody Piper. Yes, leaves the room. Without sweeping up any of the flour, throwing away the excess poo-colored icing or washing up the bowls. He just leaves them for me to tidy up, consciously or not. For every good thing he does, another bad one follows— the yin and yang of our partnership. I breathe in through my nose and out through my mouth like I was taught in yoga. (Now if ever there was an inappropriate form of exercise for the woman some people refer to as Scary Mary, it was yoga. All that peace and meditation stuff drove me mad. I kept on waiting for the sweaty bit to get started. I mean, what's the point of exercise if it doesn't make you drip? I soon gave it up and swapped to classes with names like Body Combat and Kick Ass, Tums & Legs.)

Later, Joel extends his culinary skills to non-scatological adult food by rustling up a nice roast chicken, which he refrains from stuffing with butter, on account of my intolerance. His repertoire veers toward the Elizabeth David end of things and he manages to not complain too frequently about the fact that he is prevented from dolloping cream and butter into all that he mixes.

9. **Is a good cook. Sure, he's messy, but sometimes it is bliss to be cooked for. Just the very act of it makes one feel nurtured and cherished. He cooks with enthusiasm and love, while I cook with practicality and ready-made sauces.**

I exceed my usual two small glasses of wine by another couple. We lounge on the sofa watching Saturday night rubbish. He rolls a joint and the alcohol has taken the edge off the irritation this usually provokes in me and I don't order him out into the cold, but merely ask him to stick his head through an open window into the garden. I don't even feel particularly irked by the fact that he's espresso guy at work (hyped up, over-zealous and frenetic) and weed guy at home (useless slobby stoner). I even have a drag myself and experience a Proustian moment from its taste, throwing me back to our courtship and afternoons spent giggling and watching black-and-white films on TV.

We lie on the sofa in a rare state of contentment. He takes my socks off and I'm mildly embarrassed about the parmesan nature of my feet, but don't care too much on account of a) being sodden by alcohol and b) it being only Joel.

10. **Gives a really good foot massage. A really, really good foot massage.**

I hope he doesn't speak. He doesn't. I feel as if I'm drifting in and out of consciousness. He moves up to my shins and then strokes my thighs through my jeans. The stiffness of the material creates an enjoyable tension, but not as enjoyable as the feeling when he removes them and begins to run his tongue along the same place. I don't know whether it's the effort of trying to think up his good points or merely being coshed by alcohol and a couple of tokes, but I decide not to stop him. "Decide"? That's the wrong word—there's no way I could stop him even if I wanted to. It's been a while.

11. Has a remarkably dextrous tongue.

He licks the very top of the inside of my thighs, while his hands remove my pants (due to a laundry crisis, they're the ones that I bought for my last post-partum hospital stay and come up past my waist) and then move under my bra and onto my breasts. His tongue now moves up and into my untamed pubic hair, past the episiotomy scars and expertly finds the right place to concentrate its attentions. One hand stretches out to my nipples, while the other puts a finger gently inside me and out, inside and out, all the while his tongue playing me like the strings on a violin.

I am now lying back on the sofa, while he is on his knees so that his head is at just the right place. I don't want it to go on too long, but neither should it stop just yet.

I can't wait any longer and I pull him up and into me and his head is now level with mine. I tilt my head to kiss his neck.

"I love you," he says and I'm embarrassed and try to avoid his eyes. That's almost too personal for me, too intimate, it's as if I need to make a stranger of him. Whatever they tell you in women's magazines, sometimes sex is easier with strangers. All the talk and abandon and the looking into each other's eyes in the moment should be easier with someone you know as well as we know each other, but I need him to be either the man I knew a long time ago or a man I've yet to meet. I move my eye-line to his expansive chest and it works, it makes him feel fresh to me once again.

I feel stoppered by him. I've forgotten how completing it can feel. I think I hear a child crying, but it's a cat wailing on the street, or a police siren, they all have the same note of distress. I work hard to get back in as I'm almost there, almost, I can get there, just not quite yet. "Not yet," I whisper, "almost." He stops himself and then starts again. I work to get back into it, refusing to allow myself to be distracted by street noises that my imagination mutates into the sound of crying children. I try to stop the random faces that enter my head from preventing me as I am almost there, I don't want it to go, I must let go. A last face falls into my consciousness. It's Cara. I finally let go, calling out to let him know, followed seconds later by a relieved Joel.

12. **He's really not bad in bed. Not bad at all. What am I saying? He's great. The only man in my not-very-extensive list of lovers who has always been able to get me there. It didn't help that the other handful were all chosen purely on the basis of their pretty-boy looks—some sort of competition I was running with Jemima, I think, as to who could pull the boy who looked most like a member of Take That first time around. As a consequence, it was as if it was enough that they deigned to sleep with you—that was pleasure enough, surely?**

I stretch across the sofa, woozily plea-bargaining in my head once again. If, I say to myself, you go and find a wet wipe to help clear up the patch on the sofa, then I will destroy The List. You will have passed my test before it has even begun. We lie there. I feel twitchy about the dribble running down my thighs and onto our already stained and manky sofa. He rolls over and adds a Turin-shroud-like imprint of his cock onto one of the expensive cushions that I bought in a fit of interiors improvement. He gets up and I hear him stumble, joint- and sex-stoned, into the bathroom. A flush sounds.

"Get some paper or a wipe, get some paper or a wipe," I silently implore, still feeling a tingling good will. "Get some paper or a wipe."

He comes back. He is empty-handed.

4

An Incredible Cook

"If you want, you can sleep in; that's my present to you, my love," says Joel with a kiss on the morning of my thirty-sixth birthday, as the boys bounce around us.

"Why, thanks."

"Just wait here and I'll go and do my thing."

Oh, god, here we go: crime number 48, the extended session in the locked toilet. My birthday good will dissolves like a vitamin C tablet. After 20 minutes, the boys, who've been jumping on the bed, and I become restless and go into the bathroom.

I reel. "It's a wonder you don't asphyxiate yourself."

"What, and your shit don't stink?" he replies, the swear word causing us both to reflexively glance at our oldest boy child.

"Well, I don't sit there like a prince on a throne for three hours. I thought I was getting a lie-in."

"You are."

I gesture at the boys. "So relaxing."

"You just need to look after them while I make you your special breakfast."

"Not much of a lie-in then, is it?"

He sighs. "All right, all right, but you know how difficult it is to cook and look after them."

"You don't say."

"Happy birthday, sweetheart. You don't look a day older than when I met you."

"Unless I was a particularly raddled-looking twenty-seven-year-old, I'm sure I do. God, thirty-six, I'm way nearer my forties than my twenties now," I say, peering into the mirror, which due to the fact that neither of us have changed the lightbulb that blew a fortnight ago, casts a not unflattering glow. Perhaps he's right, perhaps I am weathering well despite all the anger and bitterness I'm feeling. You'd have thought it would be showing in my face. There must be a photograph of me somewhere in which I appear shriveled with ill will and resentment, allowing me to look, well, all right, I suppose.

"No, really," he says. "I was looking at you talking to Becky and Mitzi and you'd never know you were all the same age."

I give mental thanks to the trichological Botox known as a fringe and decide at least to try to enjoy my birthday. I am leavening the load of XY chromosomes in this household by inviting my sister Jemima. She's the only one of my family, my first family, that I've got down south and introduces into this house the pleasantly familiar elements of my hometown, food obsessive-compulsiveness and impractical footwear.

My birthday resolution to be happy is further tested as I go downstairs 20 minutes later to view the carnage left over by the preparation of pancakes with maple syrup and blueberry compote. There's a huge bunch of flowers, from an expensive celebrity florist. They are undeniably gorgeous. Joel is good with such things.

"Brassica and French tulips," he says. "They're grown in Kent, not Kenya. I checked."

I don't bloody want apple blossom and French tulips, I think, I want wiped worktops and dressed children. I look at the flowers again. They are so perfect and sculptural that I feel our kitchen is unworthy of them; they deserve work surfaces like Mitzi's to showcase their loveliness. I'm wrong, it's not that I don't want these flowers, I just want the life to match. "Thank you, they're beautiful."

"And so are you."

These are the sort of words he's lavished on me from the moment we first got together. They brought me to a stupor of love, but now that love is hungover. His compliments have become habitual.

He gives me flowers, but he doesn't put them into a vase. He shows them off to visitors, but he fails to empty the water, even when it's slimy with age.

I take out a shepherd's pie from the freezer for lunch. Or "just shepherd's pie," as Joel always refers to it, despite the fact that it's actually a total pain of peeling and chopping to make, and always ends up keeping me up until way past my bedtime mashing potatoes. I'm good at "just" type of recipes—bolognese, macaroni and cheese, sponge cakes—while Joel excels at "Wow, look at that, you spoil us" food. Which may in fact be rustled up in minutes: pan-fried scallops with a balsamic jus or a steak with homemade Béarnaise sauce.

Jemima arrives, ostentatiously wearing a pair of sunglasses amid the winter gloom. I hug her and enjoy the fact that she is my size. Not as huge and bear-like as my husband, not as small and terrier-like as my sons. She smells delicious and clean and unfrazzled.

"Do you mind?" I gesture toward her shoes and the pile of outdoor ones we've left by the door.

"A bit. I mean, have you seen them?"

They are spindly-heeled, complicatedly strapped and pointy-toed. "They're fabulous," I say, slipping easily into the shoe-language of yore. These days I tend to reserve the words "gorgeous," "exquisite" and "fabulous" for people's new kitchen units. "Absolutely stunning. They're far too nice to join that hell-hole shoe mountain. Why don't we go and put them on the dresser where they can be properly venerated?" She takes me at my word and carefully conveys them toward the kitchen.

"You're looking thin," she says. "Have you lost weight?"

"A bit, I think," I reply.

"Almost half a stone, I'd guess, maybe a bit less. Five pounds?"

"All right, it's six pounds. My, you're good," I say. "You're like one of those boys who can guess a woman's bra size to within half a cup just by looking."

She giggles. "I try. Do you think I can market this particular skill in some way?"

"Additional skills and interests on your CV? Anyway, you're one to talk. You look fantastic. Really toned. Have you been going to the gym a lot?"

"Three to four times a week."

"Lucky you. I never get a chance to go anymore. Although I'm now quite thin, I'm skinny-flabby, do you know what I mean?"

"It's a small price to pay," she says. "For all this." She gestures around the kitchen, which looks like a bad TV drama version of a family home, rather than the real thing. All the obvious clues are there—the children's daubs stuck to the walls, invitations to birthday parties hanging off fridge magnets, piles of picture books on an old pine dresser, brightly colored crockery hanging on hooks. And me, too, I'm just set dressing—I can't be the real mother at the heart of this hearth, I'm a bad actor pretending to be a grown-up. I'm a fake materfamilias. Martyr-familias, perhaps.

Jemima looks wistful, as she does when the subject of her

single and childless/child-free state arises. I am not to complain of my life or describe it as less than perfect. She brightens as Joel enters the room.

"Darling," he says, enveloping her. "Nice sunglasses."

"We call them sunnies nowadays."

"Oh, you crazy young folk. Come and tell me all about what life is like out there." He gives a theatrically wistful sigh. "Are you still doing the Internet dating thing?"

I wince, waiting for Jemima to do the hurt, single-girl look, but she swings back to anecdote mode for his benefit. "I'm on three separate sites. On one of them, I've got the seventh most visited profile. It's exhausting sifting through all the emails. God, there are some freaks out there."

"But some not-freaks too?" I ask.

"Oh, yes. There's this surfer guy who wants to hook up. He is hot to trot."

"How old is he?" I am so boring and predictable.

"Twentysomething. Late twentysomething, I think."

"I'm not surprised you're inundated," Joel says. "It's brilliant. A smorgasbord of possibilities with none of the stigma of dating agencies of the past. I mean, if someone like you goes online... If I were single and went onto a dating site and there were girls like you—well, it's like the sort of thing I used to fantasize about as an adolescent."

I wonder if he still does.

"You do look fantastic, Jemima," I say, falling into an age-old but strangely comforting routine of everything being about her, even on my birthday. It's always a relief to cede attention in her direction. Her eyebrows are plucked, her skin exfoliated, her clothes fashionable. "We could be a 'before and after' shot on one of those cosmetic surgery makeover shows. You're the physical embodiment of what I'd look like if I hadn't had children."

"Or been born with red hair," she chips in. "Not that it isn't lovely. I've always loved your hair."

"Flame," I say, "as in flame-haired temptress."

Joel laughs a little too heartily.

"Do you want to go and check that the boys aren't killing each other?"

"They're fine."

I give him the look that conveys this was a rhetorical question and he slopes off.

Jemima physically slumps once Joel leaves the room. "It's not that great, you know."

"What isn't?"

"Internet dating. It's all very well having a limitless supply of fresh meat, but the thing is, you don't want it to be endless, do you? I mean, the whole point is that it should end with you meeting someone great. Me meeting someone great."

"It's not the end, though, meeting someone. It's not the end of problems and the solution to everything. It's just the beginning of a whole set of new ones." How can I communicate to her, without being patronizing, that there's a whole long life beyond the chick-flick ending.

"But at least you've got the option of all these new problems. I'm beginning to worry that your thirties is like some gigantic game of musical chairs and somehow I've been left standing."

"Jemima, I'm really sure that should you choose to settle down, then you will. And anyway, you're young. You'll always be my little sister."

"I'm almost thirty-five."

"And you're gorgeous. You've always been the gorgeous one. I once heard Mom on the phone saying, 'I know, who'd have thought it, but Jemima's the unmarried one.'"

"God, she is awful, isn't she?" We snigger. Ganging up on our mother has always united us. Joel and I might not have mastered the concept of shared parenting, but Jemima and I have got shared daughtering licked. Although of late, I've been wondering whether we haven't been a bit unfair to Mom. We did nothing to help her around the house. She tried everything to induce us. Timetables, lists and bribery, but nothing worked. She did housework too well, that was her mistake. She did it so seamlessly, secretly and silently, that I never actually realized she was doing it all and how much there was of it.

"Honestly, make the most of this time," I say. "What may follow is not an endless honeymoon of perfection. I always think that being single is like being unemployed—if you knew how long it was going to last, you could have such a fun time of it."

"It's not fun anymore," she says. "I'm so bored of it. I'm bored of the bloody dates and the swapping childhoods and the 'Did you have any pets when you were growing up?' and the phoning and the not phoning. There are so many ways to be not-called these days. They can not-call you by email, by Facebook, by mobile, by landline, by office phone, by text. Fuck, I'm sick of it. Do you know why I go to the beauticians so much?"

"To look as good as you do?"

"It's because I want to be touched. Oh, god, that sounds really pervy, doesn't it? When you're single, you crave being touched so you end up paying for face massages and full-body seaweed wraps. You crave human touch and it's better to pay for it this way than have stupid one-night stands with men you don't even particularly like but who still manage to make you feel shit if they not-call you. And guilty if they do because you have absolutely no intention of ever seeing them again."

"I have too much touch in my life. I'm always picking them off, like tics."

"Who, Joel or the boys?"

"All of them. Urgh." She smiles. My ploy to make her feel better has worked. It's a lie, of course, at least partially. I love that my boys are like hooks of Velcro, ever-ready to attach themselves to the mother loops. I grab at them when they walk past me to crush their skinniness into my chest, pulling them in so tight it's as if I want to be one again, as we were in pregnancy. It's a wonder to me that I have this constant and accommodating source of physical comfort and I dread the day, which cannot be too far off, when it will end. Joel, though, with his clammy arms at night and the way that he is rendered on a different scale to Rufus and Gabe—I was telling the truth about that.

"I'm sorry you're feeling like this, Jem. Maybe twentysomething surfer boys aren't the way forward." Jemima still has her penchant for pretty boyband member types, which was a good look when she was an equally exquisite young thing, but doesn't make for ideal settling-down material.

"You think I should lower my standards?"

"Not lower so much as change them. An actuary rather than an actor this time? Dad's fat whistling man, you know, the one he said he wanted us to end up with."

"He's fat because he loves his food."

"And he whistles because he's so jovial and contented."

Jemima puts her head in her hands. "Oh, god, I don't want that. I want thin angsty man."

"And I just want you to be happy."

I do want her to be happy. Despite all the fighting and the dieting and the clothes-stealing, that's all we've ever wanted for each other. I want her to have what I have, I suppose—the marriage and the children—but what arrogance is it of mine to think that's what will make her happy? I mean, it's not exactly working for me, is it? I worry that in fact, I want her to meet someone and settle down not because I want her to be happy like me, but because I want her to be *unhappy* like me.

She perks up once again as Joel returns. People do that, around Joel—he can make everyone but me glow. He's well on his way to becoming fat, though I haven't heard him whistle much of late.

"Joel, do you think you can tidy up the breakfast things so I can get on with laying the table?"

Jemima makes that rising-inflection "ooh" sound that children do when their teacher gets annoyed, as in "Ooh, Miss has got a bit batey." "Mary," she says, "nobody would ever guess that you kept your side of our bedroom so messy that there were things growing in it."

"I know, she was wonderfully untidy," says Joel. "It was one of the things I fell in love with, her fantastically slatternly ways."

"Yeah, well, you have to do a bit more maintenance when you've got children, Joel."

"Do you remember," Jemima says, "how you used to make a line out of tights across the room. Do you remember those really thick woolly ones that Mom used to try to get us to darn if we got holes in them?"

"Make do and mend, she used to say. Don't know the last time I darned a sock."

"I've got some you could work on," says Joel.

"Very funny," I say. "I do remember the Maginot Line of tights. You weren't allowed to step over it or put any of your stuff in my territory."

"You used to move it a few inches further into my side of the room every day and think I wouldn't notice."

Joel laughs. "I expect you'd like to do that in our bedroom too."

"It's odd," I say, "that you spend the whole of your childhood wishing you could have a bedroom of your own and your entire twenties trying to share one again."

"But even when we were small," Jemima continues, "you used to count up the number of tiles on the bathroom wall to make sure that we had exactly half the bath each to sit in. Although there was an odd number of tiles, so you took the extra one as you said you were older."

"You were just as bad." These stories are well worn and age has weathered them from bitter battles to fond memories. "One time you wouldn't let me get out of the car over 'your side' and we were parked up against a wall, so I ended up having to climb into the boot and out that way."

"You complained if I looked out of 'your' window. And you counted the hundreds and thousands on my fairy cake just to check it didn't have more than yours."

"What about tubes of Smarties? We always had to pour them out to check that they had equal amounts."

"That was you that used to do that. You'd nick all my orange ones."

"I love these stories," says Joel, accompanied by the chortle that reminds me so much of his mother. "Go on." Being an only child, he thinks that sibling bickering is like the national dance of an Eastern European country—hilarious to witness, but mortifying to have actually partaken in. When our sons fight—which they do, constantly—he thinks it's some unique family trait that has been inherited directly from me, like the red hair.

"You've heard them all before," I say.

"But I'll never tire of them."

It's fine for me and Jemima to laugh at each other's pettiness, but not for Joel to join in.

"Have you spoken to Mom recently?" I ask her.

"Usual Sunday nighters. Just when I'm feeling most depressed and least likely to talk."

"Same here," I say. "She always rings when I'm grappling with the boys' bedtime. She sounds worried about Dad."

"She should be. He should cut down on his pork life, as the song says."

"He is fat, isn't he? Hope I haven't inherited his gene."

"Me neither." We both do a check of our respective stomachs for reassurance.

Lunch is not the Italian family feast that I always fantasize it might be. Gabe spits out his shepherd's pie, which his interpreter Rufus explains is because "it tastes like sick." Jemima and I push the pie around our plates with reflexive competitiveness, throwing little glances at each other. If it wasn't for Joel's prodigious appetite, there would be leftover mince for weeks.

Joel brings out the cake, which he made the day before. It's fudgy and sludgy and I have to concede, heavenly.

"Oh my god," mouths Jemima, "this is a-maze-ing." She dips her finger in the fudge icing and sucks it, making me want to put my own finger down my throat. Ah, happy memories of our shared bulimic phase. "Do not tell me it's dairy-free."

"It's got marge and soy milk instead of butter. Plus best-quality dark chocolate," he tells her. "And white wine vinegar, weirdly, but it seems to work."

"That is so nice of you to do that for Mary."

"It is my birthday," I protest. "It's not my fault I'm dairy intolerant." Eyebrows are raised. "What is it with everyone thinking that? You wouldn't say that if I had asthma or something. It's a medical condition."

"You are such an incredible cook, Joel," Jemima says. "You're so lucky, Mary. Why can't I find a nice man like him? How come you managed to nab such a winner?"

How had I? I had often wondered this when I'd been enjoying the first flush of our love, many years and children ago. I can remember so clearly him walking into the office; he was wearing a thick slate-gray polo neck that was shredded at the cuffs, worn-down gray cords and Converse trainers long before they were fashionable. I don't know why I keep the vision of his first appearance so pristine in my memory since at first I didn't find him remotely attractive. Being immune to the charms of Joel Tennant put me in a minority of one in the office. The other women, including Mitzi, ran around him though he was barely more than a runner himself. I prided myself on remaining aloof, but then, like the last sibling in the family to catch chicken pox, when I fell, I fell the hardest.

I look at my birthday cake. It has nine candles on it, three and six added together. When I had my ninth birthday, Jemima stripped naked and tried to do headstands, which everyone else thought was adorable. Mom made an elaborate cake in the shape of a fat little pony and found a redheaded doll to sit on top. It was back when she didn't work, so she could devote herself to her pair of ingrate daughters and slothful husband. She went back to work again when we were at secondary school, but her devotion to the house and the household remained unstinting. Dad's work within the home didn't increase in line with hers outside, and when he did make some minimal contribution, badly—laying the table or a fry-up—he'd call it "helping your mother." And if she ever asked Jemima and I to do anything, we'd shout "Why don't you ask Dad to do it? God, you're so sexist, Mom. Stop colluding with the patriarchal society!" Rather touchingly, our mother could not hide her excitement at getting out of the house to work and would carry a completely unnecessary briefcase and take "urgent" phone calls from the university office where she did admin, during which she'd talk too loudly about "faculty strategy" and return to the kitchen looking flushed with self-importance.

I think of the other times my birthday has added up to nine. My eighteenth, when I snogged David Parsons, who was absolutely gorgeous but also trying to see how many girls from our school he could rack up. Jemima turned him down a couple of months later, to her credit, although when I asked her why, she said, "Blergh, he's revolting," which made me feel small about my own feelings of triumph at having kissed him. I didn't have a party for my twenty-seventh. I felt like I was hurtling toward thirty, which at the time seemed so old and so scary. When I finally got there, I felt giddy with relief after dreading it for so long. Why didn't I enjoy my twenties more? Why didn't I revel in my youthful gorgeousness and enjoy the power that I could have yielded? I wasn't perfect looking, but my god, it was as good as it gets and I didn't appreciate it. If only I had known on my twenty-seventh birthday that later that year, I would meet Joel and become as happy as I'd ever been or probably will ever be.

"Nine candles," I announce. I have nothing else to add.

Joel ruffles my hair in the manner of an uncle to a small child. "What are your plans for your thirty-seventh year?"

"I'm going to find myself a keeper," says Jemima. "And then I'm going to have a baby. Maybe not all this year."

"My plans are..." I trail off. My plans, if you must know, Joel, are this: today is the last day of January and the last day of the phase of List Compilation. Tomorrow is the first day of February and it shall also be the first day of List Implementation. I shall spend the night of my birthday not dancing in a club nor out in a restaurant with friends, but putting the finishing touches to my Excel spreadsheet of marital investigation.

Every month you shall have an allowance of two debits a day. These are your freebies, if you like. Anything you spend over this and don't claw back by positive points will go toward your monthly total. Thanks to Becky's intervention, I won't count yin negatives that follow yang positives, does that make sense? It means that if you change a diaper, you won't be penalized for not putting it in the diaper bin, or if you make a delicious meal, you won't be penalized for not clearing it up.

Any debits over your monthly allowance (i.e., 60 in September, April, June and November; 62 for the others, save February, 56) will be added to your total score of infringements. If, after six months, this score is over 100 points, then that's it; the proof I needed that you're a selfish, lazy pig with no respect for me, this house or this family.

It needs a bit of tweaking, but it's almost there. I itch to get back to the laptop and finesse its wonder. Each month has its own spreadsheet. Across the top are written the dates. In each of the columns, I will be writing a number that can be cross-referenced to a separate tab where I have sorted the top 100 of his crimes into subsections like kitchen, bathroom, laundry and general ineptitude. There's another tab with the dozen or so credits that can offset them.

"Do you two mind emptying the dishwasher?" I ask Joel and Jemima. They slowly do, with Joel leaving the more obscure items in there for me to repatriate, as is his habit. Once I left Rufus's soup flask in there just to see how long Joel would manage to ignore it and it survived five cycles before I realized that this repeated washing was eroding the dinosaur transfer and I decided to rescue it. It's the same when he empties the plastic bags brought by the online supermarket delivery. Doesn't know where baking powder goes, just leaves it in the bag. Black-eyed peas? Sing "Where Is the Love?" and leave them lying on the counter.

I briskly wipe surfaces, pick up food from the floor and look at the way they have moved plates nearer the dishwasher but not actually *into* the dishwasher. Joel has already settled back into his chair and is looking at me with bemusement.

"Relax, Maz," he says. "Why don't we just do it later?"

"Because it will be me not we that does it later. I hate it when you say that."

Jemima gives me a quizzical look. We've shared everything from nits to knitwear, but I don't ever tell her all that I have to complain of in my life. Rufus's belief in the tooth fairy and Jemima's in the happy-ever-after are precious gobbets of innocence in a corrupted world. "Fine," I say. "Let's clear it up later then. Why don't you switch on the kids' channel, ASBO parent style, and I'll make some tea?"

Later, Jemima and Joel are playing a game with Rufus and Gabe that involves eating pistachios and throwing the shells back into the jar. Everyone finds this hilarious and I don't dare be the boring one, as usual, and tell them to throw the empty shells into the compost.

"Jemima," I say. "Do you remember how Mom used to get you a present on my birthday, so you didn't feel left out?"

"You've reminded me often enough."

"And then on your birthday I didn't get one too, and they used to tell me not to be so silly and that I was older..."

Joel and Jemima say together, "It's not fair," their voices a whining imitation of mine. They fall about laughing at that.

"Well, it wasn't..."

"Life isn't," they say again with one voice.

"No, I suppose not." I look at my husband and my sister. One large and dark, the other thin and blonde, but the same, they are the same. Both effortlessly favored, blessed by love, the people that others gravitate toward, the ones whose names are remembered. Now we are always "Joelandmary," just as it was always "Jemimaandmary" as I was growing up. I'm an idiot. I spent my whole childhood grappling for popularity in the face of an alpha girl sister and now I've only gone and married someone who makes me feel the same way. As a child, I lived with parents who seemed to prefer the other one. As a parent, I live with children who definitely prefer the other one. I'm a second-class inter-generational sandwich.

I stop scouring the sink aggressively and grab Rufus, hugging him tight to me, stroking his hair and delighting in its musty unwashed smell. Poor mite, to be so squeezed by me and to be so like me. I kiss the hair that he inherited, which I have always hated on myself and on him is breathtakingly beautiful—so many shades on every shaft, all with names from nature like ginger, conker and nut. Despite its glory, it's Gabe's hair that always gets patted in shops, those thick dark curls with their strange blond highlights ("Are they natural?" people are always asking, as if I go to the hairdresser with my two-year-old and ask for a half head of foils). It's Gabe that smiles at strangers, while Rufus is not so good on eye contact, and like all middle-class parents I went through a phase of thinking he might be autistic. He and I are underdogs, but I vow to make sure he'll never feel it.

"Happy birthday, sorry it's a week late," says Becky, giving me the well-reviewed biography of a dead female writer. It's our fortnightly Monday lunch and I'm so very glad.

"Wow, it's quite long given that she died young, isn't it?" I say, looking at the book's don't-drop-it-on-your-foot proportions.

"Do you know, she was only thirty-eight."

"She can join my 'talented women who died in their thirties' club. Jemima tells me that she always checks how old celebrities were when they had their first child, while my parents are obsessed with working out death ages in obituaries. I wonder which camp I fall into?"

"Death ages, definitely," says Becky.

"Thanks." I pick up the book again and flick through the photographs of a woman doing all that I have done and so much more. "Thirty-eight you say? Only two years off. How depressing."

"That she topped herself?"

"No," I say, "that she should have achieved so much in such a short time. My biography at thirty-eight would only be a pamphlet." Unless, I think, I could patent my revolutionary marriage-value-calculating list to both fortune and acclaim.

"What would you like to achieve?" asks Becky. I love that she asks me questions like that. I feel that she's the only person with whom I talk about things other than my children and my day-to-day tasks and expectations. Even at work, I never seem to get beyond the discussions about what we watched last night and where everyone else is going out for the evening.

"I don't know." I love that she asks me such questions, but it doesn't mean that I know how to answer them.

"Come on," she says firmly. "Don't tell me you've achieved all that you want to in life?"

"OK. I stress about where Rufus will go to secondary school, so I guess I want him to go somewhere good, or at least right for him. I want Gabe to be potty-trained."

Becky looks like she's going to bring up her seafood wrap. "Come on, Maz, what about you? What about your career? What are your goals?"

"I'm not sure I have a career anymore. I've got a job. I'm not making excuses but it's quite hard to have a career when you work part-time."

"Well, work full-time then."

"Again, not making excuses…"

"Cue excuse…"

"But it's quite hard to work full-time when you've got small children."

"Really? Because I see quite a lot of MPs, lawyers, scientists, whatevers working full-time, and some of them have even more children than you do."

"Hard in TV then. Filming is irregular, on location, in the evening and if I went back into the bits of the job I find interesting I might have to go back into short-term contracts, which is a nightmare in terms of continuity of childcare. I could have done it with just the one, maybe, but two throws the whole thing out. If I end up having to pay for childcare for evenings as well as days, I'll really be out of pocket. I have sometimes been there— when Joel's away filming and I've got some work thing in the evening and it costs me £50 in babysitting and his work can't really pay and nor can mine, but at the same time, why are we having to stump up for the pleasure of working outside office hours?"

"OK then, by the time you're thirty-eight, they'll both be at school, won't they? That will bring down your costs. What then?"

"I don't know, I don't know. Stop getting at me."

She smiles apologetically. "I'm not getting at you, love, especially not when we're celebrating your birthday. It's not you, really, it's a general thing I'm seeing and it's depressing me."

"What?"

"The wasted potential of women," she says. "Like something out of the 1950s, when I thought we'd be beyond all of that now. I have clients or clients' wives who don't work."

"Small children?"

"Yes, some of them. But what frustrates me is that there is no expectation that they will ever work again. It's like getting married to a rich man and having his children is the same as having been disabled in a workplace accident, so they should be on benefits for the rest of their lives. When the government tries to get single mothers off benefits and back into work, they make out that it's not for economic reasons, oh no, it's because they want to raise these women's self-esteem. So why's it different for these rich, divorced women? Does having money mean you don't need your self-esteem? Do they get their self-esteem from pedicures or something? It's incredibly patronizing and misogynist, but it's like, because these are benefits paid by their husbands, nobody makes a fuss about it."

I can't help but think of Mitzi, who of course has a "divine" woman in the West End who is such a specialist that she only does pedicures. She has another great find who only does brows, one for her pores, another for hair removal. "Rich men supporting their wives," I say. "Are you surprised that no one's rushing to their defense?"

"Often they're not particularly rich. And anyway, it's not them I worry about, it's the women, the ex-wives, these..." she searches for a suitably disdainful word, "...chattels. They feel like they've hit the jackpot, but they haven't because they'll never know the value of work."

"It's kind of fine for you to know the value of work, because you have an interesting job. But lots of jobs don't make people feel valuable," I try to argue, knowing that her legal mind makes resistance futile. And I know she's right, in a way—if I didn't escape the house to work I might feel even more oppressed by the tide of filth. "And I know it sounds weird and anti-feminist of me to say, but at the same time, if those wives didn't work while their children were small and then ran the home so that their husbands could earn lots of money—"

Becky hurrumphs. Nobody hurrumphs quite like Becky. "Ran

the home? I'm sorry, I didn't realize we were meeting for lunch in Edwardian England. I know, I know, it really is a full-time job organizing the servants, writing thank-you notes and planning the dinner-party menus."

"Do you want a coffee? I'll get them."

As I stand in the line at the counter, I find myself fingering the bracelet I'm wearing. Rufus made it for me at school, and its beads made of painted penne pasta become a sort of rosary as I say a prayer for a good argument to use with Becky. I love her, but she has a knack for making me feel so inefficient.

"Don't you ever think it would be nice to have a wife, Becky?" I say when I return to the table with our hot drinks. "An old-fashioned one who picked up your suits from the dry cleaner?"

"I never dreamed of having a wife as much as I dreamed about being good at my job. I'm not sure it's a coincidence that of all of us who went to university together, the woman with the most successful career should be the only gay one. Even when I thought I was straight, I knew I'd always support myself."

"What do you mean? It's not like all of us have got married or had kids and stuff. We've got loads of single friends from that time."

"But they would have made their career choices with the expectation that they would have a get-out clause somewhere along the line," she says. "The fact that they haven't ended up with a man who could partially support them is beside the point. Subconsciously or otherwise, they—all of you—thought that you would have the option of stepping off the career track for a few years and rethinking or retraining."

"Becoming a teacher, acupuncturist or psychotherapist," I say, thinking of the second-wave careers of the mothers from Rufus's school. "Or opening a shop selling hand-knitted children's jumpers. Or a child-friendly café."

"Exactly!" Becky bangs the table and the soy froth on my coffee bounces. "I'm so depressed by the wastage I see in my profession, in both the female lawyers and the clients. And do you know what I blame?"

I shrug.

"I blame improved maternity rights. You know, your extended maternity leaves and your flexible working rights, your part-time jobs and I must leave the office at 5 p.m.s."

"What?" I'm genuinely shocked. "That's heresy, Becky. You talk about women fighting for the right to work but we've fought just as hard for the right to maternity pay. You can't seriously blame them for . . . I don't know, what do you blame them for?"

"Do you know that almost all the top family lawyers at the moment are women?"

"Great . . ."

"And do you know who the top ones in ten or fifteen years' time will be? Men, they'll all be men."

"And you."

"Yes, and me, thanks. I shouldn't complain about the elimination of competition, but it's so frustrating to see all this talent slip away."

"But surely improved maternity rights keep talent in? If mothers didn't have the chance of taking a year's maternity leave and then working flexibly afterward, then maybe they'd leave the profession altogether."

"The lightweights would, yes, and many of them still do. But the rest would have worked full-time after three months off and it would have been bloody hard for a few years but then they'd have a brilliant and interesting career for when the children go to school."

"They're only at school for six hours a day . . ." I try to interject.

"That's just the sort of defeatist talk I get all the time from colleagues. Feminism is about equal pay for equal work and if you're not working flat out then you shouldn't be paid flat out."

"Maybe it's not working mothers who should change, but the system. It's such a male-created structure. Why should anybody work flat out?"

"Don't be daft, Mary. I can't charge clients £300 an hour and then swan off for long weekends."

"We don't 'swan off.' If only. Jeez, Becky, what's brought this on?"

"Nothing. The political isn't the personal in this case." She sighs. "I suppose I've been thinking about children a bit, because of the polycystic ovaries and all that, and what I would do, work-wise, if I had them. I would work full-time, you see, and I'd go back after a short maternity leave. I'm damn well not letting those smug men I work with climb the ladder ahead of me."

"I've been thinking about all that. Here," I open my bag up and pull out a sheet of A4. "I know you were skeptical but I did you a flow chart of all your decisions and how they feed off each other. It might help a bit."

Becky smiles. "Bless. Thanks, Mary. I think."

"Where have you got to with the baby idea?"

"I don't know." She presses her fingers to her temples and looks as uncertain as I've ever seen her.

"Whether you want a baby or not?"

"Whether I want a baby, can I even have one if I do want one, do I want one with Cara, do I want a baby more than I want to be with Cara, do I want to be with Cara at all, does Cara want to be with me?"

"That's what I was trying to express." I point at the piece of paper. It looks pathetically inadequate in the face of such life-changing decisions, but I wanted to help and it was the only way I knew how.

She looks down at it. "This is really great, you know—all these issues are all dependent on each other. I can't answer any of them before answering the others, and round and round in circles I go. Anyway, how's your plan to divorce Joel for not polishing the silver?"

"Ha ha."

"That depresses me too. Your marriage. You and Joel could be asking really interesting questions about what the heterosexual marriage means in the twenty-first century, you could be reinventing the institution entirely. But instead, you're bickering about the washing-up. It's so retro."

"You sound like Ursula."

"Thank you. I'll take that as a compliment."

I return to the office. As the new production gets underway, it becomes populated. Where once just Lily and I sat, now a chattering rabble of researchers, celebrity bookers and directors teem.

"Mazza," one of them whines at me, while simultaneously surfing his iPhone. "When's the archive researcher going to start?" His name is Jude and he wears T-shirts with a very low V to reveal a hairless chest. I don't know if his torso baldness is because he waxes or because he's too young to have grown body hair.

"Beginning of March, assuming we find one."

"But I'm having to do too much of that shit now."

"Well, talk to the exec about it."

"But he's not here. Why isn't the archive person starting now? We really need one otherwise we're going to get behind. Why aren't they starting yet, why?"

Count to three and breathe. "Because that's what's in the budget."

"Why?"

"Because it is," I say, my voice emphasizing the full stop of my statement.

"But why? Why have you got a director starting already and no archive researcher? Why?"

I am being dragged there, the place of no return, the place I do my best to avoid when at home with the boys: the cul de sac of why.

"Because I say so," I shout and escape to the loo, hoping that the hordes of new and thankfully temporary employees won't mess up the office or play with scissors in my absence. I lock myself into a cubicle. A pair of scarily high boots clips past the bottom of the toilet door. This lot are undeniably well heeled; how, I'm not sure, given their measly rates of pay.

"Mary," says the voice above the expensively shod feet, feet that are topped by skinny jeans and even skinnier legs. "What time does the dev meeting start?"

"Why don't you check Calendar?" I shout through the cubicle door. I know exactly when the development meeting starts.

"Oh, right. Good plan," says Poppy or Posy or Rosie.

How did she even know it was me in here? I look down at my feet and see the pair of flat, scuffed boots that would have been visible under the door.

I get my papers together and start touring the desks of my fellow employees. "Everybody, meeting, five minutes' time, are you ready?"

"Oh, man," Jude says. "I am so busy."

"Have you got a pen and paper? Well, get one from the stationery cupboard. You too," I say to the girl whose name I don't remember. "Where's Lily?"

"Think she had to go somewhere after lunch."

"Right, I'll text her. She's supposed to have printed out and distributed the agenda. I'll do it. Can you round up everyone else? I want this to start on time for once."

I bustle them into the meeting room where we wait for our creative director, Matt, to arrive. He is someone who emphasizes the creative part of his job title and seems to think it gives him license to arrive late for everything. When he finally turns up, Lily is nowhere to be seen, so I end up taking the notes and writing the abbreviation AP for Action Point next to my initials more than is ideal.

"Right," says Matt toward the end of our allotted slot. "We need more commissions." There's a collective groan. We always need more commissions. "I've got some pitch meetings lined up next month so I need as many basic format ideas as possible."

"I think we should do something that needs filming in the Caribbean," says Jude, at which the class sniggers.

"Do you know what?" says another pretty girl whose name doesn't seem worth me remembering. "There's not enough fashion on TV."

"Almost every single fashion show that's ever been broadcast hasn't worked," I say. "I think there's something intrinsically unfashionable about TV. You know, like your dad dancing to rave."

"Nothing wrong with dad dancing," says Matt in an attempt at self-mocking humor, with which the girls in the room enthusiastically agree. Joel and he occasionally go out for a drink together to talk about work, when, according to Joel, Matt actually tells him in forensic detail exactly what he'd like to do to the various young women in the office, before going into sentimental reveries about just how much he loves being a father.

"I think the problem is that the programs haven't ever decided whether they want to be street or high fashion and so fall somewhere in between," I say, aware that this meeting needs to get moving if I'm to leave on time. "If you could make a quite low-budget, grungier, more handheld sort of show for one of the digital channels, then that might work better."

"Yeah, good. Flo, why don't you have a think about that. Any other ideas?"

"Yes." I am surprised at myself. The things that Becky said at lunch have triggered thoughts both professional and personal. "I keep seeing shows about the history of feminism, but I don't see anything about its future and where we are at the moment with sexual relations."

Jude sniggers.

"Gender politics. Not the top-level stuff about equal pay and quotas for board members or politicians, but more in the domestic sphere." Somebody yawns. "I was reading the other day that even when a woman works outside the home, the amount of housework her partner does doesn't increase. I'm sure there must be a way to explore this in a documentary, but in a fun way."

"A fun look at housework?" asks Matt.

"I know, I know. But everybody does it, even if nobody talks about it. I thought you could take a variety of different household setups—single parent, working mother, non-working mother, house husband—and monitor what they think they do and what they actually do. Then we could question the participants to see if there was a direct correlation between marital satisfaction and equal participation in household chores. Even if there was a link between that and how much sex they have. There could be some tests common to all of them, like a mug left in the sink, how many minutes it stays there before the various different participants clean it or whether they notice it at all. I remember there was a documentary about sexual attraction once, where they had these cameras which could track the gaze of men and women, something like that. You could keep upping the ante, with more and more extreme traps left for those men, or women, who never notice."

"Yes," says Lily, who has finally made it to the meeting fifteen minutes late, and whose presence I give silent thanks to for the enthusiasm that only she is expressing. "We could set up like this really gross reality house where it's totally disgusting by the end and filled with really good-looking students."

"*Big Brother* meets *How Clean Is Your House*? I like it," says Matt. "Why don't you try to flesh it out a bit, Lily, and we'll think about pitching it to Factual Entertainment."

"Hang on," I say, "it was my idea. And it's for Documentary."

"We need you to coordinate the productions. You're so good at it."

"That's like saying someone's good at the washing-up."

"You're probably very good at that too."

"I could do both. Developing the format and coordinating, I mean, not the washing-up. I can do a pitch based around a more serious approach to the subject."

"Don't think so," says Matt. "What with all your time off and stuff."

"It's not time off. I'm part-time." I'm sure you could be too, I think, if you'd sacrifice a large chunk of your salary and be prepared to answer calls and emails on your non-office day.

"Yes, that's what I meant," he says, dismissing both me and the meeting.

Valentine's Day was never a golden date in my diary. Just a couple of weeks after my birthday, it only added to any lingering disappointment at the lack of cards/surfeit of obviously re-gifted gifts of my own anniversary. In my late teens I feigned a posture of antipathy, snarling that it was a tacky Hallmark invention of the consumerist society. By my mid-twenties, this posture had calcified into authenticity.

Meeting Joel changed all that. The syrup of manufactured sentiment was made savory by a combination of my self-transforming love for him and his ability to find freshness in the most hackneyed of situations. I loved him so much that I allowed myself to be one half of a couple that mythologized its own specialness, the uniqueness of its love, and so was allowed to indulge in all manner of nauseating activities.

The first Valentine's Day, he had a pliant café worker deliver to the office a be-ribboned latte, made with a double shot of espresso and soy milk, just the way I like it. He had decorated the mug himself, with Keith Haring–like doodles of hearts and flowers, using some specially bought ceramic paints. My boyfriend, I thought, is so artistic, so quirky, so cute, so in love with me and I with him. I kept the cup and used it only on special occasions, washing it gently afterward not with washing-up liquid but my own expensive handwash. It's still in our crockery cupboard, only now the colors have long since faded, having been put through a dishwasher cycle one too many times.

The second Valentine's Day, my true love made for me a treasure hunt that began with a clue attached to the collar of my flatmate's cat and ended with a photo taken of us at the top of Ben Nevis, which he'd blown up to four foot by two foot proportions and managed to slip inside the front of the vending machine at the office. I was hugely embarrassed, of course, but since everyone there knew and adored Joel, I was secretly rather pleased too. Glad, at the same time, that we'd gone on holiday to chilly Scotland that year, not anywhere that might have involved the wearing of a bikini.

By the third Valentine's Day the ante had been raised and

nothing less than a proposal would satisfy me. It was pathetic and I hated myself for it, but our relationship had started at such a fever pitch that I wanted to maintain this pace and excitement. Got a hand-knitted scarf with my initials embroidered into it. I tried not to be churlishly disappointed and felt silly when we did get engaged not long after, though in circumstances that fell short of the tales of romantic derring-do that I and others expected of Joel.

By the fourth Valentine's Day we were married and I was pregnant. He still played the game, though, even now that he had me for life. He set up a dining table in the spare room of the first flat we owned together, blacked out the windows and turned off the lights. This was to re-create the ambience of a recently opened restaurant which offered the particular USP of serving food in pitch blackness. He then fed me a five-course meal that Heston Blumenthal would have been impressed by. To be honest, the experience of eating rich and complex food in total darkness made me feel rather nauseous, as well as worried about some of the oysters (that I had to spit out on account of being pregnant), getting ground into the new carpet. The meal culminated in a bout of frenzied sex and some weird stains on the paintwork that I was acutely conscious of when we had estate agents' viewings.

The next few years blur into one another. The gestures were less dramatic, but there were still small surprises: Post-it note treasure hunts through the house; messages of love iced across fairy cakes; a first-edition book. Even last year, when we were well into our lives as stressed and stroppy parents of two, Joel hung up a banner painted with the help of the boys.

And now it is our ninth Valentine's Day together. I'm scrubbing at the floor beneath the boys' chairs.

He rips open a packet of Rice Krispies. I stop myself from pointing out that a) there's a packet already open and b) why doesn't he cut the packet instead of ripping it, which would mean that it wouldn't spill out over the work surface or accumulate at the bottom of the cardboard box and thus spill out when I collect up the cereal boxes to take to Rufus's school for junk modeling. No, I breathe to myself, I shall just put these two points onto The List, which is safely stored on my laptop. And anyway, although Valentine's Day is obviously a horrible consumerist construct, it is one that I will suspend animosity for. Or if I am feeling particularly generous, I may give him some get-out-of-jail-free passes to use against his miscreant behavior with dried breakfast products.

I continue watching him and then can bear it no longer.

"Do you know what day it is today?" I ask.

"Monday."

"Yeah, but what day of the year it is?"

"Valentine's Day."

"Right, you do know," I say.

"You don't believe in Valentine's Day, though, do you?" he says. "Or romance or flowers or in fact being very nice to your beloved, do you? Or even being civil to them and saying good morning?"

"Yes, obviously I think Valentine's Day is silly. You're the one who always makes such a big deal about it."

He starts singing "The Times They Are a-Changin'" and saunters off to the loo, leaving me with the post-breakfast, pre-departure flurry of bad tempers, missing nylon book bags and papier-mâché-like encrustations of Cheerios on the wall.

I spend the day pondering his elaborate subterfuge and wondering what surprise he will have planned for me that evening. One year, post-Rufus and pre-Gabe, he managed to organize babysitting for us to go out, despite the fact that all childcare was and is my provenance to the extent that he'd had to look on my mobile to get the number of the babysitter. That he ended up phoning Maria my old school friend rather than Maria the nice Polish lady who looked after the baby occasionally was beside the point. And it was very kind of Maria my old school friend to come around to keep an eye on the baby monitor and watch our TV for a few hours, though as a City accountant, her rates were probably usually somewhat higher than our £6 per hour.

This intrigue sustains me through the day and I make myself up in honor of the surprised face I shall be making. I pick the kids up from Deena's and I wait. And wait. Joel arrives back after their bedtime, one that has involved a three-way row between Rufus, Gabe and I, the kind of opposite of a group hug.

It's now ten thirty and still I wait. For the first time in nine Valentine's Days, the surprise is that there is no surprise. I open up my laptop in bed and add a few more things to The List.

February Good Housekeeping

	A	B
1	February allowance	2 per day, total 56
2	Total no. of debits in February	73
3	Breakdown of infringements	22 kitchen; 13 bathroom; 5 laundry; 4 bedroom; 9 invisible woman; 9 parenting; 11 general ineptitude.
4	Infringement of the month	Leaving Gabe's sodden diaper on my side of the bed, kind of like one of those chocolates you get at chintzy hotels. Well, kind of.
5	Positives to offset	5. Three compliments; went to fishmonger; tidied out the car without being asked.
6	Feb debt	12 (73 offset by February allowance of 56 and 5 positives)
7	Total remaining	88 over next five months (100 minus 12)

5

The Lost Keys

"You do remember I'm off to book group this evening," I say to Joel.

"But I've got to go out with everyone from work. Celebrate the commission."

"I told you ages ago."

"No, you didn't."

"Look, it's on the calendar," I say triumphantly and with some relief because until that moment of checking, I couldn't have been entirely sure that it had been marked.

"Shit."

"Don't swear."

"You don't even like book group."

True, I thought, there had been tears when somebody questioned another's assertion that *The Time Traveler's Wife* was the best book ever written.

"That's not the point," I say.

"What is the point, then?"

"The point is that you never respect my plans even if I've reserved going out first, which I did. It's like my plans are secondary to yours, or like it's my default role to look after the children so I have to get express permission to get out of it, while you can just automatically assume that I'll be around to pick up the slack while off you go, gallivanting into the night. Even if it's a work thing I've got to do, it's still secondary and I end up not doing it or I end up paying for the pleasure of working in the evenings, because childcare costs aren't something we're allowed to put on our expenses claims, while vast quantities of booze are."

"Blimey, have you finished?"

"Yes."

"Me going out is hardly likely to be fun. It's work," he says.

"Right, that trump card. Paper scissors stone, your work, my work, the children. Even when I've had a work thing to go to on the same night, I've always had to find a babysitter and pay for them, or cancel. Your work beats them all, doesn't it?"

"Pays the mortgage."

"And mine doesn't? And remind me, how does going out for drinks after work pay the mortgage?"

"It's important for morale."

"That you get drunk?"

"Yes," he says, very matter-of-factly. "I can't be seen to be some sort of teetotal killjoy."

"So what, when I don't drink because I'm pregnant or breast-feeding or driving, I'm a teetotal killjoy, am I?"

"I didn't say that." He sighs. "Can't you just get a babysitter?"

God, but he is feckless with money. The whole point of going out separately is that one of us stays at home so we don't have to pay a babysitter. It is very aggravating to have to pay out all that money before you've even bought a drink. And I'm the one who has to ring around to get the babysitter—and I'm the one who pays them, too, as childcare's one of my expenses, which is why he's the one who can say that his work pays the mortgage.

What's more annoying is that, while I don't actively dislike book group, I don't like it so much that I want to be shelling out £30 of babysitting money for the privilege of attending to the literary thoughts of Mitzi's random assortment of mom friends.

Breathe in, I tell myself. "Yes, all right, I'll try to get a baby-sitter," I say, while thinking with some glee about the huge accumulation of negative points for The List this short conversation has amassed. A point for not bothering to ask if it was fine that he goes out, a point for his going out trumping mine, a point for the fact that I pay for all the childcare, a point for his general uselessness with money.

"Thank you, darling." He sounds surprised at my acquiescence. He gives me a kiss on my forehead in a patronizing style and skips off to work with nary a look back.

We are gathered at the home of Alison, who is Mitzi without the charm and humor. Or looks, charisma or generosity. In fact, she is Mitzi with a big bag of bitterness and resentment. So I guess, nothing like Mitzi at all, except that her house is fastidiously tidy, though lacking those dashing touches, those little stylish details, that save Mitzi's from sterility. Alison is opining on the protagonist of this month's book.

"She was such a whiner. I mean, she was so lucky to have a house with a proper garden."

"Yard, they call it," adds Daisy, helpfully. "They call it a yard in America. Diaper, that's a funny word, isn't it? Faucet."

"But she had everything—a husband, two children, one of each—what did she want to keep whining on about Paris for?" continues Alison, in what can only be described as a whiny voice. "Why didn't she just go there for a mini-break?"

"I think that's the whole point," I say, though my heart's not in it. "That they'd got *the* American dream, it just wasn't her dream. There's no joy in achieving someone else's dream, is there?"

"Well, it's a very nice dream. She should shut up and consider herself lucky."

"She was lucky to wear such nice clothes," says Daisy. "And drink so many martinis."

"You so haven't the read the book, have you?" I ask Daisy. "You just watched the film on DVD."

She giggles. I love Daisy. She is the laziest woman I've ever met. She is like Lady Bertram without the staff and her standard answer to anything is "I so couldn't be arsed." This can include anything from applying to competitive pre-prep schools or getting a job, to wiping her children's faces or changing an infant's graying babygro on special occasions. "The film was good, though," she says apologetically.

"Unbearable," I say. "Talk about cinema verité. I thought I was trapped in my own fly-on-the-wall documentary. Next time I'm getting a nice science fiction DVD for some proper escapism."

"But honestly," says Alison, "didn't you think she had it easy? It's not like she had to work or anything. She was just a stay-at-home mother." Alison does something very busy in the City that no one quite understands, not least because it doesn't seem to make her millions of pounds in the manner of a banker, but merely causes her a great deal of self-important stress. Something to do with risk assessment, I think, which is ironic given that she appears to be doing everything she can to eliminate any possible risk to her children's lives, such as banning them from kicking a ball around the park for fear that dog poo will make its way from the ball to their eyes and blind them.

"*Just* a stay-at-home mother?" asks Mitzi, bringing in a basket of multi-colored macaroons that, alongside an expensive bottle of Chablis, is her contribution to the evening's food.

I don metaphorical body armor and wait for the grenades to get thrown.

"You've got four children, Mitzi," says Alison. "And two homes. I'd hardly call you just a stay-at-home mother."

"I've only got two children and one home," pipes Daisy. "And I rarely go out. I'm a stay-at-home-and-watch-daytime-TV mother."

"I work," says Henrietta with the pride of a child who's just started big school. "But I work from home. What does that make me?"

A woman who crochets lumpen jewelry to sell on an Internet craft site.

"And I only teach two days a week," says Beth, "and only then at a private school so I can get money taken off the school fees."

"Yeah," cheerleads Henrietta.

"And my therapy is part of my training so it counts as work," says Jennifer. "I'm constantly having to work through my past in order to be a better therapist. It's exhausting, much more so than any office job."

The other five women look at Alison expectantly and I glance from one to another as though this were a magnificent multi-player tennis match.

"Being a working mother is really tough," says Alison, but she no longer has the fight, nor did she ever since the moment that alpha girl Mitzi nailed her colors to the mast. "I mean it is for any sort of mother, but going out, to an office, to work on top of everything else..."

"Being a mother is the hardest job of all," says Beth.

"My friends who work say they go to the office for a break," says Daisy. "It's easier than being at home."

God give me strength, when will the clichés stop?

"There's no such thing as a non-working mother," says Henrietta. "The work never ends for all mothers."

I shall intervene, I think to myself, when someone mentions cupcakes. Someone always mentions cupcakes.

"Yes, true," says Alison. "But I'm having to do all the mother stuff you do, but also juggle stressful and complex financial negotiations. If I make a tiny mistake I could lose my firm millions. If you make a mistake, I don't know, your cupcakes might not rise."

Bingo. "Isn't the reality of working and parenthood a bit less black and white than working mothers versus stay-at-home mothers?" I say. "I mean, that's the way the media always portrays it, like there's women in suits armed with briefcases on one side and women in pinnies throwing those bloody cupcakes on the other. In fact, it's funny, because the more high-powered a woman's job is the more cupcakes she actually makes anyway, because she's over-compensating."

"Speaking of which," says Alison, "ta-da." She brandishes a plate of fairy cakes with bright pink icing. Does anyone actually like cupcakes as much as a good old-fashioned bar of chocolate? It's as if all women's ambitions and aspirations can be boiled down to just two things: twirly-iced cupcakes and high-heeled shoes. "I picked Grace up from school, did her two math worksheets, kept up with work on my BlackBerry and made two dozen of these."

"Alison, you're making me feel tired just thinking about your achievements," says Daisy.

I'm not to be deflected. "And anyway, in reality, most of us work but usually it's part-time, and whether it's at home or in an office, it's a job not a career. I think it's something like 75 percent of mothers of under fives." I'm making up statistics. "Most of us muddle through doing neither one thing nor the other, do you know what I mean?"

They look at me blankly. Henrietta is desperately twiddling one of the earrings that she's showcasing from her crocheted collection as if it were an earpiece through which a researcher was going to tell her what to say.

"Go on," says Alison, waving her hand in encouragement.

"Thanks," I say. "For instance, I work four days a week, depending on what's in production."

"I meant go on everyone, tuck in to my cupcakes, you know you want to."

I stumble on, drunk on white wine and my own rhetoric. "Henrietta works at home, Alison's four days a week and then one day from home, isn't that right? Mitzi's thinking of starting her own business. We're all sort of working and sort of not working and that's before we've even got onto the business of whether looking after children should accurately be called 'not working.'"

"Oh my god," says Beth. "These are amazing, Alison. You are naughty, I just can't resist."

"I don't know," I say. "It just seems to me that this whole mommy wars thing is a bit of a myth, that's all. Surely the divide is not between those who work and those who don't, but between those who have childcare for when they're not working. I mean, the stay-at-home mother with no time off is just as harried as the working mother. And the only relaxed women are those with spare capacity childcare, like, I don't know, those who work three days but have a full-time nanny, or don't work but still have an au pair." I'm thinking Mitzi, but I don't say it. "It should be those with no time away from the office or their children versus those with time away from them. Or nobody versus anyone, in fact—I mean, there's more that unites us than divides us, don't you think? In fact, let's not fight each other, let's fight men. Yeah!" The rabble-rousing tone of my final word fades.

There is a pause.

"More macaroons?" asks Mitzi.

It's always like this, I think; always chitchat, never conversation. At university, I used to have those giddy, drunken discussions about what were the limits of the universe or how we knew we weren't in fact computers or whether it might be true that we were all living in a gigantic other being's imagination. Now I never seem to get beyond drinks-party babble. Back in my twenties the drinks were stiff, the drugs soft and the conversation flowing. Now the medium-priced wine flows, the drugs are absent and the conversation hard. Whenever these mothers and I get together with the children, at parties or in the park, I feel like our discussions are always teetering on the edge of a precipice of interest or revelation, only to be interrupted by a child at a crucial moment. It's as if our sentences can only come in fragments, like those fridge magnets of random words we all have to help our children read, and if only we had more time we could assemble them into interesting wholes. And yet, when we do convene without the children, I realize that those interrupted half-exchanges are actually more interesting than these completed ones, for they hold the allure of what might have been said. Our minds are too busy still multi-tasking away, uselessly spinning.

Sex: that was another thing my friends, my old pre-children friends, and I used to talk about. These conversations about sex were almost better than sex itself. Lubricated caps that pinged across strangers' bedrooms; competitions with bananas to see who had the least sensitive gag reflex; detailed discussions about what made you good in bed. Mitzi and I were young and single when we first met. I look over to her now, gracious hostess as always, even in somebody else's house, and I find it difficult to remember the chaotic, hilarious promiscuity of her youth. Nobody could tell as good a morning-after story as Mitzi. She was poor and scruffy then, yet even her smoky-eyed, dirty-stop-out-in-last-night's-dress look was stylish. She made you want to leave your makeup on overnight and come into work wearing two-day-old clothes because that wantonness was so damn cool. Her laugh was as filthy as those frocks. And those stories... "Acorn boy" who never grew a mighty oak; the pop star who liked to suck a dummy; the sitcom actor who made her watch footage of his rivals and shout "You're the funniest, you're the best" over and over mid-coitus; the endless meat metaphors deployed to describe the anatomy of the then lowly sous-chef, now of course a well-known restaurateur. Our present-day anecdotes about our children's reading ages are never going to be as funny.

Everyone is playing musical sofas to avoid being stuck with Alison and her haranguing on how hard she works, combined with her ability to make you stress about whole new, hitherto unexplored areas of anxiety. She has a special trick of being able to denigrate and exalt her children and husband simultaneously. "I'm fed up with Oliver," she'll say of her six-year-old, "always on at me to explain cloud formations. And I bought him the unabridged *Hobbit* and he finished it in two days. Does he think I'm made of money? And as for Grace," she sighs of the four-year-old, "I don't think people realize that being gifted is as much a special need as being autistic or having attention deficit disorder."

"Do you remember," I say to Mitzi, "when we used to talk about sex?"

Daisy overhears me and giggles. "Do you remember when we used to actually have sex? I really can't be arsed anymore."

Mitzi purses her lips into a smirking pout.

"Do I take it you can be arsed?" I ask her. "Unfortunate choice of word."

She simpers again. Really? One way of avoiding conceiving more children, I suppose. "Don't go all enigmatic on me now, Mitz, do tell."

"I don't think we need know about anybody's sex life, thank you very much," says Alison, while everyone else tries to ignore her.

"But we do," I say. "Mitzi used to tell the best anecdotes when we were younger. Do you remember that time with the chef and the giant truffle? Not one of those chocolate ones covered in sprinkles, a proper one found by a pig in the woods and all that."

"I don't think we need to go into that now," she says. Of course, that's all in the past and in her present, these women only know her as the elegant lady-wife. "Let's just say," she murmurs to Daisy and me in an aside, "that I am finding age is not withering Michael's and my boudoir activities." Her bedroom bloody is a boudoir, too, all sumptuous drapes, a velvet-covered chaise longue and one of those extra-wide beds you get in boutique hotels.

"But you've got four children," says Daisy. "Two of them are twins. How do you have the energy?"

"Priorities."

"And staff," snaps Alison, shuffling over to join in.

"But sleep. You can't get staff to sleep for you. You can't subcontract out everything," Daisy says.

"Least of all sex with your husband," I say. "Although, actually, I believe you can do that."

"Maybe I should," says Daisy.

"Please, do we really need to be talking about this?" says Alison. We continue to ignore her.

"Seriously, Mitzi, what grown-up mature activities do you get up to in the bedroom—sorry, boudoir?" I ask. "Go on, inspire us."

She smiles enigmatically. In the old days, she'd have been launching into scurrilous detail, but ever since I got together with Joel she's been all about secrets. She does that face, the one she puts on when she's talking about my husband, that hints at things the rest of us shall never know. "You have to use your imagination."

An image of Michael, all alpha and hairy and imposing, pops into my head. "I'd rather not."

"I mean," she says, "you have to use your imagination with your own husbands. Don't you with Joel, Mary? Honestly, there's no reason why sex can't get better and better with age."

"There are a million reasons," I say.

"Or just two in my case," says Daisy. "Three if you include the man I married."

"If you let them. Like I say, it's a question of priorities and I choose to prioritize my sex life. Michael is a very powerful man and it's important to me that I make sure that power is sated and that I am as sexually desirable to him as the day we met."

When he was married to somebody else, I think. "Go on," I say.

"I make sure that my behavior and my appearance is far from mumsy."

I bet Mitzi has really nice expensive undies. Mine still include some post-partum big knickers and a couple of nursing bras. Becky is a fan of the ones that look like sports bras, those that bind rather than build. I wonder what underwear Cara wears. Is it utilitarian or silky? I think it may be quite sculptural, almost old-fashioned, a bit Rita Hayworth.

"I don't know, Mitzi, sounds a bit surrendered wife to me," I say. "Servicing a husband's powerful urges and all that."

"Believe you me," she says with that smirk again, "I'm not always the one surrendering."

It shows me how far I've come from the world of sexual intrigue and the days when we used to swap top sex tips that I have absolutely no idea what she can be talking about.

* * *

It wasn't just sex that Mitzi and I talked about when we first met, it was everything. It was one of those friendships that was like falling in love, when we stayed up all night swapping pasts and futures and I used to store up funny things to tell her.

It was my first day at my first proper job. I had an idea that working in television was going to be glitzy, a preconception that everyone I had met in the interview process had contradicted with their clothes, which were disappointingly dowdy. All I had to do in my entry-level job was type, but I felt like a media hot-shot just being allowed into the building.

My excitement was waning after only an hour in the office. My face ached from all the smiling and my brain flagged from all the names I had to remember. I know now that there are the same types in every workplace and that in my twenties I'd always get befriended by the office joker, but back then it was all new and exhausting to me.

People came up to me and I put my smile back on but they only ever wanted to know where Mitzi was. I didn't even know who she was.

Then she walked in and I knew it was her. It sounds corny, but it was as if she was accompanied by a choir and a special light filter. I wanted to be her friend so much that I could barely look at her.

I couldn't believe that she would like me and the mere fact that she asked me if I wanted to get a sandwich with her allowed me to become my most witty, best self. Looking back, I might have become a bit Single White Female, with my Mitzi-inspired taste for vintage dresses and newfound enthusiasm for shoes. The first time she asked me if I wanted to meet up to go shopping at the weekend, out of office hours and everything, I felt as happy as if I'd been proposed to. Our trip to the shops was like a budget, girls-only version of that scene from *Pretty Woman*, as she kitted me out in stylish high-street fashion finds.

One day, she was away from her desk and I answered her phone, this being before everyone got called on mobiles. Personal calls for her were usually from men, but this was a woman, older sounding and with an accent that roamed around the globe in one short sentence. She sounded polite, yet pleading. "Can you pass on a message to Mitzi?" she asked.

"Of course."

"But you will make sure she gets it. I don't think my messages have been reaching her."

"I've got pen and paper right in front of me."

"Tell her to call her mother. Take down my number, in case she's not got it."

I hung up and felt ashamed, as if I had intruded on something Mitzi did not want to share. When she came back I passed on the message and I saw her look unnerved for the first time.

"Oh fuck," she said, with one of those posh voices that can get away with it. "She's back. Do you know what? In tribute to my old soak of a mother, I think we should go out and get very, very drunk tonight."

Later, as we bought cocktails we couldn't afford, she leaned forward to tell me, "I really don't like to talk about this so you must keep it very secret."

"Of course." I was thrilled.

"My mother is a love addict."

These days, celebrities are always claiming to be sex addicts, but back then the term wasn't quite so widely used. It sounded very glamorous. I couldn't imagine my parents being addicted to anything, though they did get a bit twitchy if they missed two consecutive episodes of *The Archers*.

I nodded, not wanting to admit my ignorance. "In what form does her addiction manifest itself?"

"Men, of course."

"I see."

"I'm sure you don't. She's had five kids by four fathers."

"Really? It must be nice to have so many brothers and sisters."

"Haven't any full ones. I was her only one by a good-looking bit of rough."

Of course, Mitzi's parents were bound to be good-looking. "Who was he?"

"Local builder. She left my brother and sister's father for him. I was the result of her first transgression. Didn't last, of course. Nor the next one, rich old bastard. A few after that. This one's being going on for about ten years, but it's probably on the rocks, guessing by the fact she's ringing me."

"Do you get on with the rest of your family?"

She shrugged. "Have you any idea what it's like for your siblings to be much, much, much richer than you?"

"How much richer?"

"Lots and lots. Mom's first husband has no chin but he owns a nice chunk of Somerset. His kids don't like me because Mom left their dad because of mine and, to be honest, they're not much to look at. My younger sister's dad has died already and left her enough money to buy a flat when she leaves university. Jake's poor like me, though, but with the most amazing eyelashes."

I imagined the feeling I used to get when Jemima got a more generous Christmas present, and multiplied by a hundred to try to imagine what it must be like to have very different financial means from your own siblings.

"It sounds very complicated."

"You've no idea. Honestly, Mary, my childhood. It was like some sort of Catherine Cookson novel, except set in the West Country. They'd come in, father a child, leave again. There'd be a few in between them too. She's always got to be 'in love,' you know—always got to be mooning over a man, has to pretend they're Darcy or Mellors or Heathcliff or whoever. So immature. Love's not like that."

"No, it's not." It hadn't yet been for me. "How did you cope?"

"I'm smart." As if I didn't know. "Wherever we lived I'd find the girl in my class with the most sensible family and latch on. Those stay-at-home mothers loved me. They used to bake cakes every day and proper puddings. It's a wonder I didn't get fat. I'd basically live with them until we moved on."

"Mitzi, I'd never have guessed. You seem so, I don't know, confident."

"I got out as quickly as I could. I left home at eighteen and I've looked after myself ever since. I tell you something, my children are never going to be poor."

"Are you going to try to make lots of money, then?"

"Or marry it," she said and raised her glass.

The next day in the office, Lily is sitting at her desk and sighing. I ignore her. She sighs some more, so much that it begins to sound like panting.

"What's wrong?"

"My pitch—you know, the one about the dirty house. I'm supposed to have finished it by now."

"The one that came out of my thoughts about gender inequality in the home?"

"Did it?"

"Yes, I said we should do something on the ways in which the real story about relations between men and women actually centers around household chores. And somehow it mutated into your dirty house reality show."

"Oh, right. So you can help me with it, then."

"Not with the format so much, but maybe I can with the background. Look." I open up a document on my screen. "I've been collecting up research about the issues and what current levels of participation are."

She peers at it. "Do people really argue about it more than money?"

"They do. It's more important than sex."

She looks skeptical.

"Listen, why don't I write you an introduction and then you can concentrate on the format."

"Thanks Maz, you're a star. You'll have it done by tomorrow, won't you?"

I'm not going out tonight, of course. "Will do."

Joel is not having a good month. He's already used up his March quota and we're not yet halfway through. The book-group night babysitting fiasco bumped it by five debits. He's not made it back for bathtime once and, while introducing his firstborn to the joys of video-gaming, he has now lost the cable that attaches the DVD player to the television, thus denying me my box sets. He's used the word "hormones" three times, as in "Is it your hormones?" followed by a skyward look if I should ever dare criticize his behavior.

I check his chest of drawers: three balled-up tissues (one with what looks like a lump of hardened phlegm encrusted onto it); two receipts for lunches that cost way more than my frugal packed ones or my occasional forays with Becky; a selection of foreign coins and a packet of Rizlas. Those receipts will never get converted into expenses, another debit on The List. He is rubbish with money perhaps because, until he had children, he never really needed any. The small stipend from a trust fund courtesy of Ursula's illustrious forebears coupled with a natural taste for shabbiness meant that he never needed to worry. Lucky him, able to bum around with the band for all those years, then waltz into a job when necessary.

God, the band. There's a whole section of The List devoted to The Spitz (named for the 1970s swimmer Mark and that gloriously camp image of him with his big haul of medals and even bigger mustache). They happily reconvene for every fortieth birthday party in the Greater London area, requiring endless practice sessions. These, naturally, occur at weekends and in the evenings, so I'm left doing all the childcare. I cannot think of an equivalent female activity that would allow me to take time off, legitimately, with no one questioning it. "Mommy's off doing her creative writing course this weekend again"; "Mommy will be off knitting again."

"You're stifling my creativity, man," Joel will self-mockingly say if I try to put the kibosh on these musical excursions, as if by acknowledging the ridiculousness of a bunch of middle-aged men playing their new-age-indie-punk-rave he is thus excused.

Music invades not just his childcare duties, but also my senses when I'm feeling delicate on a Saturday morning. The radio dial does a little dance as I swap between stations.

"Bloody hell, have you messed with the pre-sets again?" I say, laboriously moving it back to the gentle chat of Radio 4.

"When did you get to be so old?"

"I'll always be younger than you."

"Technically speaking."

"Listening to rock music"—I do a sad little strum of an air guitar—"does not make you young."

"Well neither does listening to this."

"You know, maybe you ought to grow your hair long and wear a tour T-shirt. I think the boys will think their dad is, like, way cool."

"Do you know, my darling," he says, "I think the moment I fell in love with you was when we were in the car and you turned the music up louder. You were the first woman I'd ever met who turned the dial up rather than down. I remember thinking, now this is a woman I could spend the rest of my life with." He sighs.

"Yes, well, things change. Though not enough. While we're talking about music, can we have our regular chat about the boxes of vinyl in the living room? You don't listen to them anymore, so why are we keeping them?"

"I like looking at the sleeves. I get sensual pleasure from the flip they make as I flick through them." He gives me a look. "I need to get sensual pleasure from somewhere."

"Could you not get some sensual pleasure from putting them in plastic boxes and moving them to the attic?" The attic is a possessions' purgatory where stuff goes to spend a couple of years in limbo before being cast into the eternal damnation of the charity shop.

"Don't make me do that."

"But you can see all the stuff we've got now. The boys need more room for toys and books. It's not even just the records, it's the programs and the tickets and the *NME* back issues and your fanzines." How can I convey to him the illogicality of those boxes full of records he never plays and ephemera he never looks at? It is matched only by the wardrobe of shirts with frayed collars or garish patterns that he refuses to throw out. "We don't live in a house as big as your mother's. In fact, why don't you move all this stuff to your boyhood home? It would seem appropriate."

"It's not the size of the house," he says mournfully. "You'd still be asking me even if we lived in a palace."

"Please."

"All right, whatever."

"Is that a yes? Will you move them?"

"Yeah, right, will do."

"When?"

"Laters, Maz. Chill."

It's not going to happen. I open my mouth to ask again. Or "nag," as is the terminology when a woman asks a man more than once to do something. "Fine," I say instead. One more for The List.

My mood is not much improved after lunch when the doorbell rings. I feel panic, like I did in the olden days when you were caught makeup free and wearing pajama bottoms in the newsagent by a boy you fancied. If houses were people, at this moment mine would be a crazy-haired lady pushing a supermarket trolley full of old newspapers. The recycling box has been emptied and its contents gaffered to the banisters and stairs to make a marble run stretching from the top-floor landing all the way down to the hall.

"Gabe," says Joel to his second born. "Don't pull that off, it won't work if you do that."

Gabriel continues to tug at the admittedly impressive midsection of the run, which consists of the cardboard tube that came inside a roll of wrapping paper, a couple of sawn-off plastic water bottles and a cling-film suspension bridge.

I stand there, trying to debate which bit of the house to try to clean or whether just to ignore the doorbell. It goes again. "Coming," I shout, "give us a minute."

"Why do you have to ruin everything, Gabe?" whines Rufus. "It's ruined, it's completely ruined." He storms off to throw his distraught body on the bed for all of ten seconds before emerging with a gobstopper-sized marble, which ricochets down the run before pinging to the corner of the hallway that is already a jumble of wellies and scarves.

"Did it work?"

Joel whoops his affirmative before jumping up the stairs, two steps at a time.

I do a quick survey of the kitchen as the doorbell rings insistently once again. On the floor, circles of rice ring the boys' chairs, though they are dwarfed by the mountain that lies below Joel's. A pair of boy's underpants—skid-mark free, thankfully—lie by the cooker. There's a crunch of breakfast cereal underfoot and damp clothes drying across busted radiators. I kick what I can aside as I run to the door, hoping that it's someone ringing the wrong bell or one of those ex-miners selling cleaning products.

It's not, and I can barely hide my surprise at the uninvited guest. "Hello, Alison."

"My word, what were you doing in there? I thought you'd never answer. Am I interrupting something?" She tries to peer around the door.

"Oh, god, no. No, really no." Does she think I've been inspired by Mitzi to sauce up my daytime love life? When she sees it's an egg carton, not underwear, strewn across the house she'll be disabused of that idea. "What are you doing here?" We know each other, but we are not friends, especially not the sort that drop in on one another unannounced. I am about to say something along the lines of "Not that it's not a pleasure to see you," when I realize that that would be a lie. So I don't.

"I've just dropped Oliver off at a birthday party around the corner and Chris, for bloody once, is actually looking after his daughter."

"Right. Great." Alison is always furious about something. She even makes me feel positively Pollyanna-ish by comparison. Well, occasionally.

I hear squeals and hollers of marble-rolling encouragement. I try to open the front door a little further but find progress impeded by a scooter. I am left to look out through the small crack allowed me like a nervous old lady with a chain on the door. Which is not unlike how I feel, faced with Alison and her permanent scowl and her ability to make one feel both pity and competitiveness in her presence.

"Actually, I come bearing gifts," she says, waving a bulging plastic bag in my face. "You were saying that Rufus is struggling with his reading..."

"No, it's not that he's no good at it, it's just that he's reluctant—"

"So I brought you all our early reading books."

"Won't Grace be needing them?" Grace is a full year younger than Rufus.

"Oh no, she taught herself to read when she was three. She's loving the *My Naughty Little Sister* books. She'll be begging me for *Harry Potter* by the end of the year."

I move my arm out to get the bag, but realize it is so full that I won't be able to squeeze it in unless I open the door further. I force it open an extra couple of inches, which Alison takes as an invitation to come into the house.

"Gosh," I say. "A couple of hours without the kids—bliss. You must have so many things you want to do."

"Absolutely." And with that, she's in. I remember Mitzi saying that Alison would ring her up and want to chat for hours on the phone, and we would wonder where her real friends were. And then, Mitzi realized, she *was* Alison's real friend.

"Goodness," says Alison, surveying the hall carpet patterned with gloves, hats and, inexplicably, a children's UV sunsuit. "Have you been burgled?"

This is what passes for humor in her world. "It's the weekend, you know. If you'd let me know you were dropping by..."

I hear a shout from the top landing. "Ready, steady, Geronimo..." cries Joel, followed by an ominous thudding as Rufus snowboards down two flights of stairs in a *Cars* Snuggle

Sac, trying to beat the marble to the bottom. He and the marble land with a thud at Alison's feet.

Joel and Gabe come rushing down behind him.

"Be careful on the stairs," I say.

"Will do."

"Not you, Joel. Gabe. Slide down on your bottom, sweetheart."

"Did it work?" Joel asks Rufus.

"Yeah, it got all the way down and I didn't have to push it once and I won, I beat it but it was going so fast and so was I."

"You know Alison, don't you?" I say, although she is always referred to in this house as Angrison.

"Yes, we've met," says Joel. "Do you want a go of our marble run? It goes all the way from the top of the house and it's taken us two hours to make. Look," he says, pointing at the avocado basket that has been designed as the marbles' final resting place. "All made from the recycling."

I expect her to appear unimpressed by the fact that it looks as if the recycling box has been involved in an overly successful breeding program, but instead she giggles. I'd go as far as to say she giggles coquettishly.

"It looks amazing. You're so sweet, Joel. What a wonderful father you are. You're so lucky, Mary. I wish bloody Chris could do something like this, though I suppose he's so busy at the moment building up a client base that he can't really expend his energies on building a marble run, lovely as it is. Did I tell you he's getting a record bonus this year? I know, despite all the gloom."

She walks straight through to my kitchen, stopping to remove a half-eaten apple that has grabbed her foot.

"What can I say? It's the weekend," I repeat.

"You know, I really admire the way you're so laid back about mess. I wish I could let my house go like this," she says.

"To be honest, I don't like it much either. I wish it weren't such a state."

"Have you tried tidying up as you go along?"

"This *is* after I've been tidying up as I go along. If I didn't, you wouldn't have been able to walk into this house. In fact, you barely could as it was."

"Poor you, it can be hard to cope."

"I am coping; my house just doesn't happen to be as immaculate as yours, that's all."

"Do you want to know the secret?"

"There's a secret?"

"Oh yes. There's a secret. Shall I tell you?"

She leans forward. I lean forward. "Of course," I find myself whispering.

"Are you ready for this?"

I nod.

"It will change your life."

And it could, I think, save my marriage.

I don't know what I expected from Alison's great revelation. Some sort of voodoo, perhaps—an incantation that could lure the magic cleaning pixies into my home. Maybe, I thought, she's going to admit that her family doesn't eat normal food but is fed Complan intravenously through stomach tubes, thus saving on all that endless shopping-cooking-washing-up. Or that they have clothes that are made by NASA and repel dirt and germs. That her family are aliens and so don't make a mess or need to wash. That she has a robot which does all the tidying—or, failing that, a very cheap illegal immigrant who lives in the cupboard under the stairs.

What I got was a scribbled name on a piece of paper.

"What's this?" A guru, maybe. A goddess to come around to my house and wave a wand that will sort out the wayward cables and put the outgrown clothes into bags to take to the charity shop.

"It's a website. For people like you. I used to be like you, Mary, but I found the way. Follow the way, Mary, and you will have a tidy home. And you will become happier, too." She spoke with all the evangelism of an AA member, but her sermon was made a little less convincing by the fact that she is still the grumpiest person I've ever met.

"Has this website made you happier?"

"Oh yes. I'm so calm these days, ask anyone. You won't believe it, but I used to shout at my family all the time. And now," she smiles, beatifically, "we live in calm."

"Sometimes," I said to her, "I feel as if my house is a physical manifestation of my mind, and it's all scraggly and messed up, and if my house was this white, empty space then my mind might be, too. Empty in a good way, I mean."

Alison's mobile rang. "For god's sake, Chris," she snapped. "I'm only requesting that you look after Grace for two hours. Is that too bloody much to ask for? It's in the cupboard by the front door, of course, where it always is—which you'd know if you ever bothered to take your child to the swings. I'll be back by six, do you think you can manage until then? Hmmm? Too much for you? How do you think I manage when you go off on those infernal golf weekends? Funny that, isn't it, since I'm the one who earns more money and yet still has to do more childcare?"

She put the phone in her pocket and then gave me one of those cocked-head, sympathetic looks. "Try it," she repeated. "I really think you need it."

I hole myself up with the laptop and with near-trembling anticipation, I type the website address that Alison gave me. Speak to me, I silently intone to the computer, speak to me.

Instead of the virtual magic I've been hoping for, I'm faced with one of the messiest looking web pages I've ever seen, with the exhortations "Declutter!," "A new program for home executives!" and "Shiny happy sinks!" I am very confused. Is this really the life-saving secret that Alison has bestowed on me?

I read on, though I am itching to get back to The List to tot up today's many transgressions. I force myself through the myriad exclamation marks to try to make sense of it all. The website tells, I finally discover, of a system by which your house will be spotless and permanently guest-ready, without you having to spend more than fifteen minutes a day on it. Florid testimonials tell of lives and homes transformed by the mere application of the "dance of disposal," where the home executive will put on a three-minute song and throw away as many things as she can in its duration. Others speak of the elimination of their "toxic spots," which sounds like something I haven't done since I had adolescent acne. All write eulogies as to the transformative powers of the creation of a "Golden Notebook," a ring-binder of to-do lists, menu plans and household zones. Doris Lessing, I think, must be so proud.

I read on, hoping to discover the secret of how you can inspire those that you share your house with to take as much interest in purging household junk as you do, while at the same time wondering why the women behind this site didn't think to perhaps try to declutter some of the excessive exclamation marks littering the prose. My eyes are glazing over just thinking about these commands to enjoy the daily cleaning of my toilet bowl and to have fun while throwing out junk. It makes me yearn for the exclamation-mark-free, joyfully joyless zone of The List. My List.

But still, I concede, can all these women (and they are all women) be so wrong? Alison did say it has changed her life, transformed her from Angrison to Airy-fairy-son. Maybe I too shall go from Scary Mary to Merry Mary. Before I can change my mind, I sign up for email reminders of how to "Work the System!" and resolve to give the "ClutterNoNo!™" system of home-executive efficiency a week's trial.

Day 1. By the time I check my messages at work on Monday morning, I have 39 emails from my new friends at ClutterNoNo. I'm confused before I've even read them. How am I supposed to find time to wade through the household detritus if I have to spend all my time wading through my inbox?

I soon discover that I'm already falling woefully behind. I should have set my alarm to get up half an hour before the rest of my family in order to get that toilet bowl really sparkly, as well as making sure that I have put on a "face"—by which I think they mean makeup, rather than just pulling one.

I'm frowning at my screen when I'm interrupted by Lily. "Matt told me to tell you that he needs all the costs added to the schedule by the end of today. Or something. Whatevs."

I'm hearing her words at the same time as reading "Go empty the dishwasher! No excuses, right now, girlfriend!"

"Sorry, what was that, Lily?"

"I don't know, Matt said something about schedules and costs. He needs them."

"Shall do. If you see him, tell him it's under control." But, I think as I read the fourteenth nagging email reminder from ClutterNoNo, I don't have all my closets under control, do I? Apparently, my mind will never be clean until the closet is. It even talks of a "coat closet," which I guess is what some people in a parallel universe have instead of the matted jumble of outdoor wear that slithers down the wall from the pegs in the hall. And what about dusting the underside of the dining-room chairs? I don't even have a dining room. And must I really create my own "signature air freshener" out of fresh mint and rose petals?

I spend the office day trying to wear two hats, that of an efficient home executive (what hat would that be? A hairnet, perhaps?) and that of an equally efficient overseer of production management at a thrusting independent television company (a beret worn at a jaunty angle?). I hardly dare look at my emails for fear of seeing more exhortations to refill my bird feeders and to love myself. Oh, god, ClutterNoNo is right, I really should clean out the boys' bath toys more often to prevent the frequent occurrence of them vomiting out gray bilge instead of bubbly water when squeezed. And if I had a laundry room, I would go there to look behind the appliances for odd socks.

Since I haven't had time to buy the ring-binder necessary to create a Golden Notebook, I scribble out a to-do list on the back of a production meeting agenda and go home full of resolve to at least give the ClutterNoNo system a try.

I barely have time to speak to my children, so frenzied am I in my race to tick off tasks. In a bid to have decluttered my allotted number of things, I am forced to throw away the artwork that Gabe has brought back from playgroup. He looks a bit upset, but I sometimes think this endless supply of daubs is all about appeasing the parents rather than bringing out any artistic talent in the child. And, to be honest, they weren't very good.

At dinner, I put newspaper under everyone's chairs as instructed and then whip the sodden pages into the bin afterward, along with the wet wipes that I have to use to get my toilet bowl "shiny shiny," and the dying plant that Ursula gave me as a Christmas present (gee, thanks). Then I have to empty the bin because it's so full of the fruits of my labor, as well as the moldy contents of the fruit bowl. I want to throw Joel in there, too, when he comes home and tells me to "chill." Using funny teen-speak laden with irony doesn't make it OK, husband of mine.

Day 2. The house doesn't look much better than it did before. I find I am spending so much time trying to create a nice-looking Golden Notebook that I don't have time to get myself looking "nice 'n' pretty" for the day. I spend the day at work, juggling the yet again reduced budgets and revised crew lists, before coming home and attempting to purify at least one of my household zones. Before collapsing exhausted into bed at night, I have to tidy the living room and kitchen, lay the table for breakfast and plan what I shall be cooking for that meal. Sugar-laden cereal, as it happens. My woman's work is not done even when I finally get to bed, for I must reflect on my day's achievements and write a list of all that I have to be thankful for, as well as making time to share with my "dh"—short for "dear husband." I think this last exhortation might be a euphemism. Either way, I don't do it. Nor do I fall asleep, as ordered, "with a smile on my face."

Day 3. What I am asked to do: fertilize the plants, write outstanding thank-you notes, buy the groceries, balance my check book and change dead lightbulbs in the cooker hood. I must tell each member of my family that I love them, and one thing that I think is awesome about their personalities. I must tell myself that I love me, and find five things that I think are awesome about my personality.

What I actually do: scream.

Stop it, stop it, stop! You stupid idiotic women! Leave me alone, stop hassling me, why are you on at me all day long? For Christ's sake, stop nagging. Does it really matter if I haven't shampooed the carpet on a Thursday? You're all flaming crazy. Fuck this, fuck this, fuck this (I just know the ClutterNoNo ladies would not like their home executive to be such a potty mouth).

I put my head in my hands. Luckily I haven't given my hair the ClutterNoNo requisite "perfect blow," so it doesn't matter that I'm mussing it up. I am filled with both admiration and pity for Alison. No wonder she's always in such a foul temper. She's being electronically nagged all day long. And what's more, she's acquiescing. I will go mad, madder than before, if I keep this up.

I find the unsubscribe button and then declutter my email inbox of every single last reminder, all 103 of them, from that source of 1950s pinny-wearing nonsense. I breathe out. They're right about one thing, those ClutterNoNo ladies, it does feel wonderful to expunge unwanted crap.

I open up The List, which has been ignored these last three days. It is so neat and lovely. I want to kiss the screen. What the ClutterNoNo people failed to suggest was that husbands, or "darling ones," took any part in this home executive efficiency. The List, on the other hand, does. I shall, I think, patent it and set up a website for everyone in my position to sort their lives out as a rival to ClutterNoNo craziness. And who knows, taken to its ultimate conclusion, The List might involve me throwing out the biggest piece of clutter of all.

March Good Housekeeping

	A	B
1	March allowance	2 per day, total 62
2	Total no. of debits in March	99
3	Breakdown of infringements	19 kitchen; 19 bathroom; 7 laundry; 11 bedroom; 23 living; 8 parenting; 5 general ineptitude; 7 finance.
4	Infringement of the month	Shouting out one morning "What have you done with my keys?" "Nothing." "Are you sure, you're always tidying things away. I really can't be late today, where are they? I'll have to take yours." And then going off, leaving me to swear through the house trying and failing to find his, before getting the spare ones off the neighbors. When he came back later, it turned out that his keys had been in his pocket all the time. He thought this funny.
5	Positives to offset	7. Some creative play with the kids and a few compliments. That's about it.
6	March debt	30 (99 offset by March allowance of 62 and 7 positives)
7	Total debt from February and March	42
8	Total remaining	58 over next four months (100 minus 42)

6

The Yellow Toothbrush

"Shit."

"Mommy, you can't say that," admonishes Rufus.

"Actually I can, because it's not an expletive, it's a factual description of the situation." He looks puzzled. "Why, why, why, do people let their flaming dogs poo all over the roads? It's disgusting," I shout, at nobody in particular, perhaps hoping to catch some recidivist dog owner. Or a recidivist dog, I suppose. "Oh, god, it's all over the buggy wheels. And your shoes, Rufe. Why did you not look where you were going?"

"It's not my fault."

"No, I know it's not. It's the fault of those flipping dog owners." I raise my voice once more. "And it's my fault, I suppose, for being in such a hurry to get you to school on time that I didn't check where we were going." Joel says I'm obsessed with dog poo. In truth, all mothers are obsessed with dog poo. We walk with an internal radar system that is constantly beep-beeping along the streets, ready to scream at our children to stop right where they are as we pull them into the road and into the path of a speeding car just to avoid smearing shit all over the buggy wheels. Joel, too, might become obsessed with excrement if he ever had to use a pencil to dig it out of the grooves of a sneaker or clean it from the axles of the buggy wheels.

For some inexplicable reason my dog waste radar failed me this morning. "Shit, shit, shit," I mutter.

Not only has the dog shat in the middle of the pavement, but also in the exact midpoint of our journey from home to school. I'm frozen for a second, then I spin the buggy 180 degrees and drag Rufus too hard by the arm to get home to deposit a pair of shitty school shoes in the sink, where they'll remain until I get home from work.

"But I don't want to wear those sneakers," he wails.

"Why not? I thought you loved these sneakers. They light up when you walk."

"They're for babies. Gaby baby Gaby baby."

Gabe retaliates with a blood-drawing swipe. "Oh, god, I've got to cut your nails." Rufus reacts as if he has been slashed with a machete.

"I'm sorry, darling, poor you, but get these sneakers on. It's these or slippers. Or bare feet."

He wails some more.

"Please, I don't have time for this," I say as I use an old yellow toothbrush to dig out the shit from the buggy wheels, while trying to hold my breath.

He wails even louder when he gets a late card at school. They're zero tolerance about punctuality, though the fact that some bastard's tied his muscly dog to the school gate is apparently fine. I want to do a DNA test on the scary-looking Staff cross that's blocking our way to find out whether it matches the crap accumulated on the pair of shoes sitting in our kitchen sink, the crap that is getting harder and glueier all the while. I bet it is the same dog. I want to find out where its owners live and rub their noses in the fly-covered shit on the street. Or post one of Gabriel's diapers through their letterbox. When he's got diarrhea.

Smiley Kylie, the PTA big cheese, comes up to me with her characteristic glow of good will. "Don't forget it's the Year 1 cake sale later today. You can leave any contributions in the PTA cupboard," she says brightly.

"Some of us work," I growl at her. I swear I hear her mutter "Bitch" under her breath.

"No worries," she says brightly.

I run, using the buggy as a sort of Zimmer, and try to drown out the sound of Gabriel telling me he wants to walk. He starts crying. People look at me as if they're about to call social services. I don't even go into Deena's house, but deposit Gabriel on the doorstep as if he were a catalog purchase. Much like the average courier, I'm tempted to ring the bell and not even wait to see that someone's there to take receipt, but instead just leave both Gabriel and a "While you were out" card. I say, "Here he is," thrust a bag of clean pants at the ever-fragrant Deena and peg it to the office.

There are no buses, as ever. I would get a late card if my office issued them. I am still, of course, earlier than most of my colleagues, but this won't stop them looking at me and muttering "Part-timer" when I leave on the dot of 5:30 p.m.

Even standing squashed on the bus, I feel like I can breathe for the first time since 6 a.m. I do this briefly and try to run through the day that awaits me. I've only got as far as 11 o'clock in my head before we arrive at my stop and I run to the office. There, I am immediately assailed by a constant stream of questions and whines from the incoming masses.

"Mary, you've got to shave 5 percent off this budget. I don't care where from, I'll operate the camera myself if I have to."

"Why aren't we getting per diems for while we're away? It's not fair. Like, are we supposed to pay for our coffees and lunches out of our own money?"

"Oi, La Roux, this schedule is a nightmare, we're never going to get everything done on time. It's like a piece of science fiction. And I'll be the one who gets blamed."

No, you won't, I think to myself. I'll be the one who gets blamed. That's what I am, a blame-sponge, the here that the buck stops at, a whine-magnet.

"Isn't it exciting?" Lily says to me.

"What?"

"That filming finally starts this week. Such a buzz."

The filming *is* a buzz and it is a relief to have a commission in these straightened times. I force myself to feel proud of the production, even if it is a rather hackneyed panel game show based on knowledge of celebrity magazines, to be broadcast on the outer reaches of the satellite listings. When filming starts, it is the play finally being performed to an audience; it's like the process of decorating a house after the boring bits involving foundations, repointing and joists; it's the race being run after hours of training. Sadly, now that I work as a backroom girl, part-time and with my regular hours, I'm part of all the build-up without the adrenalin payoff. I wonder for the umpteenth time whether there is any way I could go back into the hot seat of being a producer-director, or whether it would mean too much time away from my boys and an even greater proportion of my time, when I finally did get back to the house, on all the boring admin instead of playing with them.

"I feel like all my babies have grown up," I say of the runners, production secretaries, directors and producers, "and now they must flee the nest and go out into the world. Run free, little ones." I've wiped the metaphorical bottoms of the crew, I've weaned them and trained them, and now they're off into the university of life as lived during production. They've left me behind and now, just like students in freshers' week, they'll be getting drunk, getting high and getting off with one another. I'm hoping that they'll also be getting the job done. If they don't, I'll be blamed.

"Are you not coming to filming on Friday night?" asks Lily. "Go on, we'll all get so wasted afterward."

"Not on the hospitality budget I've drawn up."

"Spoilsport."

I am the boring one now. I wasn't always. It was on a production much like this that Joel and I met. We flirted, then we didn't, then we got together. Well, that's the abridged version. The more complicated one has a cameo role for Mitzi. But when we finally did get together, I loved him so quickly and so fearlessly. I never had to worry that he wouldn't call or that he would go off me. Joel's confidence allowed him to love and to be loved generously. I wore his frayed sweaters and his warm smile. At the age of 27 and a half, I had my first true love. I carried in my stomach that wonderful feeling of always having something to look forward to. I wanted to scrawl his name onto my bag and walk with my hand in his jeans' pocket. I felt 17. No, not 17 again, not like I did when I was really and truly 17, for that was miserable and insecure and angst-ridden. No, I felt 17 like one is 17 in the movies: flushed with love, optimism and possibilities.

I don't know how we got any work done. We partied with our friends from the office, enjoying their audience to the perfection of our love; they were our own Greek chorus, speaking of what a great couple we were. Then we'd go home where we'd have sex for hours, our sessions elongated not by complicated tantric moves but by the fact that we couldn't stop talking. I loved the stories from his bohemian childhood, he found my tales of Northern respectability equally exotic. We'd go to bed talking and then wake up talking. Mouths made for talking, kissing, smiling.

"Go on—can't you just, like, get a babysitter?" I am snapped out of my reverie by Lily.

"But Lily, a babysitter's not there the next day when I'll have a hangover and two hyperactive boys."

"Well, just get a babysitter that stays the night, then."

"Maybe." As if.

My hands seem to carry with them the stench of turd, however hard I scrub at them, Lady Macbeth–like. I think of ways to blame Joel for this morning's debacle. If he had taken Rufus to school instead of leaving me to drop off both him and Gabriel, it would never have happened. Well, it might have happened, but at least it would not have happened to me. If men like him shared the maternal angst about dog shit, then maybe laws would be enforced and dog owners properly punished. If I hadn't had to wipe up his endless rings of milk from the kitchen counter after breakfast then I would not have been in such a rush this morning.

I decide to nip out to the shop to buy chewing gum in the vain hope that making my mouth minty fresh might finally expunge the aura of dog shit that clings to me.

It's then that I see her, Cara, walking—no, gliding—down the street toward me. I wish that I could have bumped into her on the way back from the shop, mouth fully minted, rather than on the way there. But then I would have had gum in my mouth and I'd hate to have to talk to Cara while chewing gum; it would be, I imagine she might say, so déclassé.

It's too late for me to duck into one of the alleyways that riddle these old industrial streets, so I concentrate on looking ahead so that I can act surprised when I get near her. Or should I catch her eye now and give her a warm smile until we are near enough to speak? But then that would be warm smiling for a very long time and I'm not sure my facial muscles would cope. I ponder all these things until we are upon one another.

"Good morning, Mary," she says, kissing me on both cheeks, not sullying the gesture with any fake "mwah" noises.

"Hello, Cara, what are you doing here?"

"It's where I live and work."

"Of course. I'm just going to the shop."

"Good." She always has a look of amusement on her face. I wish I found the world wryly amusing instead of verily irritating.

I plug the gap with a garbled, "How's Becky?" I feel intrusive, like a tabloid reporter, for asking a question that would be innocuous to anyone else.

"How do you think she is?" she replies.

"Great." Why's she asking me?

"Well then, she's great." Her expression remains the same.

"My office is really near here." I sound so eager, so keen to impress the cool girl from the year above.

"I think I knew that already. We should have a drink sometime."

"We should. That would be great; yes, definitely, let's do that." Oh, god, let's not, what would we talk about? I can't even manage a straightforward conversation on the street. I can see how Mitzi might be her friend, but not how on earth Becky can be her girlfriend. Her lover. In theory I think I know what they might get up to, but they are so different I can't even imagine them sharing a kitchen, let alone a bedroom. It's a same-sex relationship, but they come from different planets.

"I like your coat," she says and touches its sleeve.

"Really? This old thing." I laugh, though I'm not sure what the joke is or who it's on.

"I must go," she says. "I've got a brunch meeting." I picture her in a fashionable restaurant with eggs Benedict and a glass of champagne that she sips, not glugs.

"Bye, then." I walk away and then break into a trot. This is pathetic. She is my best friend's girlfriend. She is not prime minister or a top brain surgeon. I am a grown-up; a mother of two; I have a good degree and oversee budgets that run into the hundreds of thousands and I have never once made a major mistake in my professional career; I can order about "talent" without offending them; I can even manage Gabriel's tantrums in public, for god's sake. Pathetic, I repeat to myself.

I'm thinking about my day, half sublime half grime, as I lie in bed that evening with the computer, updating The List, which is hurtling toward a healthy total early in the month.

I check the code for the first of the day's misdemeanors. **Subsection A [kitchen] number** 16) *Never clears out the sink gunk.* I hate that one, it reminds me of when James Herriot puts his hand up a cow's vagina and pulls out a calf. I think maybe I ought to just add a point for that one every day, since it's unlikely he'll ever find his way to digging out the slime.

I cast my eyes around the room. **Subsection C [laundry]** *Leaves dirty underwear mummified into duvet.* Oh, and also, **D [bedroom] number** 4) *Leaves balled-up tissues on the chest of drawers.* He always puts these germy rags on the side. Actually, that's unfair, he doesn't always leave them on the chest of drawers. Sometimes he leaves them in his trouser pocket so that they can go in the washing machine and leave little white ball-bearings to stick to everyone else's clothes. Which, of course, is another point on The List.

"You're spending a lot of time holed up with the laptop," says Joel.

"Not really."

"What are you doing?"

"Nothing." I give my best imitation of Rufus on being asked what he did at school today. "Stuff. The Internet sometimes.

We really should get that wireless connection sorted. I wish our whole lives could be wireless," I say, feeling depressed by the spaghetti junction lying behind the TV. It'll be me that sorts it out. As well as chief home executive, I am also home IT consultant. And head of accounts, personnel and internal communications.

"Are you having one of those virtual affairs?"

"What? Of course not."

"I was joking, Mary. As if."

"Why's it so unlikely? Do you think no one would want to have an email liaison with me? I could be having an affair online."

"You just said you weren't."

"I'm not."

"Well then. So what is it, then? I'm trying to think what would be worse: you having an affair or you being addicted to one of those geeky Dungeons and Dragons type of sites, world of witchcraft."

"Warcraft," I correct him. "World of Warcraft, it's called."

"So that's what you're doing. You're spending all your time pretending to be a scantily clad superhero wood sprite called Thorday." He gives it a portentous, cinema trailer type voice-over.

"In your dreams. You're the one who seems to know so much about it."

I continue to look at my scribbled details of transgressions ready to transcribe to today's date. If I were to do a pie chart of how I spend my time in bed, there would be more minutes actively engaged with The List than with my husband. Or with anybody else's husband for that matter. Why was Joel quite so dismissive of the idea that I might be having a virtual affair? I could have an avatar of myself as a busty blonde in a leather bikini, happily cavorting with a hirsute cartoon muscleman, who is in real life a balding call-center operative who lives with his mother.

Although if I was going to have an affair, I think I'd probably make it a real one. It hardly seems worth going to the trouble of having one confined to cyberspace. "An affair"—I say the word in my head with a French accent. Lover, passion, érotique... Saying the words in French makes it sound a lot more classy a prospect, in the manner of a moisturizer that promises *luminescence pour la peau.*

I feel much the same way toward the prospect of an affair as I do about other people's perfect homes—where on earth do they find the time? The only person with sufficient staff to squeeze in a lunchtime assignation is Mitzi. And what about all the body maintenance involved? When would one find time to do all the necessary beautification to sleep with someone for the first time? If you had them over to your house, you'd have to wash the sheets afterward. And before, probably.

Joel could have an affair, I suppose. I wonder what he'd like best about having to "stay late at the office"—the sex or the missing out on the fractious bath-and-bedtime routine?

I go into the bathroom to find Joel brushing his teeth with a bright yellow, aging toothbrush.

"Is that your toothbrush?" I ask.

"Yeah. Why?"

"I thought it was an old one. I just assumed it was."

"Waste not want not. Do you know what it was doing by the kitchen sink? Next to Rufe's shoes?"

"No, I don't, sorry."

I'm sure that this Sunday will be a day of multiple infringements of The List point code-named **Subsection F [invisible woman] number** 7) previously known as number 33: *Takes his mother's side over mine.*

Deep breath as we park the car and bundle the potty, favored toys, spare clothes and, finally, children out of it and into the front garden of Ursula's house. I need to breathe deeply a) to stay calm in the face of the Tennant family passive-aggression and b) because Ursula's house, quite literally, smells. I drag my children through the overgrown garden to a front door emblazoned with "no junk mail" and peeling "No to Trident" stickers. I used to do mental makeovers of plain fellow students at university, imagining what they might look like with a proper haircut and some stylish clothes. Now I wonder what Mitzi would do to Ursula's house, a solid double-fronted Edwardian villa. She'd rip out the tatty vinyl that half covers the original tiling in the hallway and replace the missing panes in the stained glass above the door. The vast quantities of orangey-brown varnished pine would be clothed in a dove-gray shade of paint made of china clay and hand mixed by Cornish fishermen.

First of all, though, she'd have to clean it. The corpses of flies litter every windowsill, the low-energy lightbulbs are coated with a layer of dead skin and the toilet bowl shows the result of a lifetime of not flushing "if it's yellow," as a thick crust of brown limescale clings to the sides, reminding me of Ursula's nicotine-stained teeth. Piles of newspapers vie with towers of books and vast dust-covered rubber plants in big brass pots, while the furniture is a bizarre mix of priceless family heirlooms and tatty 70s junk shop—either Chippendale or merely chipped.

Ursula is the brightest thing in the dingy hall, dressed in purple velvet and a necklace made by a Guatemalan women's collective. Rufus, well trained as he is, immediately sits on the bottom of the stairs to remove his shoes. The last time he did that, his socks were so permanently blackened by the experience that we had to throw them out.

"You don't have to take your shoes off, darling."

"Why not, Mommy?"

I ponder a tactful answer to that question when Ursula intervenes. "Because shoes are for wearing, of course." She smiles at me. "And how is my favorite daughter-in-law?" It is just as well Joel is an only child.

"Fine, thanks." In the novels I read, an untidy house is always shorthand for warmth and love. A tidy house means that the owner is clinical and cold, quite possibly sterile. I don't believe that anymore. I walk into the kitchen, which has sticky brown cupboards, lined inside with graphic orange and white wallpaper. It's a warm day. Ursula ushers us outside for what she calls a "gin and French," closely related to another mysterious beverage called a "gin and It." Standing on the moss-veined patio is Becky, holding a sweaty-looking glass of rosé. She gets up to hug me.

"Becky, how lovely. What are you doing here?" I ask.

"Ursula invited me."

"Yes, but . . . anyway, it's lovely to see you." I lower my voice. "It's great to have an ally." She looks mystified.

"It's great to be here." She waves her glass, which could more accurately be described as a tumbler.

"Rebecca," says Ursula, "has been working with my good friend Suzannah Westernberg on numerous cases."

"Legendary family law barrister," explains Becky.

"She thinks very highly of you, too," says Ursula. I feel that Becky, sexual orientation notwithstanding, would make a far better daughter-in-law than me.

"What are you having, Ma?" Joel shouts from the kitchen. She is Ursula, Ma or Mater. Never "Mom" like anybody else's mother. "And you, Mary?"

He is already knocking back the gin and something, thus fulfilling transgression F3: *Assumes that I will always be the one to drive us home when we go out.* "Something soft, I guess." He doesn't even notice the sacrifice. "Actually, will you drive today? I'll have some rosé."

He swigs back the remains of his glass, rasping at the power of neat alcohol. "I think it may be too late. You don't mind, it's not like you ever want more than a couple anyway."

He is quite the host in his mother's house, busying himself with the supermarket-brand peanuts and making sure that everyone has a drink. He is much more helpful here than at home. And he won't have a word said against the food served here, despite being a balsamic vinegar sort of man from a crusty wine vinegar childhood.

"I bumped into Cara the other day," I say to Becky.

"Did you? She didn't mention it."

"It's not like we talked for very long. A couple of minutes. It was near the office."

"Have you seen Suzannah recently, Ursula?" Becky changes the subject abruptly. I wonder why and make a note to myself to ask her later. I don't want to bury myself so deep in the dirty laundry of The List that I forget about Becky's dilemma. "She's got this case that's going up to the Lords. Everyone reckons it's going to set a precedent over reasonable needs."

"Don't have those crisps, Gabe. Joel, stop him, he's ruining his appetite."

"And other things that mothers say," says Joel.

"I never did," says Ursula.

"And don't toss peanuts into your mouth. The boys will copy you and choke."

Ursula snorts, "Peanut allergy."

"They don't have peanut allergies, but it's very easy to choke on nuts. And uncut grapes."

"And yet more things that mothers say," adds Joel.

And that will be a **G9**: *Fails to back me up when I tell the children to do something entirely reasonable.*

"You've got to chill about their food."

"He's right," says Ursula. "No child ever starves himself. Joel lived on nothing but cornflakes and orange juice until he was seven."

"But I want my children to have a proper balance of protein and carbohydrates and vitamins and minerals."

Gabe and Rufus continue to mainline salty snacks, while the adults suck up the tepid rosé and faux martinis. The blossom is out and the beds are filled with tulips. The children are being unobtrusive thanks to the sedative properties of salt, while the adults bounce between the political and the personal. It is the sort of charming and bohemian scene that I used to fantasize about while growing up a bookish girl in what I considered to be a grim town. I would have imagined myself so happy here.

Lunch starts with what Ursula calls "tapas": some aging olives, pickled onions mixed with salad cream and crackers topped with cheese out of a tube. Joel pronounces it all delicious. The roast meat is overdone while the roast potatoes are mysteriously rock solid and lacking a crunchy shell—instead they feel like they have been coated with an impenetrable rubber casing. The leeks are buttered, natch.

"Sorry," says Ursula. "You know how I always forget about your dairy thing. Joel, you'll never believe it, but the Moores have split up."

"What, the grown-ups or the children?" asks Joel.

"The grown-ups. Well, as grown-up as you can be in your sixties. In their sixties." She shakes her head. "I mean, what's the point? What is the point?"

"If they were unhappy," I say. "If she was unhappy."

"Yes, but you'd have to be very unhappy indeed to go through all that bother. I mean, it's not exactly as if either of them are going to find anyone else, are they?"

"I don't understand," I say. "You're not objecting to divorce on the grounds of morality, but of practicality?"

"Of course I don't object to it on moral grounds. I'm hardly in a position to take a stance on the perfect nuclear family." Joel's father is somewhere in the States and played only an intermittent exotic gift-bringing part in his childhood. Even now, Joel is expected to get over-excited about the arrival of Oreos and Hershey bars, like a treat-starved World War II land girl welcoming the GIs. "I'm sure Rebecca can back me up here, but isn't divorce a whole load of bother?"

"Not to mention expense," Becky says. "Much of which gets wasted on people like me. And all the evidence suggests that one year on, the divorcees are unhappier than they were when they were married anyway. Especially the women, I think." She looks at me as she says this.

"It's all rather embarrassing," says Ursula. "I really think the Moores believe that they're not too old for love and happiness. How absurd. Oh dear, Mary."

"What?"

"You won't be able to have any cream with your crumble either, will you?"

"I'm not sure Mary would want to anyway," says Joel, holding up the tub. "Mother, your commitment to 'waste not want not' is admirable, but I think you may have excelled yourself this time. This cream's sell-by date is in February."

"Nonsense," she says, giving it a theatrical sniff. "Absolutely bloody fine. Hate all this hygiene namby-pambyism. Those sell-by dates are all a ruse by the supermarkets to make you buy more."

"You're quite right," says Becky. "That's what I'm always telling Cara." She pulls a face. "Especially yogurt. It's supposed to be a bit moldy."

"You are a woman after my own heart," says Ursula. "Ham is supposed to have that green shine to it. Sign that it's mature."

"Exactly," says Becky, with rosé-fueled emphasis. "The waste not want not mentality is authentic environmentalism. Not like your friend Mitzi." She hisses her name.

"That's what I'm always saying to Mary," adds Joel. "It's about buying less, not more."

"I agree," I say. "You don't have to tell me all this. I find all that hybrid-car-driving, fancy compost heap stuff sticks in my throat too, you know." Though not quite as much as Ursula's two-month-old cream would.

I clear the plates and take them into the kitchen. I decant leftovers into little bowls so as not to be accused of wastage and look in vain for some plastic wrap. The fridge is already crammed with saucepans holding useless remnants of previous meals and strange bowls of unidentifiable fat. I'm desperate for the toilet, but find the lack of bathroom locks inhibiting. Joel finds my attitude bewildering and tells me just to shout "I'm in here," if I hear someone coming.

Becky joins me. "It's bliss here, isn't it? You're so lucky, Ursula is so wonderful. This house, it's my idea of heaven."

"How so?"

"Everything shouts out a life lived. The sofas dip where bums have sat and you feel like just sitting there means you join a great pantheon of others and the good times they've had. I love that all the walls have been drawn on and that door frame has the heights etched on of not just your children, but Joel, too. I mean, how fantastic that it hasn't been painted in 30 years. You know that you could pick up anything and there would be a story behind it. A mug bought on holiday, books signed by the author, ancient cookery books with food-encrusted pages."

"Ursula doesn't really do much cooking," I reply.

"If these walls could talk . . ."

"They'd be pontificating about something or other in a judgmental, intellectually entitled way."

"Well, I think it's brilliant. I hate the way people these days get rid of perfectly usable kitchens because they're not in this year's colors, or think that there's no place for something that looks ugly but may have a beautiful story behind it."

"This isn't about Ursula's house, is it? Are you still feeling uncomfortable at Cara's?"

"I suppose." Becky picks up an ancient place mat with an engraving of a Cambridge college. Or at least, St. John's College in a mud storm, splattered as it is with vintage congealed gravy.

"But it's so perfect," I say, thinking of Cara's galvanized-steel worktops.

"Exactly. Perfection's not really me. When I look at the place that I'm living in—see, I can't even call it 'my place,' it's 'the place where I'm living'—I just wonder where all the ephemera is."

"Ephemera?"

"The stuff, the souvenirs, the gifts, the old chairs that don't match."

"Oh, the crap, you mean."

"It's not normal, the way these people expunge anything that isn't aesthetically pleasing from their lives. And then I think I'm the only piece of ephemera, or crap as you'd call it, in the whole flat. I'm the only thing that isn't shiny and new. I'm the only thing that doesn't match, that doesn't match some scheme or other."

"Becks, this isn't about the way that Cara has decorated her house, is it? We identify ourselves with our surroundings, don't we? If my house isn't tidy, I feel untidy, unhinged. The state of my house dictates my state of mind. Is something like that going on with you?"

"You're right."

"I thought so."

"No, I mean you're right about confusing your feelings about where you live with how you feel about yourself, but I think it's probably the other way around. It's not that the state of your house reflects the state of your mind. More that the state of your mind dictates to you how you feel about your house."

"What do you mean?"

"Take you and Joel. It's not your untidy house that's the problem, it's you. Just like it's not actually the fact that I don't wear white and match the painted floorboards at Cara's that's the issue, it's the fact that I don't match her. We don't match each other."

Joel walks in, carrying a tray piled with plates stacked precariously on top of one another. It really annoys me the way he doesn't put all the food scrapings and the cutlery onto the top plate when he clears the table. Not that he ever clears the table at home; this sort of helpful behavior is reserved for his mother.

Becky looks at me and at Joel, then squeezes my arm. "Think about it."

I did think about it. I am still thinking about it three days later when I should be sorting out some yet more revised budgets, or at the very least electronically skiving like a normal person working in TV.

"Done," says Lily, staring at her Facebook page. "Status updated. I'm so through with Zak."

I hadn't been aware that she had been so with Zak in the first place. "I'm sorry to hear that. What is your current status? No, don't tell me, why not just tweet me since I'm sitting all of five meters away from you."

"You're not subscribed, remember? Do you want me to sort it out for you, Grandma?"

And to think how dismissive I used to be of my parents when I had to program the video recorder for them. "I was joking. Single and happy? Single and looking? Joining holy orders?"

"Single and thinking."

"That's not like you."

"What, the single bit or the thinking bit?"

"Either?"

"Very funny." She twists her dangling scarf with the Op Art pattern. See, Lily can wear a scarf and it looks hip, edgy and nonchalant. If I wore one, I'd look like a middle-aged Labor MP. Or, worse, Ursula. "Nah, seriously, I'm bored with all these boys. I want a man. Someone like your sex-on-a-stick husband. He is fierce."

"Oh, please." Someone less fierce in any sense of the word I cannot imagine. Talking about anybody's husband, even or especially my own, as sexually attractive makes my stomach turn. When we were all on the dating scene, it was perfectly acceptable, even mandatory, to drone on about how gorgeous and studlike your latest man was and how well endowed he was, but I now find any reference to the allure of a married man distasteful. Such language about sex and men has been replaced with a new vocabulary of tragicomic celibacy and casual disparagement.

"No, seriously," continues Lily. "He's got that salt and pepper hair, big strong arms thing going on. I'm hot for that now, skinny girl-boys are very last year, don't you know? Where would I find Joel version 2.0? I'm thinking chopping wood or shearing sheep."

I laugh. "Nothing could be further from the truth. He's the least practical or outdoorsy person I've ever met. He grew up in London and was amazed to find that cows lived in fields rather than in city farms. He thinks that to light a fire, you just have to switch on the gas."

"You know what I mean." Lily is undeterred. "He looks like he would survive in the event of a global meltdown. And that's what really matters. How did you two get together?"

"I hate to tell you this, but we didn't meet while white-water rafting in the Amazon. We met at work."

Lily looks around at the fey creatures populating the office and winces. "And?"

"He started out as a runner, inappropriately since he never runs anywhere, and there weren't many straight men in our office and, well, we got together."

"Details, I want details. I love 'how we met' stories."

"OK. You know my friend Mitzi? She's come in and met me for lunch a couple of times, used to work in telly."

"Blonde, thin, rich Mitzi with all the children. Botox."

"Why does everyone know she's had Botox but me? Is it because you read all those magazines where they put big red rings around any surgery celebs have had?"

"Important sociological documents, those magazines," she says. "Go on, tell me about Mitzi and your man."

"She was working in the same place as Joel and I. She fancied him so I assumed, we all assumed, that nobody else would get a look-in. In those days, Mitzi pretty much creamed off anyone remotely attractive—the presenters, the execs, the married man who owned the company." It was an immutable law of nature that Mitzi was the attractive one. Long of leg but not too tall, slim but not skinny, blonde yet with a nose just big enough and a jaw just strong enough to save her from blandness. Her looks alone were killer, but it was also the way she carried them. Her mane naturally flicked, her hips swayed, her eyes had a slight glaze to them which made men believe she was permanently thinking about sex. The rest of us accepted her supremacy without really objecting to the presumption. It would have been like a planet objecting to having to rotate around the sun. "I wasn't sure I liked him that much anyway. I remember thinking he was a bit porky," I continue to Lily. "Mitzi said he wasn't fat, he had 'generous girth' and that it showed he loved food and drink and thus life and thus sex."

"So she copped off with him first."

"No, Joel didn't fancy her back." It was that simple, that's what I tell myself. But for Mitzi and the rest of us in her wake, it didn't seem like a credible explanation. It was as if the earth had stopped spinning on its axis. I expected frogs to fall from the sky and plagues of locusts to attack.

"And he fancied you?"

"Yes." I smile to relive my happiest triumph, its luster undimmed by what has happened since. "It's a bit more complicated than just that, or at least it seemed so at the time."

"Go on, tell me. Did bitchy Mitzi stand in your way?"

"No, no, not really. Sort of. Not on purpose, I don't think. She kind of didn't tell me that Joel fancied me, but I think that was because she'd misunderstood what he was saying and had assumed I wasn't his type. I think. I'm not sure I ever really got to the bottom of who said what and what happened myself. Anyway, Joel and I got together and that was all that mattered at the time."

That was all that mattered for years afterward. If I ever had a down moment or couldn't get to sleep, I'd just go over Joel's and my "how we got together" story and I'd tingle. It became what a friend of mine calls your "default thought," which has now been replaced by the moment Rufus first smiled or when I lay in the hospital clutching the extraordinarily beautiful newborn Gabe and Rufus gently stroked his soft skull.

The fact that I'd never really questioned Mitzi's role in us getting together, or more possibly her role in us almost not getting together, was irrelevant. I didn't want to have it out with her back then, partly because I was on such a wave of love that I couldn't accommodate the necessary amount of logic or bad feeling, and partly, less edifyingly, I wanted her around to witness my happiness.

"You know what, Lily?" I say. "There's no interesting intrigue with me and Joel. One office, two people, a lot of alcohol—isn't that how everyone gets together?"

That made it sound simple. The truth is more complicated but so much sweeter. Our "how we met" story has all the misunderstandings and confusions of a Hardy novel without the rural idyll or Shakespeare without the twins and cross-dressing. Or perhaps it was merely a bad rom-com, depending on your cultural reference point. At the time, it was a messy, non-linear business, but the years of our relationship have honed a narrative out of it. After we got together, we loved to swap our perspectives, to recount our history to one another once again, all the while finessing it, adding adorable touches, trying to give it a perfect three-act structure.

How it began. Joel walked into the office and saw me. I was putting up a shelf, since the two-bit production company I worked for didn't seem able to stretch to refurbishment and I was the most practical person there. I was standing on a desk, showing my handiness with a spirit level and power drill. I got down to say hello and gave my drill a little whirr for extra emphasis. I was flushed with exertion. Joel said later, when we were in bed together, "That slight sheen of sweat and the red in your cheeks, I knew exactly what you'd look like post-coitally. And I was right." He claims he fell in love with me then and there. But there are, in fact, many "And that's when I knew I was in love" moments from Joel: when I ordered a pint of Guinness; when he found out I'd actually read one of Ursula's books; when he saw that I could go on holiday with hand luggage only.

Despite Joel's nascent paunch and permanent five-o'clock shadow, the girls in the office fell about and acted like they were builders on a construction site and he was a big-busted blonde, just about managing to stop short of wolf-whistling. I myself find it hard to see now, but am occasionally reminded when I witness Joel's continuing effect on women. It's something to do with the contrast between the way he looks and the way he acts. He was, is, very masculine-looking, not in a waxed Adonis way, but in his big hairiness. Yet he has a real touchy-feely, talk-about-my-emotions personality. "How are you?" he'd ask, not as a pleasantry, but because he really, really wanted to know and not just about your physical health, but about how you were feeling—no, I mean how you're really feeling, tell me, tell me everything. He could say camp things like "Ooh, girlfriend, get you in your Missoni," but in that deep, chocolate-brown voice of his, like James Mason's. He could talk about the nuances of heel height, all the while wearing the same old scuffed-out shoes. He is a man of political engagement and principles, yet who likes reading women's magazines and can talk about celebrity couples and the names they've given their offspring.

"H.O.T., hot," said Mitzi after a couple of days, and the other girls hid their disappointment that a red dot had appeared on the best painting in the gallery.

"It's like he really understands women," she said after she'd managed to smuggle him out of the office for a coffee one morning.

"Watch this space," she said after she'd lured him out for a drink after work.

"He's gay," she announced after their fourth lunch break.

"Really?" I asked. I could have sworn that he'd been flirting with me, but I later found out that everyone felt the same way. He's very good on eye contact, Joel, like his second born. "Did he tell you?"

"Hmm," Mitzi said. "He's been to see *Chicago* twice. At the theater."

"But did he do that thing that gay men do, when they make sure they incorporate it into conversation at the earliest opportunity, you know, mention 'my boyfriend' or refer to 'us gay men' or something like that?"

"He says his perfect Sunday would consist of going to the farmers' market to buy some obscure cheeses before having lunch with his mother."

"Ah, that's nice. Did you know his mother is Ursula Tennant, the feminist writer? Still, that's not exactly conclusive."

"He knows the difference between merino and cashmere."

"Don't you think your definition of heterosexuality needs broadening, Mitzi? He doesn't look very gay."

"Now who's got a narrow definition of what gay men are like? He's what they call a bear. Very popular these days, all my gay friends want one. Honestly, Mary, do you think I don't know if someone's gay or not?"

By the end of the day, all the women in the office had muttered one or all of the following phrases: "What a shame," "All the best ones are," or "I knew he was too good to be true." He was still sought out, but now only for his wise counsel on shopping and haircuts.

"Didn't you realize that's what everyone thought?" I asked Joel some time after we'd got together. "The fact that all these girls kept on telling you how great you were to talk to and what a shame you were off limits."

"I just thought they all knew that I only had eyes for you."

"But Karen even asked you how to do the perfect blow job."

"I assumed she was asking me from the point of view of a recipient rather than as a recipient and donor."

Mitzi and he continued going on their cozy lunches and Mitzi continued to fund us with tales of his man-loving proclivities. His being gay gave me the freedom to admit to myself that I had joined the rest in finding him attractive. It felt so unoriginal of me, especially coming to the Joel fan club so late when I had always prided myself on being into bands long before their first hit. The fact that he was gay spared me from entering and losing the competition with Mitzi. It was comfortingly adolescent to have a crush on a gay man. My youthful obsession with George Michael had continued long after he came out; in fact, the knowledge of his unavailability to all women had almost strengthened my love for him. Of course, Joel was irritating in a way that George Michael never had been, so arrogant and entitled, waltzing around the office and saying things like "My godfather, the head of commissioning at Channel 4" and "When I went to school in California." Freed from trying to impress him, I'd mock him for these comments, which he'd take in remarkable good humor. I enjoyed the little I saw of him, especially now that I knew he was not to be claimed by Mitzi. Brotherless and educated at a girls' school, I tended to react to straight men with either aggression or awkwardness.

"Do you know," he said to me one morning as we had coincided, yet again, at the kettle, "my best friend at school and I had a thing for the Pre-Raphaelites? We called ourselves The Brotherhood and used to hang around the nineteenth-century bit of the National Gallery and at the V & A, stroking the William Morris wallpaper."

"Blimey," I said. "How old were you?"

"First year of senior school, you know, thirteen." I realized then that he'd gone to the sort of expensive school that starts at thirteen, not eleven. As if it wasn't obvious by the fact that he had been a boy with a thing for the Pre-Raphaelites.

"I think I was into Wham! and buying hair accessories at the time," I said. "But you know, Millais versus a hair grip with a butterfly on it, same thing really." He laughed. I loved to make him laugh.

"Somewhere at my mother's house, I've still got a box filled with all the postcards, with Blu-Tack on the back."

"And what became of The Brotherhood? Your one?"

"It's really quite sad. Tom, my friend, wanted to become an artist, but got into crack at art college. I don't know what he's doing now. I rather lost touch with him when I got into my band, and all that I have left of The Brotherhood is the postcards and a penchant for redheads."

I blushed and couldn't stop myself running my hands through my hair. He's gay, obviously, I told myself. Around where I grew up, straight teenage boys did not get a thing for Victorian painters.

I liked these conversations. They seemed to transcend the usual trivia and "What did you do last night?"'s. He was the only person who'd ask you what you were reading rather than what you were watching. P. G. Wodehouse, I replied one day, and he became very excited.

"That's amazing," he said. "I don't think I've ever met a girl who's read P. G. Wodehouse."

I shrugged and said, "They're all too busy reading Nancy Mitford instead. Fools."

"I wouldn't say that, I have a bit of a weakness for her, too. And some of her sisters."

"I don't think I've ever met a man who's read Nancy Mitford."

"There you go," he said. "The man who reads Mitford and

the woman who reads Wodehouse. A match made in heaven. We could go on holiday and only have to pack half the number of books."

This easy banter ended one Monday morning.

"Hi, Joel," I said brightly.

"Oh, hello," he said and walked off. I could have sworn it was a snub.

Later I bumped into him in the line at the sandwich shop. "Did you have a good weekend?" I do this when I fancy someone, I sound like somebody's mother. I was worried that any minute now, I was going to start asking him what A levels he'd done.

"Fantastic. In fact, I think I'm still hungover. Two of your very best bacon sandwiches, please." Joel, as I subsequently discovered, has the zeal for flesh that only a former vegetarian can muster.

"What were you doing?"

He looked quizzical. "I was hosting the party. You know, at my mom's place. She's on a book tour in the States."

"A party?" I tried to keep my voice bright. Maybe it was some sort of man-only thing. "Did you get lots of people turning up?"

"Yeah, loads."

Oh. "That's great." I was thinking, it's quite rude of him to be boasting about his well-attended banging bloody brilliant party to someone who wasn't invited. I felt my cheeks burn with indignation. I could tell that he had noticed my reddening and an unreadable expression flashed across his face before he quickly escaped, clutching his calorific cargo.

"Did you go to Joel's party?" I asked Mitzi on returning to my desk.

"Yes. Shame you weren't there. He didn't want to invite everyone from the office. It was no big deal."

"Fair enough." Arse. Stupid, posh boy, metropolitan,

everything-on-a-plate, unfairly promoted arse. That was that, I decided. I wasn't going to be civil to him anymore.

I maintained my *froideur* for a whole week. Coolness does not come easily to me and inside I was ablaze. These days I don't give a monkey's whether or not I'm invited to somebody's party, though I do get furious on behalf of my children. Only last week, Rufus wasn't invited to Flynn's sixth, despite the fact that they sit at the same reading table. I still entertain fantasies of pushing the little tyke off his scooter in retaliation.

The following Monday, about ten of us were sitting in an ideas meeting. Joel, despite his lowly position, was of course allowed to attend due to his family connections to the managing director.

"It's been done before," I said to the first of Joel's pitches.

"That's one of those formats that's expensive to produce yet makes for cheap viewing," I said of the second.

"Meh," was all I managed for the third.

I went into the tiny kitchen soon afterward to find myself trapped in there with him. I couldn't very well walk out, but the kettle seemed to take an age to boil. He's gay, he's gay, he's gay, I told myself. He's horrible, too. He's gay and he's horrible. In fact, he's gay and horrible and he doesn't even like you enough to invite you to his "loads of mates" party. And he's fat. I felt my whole body prickle with heat. I thought I might be sick. "How do you take your tea?" How do you "take" your tea? I seemed to have landed in a costume drama all of a sudden. Soon I'd be asking him how he found the weather at this time of year and tell him that I myself found it most agreeable. The more flustered I felt, the more amused he seemed to be. He later told me that amusement is his defensive position, just as anger is mine.

"Milk, one sugar," he said.

We both went for the same mug, our hands touching. It could

have been the moment when we looked into each other's eyes and saw the truth, but instead I reached quickly for the chipped one featuring a woman in a bikini that came off when you put hot liquids into it.

We both stared at the still non-boiling kettle. "Have you got a problem with me?" he asked in a way that suggested nobody had ever had a problem with him before.

"No." I pulled a face to try to emphasize my rebuttal. Damn my flushing cheeks once more. "Sorry, I don't know where you might have got that idea."

"In there. In the meeting—you kept shooting down my ideas."

The kettle finally boiled and I watched him put the sugar in his tea. Even now I remember the little circle of granules that was left on the peeling vinyl of the kitchen worktop. "Maybe they weren't very good."

"True," he said. "Well. I'll be seeing you."

Not if I see you first, I thought, as then I'll be diving into the toilets to avoid another awkward conversation like the one we've just had.

I looked for assurance from Mitzi, who told me stiffly that she had never heard him say anything negative about me. "Why do you care?"

I successfully avoided Joel until a post-work booze-up in the pub a few weeks later. There, I tried to ignore his presence but found myself aware of whom he was sitting next to and the conversations he was having. The seating would shuffle as someone got up to get a round in, but I never seemed to get any nearer to him—he was like some iconic skyscraper that is visible from all parts of the city but you can never seem to actually reach it. Much drink was drunk, a good proportion of it by me. Our group got larger and louder, irritating to the rest of the pub, but convinced of its own glamour and hilarity. It was back in the days when we smoked and were allowed to, and I got up to buy another packet. The cigarette machine was in a grubby corridor outside the men's toilets, which was steeped with the ammonia stench of alleyways. For years afterward, I used to get a little thrill of remembrance when I smelled concentrated male urine. Now I get a surge of irritation and flush it away.

"Damn it," I said when the machine gobbled up my coins without spitting out a packet in return.

"Need some help?" said Joel, emerging from the men's. I caught a glimpse into the strange world of urinals.

I was drunk by this point. "All right, Mr. Practical."

He looked at it thoughtfully before giving it a hard shove. He gave a silent scream and shook his hand out with pantomime exaggeration. I pulled out the cigarettes that this maneuvering had successfully dislodged.

"Thank you." I smiled at him. The corridor was narrow and we were close. I was too drunk to feel angry at him any longer and, besides, I was grateful to him for getting me the cigarettes.

"You don't like me, do you?"

I shrug. "What's it to you, anyway?" I was very drunk. "Everybody else does. Everybody else loves Joel."

He nodded. "I like being liked. What do you like then, my little fairy Mary?"

"Nobody's ever called me that before. Scary Mary, that's what everyone else calls me."

"Redhairy Mary. No, that sounds wrong. It is beautiful, your hair." He reached his hand toward it but stopped before contact was made. "What do you like?"

"I like…" I couldn't for the life of me think of anything I liked. Well, anything other than the feeling of him being wedged so close to me with his huge physical presence keeping me warm and enclosed against the cigarette machine. "Whiskers on kittens."

He laughed. "And brown paper packages."

I nodded and tried to say, "Tied up with string," but no words would come out. I just stared at him, my mouth agape, waiting for my voice to emerge.

Instead of words coming out of my mouth, I found lips coming toward it. He's gay, I told myself. I felt a delicious contrast between his stubble and his surprisingly soft lips. I immediately found myself thinking of how that contrast would play out elsewhere on my body. He moved away and looked at me.

Finally I heard words come out of my mouth without really being aware that it was me who was saying them. They had a life of their own. "I like this."

He smiled and kissed me again. He's so not gay. I kissed him back, hard. I wanted to eat him up, he tasted so deliciously of smoke and crisps and beer and himself. I thought I could kiss him forever but we had to break off to burst into laughter. We looked at each other and laughed until tears came to our eyes, then we slipped out of the emergency exit and into the passageway, where empty kegs and the pub's rubbish were kept. There, I leaned against the wall and we kissed some more—kiss, laugh, kiss, laugh. I felt him hard against my flimsy dress, harder still when I lifted my legs and wrapped them around that expansive waistline. I felt so drunk and so turned on that I had wanted him to lift up that dress and rip open my opaque tights and plain supermarket knickers and screw me there and then. Indeed, this might have happened were it not for a pub worker throwing out a bag of rubbish that nearly hit us, whereupon he sneered "Get a room." We laughed some more and then went back into the pub, walking separately back to our party. Separately, but in a similar state of discomfort, my damp pants and throbbing thighs impeding my progress.

Around that pub table there then followed the most ecstatically excruciating hour of my life. We were pretending that nothing had happened so convincingly that I began to wonder whether anything had. But then he'd catch my eye and we'd swap those smiles that had been as much a part of our seduction as the kisses. I felt emboldened and stroked the back of his neck when I walked past him on the way to the bar.

When I got back to the table, the usual game of musical chairs had taken place and I was now sitting opposite him. I felt a socked foot in my lap. He always has worn nice socks, and these were silky, striped ones. His big toe probed and I felt my pants dampen still further and my mouth open in an involuntary "Oh" of pleasure. The toe pushed on. I wanted more than anything to remove that sock and put those toes into my mouth. I put my finger in instead and looked at him. He turned away and started fiddling with his phone. A second later, mine bleeped with a text message alert.

It was a single word: "OUTSIDE."

I avoided looking at him and texted back: "NOW." I tried to find the question mark but gave up and left it as an exhortation.

He stood up and said his goodbyes, swaying slightly. I counted to 60 and then did the same. I rushed out only to find that he wasn't there. It's all a joke, of course, he's gay, he doesn't even like me, Mitzi and he are probably looking at me and thinking, poor deluded drunken Mary. Then I felt a pair of arms around my waist.

"Quick, before anybody else comes out."

"Speaking of coming out..." I was interrupted by the timely arrival of a taxi.

"Where to?" Joel asked me.

"I've got a flatmate," I said.

He told the taxi driver an address in an area I'd long coveted but would never be able to afford. We indulged in the sort of frantic, drunken snogging that taxi drivers have to put up with and came up for air outside a large redbrick house.

"My mom's."

"She's not there, is she?"

He laughed. "No, she's away. Anyway, I've got my own flat bit thing."

We walked through a large hall filled with ancient-looking vases of dried flowers and standard lamps with tasseled shades. I was torn between the desire to follow him or to explore these fantastical rooms with their tantalizing vistas. There was a kitchen with framed newspaper cartoons on the walls and piles of ancient Le Creuset, a study stuffed with books and a tatty armchair, a living room with an exotic drinks trolley. It was all so different from the house I grew up in—this was all faded Persians instead of fitted carpets.

He led me up a corkscrew staircase and then up again to the top floor, which consisted of a vast room with a kitchenette in one corner and a futon in another. The sight of the crumpled sheets made me feel both charged and alarmed. A small door led to a stunted shower room in the eaves. I looked out of the window to see the city sprawled and sparkling in the darkness. It felt like the middle of the night as we'd been drinking since five, but it was only nine o'clock. He rustled up an omelette with herbs cut from a window box that was kept on the roof of the house. I wolfed it down because I wasn't so drunk not to know that I had to eat something, but I didn't really want anything other than him in my mouth.

I suppose a thought might have flashed through my head about the wisdom of it all happening so quickly, but I was too drunk and too turned on to care. Normally I might have felt embarrassed by this point, but Joel made me feel like I had come home. In fact, his home felt like the one I should have always lived in, convinced as I was as a teenager that I had been adopted by these boring people and my real parents were arty liberal types engaging in lively debate in an exotic metropolis.

We kissed and laughed and then kissed some more. Then we drank and talked, hurriedly telling each other strange minor details of our lives that seemed suddenly so fascinating. I wanted to eat up him and his words, then I just wanted to eat some more, so we went downstairs to his mom's kitchen and ate stale peanuts and cooking chocolate. The snack food sobered me up and I vaguely thought about postponing sleeping with him. But I think I already knew what would happen that night.

It was so glorious. He slipped inside me so easily and yet with perfect friction. I wanted to keep him there forever, but I wanted him in and out. He came quickly, a beautiful sight, naked but for one stripy sock and a condom. I hadn't come, yet, but this was rectified in what seemed like seconds as he dove down before emerging with a glistening chin. Back in the days that I smoked, I used to sometimes think about the pleasure of the next cigarette even as I was smoking my current one. That was how I was that night as I came—I was impatient to make him hard again and to have him inside me, or to rub his cock gently against me until I was begging him to put it inside me. Even for the third or fourth time, I started to think about how good sex would be in the future, since it had started so promisingly when usually the first night is something just to get through without disaster.

I surveyed myself, speckled with a red flush and stubble burn on my inner thighs. I surveyed the room, which was as disheveled as I was, with red wine splashed against the wall, the sheet coming off the mattress, a saggy bean bag molded to the shape of my bum where Joel had pushed against me from above.

I didn't think that I had ever been so happy.

	A	B
1	April allowance	2 per day, total 60
2	Total no. of debits in April	82
3	Breakdown of infringements	12 kitchen; 7 bathroom; 7 laundry; 8 bedroom; 15 living; 11 parenting; 7 environment; 9 general ineptitude; 6 finance.
4	Infringement of the month	He told me not to use the tumble dryer, "because of the environment." I told him I use it for exactly that reason, to enhance our immediate environment by not having lots of dank clothes draped across the radiators. "But it's such a sunny day." "All right, I won't, if you hang up the clothes on the line yourself." He didn't, obviously – they sat in a washing-machine swamp until I needed to put in another load, so I ended up hanging them up, telling him that he at least had to fold them up when they were dry (and crispy, in fact, the way they go when they're hung up rather than put in the tumble dryer when they emerge so warm and soft that I want to bury myself in their cleanliness like one of those mad women in an ad for fabric conditioner). Then, of course, he didn't take them off the line and

		fold them, and it started raining and the clothes got streaky and the whole lot ended up in the washing machine all over again and then into the tumble dryer. Why is it that any way of reducing women's work in the home seems to be either environmentally or morally unsound? I can't use effective cleaning products without destroying the planet. I can't pay a woman from a developing nation to do our dirty work without fear of exploiting her.
5	Positives to offset	5. Three brilliant anecdotes about mutual ex-colleagues and 1 compliment, plus the fact that he didn't complain about his toothbrush being used to clean Rufus's shoes. Not that I confessed to what I had done.
6	April debt	17 (82 offset by April allowance of 60 and 5 positives)
7	Total debt from February, March and April	59
8	Total remaining	41 over next three months (100 minus 59)

7

People in Glass Houses

Subsection E [living] number 5) *Leaves me to do all the packing. Well, not all the packing, strictly speaking: he packs his own case (small, battered, belonged to his grandfather and is covered in glamorous Cunard cruise liner and early Pan Am stickers) with a few pairs of boxers and a toothbrush.*

E6) Shouts "I've finished," when he's done doing E5) and then sits around sighing while I pack for two children as well as all the general family baggage.

E7) Says "Blimey" when he sees the quantity of detritus I've packed—the snacks for the journey, the diapers for Gabe, the potty, the four times daily changes of clothes, the all-weather options, the duvet that Rufus can't sleep without—"I remember when you used to be able to do hand luggage for a fortnight's holiday," he sighs.

I [general ineptitude] number 12) *Leaves all the drawers on his chest perilously open. Does he not read the freak-accident-killing-toddler section of the newspapers? The one that warns of decapitation by electric windows in the car, choking on dried apricots and being skewered by an up-ended knife in an open dishwasher?*

"Can you at least help me get this stuff into the car?" I shout as I'm surrounded by a mismatched assortment of suitcases and rucksacks, with overspill barely contained by a couple of plastic bags. Why is packing like this? It starts days earlier with scribbled reminders not to forget various items on scraps of paper and the backs of envelopes. Months later, I might find a cryptic clue inscribed on the flyleaf of one of the boys' books, reading "monitor" or "rabbit." I also do my best to siphon off the clothes that we will be taking with us in the week preceding departure, but still find myself washing all the favorite must-haves the day before, forgetting to put them in the tumble dryer and having to take them still wet in plastic bags. They then either get hung up to dry in the car (we used to let them fly in the breeze by rolling up the windows to trap them, until Gabe worked out how to unwind the windows on the M1 and liberated a flock of damp undies), or left in the plastic bag to mildew.

In my fantasy, packing involves going into a marvelous walk-in wardrobe full of neatly folded clothes which will be seamlessly transferred to a matching set of luggage on wheels. One day, I think, I shall be the sort of person who keeps my shoes in their original boxes with photographs on the outside to identify the contents.

Mitzi says she's got packing for the second home down to a tee and can "bundle them into the car in just two minutes." I think she has been helped in this by buying duplicates of everything, including assorted bicycles and favorite scooters, thus avoiding the pile-up in a toy shop effect that our car boot is currently sporting.

Gabe is hitting his elder brother with a wooden spoon. Rufus rolls around in exaggerated agony and then begins to whine, an oft-adopted tone. In any given hour of the day, a TV production team could easily compile enough footage for "The Tennant family are finding life with two boisterous boys hard-going" segments for one of those programs where a nanny comes and sorts out your dysfunctional family.

"Please," I shout to Joel. We only ever use such pleasantries in unpleasant voices.

"Can't we just pretend that we're ill?" he says.

"Don't start that again. It will be fun." This is said in the same bright voice that I use when I'm telling my children about our forthcoming trip to a stately home.

"It will be about as fun as a botulism cocktail with an anthrax chaser."

"Have you got any better suggestions for the bank holiday weekend?"

"I wish it were just a weekend. I can't believe you've said we'll stay until Wednesday."

"Think of it as a long weekend."

"A very, very long weekend."

"It's half term. Have you got any better plans?"

"I'd be very happy to stay here."

"You know we'd drive each other mad by tomorrow and you'd mysteriously find a reason to go into the office. Look upon it as a free holiday."

"You know that nothing's ever free with Mitzi." He sighs. "At the very least we'll be expected to wax lyrical about, oh I don't know, the wonderful original features and aren't you clever to have found flagstones made from the bones of real organic orphans, and a bath hand-knitted by a thousand Hindu priests and filled with holy water from the river Ganges."

"It's a small price to pay. Have you seen the cost of renting in the school holidays?"

"All those ghastly friends..."

"Becky's staying nearby and will be coming over. You'll have one kindred spirit."

"Thank the lord."

"Come on, let's get this stuff into the car."

"I thought we were going for a few nights, not relocating our entire lives."

"Very funny. Now get it into the car before I decide to go without you."

"Now we're talking."

We have exceeded the maximum time that our family can be in the car without fear of violence. Joel and I have argued about whether we should have music or speech radio, the boys have argued about who gets to hold the portable DVD player.

"So how long did Mitzi say it would take to get there?" It is rare that Joel gets noticeably irritated, but a long car ride to an undesirable destination is enough to rile even him.

"A couple of hours."

He snorted. "We've already been in the car two and a half. Why is it that people with second homes always feel the need to lie about how long it takes to get there?"

"Maybe they've got some cunning route."

"In their time machine."

"More likely Michael's Ferrari."

"That's it. Once, Michael will have done the journey in two and a half hours at one in the morning 30 miles over the speed limit and now Mitzi feels it's completely truthful to chirp that their dear little place in the country is just 'a couple of hours away.' It's what people with country houses do. That, and tell you it's only an hour by train and 'It can take you longer than that just to get across London.' And if they move lock, stock and barrel to the country, they'll always use the phrase 'You must come and stay. We'll probably see more of each other than we do now.' Those are the three immutable laws of buying a house outside the M25."

Joel's experience of people with country houses is far more

extensive than mine, given that most of his mother's friends had "little places" they'd inherited or picked up for a song in parts of Suffolk, Sussex or Dorset, back in the days when being an intellectual seemed to afford one the life of a banker.

A full three and three quarter hours after we set off, we arrive at a large flint and brick converted barn surrounded by fields, and beyond that marshes, and beyond that the sea. Its rustic charm is only slightly marred by the look-at-me solar panels, wind-power generator and about half a million pounds' worth of cars on the front driveway. That and the sound of two small boys whining from the back seat of our battered Volkswagen Golf and my leaden heart at seeing the wet patch on Gabe's trousers.

Mitzi comes out, wearing a sailcloth slop, very fitted jeans and a pair of unmuddied Hunters. Two of her offspring follow her, wearing children's approximations of the same outfit, trailed by a Labrador and a terrier. I quickly realize that neither I nor my children have the wardrobe nor domestic pet necessary for an English coastal retreat.

"I'm so sorry we're late, it took us longer than expected."

"Almost four hours, in fact," adds Joel. It's started already, that snapping at each other that he and Mitzi engage in.

"What, did you come via Scotland?" says Mitzi.

"No, just via the same old boring time-space continuum that most of us live in."

"Well, if you'd helped me pack then maybe we'd have been able to leave a bit sooner and not got into all that caravan traffic."

"I wasn't the one who said it was going to take two hours."

"This place is amazing," I say, turning to Mitzi.

"Isn't it? Do you want to have a look around?"

"I'd rather have lunch," mutters Joel.

"Don't mind him, I think he may be a bit hypoglycemic. Why don't you get some cereal bars out of my bag for you and the boys?" I sigh. "You know what they're like, they need carbs and/or sugar every two hours."

"So we opened out the hall to make a more imposing entrance and it doubles up as a dining room," Mitzi begins. "And then of course the kitchen was so poky that we knocked it all through." We come into an expanse of light that looks out to all that flatness and all that sky.

"Wow, look at this granite," I say, stroking an island unit that's as large as most mortals' kitchens.

"Not granite, 80 percent recycled glass. And the floor you're standing on is made from old tires, melted down and woven. Stunning, isn't it?"

"Look at those views," I say, though in truth my eye is more taken by the twelve-foot-high sliding doors that divide us from the outside. They must have cost a *fortune*. "Was it difficult to get planning for this extension?"

"Yes. It bloody was. The wood for these units is reconstituted Victorian apothecary cupboards and the timber staircase is made from the planks of boats shipwrecked on this very stretch of coast. The Aga's new, I must confess, but don't you just adore that baby blue color? Oh, and that glass dividing wall is made from old milk bottles."

Beyond the hazy gauze of the recycled glass wall is a space filled with slumpy sofas upholstered with mattress ticking around a large glass coffee table.

"It's just so great to have a utility room with a shower, so when the kids come in from dune jumping or covering themselves in salty mud, they can just wash off here." The shower alone is bigger than our bathroom. Wellies and waders line the floor, while the coat pegs are laden with carefully coordinating slops and boating anoraks. "Do you want to see your room? Well, rooms."

I nod. I don't think I can speak for envy. I don't want my stuff, I want *this* stuff. I want my life to match, I want a place for everything. Mitzi is so at ease with her wealth, there is a sense of natural entitlement, of the inevitability of it, that belies her own origins or the fact that she has never made any money of her own. Does she not ever think to herself that if she'd married someone else, someone like Joel, she wouldn't be tossing up between private schools and employing environmental decoration consultants? She'd be living a life that, while comfortable by any normal standards, is not this one.

"Because we want to have lots of other families to stay, we've designed this to be like a separate guest wing with its own staircase. Can you see the way that the stairs are slatted to reference the ones that take you below deck on a boat?"

"Yes, I was just thinking that." I follow her up what I guess would be called the back stairs but are grander than most people's front ones. They emerge into two interlinked bedrooms and a large bathroom.

"I liked the idea of the bathroom having the best view so guests could luxuriate in the tub soaking up the suds and the landscape."

"It is lovely." I am fantasizing about the possibility of being able to take a bath that isn't tepid and shared with one of my boys and a selection of bath toys that spew mold when squeezed.

"The bath itself is made of recycled brake pads. And the splashback from old plastic bottles."

"Wow." I'm distracted by the shelves laden with expensive beauty products, and the two fluffy robes hanging on the door. Mitzi goes to line up the products into matching pairs of conditioner and shampoo, body wash and lotion. They sit obediently equidistant on the shelves. It's like staying at the sort of expensive boutique hotel we can't afford. I look out of the window to see Molyneux and Mahalia flying a kite, while the twins are swooping on the decking on their wooden bikes, all captured by a photographer wielding a very large lens.

"He's from one of the color supplements," she explains.

"Oh, right."

"They're doing a piece about how it's possible to make a beautiful retreat that doesn't cost a fortune or the earth. I thought it would be good publicity."

"For what?"

"You know I'm thinking of starting my own business. Very chic, environmentally sound products for the home. Ethically produced abroad. I've got a domain name and everything, so the piece can point to something when it gets published later on this year."

I stare out at the photographer, who's encouraging the children to throw grass cuttings at one another like confetti. "Is he going soon?" I ask. "They're not going to want pictures of your guests, are they?" As I ask the question I know the answer. There will no doubt be some reference in the article as to how Mitzi and Michael like to "keep an open house so that friends and family can enjoy the house as much as they do." I look down at my clothes, which are scruffy yet not artfully so. "Do we need to get changed into lovely faded vintage clothes to complete the look?"

"Hmm," she dissembles.

"And do we need to be very tidy?"

"Don't be silly, I'd never expect your family to be tidy. They did all the interior shots yesterday. No, today, they want shots of a big family lunch on the terrace..."

"Adorable moppets popping wild blackberries into their mouths, laughing adults passing carafes of wine to one another, big bowls of very simple yet very delicious pasta, type of thing?"

"Blackberries aren't in season yet."

"God, Mitzi, how do you do it? How do you manage to decorate a whole other house when I can't even get around to painting my one and only? And then you also find time to make a rustic feast fit for an interiors magazine."

She gives an airy wave of her hand as I look out and see that the children are being herded by not only their London nanny, but the back-up au pair, while a portly red-faced woman is laying the wooden table—hewn, I dare say, from the hull of a reclaimed galleon.

We come downstairs to find Michael sneering at Joel's choice of route out of London and supposedly good-humored joshing at the decrepitude of our car.

"You're right. They are very environmentally sound," says Joel to me as we pull out our raggle-taggle collection of possessions from the vehicle only recently referred to by Michael as the sort of car a 20-year-old nursery-school teacher might drive. "Even the conversation is recycled."

We survive lunch, where we are joined by local friends of theirs, a couple whose female half is a conveniently photogenic African-American, and their heartbreakingly cute daughter. My sons have somehow found themselves wearing stripy toweling beach robes belonging to Mitzi's family and so look far more appropriate for the photographer's scene than they did in their Ben 10 T-shirts. The magazine's writer, stylist and photographer have now retreated, and I thought I heard an exhalation of relief that we are no longer so publicly playing the part of perfection.

"Can I make myself a cup of tea?" I ask Mitzi. "Anyone else?"

"Rooibos?"

"No, the normal stuff."

I switch on the kettle, only to be interrupted by Michael.

"You must always use fresh water when you boil a kettle," he explains. "Otherwise you'll be re-boiling water. And use the Aga—it's what it's there for, after all."

"Okay." I take the electric kettle off its plinth and carry it toward the Aga.

"Don't put that kettle on the Aga, you idiot," he shouts. "You'll ruin it. Use the stove-top one. Have you never used an Aga before?"

"No, as a matter of fact." And don't call me an idiot. "I was joking. Of course I wasn't going to put the electric kettle on the hotplate. As if." I spy a chrome kettle with a whistle in its spout and start to fill it.

"Not that tap. This is the drinking-water tap," he says.

"Fine." He continues to lurk, watching me. I line up three mugs and am about to plonk a bag in each of them when Michael speaks again.

"Teapot. You must always make tea in a teapot. Can't you taste the difference between tea made in a mug and tea made in a teapot? It must be made with loose tea and you must always drink it in china cups." He's waiting for me to screw up as I grab the teapot with over-sized spots on it. "Mary, you must warm it first."

This is the longest conversation I've ever had with him and it's about how to make a cup of tea.

"Michael's very particular about his tea," says Mitzi, coming into the kitchen. There's no edge to her voice. She has lectured me before on the importance of not belittling or mocking one's husband. "And it really does make a difference. You've taught me everything there is to know about a good cup of tea," she says to Michael and then kisses him on his fine Roman nose. I would have poured the kettle of boiling water on my husband's head by this point, and give brief mental thanks to him for not hectoring me on how to make a holy cup of tea. Mitzi, on the other hand, is ready with the J-cloth, wiping any spillages I may have made in this tortuous process.

Michael is the sort of man who makes a big deal of beckoning the sommelier in a restaurant and discussing the merits of the various years of Châteauneuf-du-Pape. I just hadn't realized he brought such stringent tastes to tea as well. He sniffs the cup I give him and then takes a small gulp. I expect him to swill it around in his mouth and spit it out into the sink, but it seems to pass muster. I don't let him see me put soy milk into mine, which I'm sure contravenes the first rule of tea-making. I wonder whether Joel didn't perhaps have a point that sometimes there is too great a price to pay for a free long weekend. Mitzi picks up my cup of tea and wipes the bottom of it with a cloth before putting it down on the recycled glass work surface.

"Delicious lunch," I say to Mitzi. "Thank you."

"Hmm," she says distractedly. "You don't think there was too much purple and red in it, that they clashed a bit? You know, aubergines *and* cabbage *and* pomegranate seeds?"

So far our stay is anything other than relaxing. I don't know whose behavior I'm more worried about, Joel's or Gabe's. Rufus, on the other hand, is doing me proud by showing off his math skills and his preternatural understanding of division and multiplication, to which Michael keeps asking whether they teach him that at "state school" and the American asks me whether I've ever wondered whether he might be autistic.

Gabe is managing to turn every product of nature into a gun or a sword, much to the horror of the twins. Joel seems to be encouraging him by inventing a game that involves placing pine-cones on the wall at the end of the terrace and throwing sticks and stones to knock them off, complete with ka-pow noises.

So much for Ursula not allowing him toy guns as a child. I am scurrying around after all three of them to make sure that we're not leaving any mess except in the sanctuary of our bedrooms, which now look like a refugee camp for displaced peoples clad entirely in now-faded Boden.

After making another trip upstairs to repatriate our chattels, I go for a poke around the bedrooms in the other wing of the house. Rufus is doing the same, closely monitored by Mahalia.

"You can't come into Molyneux's room," she says to him. "You'll take out toys and you won't put them back in the right place."

"I will," he says. "I just want to have a little play."

"Toys are not for playing with," she declares, giving him a sharp rap to the knuckles as he reaches for the 1950s wooden plane that is hanging artfully from the ceiling.

It's going to be a long day. I can't remember what you're supposed to do in the country. These weekends usually involve some sort of trip to a local wildlife reserve or bird sanctuary, I think, which takes about three hours to marshal. I was brought up on the edge of a town that fell away into fields and a river, but I don't remember any Enid Blyton *Island of Adventure* type activities, more a crushing boredom and the discovery that time would go much quicker than you'd think if you read books all afternoon.

"Why don't we go for a walk?" I say brightly as the ruddy-faced local retainer picks up one of my son's Thomas the Tank Engine wellies and removes it to the boot room, where the pair stands at attention amid the serried ranks of outdoor footwear.

"Where?" asks Rufus, now banished from the enchanted kingdom of Mahalia's and Molyneux's rooms.

"I don't know. Just for a walk. To the sea?"

"Can I buy a magazine there?"

"No, there are no shops in the sea."

"Oh." His voice falls in disappointment. "Can I play on the Wii instead?"

The non-educational electronic games, I noted earlier, are kept in a small windowless room that was not part of the grand tour of the house nor one of the photographer's subjects.

"It's a lovely day." I can hear the fake exclamation mark in my voice and, worse, my mother's oft-repeated words. How we hated the inevitable exhortations to make the most of the sunshine by collecting wild plants to put in a flower press, or to go and see if there were any water boatmen or tadpoles in the river. Despite all the talk of how different our children's generation is to ours, I'm struck by how I have the same conversations with them that I had with my mother: the "But ketchup is made of tomatoes" and the "Chips are made from potatoes." I feel a shuddery sense that I am being physically possessed by her when I crouch over to blow up a child's armbands while they're already wearing them, or stick the parking ticket in my mouth while I reverse into a space in the car park. The strange thing about small boys is they do absolutely what you expect them to do, and have done forever. They jump in muddy puddles, they kick leaves, they put their heads through railings and their hands down trousers. Even the things that I thought unique to them, like the way Rufus began obsessively to collect the postman's discarded red elastic bands, turns out to be common to all the boys around our way, who attach them like great rubbery snakes to their bikes and scooters.

Joel helps me to dress up the children in their country-appropriate gear, mostly borrowed, and Mitzi prepares Molyneux and Mahalia, who, I am glad to say, are moaning about wanting to use the Wii just as much as Rufus. Right as we are about to leave, Merle, the girl twin, trips over the foot of Michael's lounger and scrapes her knee. He does nothing. It's almost as if he can't hear her cries, as if they're pitched like a dog whistle so that only the rest of us can hear. Eventually, the au pair comes out and envelops Merle in sturdy Bulgarian arms, while Michael continues to read all the sections of the newspaper that I ignore.

"Does Michael do much with the children?" I ask Mitzi as we walk out across the flatness toward the sea and the seals, and she begins to toss seaweed into a flat basket. "Why are you weeding the great outdoors?"

"It's samphire. It's the asparagus of the sea. Not really the season for it yet, but it's simply delicious with melted butter and, best of all, completely natural and free. I'm very down with foraging at the moment."

"Yes, I've read about that. The only thing I could forage in our neck of the woods would be supermarket trolleys, flattened chewing gum and lager cans. What does wild garlic look like, anyway? And how do you tell the difference between a mushroom and a toadstool?"

"You just know," says Mitzi. "Like choosing a lover."

"So, Michael. He seems quite hands off."

"In a domestic, diaper-changing way, I suppose he is," she says. "He works so hard and is so successful that I feel it would be very unfair of me to burden him with anything to do with the house. And he's very involved in the children's education."

"He pays for it."

"No, more than that. He was adamant that I made sure Molyneux and Mahalia could read before they went to school, and knew some French. It's really important to him."

Now I think about it, Mitzi can't walk down steps with her children without having to count them out loud, and the twins, aged two, are constantly drilled on their colors and shapes. "But other stuff?" I ask.

"Well, he doesn't do all that baby in a sling, throw the toddler in the air type of fatherhood, if that's what you mean. We can't all be married to the perfect father, you know. You're the one married to Joel."

"I didn't mean that."

"We all know you're the one who got Joel. I do wish you didn't feel like you constantly have to remind me."

"Sorry, I didn't know I did. Let me help you with your seaweed."

"We could have a completely foraged supper." Mitzi now speaks with the excitement she used to reserve for pills and booze. "We could catch crabs."

"Just like the good old days."

She giggles and, standing here, well away from Michael and the staff, she's like the girl I first met thirteen years ago. "You mustn't say such things in front of Michael."

"Does he think you were a virgin when you two met?"

"Obviously not, but he doesn't know quite the extent of my twenties. It was all so chaotic."

"It wasn't, though," I say, thinking back. "Mine were less exciting but somehow more chaotic than yours. Your adventures seemed quite deliberate, well planned. I think you even said so at the time. That you were going to have as much fun as possible and then settle down with a rich man. And you've done exactly that."

"I never said that. It's a coincidence that Michael happens to be successful. I fell in love with him, not his money. The sort of man I was going to fall in love with, powerful and intelligent, was probably the sort of man who'd be successful in his chosen profession."

"Maybe, but what career advice will you give Mahalia and Merle?"

"Are you implying that me marrying Michael was a career move?"

"No, no, of course not." Of course I am. Not since Trotsky was erased from photos of revolutionary Russia has history been so blatantly revised. Mitzi banked copious reserves of sex and fun in order to pay for a good marriage to a man as stiff as Michael.

"I wanted security," she admits. "Not financial, necessarily. You know about my mother. I didn't want that for my own family."

The children are now covering themselves in mud and whooping with delight. They throw themselves across the flats, skidding and colliding as they do, not caring that embedded shells occasionally scrape their palely perfect skin. I want to hold on to this moment, which makes me feel, for a day at least, as if I'm giving my children the childhood they deserve. I occasionally have these moments when we're all singing along to the radio and making up silly lyrics, my contribution inserting their names into the songs, theirs reliant on repetition of the words "poo" and "bum." These are the times when I know, rather than just tell myself, how much I love them and love being with them. I revel in these brief interludes of familial perfection, as I do now, watching their hair clog with Norfolk mud and their skinny limbs become camouflaged into an indistinguishable mass. I almost want to weep with the utter loveliness of it and I wonder whether this is what it's always like for Mitzi, to always have the idyll, the life that the article about Mitzi's second home will tell us we are so blessed to be living.

The morning after my first night with Joel, I didn't so much wake up in the attic at Ursula's house as not go to sleep at all. We screwed and laughed and drank, before dozing for only a few minutes at a time, then starting off all over again. We zipped ourselves to one another, creating a film of sticky sweat between us, and I found myself cursing the fact that I had two arms, for the way one of them always created a barrier between us. Our first sleepover was as giggle-infested as any eight-year-old girl's. "You go to sleep first." "No, you." "Are you asleep yet?"

"I fancied you from the moment I walked into the office," Joel said as the light poured in and we debated what to have for breakfast. "There you were, a gorgeous redhead standing on a desk, and when you stretched up to do those shelves, there was a little band of bare skin showing around your waist...this one." He leaned down to kiss the flesh above my stomach and I felt myself get wet once again. It was like when you have a terrible cold and you wonder where on earth all this liquid can come from.

I blushed. I hadn't expected this conversation so soon in. Joel didn't bother playing hard to get because he didn't need to. "But..."

"But what?"

"I thought you were gay."

"Some of my best friends, et cetera, et cetera, but what on earth made you think that?"

"Mitzi told me."

His eyes narrowed. "But she knows I fancy you."

I blushed with the joy of it, not stopping to question how I had been kept ignorant of that fact. "Maybe I got the wrong end of the stick. Or maybe Mitzi did."

"Easy mistake to make, Mary being a well-known boy's name." His head moved back down and he licked me. He emerged to speak. "I'm so glad Mary's not a boy." He delved in once more.

"And I'm so glad that you are one," I said, pulling him up and inside me yet again.

This could have gone on all day. I wondered whether I ought to pretend that I had some pressing and wildly glamorous engagement on that Saturday morning. Joel suddenly leaped up.

"I'm an idiot," he shouted, doing an exaggerated dance of panic that segued into a dance of trying to get his underwear and trousers on.

"What?" I asked. This is too good to be true, I thought; he's remembered he's got a wife and child to meet up with.

"I've got to be in Brussels for lunch. I'm meeting Ursula there. Where are the train tickets?" The room, which had been jumbled when we came in, was now in a comedic state of dishevelment. I started to hyperventilate. I have a morbid fear of missing planes and trains. As Joel flung possessions around in a wild search for socks, passport and ticket, I tried to calm myself by methodically searching through his desk. He had to make that train. If he didn't, everything would be ruined. I'd be forever the girl who made him miss the train—not just any train, the Eurostar. How impossibly fabulous, I thought in my panic, here is a man who can forget he's got a trip away, abroad and everything. Here is a man who, instead of spending the night before laying out clothes and uttering the passport-tickets-money mantra, could go out drinking and seduce a girl.

"Found them," I shouted. "Your tickets and your passport."

"I love you," he said and kissed me. It wasn't a proper "I love you," it was just the one you'd say to anyone who found your tickets and your passport. Nevertheless, it made me realize how I'd feel if he said it for real.

I love you too, I said to myself. I love that you are so damn good in bed, that you raise my game with your confidence, that you lose things and I can help you find them, that you can treat cross-channel trains like others treat buses.

Joel is always talking of those "and that's the moment I knew I loved you" moments; he seems to have had hundreds of them. But when he texted me his thanks and love from the train bound for Brussels, I knew too.

At work we had a blissful week where we kept our relationship quiet and got off with each other in the disabled toilets on the second floor. We emailed and texted when we weren't with each other, though we met up as much as we could. I didn't play hard to get. I was soft to get.

Then someone caught us in a café around the corner and I knew I'd have to tell Mitzi.

"Great," she said on hearing the news. "How sweet."

I was so relieved I didn't analyze her reaction much. "He's not gay, you know."

"No," she said. "Well, you've got to hope not, anyway."

And that was that. Mitzi's and my friendship lost its intensity and I became just one of her many disciples, as I remain to this day. Joel and Mitzi developed their own special prickly, barb-throwing relationship, a love-hate thing where nobody is sure of the proportions on each side. Sometimes he'd insist that we avoid her, which would make me insist the opposite. I didn't want him protesting too much. Then a year or so later she met Michael, and embarked on a love story more epic than anybody else's ever, with holidays to private islands in the Maldives and a wedding that made the Oscars ceremony seem under-produced.

"Could you make it a bit less evident how little you want to be here?" I snap at Joel as we sluice the boys in the recycled brake-pad bath, picking the Norfolk mud off their limbs.

"Gooey goo for chewy chewing," he says to Rufus and Gabe and pretends to put some of the glutinous soil into his mouth, much to their amusement. "I don't know what you expect me to do. You're always telling me how irritating you find it that I want people to like me. As if I should be wanting everyone to hate me."

"I just can't understand why you, who must make everybody

love you, seem so intent on being so boorish and uncharming with Michael and Mitzi. Is there not some middle way?"

"I can't win, can I? Either it annoys you that I want people to like me or I don't want certain people to like me enough."

"Don't worry—they still think you're *so* wonderful and I'm *so* lucky to have you. Everybody loves Joel."

"Except my wife, who apparently hates me."

"I don't hate you." I look nervously at the boys who are busy sudsing themselves up with expensive facial cleanser. Joel looks skeptical. "I just sometimes hate the things you do."

"Becky, it is a joy to see you." A freshly shaved and laundered Joel swoops upon her. They are both tall and broad-shouldered, with the capacity to run to fat and arms built for enveloping others. She whispers something into his ear and I see him relax for the first time since we arrived the day before.

"How's your hotel?" I ask when they've finished.

"It's nice."

"It's gorgeous," adds Cara, who gives me a kiss smelling of lemongrass. "Mitzi, you are clever to have found it for us."

"It's divine, isn't it?" says Mitzi. "Its utter fabulousness was the only thing that got us through all those boring planning meetings and arguments with the builders that we had to come up for when this place was being done."

Mitzi's holiday finds are always beyond fabulous. We are invited to admire not Michael's ability to pay for such luxury, but her cleverness in truffling out these darling boutique hotels and fully staffed villas. That she and Michael go away for the odd child-free week in the chicest of Caribbean hotels is not a sign that they've more money than the rest of us, but that they have more discernment, as well as being more in love. Good taste is a sort of morality for her. Even in our scuzzy twenties, she had a natural predilection for Egyptian cotton sheets, 85-percent-cocoa chocolate and very dry wine. She is someone who actually likes doing yoga.

"Why aren't you staying here?" I ask Becky. "There's masses of room."

"God, there's no way Cara was going to share a house with half a dozen under-eights waking up at the crack of dawn. She sleeps with an eye mask and everything." I picture Cara with a pale green silk eye mask and matching slip. I think of the cut-off tracksuit bottoms and T-shirt that make up my nightwear.

"I don't blame her. If I were you, I wouldn't want to go on holiday with my family. In fact, if I were me, I wouldn't want to either."

We're interrupted by the arrival of lazy Daisy and her silent husband.

"I didn't know you were coming," I say. "Though I'm very pleased to see you."

"My in-laws have a place down the road. Have done forever. Holiday home like this one. Though I say like this one, but a house less like this one it's hard to imagine. It's way more shabby than chic."

"It's very beautiful around here. I'm getting terrible house envy," I say. "Mitzi, I want your house."

"Oh, god, I don't," says Daisy. "Such a hassle having a place in the country, even a dump like Robert's parents'."

"A country estate is something I'd hate," sings Joel, showcasing the knowledge of musicals that may have contributed to the rumor that he was gay.

"No, really," says Daisy. "Boilers going wrong and burst pipes and all that. Such a shag. I can't be doing with one house most of the time."

"That's true," I say. "I feel that about mine."

"Although I have discovered the secret to feeling happy at home," she says.

"Do tell."

"Lowering your standards," she laughs. "I apply the same logic to my appearance. In fact, you can combine the two by having only dirty mirrors in your house. And certainly no mirrors in which you can see below the waist."

I wish I could channel the spirit of lazy Daisy.

"And drinking lots," she adds. "I need a drink after the day we've had."

Alpha male Michael is, of course, on drinks duty, giving us old-fashioned spirits rather than the cans of lager and glasses of wine that serve as aperitifs at our house. Everyone compliments him lavishly for his way with the gin bottle. It's unseasonably warm and I find myself drinking the spirits as if they were my usual wine. I notice that Becky is doing much the same.

After a few of these, I begin to feel shaky. I go to the loo to check out my mottled cheeks.

"Do you really mean it?" Becky corners me as I emerge.

"Mean what?"

"What you said about not wanting to be with your children?"

"No, of course not. Not really. It was just a silly joke."

"Does having children make you happy?"

Oh, god, here we go. Why can't Becky ever want to chat about reality television and celebrities? I am feeling as shallow as a Norfolk beach with the tide out.

"Yes, sometimes. Anxious, too. Stressed, but happy, yes, generally, I think. I don't know."

"You must know. Do Gabe and Rufus make you, Mary, happy?"

"I can't imagine life without them. My biggest fear is that something might happen to them. I would never, ever, want to unwish them. I would give up my life for them but at the same time I have this terrible fear of not being around for them."

"But do they make you happy?"

I think to myself of the way I am sometimes woken up at dawn and my first thought is, oh, god, another thirteen hours until their bedtime. Of how I want to stick pins in my eyes rather than read another page of another Thomas the Tank Engine book. Of how my favorite moments of the day are often those without them—going to the cinema, a coffee alone, even my journey to work. Of the perpetual, eternal, overwhelming chaos.

And then I think of how, when they've gone to bed, I find myself longing for them to be awake again because I miss them so much. Of how I gorge myself on Gabe's beauty. There is something in the truism that all newborns are ugly and all toddlers are beautiful. Especially my second born, who has Joel's dark skin and my pale eyes. You know when you meet an exceptionally beautiful girl and you want to put on dark glasses in order to stare at her? When you have a toddler, you can stare all you like without embarrassment and they are all beautiful.

And Rufus's endearing earnestness, the funny things that he says and his capacity to learn, they make me happy. I love that he goes through the day multiplying every number that he comes across to the power of a hundred for no reason other than that he wants to. I love how he over-uses the word "actually," draws pictures of domestic appliances, and thinks that the stories I tell him and Gabe when we've no books on hand are better than any story we could read. I love that he teaches me that however perfect you think an age is, he grows up and shows me that it just keeps on getting better. I thought that a baby sitting up or a toddler's early speech could never be beaten, but I didn't know how good a conversation with a child could be, that it could delight me in a way that none had since those early biography-swapping late-night talks in my early days with Joel.

"You'll never get a straight answer out of a parent," I finally say to Becky. "It's not a choice that can be rationalized, even by you. I'm glad I've got them, really I am, but I don't believe that on balance people with children are any happier than those without. I'm sure I've even read some study or other that says that." I have to say this to Becky, whatever I really think, because I know there's every chance she won't have children herself. I am groping for the balance between encouragement to try and platitudes if she doesn't succeed.

She sighs. "I'm still trying to weigh it up."

"You're thinking too much. You always think too much."

"I know, I do."

We sit down to eat fashionably old-fashioned British food, lots of lovage and obscure cuts of meat, alongside the samphire we picked earlier. I think it's quite disgusting, but everyone else swoons.

"What is this?" I ask, prodding at my custard-like pudding.

"It's lemon posset," says Mitzi.

"I thought posset was what babies bring up—you know, regurgitated milk." Which is frankly what this looks like.

"There's a word for that," says Joel. "You know, the opposite of a synonym. When the same word has two totally different meanings."

"Well, this posset is a wonderful old British recipe made with cream, lemon and sugar. Divine, isn't it?" says Mitzi.

"What a shame," I say. "Dairy." My plate is quickly swiped away by Joel, who looks happy for the first time all day.

"Do you want to race tomorrow?" Michael asks Joel.

"Race what?"

"Enterprises."

"Sorry, is this some sort of City thing?"

"Dinghies. It's a two-man jobbie and I've put myself down for the Enterprise class in tomorrow's regatta. You'd make good ballast." He points at Joel's posset-filled belly.

"OK." He shrugs. "Could be a laugh."

"It's no laugh," says Mitzi. "The regatta's taken very seriously around here."

"I warn you, Michael, Joel was born without the competitive gene." It had shocked me at first. He'd lose to me at tennis and he'd just offer congratulations and give me a hug, never insisting we play again and again until he'd won, or blame the racquet for his poor performance.

"Does it involve me getting up early?" asks Joel.

I give him a look. "I think what he's trying to say is, does it involve him spending a lot of time away from looking after his children?"

"Cut the poor bloke some slack," says Michael. "As far as I can see all he does is look after your children. Don't worry, under-the-thumb boy, high tide isn't until one."

"Of course you must go," I say, faking magnanimity. "And I'll find something to do away from the children in the morning and you can look after them then. It's called tag-team parenting."

"There are some dear little shops in the village," says Mitzi. "Very cute interiors, lots of lovely stripes and checks."

"Over-priced bags of fudge," says Becky. "Cara insisted on going to them today. Some rather sweet lavender-stuffed dog-shaped door stoppers, but of course I wasn't allowed to buy one of those."

"I'm going to walk across to the island at low tide," says Cara. "First thing in the morning, before all the tourists."

"Grockles, we call them around here," says Mitzi. "Isn't that too divine?" I'm not sure when she began to talk as though she were in an Evelyn Waugh adaptation.

"Why don't you come along?" Cara says to me.

"That would be nice," I say. How strange to walk at my own pace. To enjoy the journey instead of spending all of it worrying about whether the boys will be able to walk all the way back, whether I'll have to carry one of them, whether they'll understand the point of our destination. These have been the years of living vicariously. "How early is early?"

"Very. I love early mornings. So efficient. Seven o'clock?"

"That's practically the afternoon. I'd love to. You can do breakfast, can't you, Joel?" A rhetorical question. He's got an afternoon of being shouted at by Michael, I get a dawn walk with Cara. I win.

I'm having a dream about opening a cupboard door at home to reveal a whole extra wing, including indoor swimming pool and gym, that we never knew existed. "I know," I'm telling all my friends who have gathered in awe, "I suppose we're just lucky." I wake up just as I hit a small barrier of stress when it comes to cleaning out the pool, especially since I can't find my swimming costume.

"What are you doing?" I hiss at Joel, who is crashing around the bedroom trying to find a T-shirt to put on over his boxers.

"Am hungry."

"No, you're just drunk. Go back to bed."

"I'm starving. Small portions." He's got his T-shirt on by now.

"You can't go downstairs. Here, have a cereal bar."

"No, need meat. There's a whole ham in the larder."

"You're not going downstairs on your own."

"I promise I won't play with knives."

"I don't trust you to tidy up after yourself. Bloody hell, Joel, why can't you sleep through the night without a midnight snack? You're worse than a baby. A strangely carnivorous newborn."

We creep down our staircase, past the utility room and approach the kitchen.

"Shh," I say. "What's that noise?"

"It sounds like a ghost."

"Don't be daft," I snap, though it is a sort of moaning sound.

"You go first."

I open the door to the kitchen. The moaning has turned to voices from beyond the recycled glass barrier between the kitchen and the family room. Joel comes to stand beside me and we watch transfixed, knowing that we should return to our room and never speak of it, but unable to tear ourselves away. We are in darkness, but the figures are lit by Mitzi's clever combination of up- and downlighters. They shimmer behind the wobbling imperfections of the glass like cars on hot tarmac, giving their actions a hazy, dream-like quality. At first it is difficult to make them out, but my eyes quickly become accustomed, as if I have been forced to wear glasses with the wrong prescription but my vision has now readjusted. The curve of the glass and the large mirror above the fireplace increases the circus freakshow feel of it all. A tall 1930s movie lamp illuminates the scene, appropriately since it is like something out of a porn film. Not that I'd have ever watched something so specialist.

Mitzi is naked but for a pair of Marigolds and an apron that manages to cover up neither her primary nor her secondary sexual characteristics. She is holding a squirt-gun dispenser full of bright yellow liquid. Michael's top half is dressed in shirt and tie, while he is naked from the waist down. He is speaking quietly, but he has one of those public-school voices, trained in oratory, that carries.

"You're a dirty bitch," he says to Mitzi.

"I'm sorry."

"And you know how we punish dirty bitches, don't you?"

"We make them learn how to clean."

At this point Michael climbs onto the glass coffee table as Mitzi lies down beneath it. I worry that it's not strong enough, but that anxiety pales into insignificance after the next development.

He crouches down. His face strains. He crouches further.

"Oh my god," Joel whispers.

I don't believe what I'm seeing. I must still be asleep. I want to look away but I can't, I have to keep looking.

"Shit!"

"Exactly," Joel says and stifles a horrified giggle.

"Tell me what you can see, my mucky little bitch," orders Michael.

"It's beautiful. It's the biggest I've ever seen," Mitzi replies as she shimmies out from under the table with what looks like well-practiced ease. She then pulls out a wet wipe and cleans her husband's arse.

"Sniff it," orders Michael.

Mitzi murmurs as if handed a swatch of Chanel No. 5.

"Now clean it up."

We watch transfixed as she does so, just like a dog owner in the park, except she's giving the occasional French-maid-like wiggle as she does so. She appears complicit. Certainly happier about it than I am when I'm wiping up the kitchen after one of Joel's baking sessions. It's the small details, like the conveniently placed diaper sacks used to put it in, that most transfix me.

"Oh my god again," says Joel as we watch Michael piss a big M across the coffee table. "They really do monogram everything."

"Now who's a mucky pup?" says Mitzi. "I'll need to get a cloth to dry it. It will be soaked. What shall I do with the cloth afterward?"

We don't get to hear the answer to this question as she begins to walk toward the kitchen part of the room and we realize that we'll be discovered. We attempt to reverse stealthily up the stairs. Neither of us breathes until we're safely in our room with the door shut. We bury ourselves under the duvet and finally give in to horrified laughter. Every time we look at each other, we start giggling again.

We stay silent under the duvet for about five minutes, clinging to one another in shared horror and humor.

"Oh my god," I finally say.

"He has nothing to do with it."

"Godliness, cleanliness, et cetera, et cetera."

"Do you think god doesn't like dirty little bitches?" says Joel, imitating Michael's well-bred tones. We giggle again, as silently as possible.

"I don't know what I'm most shocked about," I say. "That Michael's a pervert or that Mitzi wasn't using environmentally sound cleaning products."

"Somehow neither surprises me much."

"Michael always seems so straight."

"Yeah, straight like a politician."

"Ooh, it is a bit tabloid exposé of an MP, isn't it? But still, I'm shocked—I really am."

"I was most taken aback by Mitzi's Hollywood."

"I love that you know what a Hollywood is," I say to Joel, feeling an unexpected warmth toward him. "Do you like it?"

"Of course not. Why would I want my woman to look like a pre-pubescent?"

The image of Mitzi's hairless genitals and sleek Pilates-toned body comes into my head again. I couldn't see her eyes, but I suspect that they may have been sad. Or amused. I don't really know her anymore.

"She once told me that Michael had powerful urges that needed servicing or something. I just hadn't realized they involved him—oh, god, I can't even say it. Mind you, she also told me she never ever poos in front of him as she doesn't want to spoil the mystery."

"Well, as far as we know she never does shit in front of him. She just has to clear up his."

"Don't."

"I know. My eyes, my eyes." Joel presses them dramatically.

"We should never have stayed there gawping. We should have left as soon as we saw them. If they're pervs, we are too—voyeurs."

"But we're staying here. We're their guests."

"Perhaps that's why we've got our own little wing."

"And what about all the staff?"

"They live above the garage."

"It's absolutely not our fault that we witnessed that. They must have known there's a risk. Maybe they like the fact that there's a risk. It's absolutely their fault that we saw what we did. We could sue. People in glass houses and all that. Sorry, sustainable recycled glass houses."

"What, people in glass houses shouldn't indulge in weird sexual perversions?" I say.

"Something like that. Shouldn't indulge in coprophilia. That's the technical term, I believe."

"I don't love that you know what coprophilia is."

"Homonym," he says, suddenly, slapping his forehead.

"I don't think he's gay. Though it is often these macho types, I suppose."

"No, Maz. That's the word I couldn't think of earlier. It's a word with two completely different meanings. Like posset meaning stuff a baby sicks up and that pudding we had."

"Now that was disgusting. Especially now I think about where Mitzi's hands have been. Oh, god, Joel, how are we going to survive until Wednesday?"

"You're not the one who's having to go sailing with shit-boy. And it wasn't me who wanted to come here. I knew it wouldn't be worth the free accommodation. It's like going to church because you want to get your children into a religious school. Hypocrisy never goes unpunished." He sighs. "The worst thing is that even that didn't put me off my food. I'm still famished."

"Don't even think about going downstairs for that ham. I don't want to think about what they may be doing with it."

I throw him a cereal bar. He unwraps it and gives a theatrical look of horror at the nutty nubby brownness of it. We look at each other and start giggling all over again.

I wake up feeling surprisingly rested. It took me ages to get to sleep with my head swirling, or should it be swilling, with what we had seen. At first we tried to sleep in each other's arms, the first time we'd done so for years, but laughter and cramps got the better of us and we wriggled away from each other, while the giggles continued. I look across the vast acreage of bed, but Joel has gone.

Our bedroom has gloriously thick curtains, so the near-midsummer dawn light is blocked out. I look at my mobile, dreading that it should only be 4 a.m., but am surprised to read 8 a.m. I do a double-take. I don't know the last time I woke up that late. I should get up, but I am leaden. Eight o'clock. Something is happening this morning, I had to be somewhere before breakfast.

Cara—of course, Cara. I throw on some clothes and go downstairs to find my menfolk in the kitchen, painting a rare picture of familial perfection, despite liberal scatterings of muesli.

"Why didn't you wake me?" I say. "I was supposed to go for a walk."

"You slept through Gabe and Rufus waking up so I thought I'd let you have a lie-in. Thought you might be tired." He suppresses a giggle. "Sorry, I forgot you were going out. Should have set the alarm."

"Since when have we needed to set an alarm for anything?" I look at his stubble-covered face and feel a surge of gratitude for both the lie-in and the fact of him not being Michael. But why is it, I also think, that the one and only time my husband spontaneously decides to let me lie in is the one time I don't want to? "Where are our hosts?"

"The offspring are being forced into outdoor activity by the au pair, while their parents have yet to emerge. I think they may be very tired." We both start giggling again.

"Michael!" shouts Joel seconds later with forced jollity. Michael is wearing shorts, a polo shirt and boating shoes. He looks every bit as respectable as he has every other time I've met him, except now I picture him sporting a gimp mask and being whipped by prison guards. "Did you sleep well?"

"Certainly did. All set for the regatta?"

Joel nods, unable to speak.

"Tea," I say. "Made in a pot and everything."

Michael sniffs it and I am inevitably reminded of his wife and the wet wipe. "You didn't use fresh, not-boiled-before water, did you?" He looks around at the selection of cereal packets and bowls encrusted with the fast-drying wallpaper paste of whole-wheat breakfast products. "Where's Radka? Why has she left this mess?"

"It's ours," says Joel. "Sorry. We've been very mucky pups, haven't we, boys? Dirty boys. Naughty, naughty, naughty." He slaps his wrist. He's got to stop this. He then scoops up the cereal packets and puts them in the cupboard where I know Mitzi will rearrange them in height order. I am beginning to think of ways that we can leave this place early.

Mitzi comes in, looking fresh and lovely. I haven't even brushed my teeth yet. I think it's all going to be fine, but then I find I can't actually look her in the eye. She manages to make me feel like we're the filthy ones for having stumbled across the scene, rather than them for a) indulging in such weirdness and b) indulging in such weirdness with guests in the house.

"Good walk?" asks Michael.

"Lovely," she replies.

Somehow we struggle through the next couple of days and Joel makes a work excuse so that we can leave on the Tuesday, a day before our agreed departure. We have the usual flurry of chaos to round up all our possessions and the endless screeching of "Have you seen the camera?" and "You had the mobile charger last." The boys have been whining about wanting to go home since we arrived, but now they whine about leaving their new best friends, the Labrador and the Jack Russell. We finally gather up the last of our detritus and, as the sound of Michael's voice giving us top navigational tips fades away, we breathe for the first time.

"Did you have fun, boys?" I ask brightly. "It was lovely, wasn't it?"

"Yeah," says Rufus. "Especially the Wii."

"I loved the sea. It was so salty," I say.

"Ooh, Oscar Wilde, I wish I'd said that," says Joel.

"What, Oscar in my class?" asks Rufus. Such is the quality of our in-car banter.

The loss of freedom in parenting is incremental. If it all came at once we'd drown our babies like puppies in the river. New parents are staggered by the compromises that they have to make when they are delivered of the firstborn, but little do they know how much worse it's going to get, that liberty is chipped at so subtly that you're not even aware of it—in fact, you even sign up for more in the shape of further children. The lost freedom I'm currently mourning is the ability to have conversations in the car without my children interrupting me or catching on to who we're gossiping about. I suppose I ought to rejoice in Rufus being behind in his reading since it means we can still "es pee ee el el" out taboo words like "sex," "affair" and "chocolate." I'm sure in only a few months this too will be denied us.

At last Rufus and Gabe fall asleep.

"I don't know how we survived," I say.

"It's all right for you. Can you imagine what it was like for me being trapped on a small boat with Michael? Making his strainy face every time he shouted out 'Ready about, Leo.'" He does a stomach-churning impression of said strainy face.

"What makes someone want to do those things? Is it something to do with potty training? Do you think his mother did it too early? Or too late? Did I leave it too late with Gabe? Or perhaps I made too much of a fuss about it. It's all very odd because I've always thought of Michael and Mitzi as anally retentive. When in fact he's anally expulsive. What does that even mean?" Joel is silent. "Your mom would know; I'll ask her next time I see her. Is it someone who's really disorganized and untidy and is always losing stuff?"

"A bit like me, you mean?"

"Yes."

"With Michael as the alternative?"

"I think there must be a happy medium, don't you?"

He's silent again.

"Don't you?"

"One person's happy medium is another person's obsessive compulsive."

"What's that supposed to mean?"

"What you think are normal levels of organization and tidiness might be someone else's idea of anally retentive. That's all."

"I'm not at all anal, if that's what you're saying. Mitzi and Michael, you're right, they did verge on the obsessive. I've always admired how tidy she is, but I did find the way she'd move my shoes so that the left one was on the left and the right on the right when I put them by the door a bit disconcerting."

"And the way she'd jump and tidy up the minute we finished eating. And throwing away all the newspapers when they were only a day old."

"No, Joel, that's normal behavior."

"No, it's anal."

"Well, that would make me anal then."

He says nothing.

"Am not. You're a slob, that's all. Do you think you're normal and I'm anal, or do you admit that I'm normal and you're a slob?"

"All I'm saying is that it's relative, like what that Daisy was saying. I'm sure Mitzi and Michael think they're completely normal. Well, that their attitude to tidiness is normal. I'm not sure even they would think defecating on glass coffee tables is entirely mainstream. And I'm sure you think your attitude to mess is completely normal."

"If anything, I'm way too tolerant. Obviously I'm not anal, given that the house is a dump at all times."

"Actually, though," he says, "now I think about it, you've been a lot nicer recently. A lot more tolerant."

"What do you mean?"

"I don't know, I'm only just realizing it now I think about it. Recently, you've been a lot less angry about stuff. We don't have those daily rows about the cereal and the laundry basket."

"Concentrate on the road."

"Yes, you've definitely been nicer to me. I don't know, for a couple of months or so. Not been on at me about every little thing. Have you noticed?"

"I've not noticed you becoming any more considerate around the house recently, no."

"I shouldn't mention it, I suppose. Just make the most of having the old Mary in the house again, my lovely slatternly *pelirroja*."

He gives me a patronizing little pat on the knee.

"Mommy," says a small voice from the back of the car. "What does anal mean?"

"Shall I put the DVD on?" The children safely distracted, I ask Joel the question I've wanted to ask for almost nine years. "I've always been curious about whether you've ever thought about, you know, the fact that Mitzi fancied you when you came to work with us?"

"Not really. Should I?"

"No. I just think you might wonder what it would be like."

"After last night, I don't need to wonder."

"I wouldn't blame you."

"For what?"

"Thinking about it. God, I'm not saying I wouldn't blame you for having an affair."

"I'm not having an affair." He leans forward to study the road. "There's an awful lot of roadkill around these parts, isn't there?"

"I never said you were having an affair. I know that. I think Mitzi's got her hands full with Michael."

"Mitzi is exactly the sort of woman to have an affair. She can't stand anybody having something she hasn't got."

"She was fine about us. It surprised me at the time. I remember I was dreading telling her, but she was fine about it."

He sighs. "I tried to tell you, but you never wanted to hear. She wasn't fine."

"What do you mean?"

"She tried it on with me."

"Yes, I know that. She fancied you first."

"No, after you and I had got together."

"Are you sure it was after she knew we were together?"

"Yes, I'm absolutely sure."

"Tell me."

"One evening, about a month or so after our first night, she said she needed to talk about something. Idiot that I am, I agreed to go out for a drink. She put her hand on my knee, low-cut top, all the clichés. I said no, that I was in love with you, she said that you didn't need to know, I said but I don't want to and she stopped. Begged me not to say anything to you, told me about her upbringing and how it makes her insecure, and made me promise not to."

"Why didn't you ever tell me?"

"Because I promised I wouldn't."

"Joel, you great lump, that sort of promise isn't binding."

"I know. It was really stupid of me. I thought it would hurt you more to know, so I didn't, but it was a mistake. It pushed me into a corner where Mitzi and I had a secret from you and I didn't like that. But I thought you'd wonder why I didn't tell you immediately, so it just seemed easier to keep quiet."

"For the last nine years?"

"I'd pretty much forgotten about it, to be honest."

"But what about all those secret glances between you two, and your antipathy toward Michael?"

"There are no secret glances. More like grimaces. And I don't like Michael because he's a tosser. Why did you think I don't like him?"

"I don't know. There's a lot about Mitzi I'm going to have to rethink after this weekend."

May Good Housekeeping

File Edit View Insert Format Tools Window

	A	B
1	May allowance	2 per day, total 62
2	Total no. of debits in May	87
3	Breakdown of infringements	19 kitchen; 11 bathroom; 5 laundry; 7 bedroom; 8 living; 21 parenting; 6 environment; 5 general ineptitude; 5 finance.
4	Infringement of the month	Grilled himself some cutlets and not only didn't wash up the fat-splattered grill pan, but left it hidden inside the oven so that when I switched it on to do some baked potatoes, the kitchen filled with the acrid stench of twice-cooked lamb fat.
5	Positives to offset	Though he racked up a huge tally in the first three weeks of the month, the last week of May was all positive and no debits. I spent the days after that night in Norfolk in a continual state of gratitude that Joel is a) not Michael and b) able to be so funny about Michael. I didn't actually write down any credits on The List, but am instead adding a one-off 10-point credit of "Isn't Michael."

6	May debt	15 (87 offset by May allowance of 62 and the "Isn't Michael" 10-point bonus ball)
7	Total debt from February, March, April and May	74
8	Total remaining	26 over next two months (100 minus 74)

8

Of Lice and Men

I feel like I'm living in a medieval plague house. I don't know why I don't just get out Gabe's poster paint and slosh a great big red cross on our door. I take it personally—it is as if I, too, am invaded and infested. Jennifer, the trainee therapist from the book group, would say that I am "toxic."

At work nobody knows the pestilence I bring with me. They have their own infestations: chlamydia, spliffs and cheap cocktails. We are all infected with the self-importance that spreads when we've got a program in production, bustling around barking at one another as if LIVES DEPENDED ON IT, when in fact all that will emerge from it is yet another reality entertainment show.

I open my email with dread. Seven new meetings have been dropped into the electronic calendar while my back was turned, all marked up as urgent. I have 102 unread emails, most of which I'm guessing aren't even addressed to me but I'll be one of a dozen cc-ed correspondents, all of us in there as extra cover for the sender's back. It's all so pointless; it's the professional equivalent of a kitchen surface that needs wiping only to be smeared all over again ten minutes later.

"You missed a top night, Mazza," says Lily, who is wearing a Hermès scarf knotted around her head like it's Woodstock. Another fashion that seems to have passed me by, and that definitely goes into the long look-book marked "Accessories that make Lily look charming and gamine but would make me look like a mad bag lady." I am beginning to worry that my long relied upon floral tea dresses fall into the same category, or a subset thereof: maiden aunt at wedding slash history teacher we laughed at.

"Why?"

"The whole team went out to celebrate the pilot being so scorching and Matt put the drinks on exes. Such a top bloke."

Matt is my age and has 50 percent more children. But Matt is male.

"I didn't know anything about it."

"Well you wouldn't, you were on holiday last week, weren't you?"

"Half term."

"I wish I had half terms," she sighs. "I'm knackered."

"So am I. Because I do have half terms."

"What did you do, anyway?"

"You know my friend Mitzi?"

"Ditzy Mitzi who fancies your husband?"

"Does not."

"Did then."

"We went to her house. Well, her second house on the coast."

"Cool, a beach shack. Surfing?"

"I don't think you can surf in Norfolk. Not that I'd know. And not a shack. About the size of four normal houses. Her pantry is bigger than most people's kitchens."

"What's a pantry? Is that for keeping your thongs in?" Lily grew up in a large vicarage in the home counties and I suspect that she knows full well what a pantry is.

"And it's got a utility room and everything."

"Don't know what a utility room is, either. I'm thinking somewhere you wear utility chic—you know, boiler suits and those totally fierce Louboutin lace-up boots." She sighs. "I'd like a futility room, where anyone who entered would be forced to chill and do fuck all but listen to music and talk to each other, really talk to each other. It's like everyone's so bonkers and stressed at the moment, know what I mean?"

"I do, I know exactly what you mean."

"Still, I guess you got to relax on your holiday. Have a good time, did you?"

"Yes, of course. It was incredible. The kids went sailing and swimming and beachcombing. There was so much space and light. You know those big skies they have there? It was great."

I don't think I've ever looked so forward to returning to the steaming stench-pile of my own home as I did when we fled Mitzi's. I welcomed the thought of the freedom to kick off my shoes and let them land where they fell, and to put down my sunglasses without fear that they would be sequestered. At first, the morning after seeing what we saw that night, I avoided looking at Mitzi as my mind was so scorched with the image of her in her porny cleaner outfit. And then I found I couldn't take my eyes off her. Usually I am so dazzled by her brilliance that she is just a hazy shimmer of perfection, but this time I felt that I saw her, properly, for the first time since she got married.

Before I had seen only the swan, but during the last couple of days in Norfolk, I saw the madly paddling legs beneath the glide through life. Mitzi is always cleaning. She has staff and all, but she is either telling them to clean something, doing it herself or guilting you into doing it. I'd have thought the last thing she'd want to do when indulging in a little sexual role-playing downtime would be to pop on her Marigolds and pick up crap.

If she's not physically cleaning, then she is tidying up life. Smoothing over Michael's querulousness over why there's never any bloody peace and quiet in this madhouse, and why do the children have to make such an infernal racket all the time, and where is Birgita, Radka, whatever her name is? And said quartet of children don't get to resemble the kids in a catalog that sells homemade bunting and bespoke treehouses by accident. Mitzi had a packet of biodegradable wet wipes permanently at hand to scrape their faces, and would pressure an au pair or nanny to remove them to beyond earshot should they start whining about wanting to use the PlayStation.

And all the environmentally friendly cleaning products in the world could never wipe from my mind the image of her and Michael, nor my new knowledge of how she betrayed me, her friend, all those years ago. When I thought I had seen a knowledge shared between Mitzi and Joel I had been right, though wrong about what it was they both knew.

My excitement about being back at home was matched by my warmth toward Joel. I even declared an unofficial moratorium on The List, which meant that when he dumped the bags in the hall I decided not to add in list number **D7**: *Will eventually unpack his clothes from the suitcase, but will leave all the sundry miscellaneous items—the cameras, books and toiletries—because they may be of use to other members of the family as well as to himself.*

In the kitchen, what had been a discarded half-eaten apple had been transformed into an almost-eaten apple by a crack team of ants, most of whom seemed to be still crawling over our kitchen surfaces. It was not quite the welcoming committee that I'd have chosen, but they were apple-pie baking grannies in comparison to the next uninvited visitor we encountered.

"What are these?" I asked Joel, pointing at the brown granules under the kitchen sink.

"Don't know."

I was feeling sugar-deprived after four days of someone else's food and so went to my secret stash of dark chocolate Easter eggs that I have been rationing out to myself. It is hidden behind one of the cupboards, away from the thieving hands of children, but not, as it turns out, from the thieving claws of vermin. Most of the foil seemed to have been removed and there were tiny teeth marks across my expensive dairy-free chocolate.

I dropped the bag in horror. "We've got mice."

"How can you tell?" asked Joel. He tried to stay calm but I knew he was far more terrified of them than I was.

"Those things were mice droppings. Gabe, put that down, wash your hands immediately! And they've been at my chocolate."

"Chocolate!" exclaimed the boys with one voice.

"And god knows what else. This is revolting. I feel dirty."

Joel started giggling. I wondered when the word "dirty" would cease to provoke this Pavlovian response.

"What do we do about it?"

He shrugged.

"I suppose I'll look on the Internet and I'll sort it out because I don't have anything else to do."

"You might want to look up how to get rid of ants while you're at it."

I was irritated but still protected by the armor of what we had seen together. Back at home, I only had to picture Mitzi in a pair of rubber gloves to feel all warm and benevolent. This lasted the whole of the first day of our return, despite the mice and the ants. We had sex that night—normal sex, obviously—and I began to wonder whether I wouldn't be able to put our marriage back on track.

Then he went back to work while I took time off to look after the boys for the remaining days of half term, and the dropped clothes, casual requests and general assumption of my domestic servitude began again.

"I'll need my suit for this meeting on Monday," he said to me that first morning.

"OK."

"Pick it up from the dry cleaner, would you?"

"All right, where's the ticket?"

"Don't know." He did that meaningless patting-pockets gesture. "The bloke's really nice in there, you won't need it, he knows who I am."

"So why don't you do it?"

"Got to rush."

The nice man in the dry cleaner and I spent an hour looking for the suit, while Gabriel tried to put plastic bags on his head and Rufus said that even school was less boring than this.

"Maybe it wasn't that dry cleaner," said Joel. He rifled through his wallet. "Here's the ticket. Oh, it's not at that dry cleaner at all, it's at the one near work. You don't need to worry about it," he said generously, "I'll pick it up myself."

Then on the Monday morning, when at last it was my turn to join him in the world of work, Joel's parting words to me were:

"You might want to take a look at the kids' heads. Rufus has been scratching like mad."

"Oh, for god's sake," I shouted at his departing back. "I feel like I'm living in a World War I trench."

"Not my fault," he shouted back, breaking into a trot.

I gave Rufus's head a cursory examination and managed to convince myself that since I couldn't see anything jumping, it would be fine to do a more thorough comb after work. What choice did I have? I tried to imagine Matt's reaction if I kept Rufus off school and Gabriel away from the child minder and failed to turn up to work, especially after what my boss would no doubt refer to as "all that time off over half term."

My last vision of Rufus in the school playground was of a

mother looking at him suspiciously as he gave his head a vigorous scratch. I felt guilt and anger in equal measure. Why wasn't this Joel's problem? I tried to ward off antipathy by thinking of the Mitzi and Michael Show, but it had already lost its power to protect Joel from my wrath.

I have a three-minute window between meetings, which is just enough to open a few emails and work out if any of them need my urgent attention or even my attention at all. The phone on my desk rings.

"What fresh hell is this?" I mutter before answering, "Hello."

"Hello, Mary." A voice that would taste of the cucumber in a large jug of ice-cold Pimm's.

"Cara, hello. I didn't know you had my work number."

"I remembered where you work."

I am flattered. "I'm so sorry about the walk—you know, in Norfolk. I was so looking forward to it."

"Don't worry about it."

"I never don't turn up for anything, especially things that I'm looking forward to."

"I said don't worry about it."

"Did you have a good time, in Norfolk, I mean, it's very beautiful, isn't it?" I'm gabbling. "Mitzi's house is amazing, don't you think?"

"She has exquisite taste."

"Yes, she does."

"And how's Becky?"

"In Newcastle."

"Yes, of course, that case. How long's it going to go on for?"

"A month, maybe two."

"Yes, I think she told me, depending on when it settles. Poor her, must be very discombobulating. And for you too, I guess, though it's a very nice town, I think—well, I haven't been there for years, but it always was and I'm sure it still is. Very friendly, that's what they always say, don't they? But still, it's not home, is it? Though this time at least she's got a serviced apartment, hasn't she? Are you going to go up at all?"

"Perhaps. She's back every Friday." There's a pause. "I wonder whether you'd like to have a drink sometime. Your office is near here."

"Yes, it is. I'd love to. That would be great." Something very cold in an all-white environment as opposed to a cup of tea in a cluttered kitchen.

"Tonight?"

A weekday, not a Friday or Saturday night? I think of the nit comb and am tempted to say yes, but I know that Joel has already told me he won't be back until gone eight. "Tonight's not great for me. Tomorrow?"

"No, can't do tomorrow."

"The weekend?" When Becky's back.

"No. Another time."

I think of all the times that Joel has turned up past the kids' bath- and bedtime and how that's just fine, that's no problem because I'm the default, the person who is home on time unless I have begged dispensation. I am about to acquiesce to Cara's summons on these grounds, but it is too late, she has hung up. I feel guilty, as if I have offended her and that it is ineffably rude to be unavailable for a drink at less than half a day's notice. I wonder whether I shall ever receive the call again.

Combing the boys' hair is hypnotic. Beside the sofa sits a long-toothed metal nit comb, a clear bowl of water and a bottle of cheap conditioner. We no longer bother with the toxic pesticides, not because we are the sort of immunization-evading, homeopathy-using parents, but because the little pests have become resistant to all known forms of poison. I'm referring to nits, obviously, not my sons. I'm filled with the usual contradictory desires to find nothing in their hair, but at the same time have the "gotcha" satisfaction of pulling out a few live ones.

"Stay still, Rufus, please." Normally having such an abundance of hair would be considered a good thing, but in this instance some of that stringy sparse stuff would be good. Where we live, parents of a certain class like to distinguish themselves from their neighbors by growing their sons' hair to effeminate lengths. The posher you are, the longer it gets. Rufus's and Gabe's falls into their eyes and down to their shoulders. It doesn't matter that your dad might wear a suit and would never dream of going longer than a month between visits to the barber. Mitzi's boy Molyneux has locks of fairy-tale proportions.

The nit comb makes its slow progress through the red hair of Rufus and then the near black of Gabriel's. Sure enough, I am rewarded with eleven live wrigglers, a couple of dozen eggs and a few emptied egg carcasses. I stare with satisfaction at the bowl of water where my haul floats and then my heart sinks at the prospect of having to do this every day for a week, with dwindling returns. Then at last will come the day where none appear, but you can never be sure that this is a result of your total annihilation of the enemy or your growing carelessness.

I turn off the TV and sink back into the sofa. The boys disappear up to the bathroom. I know I should follow them or use this brief respite to swish out the nit bowl or to repatriate the Playmobil knights' swords and shields, but I flop. The house is quiet. I enjoy the quiet.

I should never enjoy the quiet.

"Mommy, Mommy," shouts Rufus. "Gabe's done an enormous poo and it's gone everywhere."

I dash upstairs. "Where is it? Where is it?" I walk into the bathroom to find it looking like a dirty protest on H block. Gabriel is using a very hard, tubular piece of his own excrement as a crayon and is scribbling over the walls. I have to concede he is showing a better hand and thumb grip than he has ever managed with the felt-tip pens. He puts a finger to his face, leaving a smear, so that he looks like the birthday boy ecstatic with the joy of his chocolate cake.

"Stop that, stop that at once," I scream.

"That's what I told him, Mommy, I told him that. Mommy, I told him to stop, I did, I kept on telling him. That's not appropriate behavior. It's disgusting."

"Not helping, Rufus. Go and grab me some more wipes. Put down the poo, Gabriel. Put down the poo."

He laughs and scampers past me.

"No," I shriek. Not near the carpet. I grab him so hard that I leave red welts on his upper arms. I feel a sense of triumph. I shove him back into the bathroom and dunk him in the shower, fully clothed, while I throw the poo-crayon down the toilet and frantically wipe the walls and the floors. I take him out and he drips onto the floor, his clothes clinging hard to his body. All the while, he is screaming and sobbing. I struggle to remove his clothes and then mummify him in a dry towel.

"Stay right where you are!"

I go in search of pajamas and return only to find that he is emptying a bottle of fake tan over himself, leaving orangey streaks across his pudgy limbs. It's like the Red Queen theory of evolution, that the faster you run the more the ground goes in the opposite direction and you stay in the same place. Here I cannot tidy up as fast as my children can mess up. I shove him back in the shower.

"I never did things like that when I was a baby," says Rufus.

"Please, go and get your PJs on."

"Mommy, tell Gabe off, tell him how I never did things like that when I was little."

"You're still little."

"No, I'm not, I'm in Year 1."

"Yes, fine. Damn it, there's no diapers. Please, Rufus, can you go and get some from the kitchen?"

He dissolves into a boy-shaped puddle on the floor. "I'm so tired. Why do I have to do everything around here?"

"Fine, I'll go."

On my return, I find that Gabe has taken the trouble to move out of the bathroom, with its tiled floor, and into the hall, with its pale wool carpet, to do a wee. It's like a Saturday night with Michael around here. Though not in an erotic way.

"That is it. Bedtime, both of you."

"But we haven't had a bath or stories."

"Gabe's had a shower and you're nice and clean, so let's just get on the PJs. Gabe, why did you put the pajamas into the water? Come on, in the bedroom, now."

"But I want a story, we always get a story."

"Well, your brother should have thought of that before he pooed all over the bathroom."

"But it's not fair..."

"Life isn't," I snap.

Gabe begins to scream. Offer him a choice, I think, make him think that I am allowing him his independence. I crouch down to be on his level, just like we're always told to do.

"Here, sweetheart, let's go and choose your pajamas."

He makes to grab a pair, but then throws them back, offended that I might have thought these were suitable attire. This continues with a second and a third pair. It is as if he has been cursed with an affliction that as soon as he chooses something, it instantly becomes the thing in the world most revolting to him. He is like some metaphor for consumerism and how choice actually makes us more and more unhappy.

OK, I think, choice not good. I pin him down and wrestle him into some blue and white stripy ones. He is screaming as if they are woven from stinging nettles.

"Not these ones! Yukky. No, no, no."

"Yes," I shout, having decided to swap into bitch mother mode since nice mom proved such a failure. "You're bloody wearing them."

After putting both legs into the same hole, I finally get them on, whereupon he immediately takes them off. This is particularly annoying since he claims to be unable to undress himself whenever I ask him to. The noise is reaching intolerable levels and I'm sure that the whole street is twitching their curtains.

Rufus is cupping his ears dramatically and moaning, "Why do I have to listen to this noise?"

"I don't much like it either," I shout over the wails. I want to press fast-forward to get to the point where they are both asleep and I have a large glass of wine in my hands. I can't work out a way of getting there. There is a ten-foot wall of disobedience, tantrums and teeth-brushing to clamber over until I reach the sanctuary of my evening.

"Come on." I grab an arm apiece and drag them into their bedroom. I know I am pulling them too hard but I convince myself that it's the only way to get them there. I shove them into their respective bunks and hold the door tight behind me. I go into a sort of trance to block out their wails and the beating on the door. Finally it subsides. I feel a surge of triumph, almost immediately replaced by shame.

I go downstairs to get the damn glass of wine. It's half an hour later than I had hoped to get them down, half an hour of my precious evening, of time that could have been spent on the delights of tidying up random bits of plastic, cooking supper, making Gabe's packed lunch for him to eat at Deena's house or watching mindless TV. I pour myself a glass and slump on a chair in the kitchen. I swear I see a mouse scuttle across the room, but I am too wrung out to care. The image of a rodent is replaced by the image of the marks left on the boys' arms by my too-tight grip, which is accompanied by a soundtrack of my shouts, of the awful inconsistency of my parenting, veering between craven cajoling and uncontrolled anger. I feel my sorrow rise up inside with an almost physical presence, bubbling up from my stomach into my mouth. It tastes of bile.

Time is spent staring at the wall, only to be broken by Joel walking in. It's past nine o'clock. "Glass of wine, how lovely," is his greeting. He smells as if he has had a few already. "Boys down, then? Shame, I was looking forward to seeing them. Good day?"

I can't speak. I can't even nod or shake my head. I just gulp down another shot of Merlot. He doesn't seem to have noticed my lack of reply, or maybe he doesn't care. My mind spins off into a fearful fantasy that there are hidden cameras in this house and that the whole world shall be treated to the image of me dragging my beloved sons so hard by their arms that they might be pulled out of their sockets. There will be another camera inside their room to capture their little fists beating at the door, begging to be let out. Will the neighbors report me to social services? I would if I had heard the sounds coming out of their bedroom.

Joel looks at the bowl of water with the floating corpses of drowned lice in it. "Have I missed the de-nitting? Shame, I find it strangely satisfying. Who did they get them from, anyway?"

I shrug.

"Must have been Mitzi's kids," he says.

The shock of this accusation stirs me out of my shame-induced torpor. "I doubt that. Mitzi's children don't have lice."

"How do you know? I thought they liked clean hair."

"That's just what they tell parents to make themselves feel better. I suppose I'm going to have to tell Mitzi to check hers. Michael will make cracks about Gabe and Rufus bringing in their plagues from poor school."

"How do you know our lot didn't catch it from her kids?"

"I don't think they have nits at private school."

Joel looks in the bowl of water. "Well, these ones are wearing purple stripy blazers and bullying the oiks who don't have a second home in the country, so I think they might be."

I fizz with irritation that he has returned home in time to make smart alec remarks, but not to help me when I needed him. He goes upstairs and I follow him. I want to punish him for not being there tonight, for waltzing in as ever when it's too late, for expressing sorrow at missing out on seeing the boys when I have seen too much of them tonight. I want to punish him for getting me into a position where I punished the boys. I should yank his arms, not theirs. I watch him as he goes into our bedroom, knowing that his coming home from work ritual is good for at least three debits on The List, my only form of punishment.

The first is easy meat.

Subsection C [laundry] number 1) *Throws his balled-up socks in vague direction of laundry basket. They never go in.*

Then he goes toward the chest of drawers. Come on, Joel, you know the routine. Yes! There it is:

Subsection E [living] number 3) *Empties pockets full of change onto chest of drawers (and kitchen table, mantelpiece, bit by the door where the letters go, etc., etc., creating small foothills of coppers all over the house).*

Once he's taken out the change he begins to remove the rest of the detritus from his pockets. No doubt some receipts that won't get charged to expenses, an underground ticket or two, tissues. He stops and turns around to glance at me. He then does something that I find almost as shocking as Mitzi and Michael's glass coffee table exploits.

He picks up the pile of change, looks at it, and puts it carefully into his wallet. He puts the receipts into the top drawer of the chest of drawers. He then picks up the tissues that he has left, walks past me and puts them into the toilet.

I look at his departing back. It is as if The List works, by some strange alchemy or osmosis. I go into the boys' room and stroke their sleeping foreheads and murmur my apologies into their sleeping minds.

"Shut up, poo-pen boy," Rufus says to Gabe in retaliation for a pinch.

"That's not very nice," I say.

"But he pinched me." He pronounces it pinch-*ed*, like something out of Shakespeare.

"Gabe, don't pinch him," I say in a perfunctory way. I'm tired after falling asleep on the floor of the boys' room, then having been unable to go back to sleep on transferring myself to the marital bed. I greeted the boys effusively when they woke up before six. They looked rather scared; at first I thought it was because they were carrying the memory of their shrieking, arm-pulling mother, but it may have been their shock at seeing me so friendly at the early hour. I told them how sorry I was and they shrugged. A psychologist could tell me if this was a good or a bad thing.

I vow to myself that from now on, I will parent them as if there were cameras filming me around the house. I will be patient and consistent. I won't chat on my mobile, check emails or try to read the paper when I'm with them. I will be, as they say, in the moment. It does not help that our day starts with breakfast, the powder keg of mealtimes. All that cereal-slopping, book-finding and harrying out of the house.

I vow to myself that from now on, I will parent them as well as I love them. And I love them so much, I really do; it's just that sometimes, when I'm tired, I don't like them very much.

"Why are you calling him poo-boy?" Joel asks Rufus, smirking.

"Don't encourage him," I say.

"Gabe pooed and used his poo to draw with."

"What?"

"Nothing. He said it was monsters but it just looked like rubbishy nothing. I'm much better at drawing."

"No, I mean, what on?"

"The walls near the bath."

Joel turns to me. "Is this true?"

"Yes. It is."

He looks as though he is about to giggle. "Why didn't you tell me?"

"I didn't think it was such a great anecdote."

"It is. Are we supposed to be pleased with his fine motor skills?"

I shrug.

"Are you all right?" he asks.

"Fine."

"It's a bit odd that you didn't tell me. It's not like you can exactly forget someone getting creative like that. You'd normally at least have a whine about it."

I carry on scraping encrustations off plastic cereal bowls.

I am beginning to feel that Joel and I don't exist in the real world anymore, only in relation to The List. It is as if it holds all the truth of our marriage, and what happens or is spoken outside of it is a mirage. He was right when he said that I am being nicer to him. It's not that we are getting on well, but we are arguing less. I am sublimating all my fury, while he is spending more time in the office and less time pissing me off. When he is at home, he's different from how he has always been. "Chipper" is the old-fashioned word I'd use to describe him. He's become this jolly, clasp-hands-together and say "Right, then" type of man.

As the tally steadily climbs toward 100, I find myself playing out the moment of revelation, when I say: "Joel, I want a divorce."

I try the words out loud, just for the effect. It makes me feel sick. It's not what I want. I want to go back to the way we were, before we had children—except with the children, of course. But I'm not sure that the way we loved each other is compatible with having the boys. It was so self-absorbed. You think to love someone is an act of selflessness, but really you love the reflection of your best self that you see in their mirror. Joel's flakiness and my efficiency had a perfect chemistry before children, but our boys are like an ingredient that, though delicious in itself, makes the whole recipe go wrong.

I try very hard to imagine Joel changing so that I find him as helpful as I used to find him seductive. If he doesn't go over his allotted number of debits on The List, then I shall try to find a way to realize this Shangri-la of family life, though I suspect that it cannot exist. And if he does go over, then I suppose there is only one alternative.

I try the words out again and repetition has blunted their power to nauseate.

"Joel, I want a divorce." I even look at myself in the mirror as I say them and try to picture his reaction.

He will look shocked, he'll steal my catchphrase and say "But this isn't fair."

Oh, but it is, I'll tell him and offer up The List as incontrovertible evidence of my fairness. I shall go through it point by point and he'll know that I have been scrupulous. Maybe I should even start taking photos on my phone as visual proof.

I'm aware that it's odd to imagine the moment of asking your husband for a divorce. It's like the culmination of an anti-rom-com. A div-dram, maybe. It's acceptable to daydream about a marriage proposal but not a proposal of divorce.

When we were going out together, before we got married, I even went through a phase of wondering how he would propose. I'm mortified by it now. Joel being king of the romantic gesture, I had high expectations. Not for him, I was sure, the corniness of a ring hidden in a fortune cookie, a mariachi band in a restaurant or rose petals across the bed. Joel would, I was sure, give me a Proposal Story to end all others.

For a shameful six months, I watched his every move, determined not to be caught out by his proposal. My face wore a perpetual expression of gracious acceptance and full makeup in readiness, like a nominee on Oscar night. I didn't fill gaps in conversation if he looked momentarily thoughtful. I let him make all the plans when we went out.

After six months, I became bored of my uncharacteristically passive behavior. "Don't you want to get married, then?" I said one morning over breakfast, while wearing the previous night's slap and a pair of old pajamas. "I'd love to," he said, giving me one of his enormous grins. "I thought you'd never ask." That was that, the shortest proposal story of them all. We laughed and kissed and began planning and I honestly felt that I'd got the best proposal after all.

Since I was the one to suggest marriage, it's only right that I should be the one to suggest that we end it.

The last two months are here. Two dozen credits and counting down.

It takes a couple more impossible invitations and curt conversations with Cara before I finally find myself standing on the threshold of her flat. I'm surprised that someone so precise in her appearance should only do last-minute invitations, but this time I left a message on Joel's voicemail to ask him, no tell him, that I'd be going out straight from work and could he pick up the boys from Deena's and don't whatever you do be late. I then screened my calls in case he tried to persuade me that he had an assignation more pressing.

Cara's voice wafts out of the intercom. I can almost smell it. Some sort of discontinued Givenchy scent available only in a perfumery in a tiny Parisian backstreet. I know that Becky is still in Newcastle, though no mention was made of her.

"Come in." She is dressed in green. I am making a rare foray in heels. I nipped out and bought them in one of the weird boutiques that pepper the streets around the office, ones which always describe themselves as selling an "eclectic mix of vintage and new designers." I used to have the right foreshortened calves to feel comfortable in some six inchers, but they seem to have lengthened back to their pre-pubescent shape and now I find only flat shoes feel right.

"Hello, how are you?" I say. "Sorry again about the walk, you know, in Norfolk, and not being able to make it for a drink those other times."

"Don't worry about it."

"I love your flat. It's so white. A polar bear would get lost in it."

"Thank you. I think."

"No, really. White is lovely. Wasn't it true that in olden days, having very white skin was a sign of being rich, because it meant you didn't have to work in the fields? Having a white sofa's a bit the same these days, because it shows you don't have to worry about people getting it dirty, or sticky fingers, or dry-cleaning bills." I should stop now. "And this furniture. Is it what they call mid-century?"

"Some of it, yes. That's the Mies van der Rohe Barcelona." She points to a slippery-looking chair that I fear would defeat me.

In a parallel life, I live in a flat like this. "And it's so quiet, too." She's not helping me. I wonder what she and Becky talk about. I can't see any traces of Becky in this room. It is hard to believe that she lives here. It's hard to believe she's even been here on a short visit.

Cara stands in the galvanized-steel corner of the open-plan room. "Would you like a drink?"

"Yes, I'd love one." I think maybe I am supposed to say which drink I'd like. A glass of wine? Or am I supposed to have a cocktail? The only ones I can think of have comedy names like Sex on the Beach. I am so not asking for one of those.

"I'm having a martini." Of course she's having a martini.

"Sounds lovely."

"I'm having mine bone dry with a twist."

"Just the way I like them."

I watch her make them with the ease with which most people boil a kettle.

I take a sip. Christ, why don't they just inject you with gin instead? The effect would be the same. My mouth feels hot with the alcohol. I want to hold my nose to get it down me. I swig it all down in an effort to get rid of the taste. Cara raises an eyebrow. She's so good at the one-eyebrow raise.

"I was thirsty." The act of taking one of those inverted

triangle glasses and knocking it back felt pleasantly cinematic. I feel emboldened, either through the alcohol or the gesture. "It's lovely to be here, really lovely." Still no response. I can't think of anything to say, so I say what's on my mind. "Why did you invite me over?"

"My, you're direct."

"Sorry."

"No, it's fine. Well..." An elongated word. "I'd like to get to know you."

"Really? Why?"

"Because I think you're one of the most angry people I've ever met."

"You can't know many angry people, then."

"I wonder what you've got to be so angry about."

"Nothing. I'm healthy, my family's healthy, we live OK. Honestly, I'm not."

"Is your marriage good?"

Now who's being direct? "It's fine." I look around the machine for living that is Cara's flat and the way she matches it so perfectly. "Why? Has Becky said anything to you?"

Cara shakes her head and I immediately regret mentioning Becky's name. I try to win her back with a confession. "It's not perfect, my marriage. My life feels really chaotic and I can't work out how to tidy it up. It's all loose ends. Or bloody chargers that I can't work out what they're there for. That's my life. Both in reality and metaphorically, if you know what I mean."

"Not really. It sounds ghastly."

Is she mocking me? "I know, I know, Joel's wonderful and I'm so lucky."

"He can't be if you feel dissatisfied." She's one of the few people I've ever heard question the wonder of Joel. I think I may cry. "He must be making you this way," she continues. "You weren't born this angry."

"Don't you believe it."

"You should be happy and if you're not, change your life. You're an intelligent, grown-up woman, take control. I never put up with things that make me less than satisfied."

"I do feel like I need to change it. Thank you. I feel like I've been going mad. But, you know, when you get to my age, to our age, it's not so easy. It's not like when you're younger and you can chuck the man, the woman, you're with or throw in your job and go around the world. Things aren't as easily changed. I mean, I wouldn't unwish my boys for the world. And really, I'm so lucky. Lots of women can't have children so I should be grateful to have them. And I am. That's part of the problem, I think—there are so many women so sad about not being able to have children that it feels churlish to complain. And I'm not, really." Cara shudders as she makes me another martini. It is maybe too late to tell her I think it's an unspeakable drink and I'd really rather a glass of wine, any color. "Do you want children?" I think of Becky and then unthink of her.

"Goodness, no."

"Have you always known? I mean that you didn't want children?"

"Yes. Absolutely. I never played with dolls and gave them those fake bottles of milk. When other girls were putting on towels and pretending they were brides, I was making perfect houses out of Legos. My future always involved me living alone."

But you don't, I thought. "Funnily enough, so did mine. I used to plan to live in a grand old country house with lots of cats and a lovingly tended garden. I don't think it really means anything."

"I knew, I always knew. And I was right, since I'm too old now."

"Really? You don't look it."

"Thank you." I must learn how to do that, to say thank you when someone compliments you, to accept it as your due. Cara is the embodiment of graciousness.

I take a second martini and down it as I did the first. My throat rasps. I'm longing for a snack, some Bombay mix, but that would be out of character for this environment. She might have some sashimi, though; that is the snack that Cara would have. None is forthcoming. The heels are making me sway slightly so I sit myself down on a silk-covered chaise longue. It's not made for sitting, more for lounging, so that is what I do.

"And did you always know?" I ask.

"What?"

"That you weren't going to get married?"

"That I was gay, you mean?"

I nod.

"Yes, always. As far back as it is possible to know. Even perhaps before then." How like her to miss out on the period of confusion and the awful shambolic sex with men that Becky suffered. Mind you, we all had awful shambolic sex with men, with or without the sexual confusion.

Two drinks and I feel dizzy. This is pathetic, it's only two drinks. Maybe they were spiked with something. Actually, I suppose the thing with a martini is that you can't spike it because nothing is stronger than what it is in the first place. Except Rohypnol. "And what do you do?"

"Sorry?" Again the rising eyebrow.

"What do you actually do, you know, in bed?" I'm really drunk now.

"You don't know what lesbian sex is?"

"Yes. No, I mean obviously I know what women do, in theory, but at the same time, I feel a bit like when I'm cooking a vegetarian meal and I can't think of anything to replace the meat. I know what you do, but then I'm not exactly sure of the way it goes in reality, when I really think about it."

"And do you think about it a lot?"

"No, no, never. Well not never. Not very often. Sometimes. How does it go? In what order? I'm from the country," I offer in explanation.

"What do I do? What do *we* do?" she ponders. "It depends."

"On what?"

"On who I'm with, what sort of mood I'm in, where I am. Whether I want a quick fuck." I blanch at the bald use of this word. It's one I'm happy to use in any other context, but not that one. In fact I blanch doubly, both at it being used to describe sex and then at it being used to describe non-penetrative sex. Although is it non-penetrative? Does she use, I don't know, some sort of strap-on thing? I really don't think of two girls fucking. And then I find that I can think of nothing else and cross my legs with the beginnings of sweet pain. Cara continues, "A quick fuck or something more languorous." She draws the word out onomatopoeically.

"Today, for instance," she continues, "I'm feeling slow, relaxed. Definitely it's a languorous sort of a day, isn't it? Today, I would keep clothes on for as long as possible. Draw out the anticipation. Keep it almost innocent. Almost, but not quite." She smiles to herself.

My mouth has gone very dry now, but I don't dare break the spell by getting myself some water. Cara looks as cool as ever, while I feel beads of sweat sieve through my skin.

"Today, if I were going to do something, I would start by running my finger along their neck." She demonstrates on herself. "Especially the clavicle. The clavicle is so underrated. Don't you think? I would run my finger down, but not very far, just to here." She stops in the space between her small breasts. "Then

I would trace their face and put my finger across their lips and then into their mouth." The finger in question has a perfect pale pink manicure and is long like a pianist's. "Then I would follow this path with my tongue so that they'd know what was coming, until I'd kissed them. But only gently, I'd only graze their lips—even though they'd try to pull me near, desperate, I'd draw myself away."

My mobile rings. It's Joel. I press the red button. "And then?" I rasp.

She gives me a sly look. "I think then I'd move onto the breasts, but with the veil of clothing. I'd feel them and stroke them but only through the clothes. The friction can be so delicious. Her nipples would harden beneath the fabric of her dress, they'd snap at my fingers. Then, just as before, I'd do everything that I did with my fingers, now with my tongue. This time without the fabric between us. Slowly I'd lick the top of her breasts and as I did so I'd undo"—she glances in my direction. I am wearing a shirt dress—"the buttons. At this point, the nipples would be almost able to move toward my tongue, they're so hungry to be touched." She runs her hand across her own, which I can see outlined beneath the thin material.

"Then, finally, I'd start very slowly moving down, letting them imagine, hope, where I am going, but then I'd stop." She stops speaking. I'm scared of the sound of my own breathing, in case it should sound like panting. "And skip over, straight to the thighs, leaving them weeping with frustration."

I shift in my seat, aware of a wetness developing. Random thoughts jostle. She calls them breasts, like a breastfeeding counselor. My own have had their own evolution, from being tits before children to boobs afterward. Boobs: jokey, unsexual, pillowy, unthreatening. I wonder what vocabulary she'll use when she finally gets there. Please let it be soon.

"Stroking, stroking, stroking. So lightly. Then," she pauses and then speaks louder and more quickly, "I'd stick my finger inside her cunt, hard."

I reel just as if she'd actually done it. So that's what she calls it. I think about mine. Joel doesn't care about vaginal topiary. He says he likes a woman natural. I used to wear bikinis and have bikini waxes. Now I wear the post-partum woman's bikini, the tankini, with low legs and I don't have anything waxed. Didn't Becky once tell me that Cara liked a woman to be kempt down there? I'm not. Mitzi is. Mitzi has her Hollywood. We know that.

"I'd thrust the finger in and out, twice. Then just as suddenly, I'd take it out and she'd be left wondering whether it really happened or whether she'd just imagined it, but she'd be left wanting it to happen again more than she's ever wanted anything."

I want it, I want these things. But I want to have a wax first and be moisturized all over and to be wearing expensive silk underwear. I don't match this. I'm not good enough. I want it but I want to escape. Please don't say anything else, I will explode. Please say something else, go on, please talk, please touch me, do those things. Cara stands up.

"Then, I'd take that very same finger and start stroking the tops of her thighs and then swirling around to below her navel, making damp circles that spiral in and in, closer and closer. Until, finally, I'd get there and start flickering in exactly the right place. I always find the right place. Just a little bit higher than anyone else and a little bit lighter. I'm better even than she is herself."

The phone goes again. It's Joel. I cut it off once more and am about to switch it off when it goes again immediately. "What?" I snap into it.

"It's Gabe. He's all hot."

"Has he got a temperature?"

"I can't find the thermometer."

"It's in the bathroom cupboard."

"I looked there, but I couldn't find the plasters or anything. Just the tape measure."

"The tape measure? Why don't you try looking for the thermometer where the tape measure goes, then?"

"Where's that?"

"In the cupboard above the washing machine. Call me back."

I look at Cara and see a look of disappointment. Not her own, but disappointment in me. Like I've let myself down. "Sorry about this. I'm sure we'll be able to sort it out. He's just going to phone back." We sit in silence. I feel myself desiccating inside and out. The phone goes.

"Did you find it? What is it?"

"Forty. What's that in the other one?"

"Double it and add 30. A hundred and ten. That can't be right. Change the button on it to Fahrenheit." Come on, come on. "A hundred and four? That's not good. Have you given him some Calpol?"

"I tried." His voice is rising in panic. "It wouldn't stay in. He's sort of listless."

"Does he have any rash or anything?" Please god say no.

"I don't know, not that I can see. Let me look. He's got a rash on his tummy."

"Do the glass thing," I say, trying to keep my voice calm. "You roll it over."

"Then what?"

"It disappears."

"The glass?"

"No, the rash. It's good if it disappears. I think. Oh shit, Joel. Look in one of the baby books. Or on the Net?"

"I tried. It didn't make sense."

"Have you rung NHS Direct? Use your instinct, do you think he's really ill?" There's silence. "Do you?"

"Yes."

I breathe in. I must stay calm. There is no point in not being calm. I must be, for Gabe's sake. "Call a taxi. Take Rufus to the neighbor's and then take the taxi to the ER. I'll see you there. Try to get some more Calpol down him. Take your phone with you. Get there as soon as you can."

I grab my bag and mutter something to Cara. I don't know what. I cannot even bear to look at her. It's my fault. Gabe has meningitis or septicemia or something and it's all my fault. I am a bad mother. I am being punished for drinking martinis and listening to a seductive woman talk sex to me. I am being punished for liking it so much.

"There you are." I run toward Joel and Gabe, who are sitting on a bed in the children's section of the Emergency unit.

"How is he?" Gabe is asleep across Joel's lap. I want to rip him away from Joel and hold him close to me. It's me that looks after the children when they're sick, it's me that they fall asleep on.

"He's asleep. He shouldn't be asleep, should he?" Joel's voice is cracking and his eyes are filled with tears. I want to be able to cry, but I can't and I envy him his ability to weep.

"It's eight o'clock, he'd normally be asleep. Has a doctor seen him? Have they seen his rash? Where is everyone?"

"A nurse did triage on him and said she'd get someone."

At that moment a young woman walks in. She has that natural, glossy-hair-scraped-back-into-a-ponytail look of a beautiful actress playing a doctor in a busy ER, which makes her a completely implausible real doctor in a real ER.

"I'm Dr. Harcourt, the pediatrician. This must be Gabriel."

"Have you seen his rash? He's got a rash," I say. "Did you tell them about the rash?" I ask Joel.

He gapes wordlessly.

Dr. Harcourt takes my sleeping boy's temperature and then looks at his rash.

"Is it meningitis?"

"Possible but not probable," she says and I feel patronized. "We need to rule it out, though, so we'll take a lumbar puncture and do some blood tests."

"Lumbar puncture?" I feel sick.

"It's not as bad as it sounds. I'll be back shortly."

"Was that good or bad?" asks Joel.

"I don't know. Possibly good. Probably good."

"Ursula says that meningitis is the most common falsely self-diagnosed illness that hospitals see."

"What does that mean? Why were you talking to Ursula about it?"

"I rang her."

"Why the hell did you ring her?"

"When I couldn't get hold of you. Where were you, anyway?"

"Out."

"Not answering your phone."

"So this is my fault, is it?"

"No."

"You could have brought him here sooner."

"So it's my fault, is it?"

"I didn't say that. But you could have taken his temperature."

"Not if I couldn't find the thermometer."

"This is why I'm always telling you to put things back where you found them. So we can find them again later."

"And you always put things back, do you?"

"Mostly, yes."

We sit in silence with poor Gabriel still lying floppily across Joel's lap. His lashes flutter against his cheeks. He must be OK. Of course he'll be OK. Things always are. He moans slightly.

"He kept on saying his head hurt. He wanted it to be dark," Joel says.

Finally we are ushered into a room where Gabriel wakes up and seems embarrassingly perky, though his mood is soon spoiled by the lumbar puncture and the blood tests. As I hold his arm tightly to be leeched by the needles, I am reminded of the last time I clasped him this hard and feel another geyser of shame. When the needle goes in, his beautiful eyes water with hurt, the look that silently says "How could you do this to me?" while his full lips make a moue. His body is spatchcocked across an examination table as they prod the now almost disappeared rash and shine torches into his eyes. The scream is no longer silent, it's echoing around the wards. It's all my fault, I think again, it's all my fault.

Eventually the doctor says that oft-repeated medical phrase: "It's just a virus," followed by that other mantra: "Give him lots of fluids, Calpol every four hours and keep an eye on him for any behavior that's out of the ordinary."

"It's definitely not meningitis?" I ask.

"As far as we can tell. It would seem highly unlikely," Dr. Harcourt says.

"But don't you think you should keep him here overnight? For observation?"

"I really think you'd all be better off at home than in a hospital. You live nearby and can come back if you see anything to worry about."

"But what about all those stories in the newspapers? The ones where the parents go to the doctor and the doctor says it's just a cold and they keep coming back and then it turns out to be meningitis all along."

"My wife is obsessed with those stories," adds Joel. I really hate him now.

"Like I say," says the doctor, who has let down her hair now, to full flicky effect, "you must come in if you have any concerns, but we are as certain as it is possible to be that Gabriel has a virus that will right itself."

"Thank you," says Joel.

"Yes," I repeat, dazed. "Thank you."

Gabriel is settled in our bed and we're sitting in the kitchen. My head hurts and I feel like I have a premature hangover. I'm desperately tired yet feel like I've been mainlining espressos and will never be able to sleep again. I look at my phone. There are no messages. I think about Cara and then I feel ashamed that my thoughts can drift in her direction after what has happened. I know I shall never hear from her again. I have disappointed her.

"He's fine, Maz. We'd both better get some sleep."

I shake my head. "We need to check him every few hours."

"OK, we'll check him. I'll set the alarm if you're worried."

"Of course I'm worried. We had a son who went floppy with suspected meningitis this evening."

"But he's fine. You heard the doctor. I don't know why you can't let it go."

I'm about to make some smart answer to this, but the words don't come out. Instead I hear an unfamiliar sound and my eyes begin to itch. I begin to cry, to sob like I haven't for as long as I can remember. Great wracking, snot-inducing sobs. I want to say something to counteract these tears, but I can't speak. I don't cry, I scream inside, I am not a crier. But clearly I am, I am crying and I am not speaking. This is not me.

The tears continue. I don't know where all the water comes from. How can I have been wet with my own bodily fluids twice in one day in such different ways? Joel looks momentarily shocked and then stands up and puts his arms around me. They are so enveloping. I feel as small and helpless as Gabe looked when he lay with his head in Joel's lap at the hospital.

It is as if all the tears unshed from the last 20 years have finally found an outlet. I'm an over-filled water butt, a flooded river, a tube of yogurt squeezed by Rufus. I am so tired, I have six years of cumulative tiredness catching up with me and I shall never feel rested again. This makes me cry some more. Joel holds me, then leads me upstairs and lies me down next to my son, where we will both sleep fitfully until morning.

The List isn't updated that night. Funny that in all my list-making, I didn't write a debit one for me that included the transgression: *Contemplated hot sex with a cool brunette.*

File   Edit   View   Insert   Format   Tools   Window

	A	B
1	June allowance	2 per day, total 60
2	Total no. of debits in June	89
3	Breakdown of infringements	14 kitchen; 15 bathroom; 11 laundry; 4 bedroom; 14 living; 15 invisible woman; 12 parenting; 4 general ineptitude.
4	Infringement of the month	Bath. Bedtime. Never there.
5	Joel's positives/my negatives to offset	Martini-meningitis night. 20 points to Joel.
6	June debt	9 (89 offset by June allowance of 60 and 20 positives)
7	Total debt from February, March, April, May and June	83
8	Total remaining	17 over next month (100 minus 83)

9

Ruskin's Wedding Night

I'm lying across the sofa with my laptop, totting up transgressions. A hundred was the grand total that I allowed Joel for six months, over and above the two daily debits he is allotted. He would be over the limit already were it not for the 20 positives I gave him in compensation for what happened or nearly happened that night. In some way, then, you could say that my near-miss with Cara or Gabriel's near miss with a fatal illness saved our marriage.

Though both did not so much save our marriage as offer it some reprieve. There is still a month to go and not much allowance left. He is tottering toward the limit. Sometimes this makes me feel sad and frightened. At other times, I am filled with a giddy sense that something, at last, will change. Something has to change.

I'm just relieved that the something didn't involve a child with a life-threatening infection or me indulging in a bout of Sapphic eroticism with my best friend's girlfriend. And I know that whatever other calamities might befall us, Cara will never call me again.

"You look nice," says Joel as he comes into the living room. I look down at my old jeans and stained T-shirt with surprise. "You do natural so well," he goes on. Is "natural" a euphemism for unkempt, I wonder, like curvy being one for fat? "Would you like a foot massage?" he continues.

"Thanks. What's this in aid of?"

"Nothing. Can't I give my wife a foot massage?"

"Of course you can. Hmm, that is nice." The laptop is propped up on my stomach and I take care to shield it from him.

"I picked up some scallops at the fishmonger near work. I thought I'd pan fry them with some bacon for supper tonight."

"Delicious. Why do they talk about pan frying? What else can you fry a scallop in?"

I look down at my lap and refer to the positives section of The List, find the code for compliments, foot massages and fine cooking, and add P1, P3 and P8 to today's date. For the first time ever, Joel is heading for a day when his positives outweigh his negatives, a debit-neutral day. It's like he's just taken a flight but planted a whole rainforest. I switch the laptop off, enjoy the massage and look forward to my shellfish supper.

"Let's sit outside," says Becky. "I'm smoking."

"You are looking pretty hot," I say.

"Ha ha, very funny, but I look like shit." She does. Becky's looks walk such a fine line between handsome and odd that it takes only a throat infection or unwashed hair for her to cross over to the dark side.

"Since when are you smoking again? You weren't smoking in Norfolk, were you?"

"No."

"Was it being in Newcastle that made you start again? Was it very stressful?"

"No, it's coming back that's got me reaching for the smokes. How long is it since we've seen each other?"

"Over a month. No, longer, Norfolk was the end of May bank holiday."

"Whatever happened to our regular Monday lunch?" she asks.

"You're the one who's been working away. I'm always here."

"Well, I'm back now."

"Yes, you're back at home. And smoking."

"God, don't. You sound like Cara. She can't bear me smoking. Well, I think it's the smoking she can't bear, actually maybe it's just that she can't bear me full stop."

"What do you want to eat? I'll go and get it. You wait here, no problem. I'm sure I owe you."

"Surprise me."

I surprise her with something called a "Superfoods Salad." I feel she might need an injection of her five-a-day, as well as a glass of wheatgrass juice.

"I suppose I can make up for it with coffee and a cake afterward," she says, looking skeptically at the bean sprouts.

"Is work still very stressful?" I ask.

"Not particularly."

"Everybody's feeling a bit low at the moment. There's lots of summer colds going around, aren't there? I've been feeling fluey for weeks now."

"I'm not ill."

"We haven't had a debrief on Norfolk yet. That seems like ages ago." I am tempted to tell her about what Joel and I stumbled across that night. In my head I start with us creeping downstairs, but then when I try to think how I might describe what we saw, I realize that some peccadilloes go beyond even gossip.

"It was all right."

"What did you think of Mitzi's house? Amazing place, isn't it? She's got exquisite taste."

"That's what Cara says."

"Does she? Yes, I suppose we can all agree that Mitzi's got exquisite taste."

"I think it's stupid. Her house is stupid and pretentious and vaguely immoral."

"Immoral?" I ask.

"To pretend that having a second home is some great eco-logical gift to the planet when it can never be anything but quite the opposite."

"And that's what Joel says."

"Maybe we should wife swap."

I giggle nervously.

She lights a cigarette, right when she should be tucking into the avocado, and sighs. "But I think that may have already happened."

"What do you mean?" I keep my voice airy.

"I think Cara's seeing someone else."

"What makes you think that?"

"She's been so absent. She doesn't seem to even notice that I've come back. We've stopped having sex. I thought me being away during the week would perk up our sex life at weekends at least. At first I thought it was just standard lesbian bed death, but I don't think so now. She seems more alive than she's been for months. She's like she was with me, in the beginning. She is so having sex, just not with me."

"Aren't you jumping to conclusions?"

"I spend my working life telling people not to jump to conclusions."

"Exactly."

"But just because the conclusion is jumped to, doesn't mean it's not right."

"Do you want the rest of your salad," I ask, "or shall I go and get that coffee and cake for you? I think carrot cake counts toward your five-a-day."

She scratches her head vigorously.

"You all right?" I ask.

"My head's itchy. I think it's like some sort of nervous tic or something. I think maybe it's a physical manifestation of all my indecision about everything in my life at the moment."

"Becks, I'm so sorry." I scratch my head in sympathy. I hope I haven't got nits.

"About what?"

"That you're having such a rubbish time at the moment. But don't let your feelings about other things force you into making assumptions about Cara. You'll probably find out that she hasn't actually done anything. Maybe she's just thought about it."

"That's just as bad."

"Is it?"

"Perhaps not. But I tell you, she doesn't get the sexed-up glow just thinking about it."

"Have you asked her?"

"I know, I know, I should just talk to her. Ask her directly what she's doing. But I'm too scared to."

I say nothing. I feel like my Superfoods Salad is going to come back up.

"She's married," says Becky.

"Cara?"

"No, the bitch who's shagging her."

"How do you know?"

"That's the way Cara likes them. Straight, I'd guess, certainly bi-curious, heteroflexible, whatever. God, the number of straight women with girl crushes on her, it's ridiculous. There's a lot of them about and they all fancy a pop at my girlfriend. And she fancies a pop at them. Especially if they're married. A more exciting challenge. Less likely to want to move in with her and mess up her precious flat. I'm the exception and Cara regrets that. She needs to live alone."

"Some people do, they just know they want to be alone. From when they're little."

"That's what Cara says. That she's always known. Well, she doesn't have to live with me anymore. I'm leaving."

"Don't be hasty."

"I'm not. Even if she's not fucking some other man's wife, I don't want to carry on feeling like I'm a stain on the polished limestone floor anymore. I've worked so hard to get to where I am and I feel like I'm falling backward every day."

"Will you go back to your flat?"

"Sold it."

"I never knew that. I thought you were keeping it. As insurance."

"I thought you'd tell me to be sensible and keep it. That's what I'd have told anybody else to do. It was an act of faith to sell it, like my clients who refuse to get a pre-nup. Idiots," she snorts. "I've got some plans. In my head." She smiles and her looks are transformed back to handsome once again. "I hadn't said it out loud. I hadn't dared. But you know what? It doesn't make me feel so bad to be talking about leaving her. I can't feel any worse than I've been feeling."

"Oh, Becks, I feel so awful. I had no idea. I'm so sorry, I really am sorry. I've been so wrapped up in myself that I've been a terrible friend. A really terrible friend." I think I may cry again. It's like now that my eyes have learned how to cry, they're never going to stop. I feel like I'm standing at the end of a very tall diving board. All I've got to do is leave the board. It's that split second of jumping that counts, not the entry into the water. If I say anything, I will say everything. I take a deep breath and then I jump. "I had a drink at Cara's, at your place. Did she tell you?"

Becky is rummaging around in her bag and pulls out her mobile. "Look at this."

I look at it. "It's a text message. From Cara."

"To Cara. I found it on her mobile and forwarded it to mine. Open it."

"Wasn't there a name attached to the number?"

"It said Plumber. It's not really the plumber, that was just a pseudonym, I'm guessing. Unless she's sleeping with the plumber, which is unlikely since he's a fat Ukrainian."

"And you didn't recognize the number?"

She shakes her head. "I should have written it down but I thought it would come through when I forwarded the message to my number. Stupid mobile. I managed to take a look at Cara's mobile the next day, but the message had disappeared. Been deleted. Read it."

Your smell is on my fingers.

"Yuk," I say. Becky looks at me skeptically. "No, it's not the girl smell thing. I love the girl smell thing. Well, not literally. I don't know, other people's dirty texts are probably always a bit embarrassing."

"They also sent a photo."

"What of?"

"A very depilated muff." So that's what Becky calls it. "So much so, it was quite hard to tell what it was. I thought it was an ear. Not my scene, you see. Though Cara is, obviously, very well tended in that area."

"Do you know when they were sent?"

"Two or three weeks ago."

I feel a flash of jealousy. I look at Becky and I hate myself for feeling that. I feel ashamed once more that I could have ever even entertained the idea of doing anything with Cara. And I feel gladder than ever that nothing happened, though this may be as much to do with finding out that I am not the only object of Cara's advances as it is to do with not betraying both my husband and my best friend. I almost jeopardize my family with some hot sex with a woman and it turns out that she's indiscriminate in her approaches. Becky clicks her phone and shows me a photo on it displaying an image more gynecological than pornographic, all smooth and toned and hairless. It's unthreatening and clean, except for a neat scar at the point where the top of the pubic hair would be were there any. "Wow." I turn the camera upside down. It's difficult to tell which way around it's supposed to go. "That really is bald." I suspect that maybe Cara would have recoiled at the sight of my nakedness in the same way that Ruskin supposedly did at his poor pubic-haired wife on his wedding night.

"And you think something's still going on?" I ask.

"It's a bit irrelevant, isn't it? Something has happened and it will happen again. It wouldn't even surprise me if there was more than one person. She's vampiric like that."

"But you don't want to throw all you've got away without at least trying to talk to her."

"I'm not going to take lectures on relationships from you of all people."

"What's that supposed to mean?"

"You've talked about leaving Joel because he leaves the toilet seat up."

"No, that's not true. I don't even mind about the toilet seat particularly. Well, not about it being up. The splatter that goes on is quite annoying, yes."

"Mary." Becky looks at me sharply. "My relationship is rubbish and that's why I'm breaking it now. You've got something worth saving, not to mention two children. You know that, don't you?"

I smile in reassurance.

"I don't know about you," she goes on. "Whether you really

mean your stupid talk about your marriage, or whether it's some sad bid for attention, like a teenager taking a dozen paracetamol."

"I don't think you can ever really understand what goes on in somebody else's relationship."

"True," she says. "Too true."

I return to the office sure that I am flushed with shame, wearing a scarlet letter for my adulterous thoughts. I may not actually be Cara's other woman, but I had wanted to be. I have a vision of Joel, Becky and the boys sitting around the kitchen table, intoning, "How could you?" How indeed.

Matt is leaning across Lily's desk in a way that means his crotch is resting on it. If he were a woman, he'd be permanently wearing a push-up bra.

"So, right, weirdly," he says to her, "after hearing nothing about the dirty house format for months, we finally heard back from the commissioner."

"And?" asks Lily.

"He didn't much like it. But Jane at Documentaries saw it and she loved it."

"Really?"

"No, not really. She thinks there is something there, but that the reality-show house thing is a bit dumbed-down. Says the channel is trying to smart-up now, wants to make serious programs again and words I never thought I'd get to hear. She went on and on about how they'd like us to rework it as a serious examination of relations between men and women in the twenty-first century, who does what, two-part doc, psychologists, yadda, yadda, yadda."

"That's what I said in the first place," I say.

"Was it?" asks Matt.

"Yes. It was my idea, remember?"

He looks blank. "It was," says Lily. "Definitely. She knows all about that domestic shit. Wrote the introduction to the pitch document."

"That was the bit that caught Jane's eye," says Matt.

"Really?" I feel a buzz I haven't felt at work in years.

"Yeah, she said it didn't seem to match the tone of the rest of the pitch and to use it as a starting point for an alternative look. I was going to get you to do that, Lily."

"To be honest, I think Mary would do a better job of it."

"Thanks, Lily." My introduction was the best bit of the pitch document. Yes!

"Do you want to develop it, then?"

"Yes, of course."

"But you'll have to do it on your day off. I can't spare you the rest of the time."

"Fine. I'll do it. I'll manage."

I frown at my laptop. In all the chaos of my real world, I am reliant on looking to my virtual one for order. The List provides me with a rational framework to overlay upon the anarchy. Have you ever seen those drawings for children that make no sense until you put a transparency on top of them and then the picture becomes clear? That's what The List does to my life. It gives it some meaning. That tea bag leaving a tannin stain on our worktop is no longer just a tea bag, it's a point in a narrative that has an unstoppable momentum toward a goal. The wet towel left to fester in the bathroom becomes a neat number on an Excel spreadsheet, something rational instead of nonsensical.

But it isn't any longer. The List has stopped making sense. Joel's tally, which was so near to its completion, now races up and down in a pattern that no longer matches the months of yore. It used to be so predictable. There was a pattern to the rubbishness of Joel. If The List doesn't make sense then nothing does. I have nothing left, and eventually my mind will become the same as the disordered jumble of our house. It's as if The List is a robot with a malfunction that causes it to repeat tasks or walk around in circles. This is not the way of The List.

Yesterday, for example, Joel took off his clothes before bed and threw them one by one, slowly, in the general direction of the laundry basket. Just as I was about to clock this misdemeanor, he went over to it and put them all in. Then he took them all out and repeated the whole process. And again.

Perhaps it's just as well that we have less than a month to go. I shall miss you when you've gone. The List, I mean.

It's what Joel always irritatingly calls my "day off," which he views as an open receptacle for filling with irritating chores along the lines of "Can you pick up my dry cleaning... on your day off?" and "You can always take the car for its MOT... on your day off." I try to convey just how hard I work on my "day off," usually by ringing him up when Gabe's having one of his tantrums and just holding the phone out.

What I never do is phone Joel when I'm lounging around a beautifully tended garden while my older child is in school and my younger is being looked after by Mitzi's nanny. I wouldn't want him to get the wrong idea.

"This is heavenly," I say to Mitzi. I had meant not to see her for a while, but then she rings up and asks me over and her house has the best toys, an enormous paddling pool and a sprinkler system. It is more enticing than the alternative, a trip to the supermarket.

"I feel like the garden's coming together at last. It's been such a nightmare trying to get a gardener who knows his arse from his elbow. Or his Alchemilla from his Echinacea, so to speak."

"You could have a garden filled with Astroturf for all it matters to me. It's having Gabe taken care of by your very capable nanny that's the real treat." I look over to see one of the twins crying and Gabe standing worryingly nearby. I choose to ignore the scene and instead look over to Mitzi. It's remarkable how quickly you can get back to normal with someone who you've witnessed indulging in revolting marital peccadilloes.

"I do need to do some more pruning, though."

I suppress a giggle. Well, *almost* back to normal.

"Thanks again for Norfolk."

"It was fabulous, wasn't it? We all had such a lovely time, didn't we? I feel like you got to know Michael a bit better, too."

"Yes, I feel like I've seen a lot more of Michael now."

"He is unbelievable, isn't he?"

"Yes. Unbelievable."

"People are always amazed when they meet him because I think they're expecting some sort of gone-to-seed banker type and there he is, so absurdly handsome."

"Yes, he is very handsome. In an older man sort of way."

Mitzi laughs. "He's not that old."

"He seems it. Not in a bad way, but in an authoritative way. I wouldn't want to mess with him."

"No, you really don't want to mess with him. I think anyone he works with could tell you that. And how all the secretaries are all over him. I know that. I'm very lucky to have him. I'm really very lucky."

"Yes, you've done well for yourself."

I can't read her eyes behind the designer sunglasses. I could swear she is looking for reassurance.

Mitzi's mobile bleeps with a message. She picks it up and smiles. She opens the message and smiles even more. She sees me looking at her and blushes beneath her light tan.

"Who's the message from?"

"No one." She cannot suppress that smile. "A friend."

"A very funny one, judging by your smirk."

"I wouldn't say funny. No, funny's not their thing, not at all." She's still staring at the message. She uncrosses then crosses her legs. She puts down the phone and it reverts to its screensaver of all four of her children hugging and smiling. I can't even get my measly two to smile at the same time.

"Damn it," she says, scratching her head. "Radka," she calls to the nanny. "Have you been nit-combing the children every day like I asked you to?" She turns to me. "Bloody nits, it's disgusting, I just can't seem to get them out of the kids' hair. I suppose I should just shave their heads and be done with it, but they do all have such incredible hair, don't they? I envy these parents whose kids have normal hair, but my children just have so much hair, it's so thick, there's so much of it. It takes Radka an age to get through them all. Honest to god, I don't know why we're paying all this money out to that school for them to still come home with bloody nits."

"I'm sorry, do you think they got them from mine?"

"Quite possibly. They've had them off and on for months."

"Mine only got them after Norfolk, so it sounds more likely it was the other way around," I say in defense. "And they don't have them anymore. I got rid of them really quickly." I glance over at Gabriel, whose head is bent toward Merle's.

"It must be so much easier when your children have thin hair."

"They've both got quite a lot, actually."

"Of nits? Isn't it horrendous? It makes my head itch to even think about it."

"Do you think you've got them?" I ask, scratching my head in sympathy.

"Of course not! I'm sure I haven't. Only children get them, like chicken pox."

"I think the reason children get them is because they're always in such close proximity to one another, which adults generally aren't. If they come into your bed they could give them to you and I guess you could give them to Michael."

"You don't think I could have them, do you? I won't be able to go to the hairdresser. Could you have a look for me? Oh, don't actually, it's too disgusting."

"You could ask Michael to take a look."

"God, no, I'd never ask Michael. How humiliating."

But parading around in a crotchless French maid's outfit and picking up his shit is empowering? I nod, while thinking about how happily I could ask Joel to nit check my hair. In fact, I have done, on more than one occasion. "You could probably check it yourself—they go for the back of the neck, but also the bit at the front." I gesture around my hairline, while squinting at hers.

"You do know a lot about it."

I shrug.

"Excuse me," she says and disappears to what estate agents call the "guest cloakroom."

Gabe is pulling the petals off roses. I'm about to warn him about thorns when I change my mind. It will serve him right. Mitzi has left her phone on the ground; I can reach it without getting off my seat. I look over at Radka, who has now taken the three children off to the trampoline hidden by a parterre at the bottom of the garden. I look back toward the house and then down at the phone again. If I'm quick.

It's a new-fangled one with a thousand applications. Text, text, text? I look back toward the house again. Why is it so complicated? Text, here, inbox, last message, from "Gardener." Gardener? I open it up. "3 it is. Have lube, vib, fist. Now u."

Are these horticultural references? I put the phone back where I found it. She did say it was hard to find a good gardener these days.

"Find anything?" I ask Mitzi. "In your hair?"

"I wasn't really looking. Did I tell you I've got to be somewhere at three?"

"No, you didn't."

"Sorry. I can't really get out of it."

"No problem. I've got to pick up Rufus anyway. Anywhere nice?"

"No, boring, dental work. Harley Street."

No it's not, I'm thinking. Is she having an affair with her gardener? What next, the plumber?

The plumber. Of course, the plumber. I look at Mitzi and cannot help but let out a little gasp of realization. The plumber and the gardener. Mitzi and Cara. It's so obvious. Of course, it's Mitzi and Cara. The lesbian who can't resist married women and the married woman who can't resist a novelty. Mitzi would never be so unoriginal as to have an affair with a man. There would be no point to that. She needs the opposite of a man, the opposite of Michael and all his alpha maleness. She wanted an anti-man—in the same way, I suppose, that I did, for very different reasons.

It's so obvious that I feel like hitting my forehead and shouting "Doh!" The walk, in Norfolk, Mitzi went instead of me. Cara was courting us both. She was probably even playing us off against each other. The nits. Becky's head-scratching. It wasn't a psychological tic, she really does have an itchy head. Mitzi bloody does have nits and she's given them to Cara who's given them to poor guiltless Becky, like some sort of pre-school version of syphilis in an Ibsen play. And that picture of the hairless vagina, that scar was from a cesarean. Mitzi had to have one because one of the twins was in a transverse lie (after breezing through her previous births saying they didn't hurt a bit because of all the yoga she'd done). Only someone as unself-consciously vain as Mitzi would ever take a photo of her vagina and send it on to her lover. Everyone else would assume theirs was too ugly, like their knees or feet. Cara is pleasuring Mitzi and vice versa. I feel a pang of envy at this point and a small twinge. A sadness that it will never happen, followed by relief at avoiding the scary prospect of fisting, a practice I've not given too much thought to, but which does make me instinctively cross my legs. I can only presume that it is not something for a first date and that Becky was right, this has been going on for a while. I wonder whether it happened on the marshes of Norfolk, when Mitzi was there instead of me. Is that when it started, before my martini night with Cara, or was it later, after I had disappointed her? Who was Cara's first choice? Did they walk out in the early Norfolk morning and lie down amid the long seagrass, hidden from dog walkers and the children making first expeditions to the beach? Who made the first move? Did they only kiss or did the taste of Mitzi mingle with the saltiness of the air? Was that grass scratchy? Would it all have been different if I hadn't overslept that morning?

"So I'd better go and get myself ready in about ten minutes," Mitzi says.

"For the dentist?"

"You know how it is, you feel you'd better give yourself an extra-vigilant floss when you see the dentist."

"Yes, a floss," I nod. She looks so happy that her skin is glowing as if she's just come back from a long walk in the country. She looks like she used to look, when we first met. I thought it was age and the gym that had hardened her face, but it was Michael.

"Mitzi?"

"Yes."

"Completely and utterly hypothetically, would you ever leave Michael?"

"No, of course not. What do you mean?"

"I mean, if he wanted you to do something horrible or if he treated you badly in some way, would you leave him? I mean, I know he wouldn't, he's great, obviously, but are you one of these people who would stay with their husband, whatever?"

"I would always stay."

"Whatever?"

"I don't know what the whatever you might be thinking of is, but yes. Infidelity I could cope with, I'm sure we'd manage with less money, we understand one another. I really can't imagine anything that would make me think it was worth upsetting my children's lives over. You know about my childhood, don't you, about my mother? Why would I ever contemplate bringing even a small fraction of that sort of instability into this..." she gestures toward the house and the garden "...into this life I've worked so hard to create?"

"Of course." She is the stylist, her children the props and her life is a six-page spread in a glossy magazine. How could she bear to let it be seen to be anything less than perfect?

"I'd better get going with my flossing." She smiles, displaying her already perfect teeth.

"Yes, you'd better. Gabe, five minutes, then we're going. Good luck at the dentist's. Hope it's not too painful," I say, "at the dentist's."

The List has become so complicated with plus and minus points that I am finding I need to update it at least every night. I am just delving into the "general ineptitude" section to cross-reference the right numbers on my spreadsheet.

	I
8	Doesn't open his mail.
9	Eventually opens his mail, but acts as if merely opening it counts as having dealt with it.
10	After a month, takes the mail out of the envelope and leaves the empty envelope lying around for me to put in the bin.
11	Points out that actually envelopes should go into the recycling rather than landfill bin.
12	But only if I make sure that I remove the little clear plastic address window first.

These are all interconnected with various points in the "finance" section, related as they are to his inability to do his expenses and his lack of comprehension that if he pays out money in the course of his work, if he gets it back it is not "free money" that he doesn't really have a right to receive. As I'm doing so, I notice I115.

Doesn't put cordless phone back on its cradle.

I don't remember adding that one. It's a crime that Joel's always accusing me of—unfairly, since I barely ever use our landline.

The clutter has finally reached the biannual point at which I start screaming that I can't stand it, you hear me? I can't stand it any longer, I'm going mad, mad I tell you, and Joel takes the boys out on an expensive and sugar-fueled trip to a tourist attraction in order that I have a mammoth session of identifying toy parts and clearing out cupboards. When he bumps into anyone we know on these trips, he'll always tell them that he's doing it "to give Mary a break" or to "let Mary do her thing" and they sigh with admiration at him.

I look forward to these cleansing Sundays, though am left

disappointed by the fact that I never achieve all that I had hoped and my life is not left magically improved by a temporarily ordered toy cupboard.

My menfolk venture forth into the outside world armed with nothing but a pair of juice cartons and a bag of dried apricots, while I survey the home front. It takes at least half an hour of my precious declutter Sunday to tidy up after breakfast, followed by a guilty fifteen minutes reading the paper. I can then put it off no longer and, rejecting the temptation to start off with something easy and entirely selfish like my wardrobe, head for the area behind the television. Or to give it its correct title, the Area Behind the Television, to convey the full screaming-strings-from-*Psycho* horror of the most neglected and terrifying trouble spot in our home.

There are stacks of CD cases and an equally large one of loose CDs. I begin to try to match these two piles, but there seems to be no correlation between them so I give up and throw them all into a plastic box which will go to the purgatory of our attic. I then start on the books, becoming absorbed in a radio program as I try to put them back into their alphabetized homes. Unfortunately the pile includes ones by Amis, Ballard and Cartwright, which means that all the McEwans, Rushdies and Tylers have to be correspondingly shifted along to create spare acres of shelf in the earlier parts of the alphabet.

I move onto the box sets of DVDs, most of which we've only ever got halfway through after gorging night after night on the early episodes of whatever quality American import we're currently watching in order to pretend that we still have some grip on popular culture. I stand up to stretch my back and contemplate making myself a cup of tea, but then realize that I'll never get back to the hellhole of forgotten possessions if I allow such distractions. I purse my mouth in determination at my next and most horrific task: the video cassettes. Technology is conspiring against me to create endless graveyards of discarded plastic. I make a pile of the dozen or so cassettes and grapple with the red and blue cables behind the television to reconnect our old video player. I feel a small pang of nostalgia as I remember the excitement that my family felt when we bought our first video recorder, one using the Betamax format.

If I can get the video to work, I can play these old three-hour cassettes. And if I can do that, I can put them into two piles. One will be for cassettes with contents worth saving, which I'll take into work to be transferred onto DVD. The second pile is for the black bin liner, to be discarded like a dumpy first wife. And if I do that I can get rid of the video recorder, which means there will be two fewer cables. Two fewer cables until we give in and buy some sort of games console for the boys.

Bingo, it works. The first cassette has a few old episodes of once loved and now fuzzy with age television programs. The second is, marvelously, our wedding video, shot by a mutual friend we used to work with, a constant presence in our lives for a period of two years but now as obsolete as a VHS tape, seeing as how he still gets drunk, takes drugs and has one-night stands. I wonder what has become of him. It's not so much the director's cut as the director's half cut, since the footage mostly consists of some zoom-ins to pretty female guests' cleavages and some wobbly ones of our speeches.

The next three go into the bin bag. There's one marked "Bob Dylan." I'm about to throw it straightaway when I think I'd better check, just in case. I hate Bob Dylan. All the whining. I realized early on in my dating career that it's best to keep one's dislike of Bob Dylan and his fellow moaners (I'm talking about you, Leonard Cohen) quiet. There's a certain sort of man of a certain sort of age who feels personally wounded if you say you just don't get the point of Bob Dylan.

The screen is fuzzy, then a handwritten board appears, reading "Mary Homesick Blues." I watch on to see Joel standing at the side of the black-and-white screen, holding a pile of placards. He's thinner than he is now and I recognize the sweater he's wearing as one that has long since disintegrated to the point where it bypassed even the charity shop. As the music plays, he begins to throw down these placards one by one, in homage to that famous Dylan video. They are all handwritten in curly marker pen and Joel discards each one with the same mock disdain that Bob displays in the original, but there's no hiding a nervousness in his face. I read the placards that he holds aloft in sequence.

"Mary" says the first.

"I'm happy" says the second.

"With you."

"And very unhappy"

"Without you."

"You're too funny and clever"

"For me."

"But even so"

"Will you"

"Marry me?"

I bring my hands up to my mouth, which is smiling, and I feel my eyes well up. I feel a little fraction of what I would have felt if Joel had played me this video, or let me find this video, back when we weren't married. All that resentment I felt at him never asking and the shambolic way we got engaged could have been avoided. This was the Proposal Story that I had longed for, that would have been in keeping with our courtship. Bless him, I think; though I am not religious, I want to touch his forehead with balm. Watching this video awakens in me a surge of the tenderness I used to feel toward him every moment of every day, that mixture of wanting to hug him like a child and to have him screw me hard against a kitchen unit. We were so young and he was so handsome. He is still—paused on the screen—and I yearn to rewind our life and stop it right there. Our world felt like a perpetual Friday afternoon of anticipation and excitement, instead of today's permanent Sunday evening. I ring his mobile.

"I'm just tidying up behind the television."

"Not behind the television."

"And I just found your Bob Dylan video."

"Uh-huh."

"You know, with the proposal." I want to have some of the moment that we would have had back then and to have it now.

"Right. Gabe, stay near me. It's Mommy on the phone. Do you want to speak to her? Don't, then."

"When did you make it?"

"I don't know. About six months before we decided to get married."

"How were you going to show it to me? Were you even going to show it to me? It's lovely."

"I don't know. Yes, actually. I had it all planned. I was going to pretend it was a tape that had one of your favorite programs on it, then put it on and wait for you to get all sweary and annoyed that it wasn't, and see your face when you realized what it was."

How happy I would have been. Three sorts of happiness—some just for me, a bit more for Joel and I to toss back and forth between us like a bean bag and then an extra dollop to broadcast to my friends and family. "Why didn't you? I mean, why go to all the trouble of making it if you didn't ever show it to me?"

There's an almost audible shrug at the other end of the phone. "I don't know."

"You must do. Why didn't you?"

"You were just always going on about how marriage was stupid and an institution that you didn't want to be a part of, so I suppose I was scared you'd say no. Between you and Ursula I was getting the message. And then you asked and so you saved me the bother."

"But it's so amazing. I wish you'd shown it to me." Did he show it to anyone else, I wonder? Sometimes I think that Joel's romantic gestures aren't necessarily for my benefit anyway. "Still, we got there in the end." As if our marriage is just a theme park in an unfamiliar part of the country which we've managed to locate after some tussles over the road map.

"I suppose. I'd better go now, the boys have gone AWOL."

I put down the phone, the balloon of renewed warmth deflated. Playing the video seemed to have revived feelings in me that were not to be reciprocated by him. He sounded pissed off. I don't know if it was at me for having played the video, or me for having denied him the chance to use it all those years ago. I'm not used to Joel being the stroppy one—he's the dependable one, the unchanging one, the loyal one. I'm the one with emotions and grievances and anger. I watch the video again and instead of feeling the love that I did five minutes ago, I feel sadness about a relationship where things could be different but never are.

There's nothing to do but get on. I shall have a clean and uncluttered house if nothing else. I finish going through the tapes and throw out the video recorder and its attendant cables. I decide then to do the blackspot of Joel's chest of drawers. Maybe I'm trying to eliminate him already in anticipation of The List's final damning conclusion. The top of the chest of drawers has the usual collection of coins, receipts and tissues. I check inside the first of his drawers to see if there are any more receipts and find a further two dozen in a jumble of paperwork, along with an envelope containing a few more. I close it again, then decide that I might as well tackle them for the sake of our bank balance if nothing else. Every receipt unclaimed for is the price of a school trip or more.

I dump the whole lot on the floor and begin to make some piles according to their dates. Anything older than three months goes into one big pile, which is too late for claiming. Joel will get a minus point on The List for every £10 of unclaimed expenses I find, wasteful idiot that he is.

I lose myself in the paperwork and the radio, finding solace in a task that can be completed, unlike the endless groundhog day of most domestic tasks, the washing and the wiping. May's pile comes to over £100, June is maybe more, April far less. As I whisk through the bits of paper I find myself thinking of those months. All time is now measured by The List, just as my babies' development used to be remembered in terms of what they could do on various holidays as our photo albums jump between beach and birthday shots.

There was that week in April when he had to go to sort out a floundering production up near Manchester. That week before half term back in May when he was out every night and I was left doing solo bath- and bedtime and trying to get everything washed before we went to Mitzi's house. The pile for June is getting larger and flicking through them provides an aide-mémoire to the last month, reminding me of all the times Joel was out and got back tipsy or even drunk. June was a very bad month.

I pull out another receipt. June the fourth was that particularly bad night, I think, when I lost it with the boys, Gabe smeared poo on the walls and I felt myself delight in holding their arms a little bit too tightly when I dragged them off to bed. Joel came back well after the boys had gone to sleep, all cheery and beery. Out with the whole crew was what he told me. I look at the receipt from that night, expecting to see the usual roster of beers for the boys and bottles of wine for the girls. Instead, I see four champagne cocktails and a meze selection with the name of a very chic boutique hotel emblazoned at the top, coming to a grand total of over £70. I try to think who he's working with at the moment and who would have ordered a champagne cocktail. It seems unlikely since, Joel excepted, they're all laddish types and would probably deride such a drink as "gay." I don't get out much with work anymore, but this is more like the sort of drinks that you would have to celebrate a commission, or if you were schmoozing a reluctant celebrity to take part in whatever lame reality format was currently under discussion. Again, I couldn't think what production that would have been in relation to.

I stare at it for a while, feeling sure that it's telling me something, if only I could interpret the oracle. I go to the laptop and see what I logged for that night. Not very much, as it turns out, though I remember I had intended to punish Joel for forcing me into punishing the boys. I stare at the computer screen for clues. He came in that night very cheerful, conciliatory even, expressing enthusiasm for the nit comb. Was there nothing List-worthy that he did on his return? He's usually good for at least an emptying out of the balled-up tissues and random receipts onto the chest of drawers, but here—nothing. Nothing. That's it, nothing. Nothing is my clue. He threw the receipt on top of his drawers and then he put this receipt away, into the envelope tucked in the drawer. He never, ever does that. Joel is nothing if not reliably unreliable. He didn't want me to see this receipt.

I look at the receipt again. This is not the receipt of some celebratory after-work drinks or even the schmoozing of a contact. This is the sort of receipt you'd be left with after a first date. I keep staring at The List, hoping it will offer me a further explanation. Something else leaps out at me.

Leaves the plasticky packets from disposable contact lenses lying around.

Joel doesn't wear contact lenses. I do.

There's another.

Buys extraneous Tupperware.

Joel has never bought a transparent plastic food-storage container in his life. I see another, one that proves beyond doubt what I realize I have been suspecting for weeks now.

Sighs in over-dramatic way when tidying up.

I hear a key at the door and then footsteps coming up the stairs. Gabe and Rufus leap into my arms and show me their purchases from the museum shop, where they spend the bulk of their time on these educational sorties. Joel sees me with The List open and I look at him.

"You found it, didn't you—you've read it?" I ask.

"And you've found my contributions to it. The next point I was going to add was going to be 'Makes self-righteous little lists of partner's misdemeanors without ever questioning own behavior.'"

"I can't believe you've been snooping through my computer. That's like reading someone's diary."

"Come off it, Mary, you didn't exactly make much of an effort to hide it. On some level, I think you wanted me to find it."

"Much like this," I say, waving the receipt from the fourth of June. He comes closer to peer at it and reddens.

"Oh," is all he can manage, and that short word tells me I had been right to suspect. "Where did you find that?"

"You didn't exactly make much of an effort to hide it," I parrot. "On some level, I think you wanted me to find it."

He shakes his head.

"We've got a lot to talk about," I say.

*　　*　　*

We make it through to the boys' bedtime with much ventriloquism.

"Gabe, what was the best thing about your day?" I ask.

"Yes," says Joel. "Gabe, was it the bus or the museum or the lunch that came in a cardboard box?"

"Did you eat much lunch, Gabe, because you're not eating much now?"

"Rufus, will you pass these plates to your mother? Good boy."

We silently clean up after them as they watch television.

"Gabe and Rufus, who do you want to do your bath? Mommy or Daddy?" I ask. "Why not Mommy, since you've been with Daddy all day."

"And I'd love to read you two your books," says Joel.

"Rufus, do make sure you actually do some reading yourself. Show your daddy how good you are at reading now."

I usually long for their sleep, but I find I am dreading it and pour two large glasses of wine in preparation. I am onto the glass that I poured for Joel by the time he gets downstairs, half an hour later than we have usually put the boys down. He's procrastinating as much as I am.

"I've had a bit of head start," I say.

He swigs back a glass in compensation.

"Let's talk about this," I say, holding the receipt.

"No, let's talk about your thing," he says. "Your computer thing."

"I said it first."

"Turn around, touch the ground..." he attempts.

"Toss for it. Heads or tails? Bagsy heads. Heads it is, I win. We need to talk about this receipt."

"I don't understand what you mean," he says.

He's always been a rubbish liar. I loved his inability to

dissemble at the beginning. "Yes, you do. What's going on?" I wave the receipt again.

"I went out for some drinks with someone from work."

"Some *one*. One person from work."

"Yes. It's not a crime."

"A woman?" He doesn't answer. "Let's be more accurate, shall we? A girl?"

He finally nods. "I didn't do anything. What are you suggesting?"

"I don't know. Nothing. Well, I would have said nothing, but you're being so weird that I'm thinking maybe something."

"Like what?"

"I don't know, whatever you do with nubile girls from the office after you've downed some expensive champagne cocktails and a meze selection."

He makes a puffing sound with his mouth in dismissal and then moves into a Southern drawl. "I did not have sexual relations with that woman." He giggles nervously.

"It's not funny, don't put on a silly voice at me. Especially not a bad Bill Clinton impression. He was bloody lying. Is that what you're telling me? That you didn't have sex with her, but she gave you a blow job?"

"No!" He is outraged. Like I'm the one in the wrong.

"Enough of the semantics, just tell me what's going on."

"Nothing is going on."

"You're doing it again, you're saying 'is' so as to avoid lying, but something did go on, didn't it? Something *went* on."

"Not really." He slumps—all the fight's gone out of him. The atmosphere has changed. I know now that the interrogation must end and the gentle prodding must begin. It pains me to repress my anger, but the longer I do so the more I'll hear. "Tell me."

"There's a girl at work, one of the researchers."

"Name?"

"Kitty."

It would be, I think.

"She laughs at my jokes."

It's so hard to stop myself from mocking. "Right. And?"

"It's not like I fancied her, particularly. It might sound strange to you, but physically I still fancy you the most. I've never been attracted to anyone the way I was, the way I am, to you."

"She's young, though, isn't she?"

"I suppose. Yes, twenty-three or twenty-four, I think."

I feel a pain in my stomach. "Go on."

"She just made me feel like I was great. That I wasn't just the most irritating man on the planet, but that I was funny and fun and clever. Almost everything she said started with the words 'You're so right.' Or no talk, just laughter. Everything you say starts with 'Can't you just . . . ?' or 'Why don't you ever . . . ?'"

"And?"

"It made coming home more bearable to have that to look forward to when I got to work the next day. Being made to feel like I had some worth. It was like swimming in a heated pool on a cold day—I dreaded getting out and having to face the freeze of being with you."

It's my fault, then, I stop myself from saying. "So what happened?"

"I found myself spending time with her. Going for lunch. Innocent."

"Innocent," I repeat.

"Nothing happened, Mary, not really." He reaches for my hands.

I shake him off. "Something happened."

"I would never jeopardize this house, this home, the boys. I would never do that."

"But you did?"

"No, you did, Mary."

"What do you mean?"

"I found your list thing, your catalog of my faults."

"I know that. But how?"

"The night Gabe got ill; when you didn't answer your phone, I thought I'd better look on the Net to see what I should be doing. I'd left my laptop at work so I used yours. You don't usually leave it lying around, but you had. I clicked on the most recently opened document by mistake, and something called something like 'May home work' came up."

"May Good Housekeeping."

"That's the one. I found this weird Excel document and I just saw something about wet towels, then I went to the health site to try to find out about rashes and forgot about the document, until later, when I saw you looking at me and then typing things. Next time you were out, I had a look at it."

"About three weeks ago," I say, thinking of his behavior and matching it to The List, the sudden flurry of positive points.

"Yes."

"Would you read someone else's diary if you found it hidden in a cupboard?"

"You could have password-protected it. On some level, you wanted me to see it."

"On some level, I don't know how to change the password on my computer. That document was buried about five layers back."

"Well, I found it."

"Just like I found the receipt of your little jaunt with Kathy, sorry, Kitty."

"Bring it back to her."

"Yes, I am bringing it back to her. We are talking about you and her first, then we'll move on to The List."

"But they're connected, aren't they? I worked out that it was a test for me, though I wasn't quite sure of the scoring system or what was going to happen if I failed. What *was* going to happen if I failed?"

I shrug. "Don't know."

"Or if I passed? You were going to be nice to me again?"

"Back to the girl," I say.

"Do you not know what was going to happen or are you not telling me?"

As he asks me, I realize that I don't know, really. What would have happened had he passed was even more opaque than if he failed. I can't tell him I thought about divorce because I don't think I ever did. Not truly. "Look, let's talk about the girl and then we can talk about The List."

"OK. At first I tried to do all the good things on your list, like complimenting you and doing cooking and craft with the boys. And clearing up the mess afterward, obviously. And I'd go and check your spreadsheet and see if you'd noticed these things and most of the time, you had, you were adding them on. Or taking them away, whatever way you want to look at it."

I nod. "It's very fair, The List."

"But I also noticed that it didn't make much difference. Not in comparison to all the things I was doing wrong. But I noticed that the more I was trying to be nice, the more crimes I seemed to commit just by breathing. So I thought, fuck it, I might as well do them all anyway and then see what happens."

"So that's when you started pissing around doing the same misdemeanor over and over again. Making the tally go haywire."

"Yes."

"So that then you'd be allowed to get off with that girl, Carly."

"Kitty."

"Get off with Kitty in the meantime."

"What do you mean?"

"Doing that old male trick of behaving so badly that your girl-friend dumps you and then acting all wounded and hurt when she does."

"I didn't want you to dump me. I don't want you to dump me. The boys."

"So did you sleep with Kitty?" I hiss her name.

"No, I didn't sleep with her."

"But you did get off with her?"

"Once. That night you're talking about, the one with the champagne and the meze selection. It was very garlicky. And very small—you know what these posh hotels are like."

"No, not really. Only then?" My head is trying to understand the chronology. "Was that before you found The List?"

"Twice, it happened twice. Yes, that's right. I was deter-mined that nothing should ever happen after that time, I felt so ashamed. But then, I went back after I read your list."

"And did what? Kissed? Felt her up? Oral? What?"

"Kissed."

"With tongues?"

"Yes, obviously with tongues."

"Don't you dare get stroppy with me."

"I'm stroppy with you?" he says. "Mary, you spend your life in barely disguised fury with me."

"Is it any wonder, with you spending your time snogging teenagers?"

"She's twentysomething. And it was once." I look at him. "OK, twice."

"It doesn't matter how many times you got off with her. It's the fact that you wanted to. It's the fact that you wanted to be with her and not with me. It's the fact that I don't find you funny when I'm knackered. It's the fact that you were glad when you saw my list because you thought it gave you permission to sleep with her, didn't you? It absolved you of your guilt in snogging her and gave you the green light to shag her. And what stopped you?"

He shrugs.

"She did?" He shakes his head. "Was it just that you hadn't gotten around to it? Were you just waiting for the right opportunity? God, Joel, I suppose I should be pleased that you're always starting things you never get around to finishing. Or was it that if I hadn't found the receipt it would have happened?"

"I don't know."

"So it would have happened eventually. And all because I wrote The List. You thought that meant you were allowed to do anything?"

"Doesn't it?"

"No."

"What did it mean, then? I don't understand. Was this list a test of our marriage?"

"Less so than whether our marriage could survive you getting off with someone else." I'm shouting now, I think, but I can't really hear my own voice or his, it's like I've lost the volume control.

"I know, I know. I'm sorry." He starts to cry now, a currency that is debased since I saw him weeping while watching *Magnificent Obsession* at the weekend. "I don't know what came over me. It's just that all the things that were so great about us now seem so horrible. You've changed."

"And you haven't. That's the problem, Joel. You're still a people-pleasing child-man, who has to be loved all the time. And if I don't have the energy then you'll find it elsewhere. There will always be those women in the office."

"What are you going to do?"

"I don't know. What are you going to do?"

"I asked you first."

"I need to digest it." Though I feel physically sick. "I can't look at you right now."

"I'll go."

"Where?"

"To my mother's, I suppose."

He's leaving me? "If that's what you want."

"If it's what you want."

I shrug. I cannot speak for sadness.

"What will you tell the boys?" he says.

That Daddy's left us? "You've gone away for work."

I watch him pack, lightly with just a few pairs of pants and some clean T-shirts. He's always kept a toothbrush at his mother's and it's been waiting for his return, as if this was always going to happen.

He looks at me. "Bye, then."

"Yes, goodbye."

I want to say something to make it all better, but I don't know what or even if such words exist. The awkwardness is finally relieved when he turns away from me. I expect him to open the front door, but he goes back toward the bathroom. I follow him and watch him pick up his flattened yellow toothbrush and pop it into his pocket. My legs wobble and my mouth fills with a foul taste. Oh my god. The words are very clear and separate in my head, they run like a subtitle in bold letters. Oh. My. God. The yellow toothbrush is leaving its place beside a Spiderman electric one and a Disney first toothbrush, and instead will sit in a filthy mug at a chaotic twentysomething flatshare in an edgy part of town, where Kitty and other young girls wander around in their underwear and boys smoke weed and argue over the

Xbox, where nobody nags about stuff at the bottom of the stairs because there are no stairs and besides, nobody cares.

"Goodbye," he says again.

I can't speak. Please stay, one voice says. Just fuck off, says the other, furious that our discoveries have led to this permission of what he's wanted to do with Kitty all along. This was not supposed to happen, this was never part of The List, he is going to get what he wanted from the start, chaos and sex, things that go together.

After he goes, I sit at my computer and stare at it. Out of habit, I type in an attempt to order my thoughts. I add his newest crime into the debit column in the hope that seeing it on the screen will mean that I understand its significance.

Has emotional affair with young woman at work and eventually kisses her, leaving me to deal with the domestic detritus in his absence, emotional and actual, while he escapes to her house for dirty sex in both senses of the word.

I stare at it for a while but I don't feel any nearer to knowing what it means or what I should do. I begin to type again, this time on the page of offsets.

Writes list of every annoying thing he does or says with aim of using it in evidence against him, while at the same time lusting after the ordered life and thighs of best friend's girlfriend.

I delete them both. I take the whole damned folder called "House admin" and drag it into the recycle bin. Then I drag it out again. I realize that I can't delete the last six months, anymore than I can delete Kitty.

He's left me, he's actually left me. Of all the outcomes that I envisaged when I started The List, this was never one of them.

10

The List V2.0

I don't want to work and I don't want to have lunch with Becky. I try ignoring her calls, but she is as insistent as a child tugging at my sleeve.

"I'm really busy, sorry. Frantic production, et cetera, you know, frantic," I tell her on the phone.

"You still have to eat."

"Sandwich at my desk."

"I'd have thought you'd hate the way crumbs get into the keyboard."

She's not going to give in. "All right, but we have to be very quick."

I put the phone down and see Matt hovering, no doubt waiting for the arrival of Lily so that they can giggle over funny videos sent over the Internet and cool additions to their Facebook pages.

"She's not here yet."

"It's you I wanted to speak to." He throws a document onto my desk. It's my pitch about housework. "She love love loves it."

"Who? The commissioner?"

"Yeah, Jane, obviously—says it's exactly what she asked for. Says all women will love it, like it's female Viagra or something."

"That's great."

"Wants to have a meeting ASAP." He pronounces it as one

word: *a-zap*. "Wants to thrash it out a bit more, but I reckon she is this close to commissioning it as a three-parter. This is exactly what we need at the moment. Genius."

"Thank you."

He looks at me to emphasize that he was using the word in its blokey, double thumbs-up way, rather than as an accurate description of me and my contribution to this triumph. "You can make?"

"Yes, sure. I'll fit it in."

"And you can work on it if—no, when—we nail this baby?"

"If you mean when we get the commission, yes, I'd love to. I have to. I've nurtured it. I suppose it is my baby."

"Good. Though you might want to rethink your hours. You're not the only parent around here, you know."

Not even Matt can dim my excitement. I'd forgotten this feeling. I love my boys, obviously, and they are the mattress that my life lies upon, but a work high is like a silk eiderdown to wrap myself in. I am a genius. I had forgotten this, but I am really quite clever. I am better than other people at my job. I can do the interesting stuff as well as the boring bits of it. I want to ring someone to tell them. I realize that I want to ring Joel. My good mood evaporates. My eyes start to prickle only seconds after I've been smirking with professional triumph.

I have cried over Joel, but not last night when he left. At first I was too shell-shocked by what had happened that I mooched around, unable to know what to think. Then I read a trashy novel until I fell asleep with the light on; anything to avoid being alone with the swill in my head. I wanted to sleep forever and not get out of bed for months or years, but the boys were unaware of this and jumped on my bed at their usual ungodly hour, not even noticing that Joel wasn't there, assuming him to be in the shower or down in the kitchen.

No, I didn't cry until breakfast this morning, when the boys finally realized that a quarter of our family was missing and asked where Daddy was. It was the cinematic poignancy of their questioning coupled with my desire to hide anything ill from them that set me off.

"Where's Daddy?" they kept on asking. "I miss my daddy," until I could bear it no longer. I hid in the loo to make sure they didn't see my tears. They banged over and over on the door, while I shouted, "I'm doing a poo," to keep them at bay. That last bit was less like a movie.

When they had finished being winsome, they moved on to moaning about how much they missed him in a way that they never do when he has to go away for work. It was almost as if they knew. Any minute, I expected them to put on American accents and say, "Why don't Mommy and Daddy love each other anymore?" It felt like a horrible vista into the future when we would have to tell them. What am I going to have to tell them, anyway?

"I'm so glad you came," says Becky as we sit at our usual low-rent, high-fiber lunching place. "I got the feeling you were trying to get out of having lunch with me."

"No, no." I glance at my watch. "I just thought I wasn't going to be able to make it. And I can't stay long. I'm expecting a phone call summoning me back to the office at any moment."

Becky clutches my hand. I'm alarmed at this physical contact. She doesn't know her own strength and the gesture is more bone-crushing than soothing.

"Do you want to tell me what's wrong?"

I decide that I do. "It's Joel. He's gone."

She nods as if she already knew. "Why? Is this about your list?"

"Partly. Not really. He did find it a few weeks ago."

"Did he read it?"

"Yes, every last point."

Becky looks horrified. "He read your list detailing everything that you don't like about him?" I nod. "Well, I'm not surprised he left."

"The list's not the half of it. Please don't tell anyone what I'm going to tell you." Becky motions a cross over her chest. "Joel had some sort of dalliance with a girl at work. Her name is Kitty." She gives the look of a child who's just been told Santa doesn't exist. I find myself wanting to defend him, to explain that it's not his fault really and tell her not to judge him, but then I think of the yellow toothbrush. "He didn't sleep with her. That's what he says, anyway, and I believe him actually. He hung out with her in a not entirely appropriate way and they kissed. And he wanted to sleep with her. May have even been planning it. I don't think anything more has happened, but what's hard is not knowing exactly why it hasn't happened. Yet. Or hadn't happened then." I don't know whether this is true anymore. God knows what comfort Kitty offered him last night. Maybe he even told her that he'd left me for her, that he'd made this big sacrifice. Maybe that's even the truth.

"But Joel would never do anything to risk your family."

"That's what I thought. Looks like we were both wrong." I mean Becky and I, but in a moment of clarity, I realize that I also mean Joel and I. We're both in the wrong. Can it ever be that we're both in the right?

"What's going to happen?"

"I don't know. You know what you were saying about how all your decisions seemed dependent on another being made, so that you ended up being paralyzed into inertia? That's what I feel."

"You'll have to write another one of your lists," she says.

"The List was supposed to make everything clear, black and

white, but it's all messy. Life is as messy as the bloody house and no lovely Excel document is going to sort it out for me."

"We can sort it out. Let's start with your list."

"That's what Joel said. Like it was worse than the girl." And yet didn't I feel, in some strange way, that his continual insistence on blocking the plughole of the kitchen sink with breakfast cereals hurt me as much as his chasing this woman?

"It's not a question of which is worse or better. You've got to drop it with the not fair thing, Mary."

"Listen to you, the negotiator."

"No, mediator. I'm fully trained in marital mediation and I'm very expensive too, so consider yourself blessed and shut up and listen. When you wrote your list, what did you hope to accomplish?"

"Like I said, clarity."

"Yes, but clarity with what aim? If he failed"—she does a little air quotes gesture—"what was going to be his punishment?" And again. Enough with the rabbit fingers.

I shrug. She stares at me. I feel like I'm in the witness stand. "Officially, if he proved himself to be as useless as I thought he was, then that would be it."

"That would be what?"

"You know."

"I want you to say it."

"I was going to divorce him. I mean, I was going to threaten to divorce him. I was going to raise the subject of divorce, at least. We were going to talk about it. In a serious way."

"I remember you saying something along those lines," says Becky, "and I couldn't believe it at the time, either. Honestly, Mary, had you really planned to sit down at the end of his probationary period and show him your list and say, 'Well, then, let's bankrupt ourselves and scar our children forever because you squeezed the toothpaste from the middle on the fourth of March'?"

"That's not on the list—with the plastic tubes it comes in these days it doesn't really matter where you squeeze. Sometimes we even get the pump dispensers."

"Don't try to change the subject." She's fierce now and I thank god that she's on my side. Allegedly. "Were you really going to suggest you divorce over a series of petty domestic challenges? Mary, think about it, try to imagine the full conversation you were going to have."

I'd never got further than the triumphant moment where I shocked him with the revelation of the proof of his uselessness. But when it really happened, when he discovered The List for himself, my gut reaction was one of embarrassment. It all seemed so rational at the time, but I look back now and think that I was in the grip of madness. Yes, I was mad in both the angry and the insane senses of the word. This is what always happens: he does something irritating, I am justified in my anger but then I express it in a way that allows him to recolonize the moral high ground. I am justified in my actions, I say to myself again. I am.

"Come on, Mary, were you really going to ask for a divorce?"

"No," I admit finally. "I wanted change. I didn't know exactly what was to happen, but I knew things couldn't continue as they were without me killing myself or him. I couldn't change my children and wouldn't want to, it didn't feel like I could change the house, I felt like I couldn't get a new job while I'm working part-time, as who'd want to employ me? It felt like Joel was the only part of my life I could control. Like food for a teenage girl."

She shakes her head. "If you had any idea what I see in my job, you wouldn't have even let the word 'divorce' flash into your mind, let alone entertain ridiculous thoughts about how your life might improve with one."

"Improve. That's it. I just wanted my life to improve and I didn't know how."

"Well, your life's looking much improved now, isn't it? Joel got off with another woman and you're no longer living together, and I presume your boys are missing their father. Yay for your list, hey, Mary? It really made life better for you."

"I know, I know." I sigh. "And I'm miserable and he's now got the perfect excuse to live at Kitty's—you know, the girl at work—and get what he wanted all along. I can't stop thinking about him having moved in with her."

"When?"

"Last night. He went to Kitty's house. He's living at Kitty's."

"Don't be daft, Mary, Joel's at Ursula's."

"How do you know?" She can't know. She didn't see him pack his toothbrush. Please let her know, please let it be the truth.

"Because I saw him there last night and he said he was staying."

"What were you doing there?"

"Just sorting out some stuff. Don't change the subject."

"How was he?"

"In a terrible state."

"Really?"

"Devastated."

"Did he tell you what was going on?"

"Only that you'd had a row, a bad one. He was crying most of the time."

I feel a thrilling relief to hear of his misery and his place of residence.

"I knew it must be bad as he was asking me all sorts of questions of a professional nature," she says.

"Like what?" I feel my optimism being extinguished.

"What the legal ramifications of him moving out of the family home would be."

"Which are?"

"Not great for him. He damages his chances of shared custody if he vacates the children's main place of residence."

"Really?"

"Yes. What he does in these early days can make a real difference to eventual residency orders."

"No, I mean was he really asking you about custody and residence and the law?" I think of him projecting himself into a tiny bedsit where the boys will visit, and it's almost worse than the picture of him at Kitty's.

"Yes, he was."

"But that's all to do with what happens when a couple separates or, I don't know, divorces."

"Yes." She looks apologetic. "I'm so sorry, Mary. I couldn't understand it at the time, but now I've heard about what's happened, I get it. He's had an affair, of sorts, and you've written a list of why you hate him and he's read it. In my work, I see people split up over far less."

"You think I've blown it, don't you?"

She doesn't say anything.

I think I've blown it.

It's a mother's truism: "In many ways," we say to one another, "it's actually easier for me to manage when he's not around." I've said it myself, lots of times. I dare say I believed it.

The thing is, these last two days, I've discovered that it's not true. It's a falseism, if such a word exists. However useless Joel is—and he is, very—a second person to pull a child out of the bath is handy, and it's good to have someone to dish out cereal while I have a shower. I miss having someone to tell of Rufus's triumphs in his spelling test or the funny thing that Gabriel has said. The thing I've always most hated about being a parent is the relentlessness of it all, and this is even more true when you're on your own. Of course, I've been alone before. Joel was away for a month once. This time feels different, though. It feels both relentless and endless, a terrifying combination.

All I want to do is flop in front of the TV with a large glass of wine, but Jemima is coming over for some pizza with her new man. She met him on the Internet and he works in IT and she sounds smitten after less than two months together.

Fate is very cruel, I think, as I open the door to my sister, who looks happier than I have seen her for years. Is there only so much romantic happiness available to share between us, like chocolate at Christmas?

"This is Dan," she says with pride. Dan, Dan the fat whistling man, I think as I shake hands with this smiley person. Where's the six-pack and boyband good looks of her usual type? I force myself to cheer up, which is made easier by Dan, who it is difficult to feel uptight around. He enthuses about our house, compliments the photos of our boys and says that Rufus has very good writing for his age. Jemima giggles throughout.

"Where's Joel?"

"He's out, some work thing. Sorry."

"That is such a shame," she says. "You'd love him, Dan. Joel is the best." They would like each other. At last Jemima has a boyfriend Joel could talk to.

It's lucky we're eating pizza slices rather than food requiring a knife and fork, since Jemima and Dan appear to need to hold hands throughout. They use the first person plural a lot and talk about selling their flats to buy somewhere together.

"I told you, didn't I?" she says to him as I turn away to stack the dishwasher. "My sister has the perfect life."

I feel like someone's tightening a corset around my chest. The phone goes and I escape the loved-up couple.

"It's me."

I feel both terror and excitement, like the early stages of dating, though more of the former and less of the latter. "Hello, Joel."

"I wanted to say good night to the boys but I couldn't get away and I didn't want to do it in front of people."

"Don't worry."

"How are they?"

"Not great. They miss you."

"The boys miss me?"

"Yes, of course. The boys miss you. Where are you?"

"At Ursula's." I strain to hear his mother's voice in the background as proof, but there is none. Nor, however, is there the sound of raucous young people having fun. "I thought about going to a mate's and then I realized I couldn't really think of any. The ones I like have children and I don't think I could bear to be around somebody else's kids at the moment."

"I thought you'd be having a nice time doing all the things we talk about doing if we didn't have children—leisurely pints, the cinema, all that."

Silence. "Joel?"

"I'm here." His voice is cracking.

"Do you want to come over and do bedtime? Tomorrow?" I feel like I'm putting myself on the line in asking him.

"Yes."

I put the phone down and try to compose myself. Fortunately Jemima is too busy twisting Dan's curls around her fingers to have noticed the strangeness of my conversation and its effect on me.

Dan announces that he is off "for a slash." Jemima has always gone out with boys, but Dan is very much a bloke. I can't believe she is with someone so forthcoming about his bodily functions, nor that when he says such a thing she looks at him as though he's just said he's off to pick up his Nobel prize.

"Well?" she asks.

"Well, what?"

"Dan, of course. What do you think?"

"He's great," I say. "I feel like I've known him ages."

"I know, me too. I feel like I've known him forever."

"He's very different from your previous boyfriends, isn't he?"

"Better, you mean."

"Yes, that. And different looking."

She grins. "He's gorgeous, isn't he?"

I can only smile back. "He is." She seems genuinely unaware of having traded down on the looks front. Jemima has made the best sort of compromise, one that she isn't even aware of. I wish again that I could delete all I now know and all my irritations and go back to a similar state of childlike innocence with my husband.

"I'm really happy," she says.

"I can see that. I'm so glad for you."

"I always felt envious of what you had and now I know that I was right to. I want it all with Dan."

I am saved from speech by his return. They'd be sitting on the same kitchen chair if they could. I feel very old.

I am wearing makeup, I blow-dried my hair this morning and have kept my heels on inside the house. I can hear laughter coming from the bedroom but I can't join in. It's me and the kids or

Joel and the kids, not all of us together. We've broken off into two units and the circles of the Venn diagram have Joel and I separated, and only the boys in the overlap. I notice that some black slime has collected around the seal of the fridge door so I get to work on it. As I do so, I think about Kitty. This is Kitty, I say to myself, as I scour it away. I see her phantom everywhere, my own vision of what she might look like: in the mirror when I look at myself, with my children, with whom she could be Dad's fun girlfriend, in the toilet bowl that I brush with violence. The slime comes away from the fridge. There—so easy, but of course fridge-seal slime and Kitty aren't the same thing at all.

"Would you like a glass of wine?" I ask Joel when he comes down, at least fifteen minutes later than the boys' appointed bedtime hour. He hasn't shaved and looks as though he hasn't been sleeping. Kitty's sitting at my shoulder and I know that she would think he looks disheveled and handsome. I think I agree with her.

"No, I'd better be off."

"Fine. I see. Yes, you get going." He can't wait to be out the door. "Send my regards to Ursula." If that is indeed where you're going.

"OK."

"Does she know?"

"What?"

"About us."

"What is there to know?"

"I don't know."

This from a couple whose relationship was built on non-stop conversation.

"Mary?"

"Yes."

"I'll be off, then."

"Yes, of course. Go."

"I suppose so."

We're both standing up and I have no idea what the etiquette is for saying goodbye to one's husband in this situation. "Well, bye then." I want some sort of physical contact and so find myself sticking out my hand. He looks at it and shakes it. We glance at each other with shock and then laugh, very briefly. I'd forgotten what laughter sounded like. It sounds like hope.

I can't go to sleep. The bedroom feels wrong. I look toward the laundry basket which has been stripped of its usual halo of socks and men's underwear. I go to Joel's chest of drawers and unball some socks and pull out a T-shirt, which I arrange around and on top of the basket. Now I can sleep.

At breakfast I am about to rinse out the nearly empty milk bottle to ready it for the recycling when I change my mind and put it back in the fridge, complete with its mere hint of liquid. I leave the toast crumbs around the toaster and place my used tea bag on the work surface.

I throw some towels down in the bathroom, but the sink remains free from the little iron filings of stubble that usually decorate it. I leave the soap bar to soak in some water for a few minutes so that it becomes furry enough to leave a residue of itself on the basin. I wet the blue washcloth and leave it dripping onto the tiles.

As I get ready to take the boys to school, I touch Joel's winter coat. I've been asking him to take it to the spare room for months, but soon it will become cold again. I look down and see that he's left some shoes behind in the hall. I can leave for the office now.

The week creaked by. Joel came around one other night while I sat in the kitchen pretending to read a magazine. I didn't enjoy dispensation from bedtime duties as much as I always thought I would. Instead, I could hear the sound of a party to which I had not been invited. I bet he's getting bloody water all over the floor, I told myself, which didn't make me feel any better.

Again we did a waltz of awkwardness when it was time to say goodbye. This time I even offered him something to eat, but this was no more tempting than the glass of wine. He was in a hurry, it seemed, to escape. Both times he has come over, I have started out with excitement and been left with dejection and rejection.

I found the weekdays hard, but this Saturday at home is even worse. It has been six days since Joel went to his mother's. My hair stinks of chlorine from swimming with the boys and I've failed to get a chance to wash it in preparation for today's bedtime visit from him. I look at myself in the mirror. I look thin, which is usually enough to brighten my mood, but it has aged me.

I hear his key in the door and it suddenly seems to be the world's most beautiful music. My legs wobble and I realize then what I can deny no longer: I want him home. This is his home. I need to know that he has a key and that every night he will let himself in. He will throw his coat on the floor and hug the boys. He could even hug me, too. The house will be filled with his noise and his mess. I hate it but I need it. I need him. I can forgive him if I know that he can forgive me, too.

He is fumbling with the key, not realizing that I have taken to double-locking in fear of being in the house alone. He comes in and I smile at him, especially when for once he hangs his jacket up on the hook. Now I see even more clearly. I need him home, but I do also need him to hang his coat up. The List cannot have been in vain.

The smile he gives me in return emboldens me. He was the

one who put his pride on the line to get us together all those years ago and it is only fair that I should do the same to get us back there again.

He turns toward the street.

"Come on, Ursula, you can look at the neighbor's clematis later."

I am so disappointed that I want to cry. My plans to ask him or even tell him to get home where he belongs dissolve. He can't want to make it work if he's bringing his mother here as a human shield. How was I going to do it, anyway? We're beyond the point where I could put on some sexy underwear and surprise him on the kitchen table. I imagine Joel and I doing exactly that and the thought of it leads to an unexpected warmth between my legs. I fancy my husband, I realize with surprise, just at the point when I can no longer have him. How could I have wasted all those opportunities when he slunk across the bed to me when now I may never have the chance again?

He looks apologetic. Ursula comes in and hugs me, clutching my arm too hard.

"Sorry," he says when we go upstairs with the boys. "She said she needed to talk to us both."

"What about?"

"I don't know."

"It's not anything to do with, you know, us?"

"No, no. I'm sure it isn't."

"Good."

"Mary, what is us?"

I shake my head and leave the room.

Ursula is a lot easier to read than some of her later books. She builds her confidence through the wearing of dangly earrings and brightly colored scarves. The television appearances have long tailed off, but back in the days when she appeared on late-night discussion shows, she was fairly swaddled in vermilion and violet, while the little wooden parrots hanging from perches in her ears careered wildly as she swung her head to emphasize her points.

Despite the July heat, Ursula is mummified in purple velvet. Her earrings, jade fashioned into bunches of grapes, almost scrape her shoulders. She has something to say. I pour out three large glasses of wine now that the boys have gone to bed.

"I have a proposition," she announces. She is giving us the sort of oratory that comes only with an expensive girls' school and one of Oxford's oldest women's colleges. Many still speak of her barnstorming performance in support of the motion "This house believes that a woman needs a man like a fish needs a bicycle."

Joel knows Ursula well and is beginning to look nervous. "A proposition?"

I think, entirely inappropriately, how this word is almost always sexual in its connotations. I'm sure Mitzi's Michael makes propositions. I shudder at the thought of Ursula and Michael together, the least likely coupling in Christendom.

"Not that sort of proposition," says Ursula, as if reading my mind. "The word 'proposition' does not always have that sort of suggestion."

I think, again inappropriately, of the sort of proposition I have just been dreaming up for Joel.

"But in modern usage, it does tend to be employcd in that context," suggests Joel.

"Perhaps a less ambiguous word is 'proposal,'" she agrees. "Though that's a word always coupled with marriage, isn't it?"

I think mournfully of Joel's thwarted proposal to me.

"Is it merely a plan, then?" he asks.

Oh, for Christ's sake, this could go on for hours. I used to love the way that you couldn't use a word without the pair of them querying its exact usage, with recourse to the vast dictionary kept permanently open on their kitchen table. "Why don't you just tell us what's on your mind and we can name it afterward?" Whatever it is that Ursula needs to say to us is of no importance in comparison to what Joel and I are not saying to one another.

"Yes, we'll name it posthumously, shall we?" says Joel. "If it requires a moniker."

Breathe in: one, two, three and out: two, three.

Ursula finally begins. "As you are aware, my house is in a state of some disrepair."

I was aware of this, as are her neighbors, who have petitioned her to make improvements for fear of bringing down the street's house prices, but I had no idea Ursula was.

"It's perfect," says Joel. "It's lovely. Who says it isn't?"

Joel loves Ursula's strangely cramped kitchen and the dried slash dead flowers in the fireplaces. He's scathing about what he calls "bashing out the back" to make outdoor rooms and a flow between spaces. Whenever we have fantasy conversations about what we'd do if we lived in Ursula's vast house, he always looks bewildered as to why I'd want to move the kitchen from the dark back alley where servants used to lurk. He believes anyone moving in would be thrilled at such a period gem, while I can hear the well-clipped tones of a hedge-funder's wife boasting to her friends of how it was "a *wreck*. Mad old woman hadn't touched the place for 40 years. We had to gut it entirely."

"Joel," says Ursula, firmly, "it's falling down."

"But I thought you liked it like that," he says. "I do." Next he's going to start whining about her threatening to throw away some of his childhood artwork or the chemistry set he got for his seventh birthday.

"Why would I like it? It's a health hazard." I feel a new respect for Ursula growing inside me. "The roof needs completely replacing, the plumbing is antediluvian, the electrics are dangerous."

"You've never had any accidents."

When I first met Joel he didn't think it odd at all that his mother's house was filled with the round-pin sockets that most people had moved away from at the end of the Second World War. In her over-flowing utility room were boxes labeled "round to square" and "square to round" filled with adaptors and plugs to snake around the house from an old electrical system to an even older one.

"Don't be silly, Joel, I've electrocuted myself hundreds of times. It's a mess and I know it. I try not to dwell on it—too, too depressing—but I don't think we can deny it any longer. Mary knows it, don't you? I can see the way you look at it and wipe the chair before you sit down."

"No, not at all. But if it is structurally unsound, then you're right, you do need to do something."

"I've been worrying about it for years and burying my head in the sand," she says. "I finally forced myself to get someone in to quote for how much all the repairs would cost. My eyes almost fell out so I got someone else in and they said even more money, so I got someone else after that and they were just as bad. So I buried my head a little longer."

My mind runs through some options as to what her proposal will be. Is she suggesting that we move in with her and pay for the repairs? I'm not sure we could afford that financially or emotionally, especially since I don't even know if there is a "we" anymore. I can't see Ursula selling up and moving into sheltered accommodation. "So what's the plan?" I ask, since Joel refuses to.

"Rebecca. That's my plan. Your friend Rebecca."

"Becky?"

"Yes. She's got no home but lots of money, I've got a large house and no money. We're a perfect match."

"You're living together?" I ask. Will Joel have to call Becky "Mother"?

"Not exactly. No, not like that," she exclaims, having seen the stricken expression on Joel's face, who now looks as though he will evaporate with relief at this reassurance. "We've got it all worked out. She's very good with money, is Rebecca. I can see why she's so good at sorting out other people's. And at making it herself. She will pay for the repairs and for converting it into two dwellings—a flat for me on the ground floor with the garden, and the floor above and the attic for her."

"My space," says Joel mournfully.

A month ago that would have been an aggravating thing for him to have said, but now it might be the truth. "That sounds like it might be a sensible plan," I say. "I don't want to sound mercenary, but you do know it's worth a lot of money?"

"I'm well aware of that, thank you, Mary. I do walk past the estate agent's windows in the high street. That was one of my problems. I knew I should probably sell it, but I couldn't bear to. My first idea was to move all of you in and you could pay for the work with the money from selling your house, but I fear we'd not have quite enough if those builders got it right. Becky's a partner in her firm and got a lot of money from selling her flat, and she has no dependents. The house is too big for me on my own, but I fear it wouldn't have been big enough for the four of you and me. You need your independence and I need mine. This way I'll have more of an income to live off as I won't have all the outgoings, as well as having Rebecca around to water the plants when I'm away." This is a euphemism, I realize, for one of those old people's eventualities like falling down the stairs and not being found until weeks later.

"How are you going to work out the finances?" I ask.

"Rebecca will have a share in the overall house worth whatever she puts in."

"A proportionate share or a value share?"

"I don't know, exactly. Obviously this all needs to be worked out, but it's the principle that you need to agree to. I'm selling off part of your family home."

Joel looks as though he's about to cry and I want to comfort him as I do the boys when they fall off the slide on the playground. These are the moments that finally make adults of the permanent teenagers that we are: the death of a parent, the birth of a child and the time when we can no longer call our parents' house our home. I look at Ursula and realize that I didn't know her at all. I thought she was unable to see that the place was crumbling around her, but all along she was aware of exactly how decrepit it was and, more surprising still, exactly how much the house was worth.

"So," I say, to break the silence. "What do you want from us?" Joel looks up. "Joel. Me."

"I need to know that everything will be all right," she says, looking at me.

There's a small voice at the kitchen door. "Mommy," says Rufus. "Can Daddy read me just one more story?"

"Of course," Joel says and leaps up and out of the room.

"Will everything be all right?" Ursula asks me.

"I don't know," I say. "I hope so."

"That's enough for me," she says. We look at each other with a warmth and understanding that I've never before detected. "I'll go now. Tell Joel that I've gone."

"And that he'll see you later?"

"That's for you two to decide."

*   *   *

After what seems to be the longest "just one more story" ever, Joel returns to the kitchen, where I'm continuing to empty a bottle of wine. I wonder what excuse he'll make this time, but he sits down and pours himself a refill.

"So?" I say.

"So," he says in a weary tone.

"Are you OK?" He shrugs. "Are you feeling disoriented about the fact that your childhood home won't feel like your home anymore?"

"What? Of course not. Do you think I'm eight or something?"

"What, then?"

"You know what. Everything."

"Joel."

"Yes."

I'm scared. I realize that I have no idea what he's thinking. He's left us and is asking Becky for divorce advice, I tell myself, but a louder voice in my head shouts that I miss him and he looks as though he may miss us too. "Come home. Here, I mean."

He gives a tentative smile and I have my first clue as to the answer. "Really? What about Kitty?"

"There's no 'about her,' is there?" Please say no.

"No, not at all."

"Promise?"

"I promise. You know how I stick to my promises. I've just given her a glowing reference to go and find work somewhere else." I feel a shock jolt of sympathy for her. It always seems to be the women whose lives get altered in these circumstances. "I'm so sorry, Mary, it was idiotic."

"It was. With someone at work, too." I shake my head. "I'm sorry, too. I was so angry," I say.

"The list, you mean?"

"Yes. I was so angry about everything. So angry that I didn't have any room for any love, at least not toward you. The dirt and the gunk were breeding and every time I cleaned away some grime from somewhere, it was like you'd stolen a piece of me. It was like the mold was breeding so fast that my heart had gone moldy. Our love was untended."

"I'm sorry about that, too. I feel unappreciated as well, you know."

"I'll laugh at your jokes more, then. Sorry, that was below the belt."

"You could, though, make me feel like you were interested in me. And I'll try to appreciate all that you do."

"I don't want you to appreciate it so much as just do it."

"I will."

"Though when you'd bloody gone, I started to think that this house was too tidy without you."

"Can I have that in writing?"

"No, obviously not." Then I realize that there is a way of getting him back without losing everything I've worked toward for the last six months. "Actually, maybe we should get something in writing. I think I feel a list coming on."

- *Neither M nor J to make jokes about male household incompetence, either as denigration or as an excuse.*
- *J to never, ever, ever use the word "chillax."*
- *Neither M nor J to refer to themselves in the third person, especially not as in the following sentence: "Mommy's tired because Daddy's made a mess in the kitchen and she has to do all the tidying up."*

It's there on the fridge door for everyone to see: The List, version 2.0.

"I don't think we should call it The List," I said when we began to compile it. "It is a new beginning, after all."

"The Pledge?"

"Sounds like something from Alcoholics Anonymous."

"Or those teenage girls who take an oath of chastity."

"I really don't want to think about teenage girls and their frustrated sex lives every time I look at the fridge."

"I do."

"If we can't decide what this thing is going to be called," I said, "how are we ever going to work out what should go in it?"

"I was never the sort of person to do revision timetables before exams."

"I was, to the detriment of my revision. I used to spend so long doing the perfect multi-sectioned, multi-colored poster that I barely had time to look at my books."

"You'd never guess."

"Well, it was all right for you, with your expensive education," I snapped back.

- *J to throw or tidy away five things before he goes to bed each evening.*
- *J to check for pile of stuff at the bottom of the stairs.*

"Hang on," he said. "Why's it all about me? What about something that you've got to do?"

"Like what?"

"Mary to not read homeware catalogs in bed."

"I do not."

"I'll extend that to décor magazines, too. Mary to not suggest that we redecorate rooms that are fully functional. Mary to not say we need a new kitchen while existing one works fine as it is. Mary to not—"

"I get the picture. Thank you."

"Mary to say thank you more often. As well as please."

"Give it a rest. Please."

- *Two laundry baskets. Colors and whites.*

"What happens with things that are gray? Or patterned so that they're both colored and white?"

"Don't be annoying, Joel."

"I'm serious."

"I'll show you the way."

"The way of the laundered."

- *M to never use the phrase "It's not fair."*

"Now that's not fair," I said.

"Uh-uh." He wagged his finger.

"No, really. I can't not use the phrase if life isn't fair. Make life fair and I'll stop using it. And don't you dare say, 'But life isn't.'"

I'd never have admitted it to Joel, but life isn't—certainly not when you have children and jobs and houses. You'll drive yourself mad making sure that life is entirely equitable, I've learned that now. But just because it isn't, doesn't mean that you have to give up trying.

- *On days that both M and J working or both not working, responsibility for children to be absolutely equal in terms of picking up from childcare, cooking boring food, getting up for breakfast.*
- *Each parent to be allotted 30-minute slot in the morning for showering, ablutions, etc.*

- *Each parent to be allotted one evening a week where they don't have to be back for bath/bed.*
- *Further late evenings to be pre-agreed.*
- *Both parents to be allowed equal amounts of time for a chosen hobby, e.g. the "band," going to the gym, shopping.*

"Remove those inverted commas."

"And you tell me I don't say please enough."

"Please remove those inverted commas from the word 'band' in the list. Thank you."

"I thought we agreed not to call it the list—you know, because of the other one."

"Does it really matter what it's called?"

"It does, it really does."

He sighed. "Maybe we need help."

I nodded. And I knew just the person.

The boys were shipped off to my parents for a whole weekend and in their place came Becky. She even stayed the night in the top bunk and said that she enjoyed the luminous stars on the ceiling when it got dark.

"As far as I can see," she said, having read a series of notes, Post-its and marital mission statements, "there are three areas of activity in your marriage."

Joel sniggered.

"No," said Becky. "That wasn't one of them."

"Well, that's certainly true," he said ruefully.

"Can we just concentrate on this? Otherwise we'll never get through it. Tell us, Becks, what are these three areas?"

"Earning, childcare and housework. They have to be treated equally."

Joel snorted.

"Equally," she repeated. "Right. I want you to write down as many tasks attached to each of these domains as possible and I'll come back in an hour."

"It's like some awful management away-day," muttered Joel.

"Or a school test," I said, cupping my arm around my pad of paper so that he couldn't copy any of my answers.

"Doctors appointments, birthday-party arranging, birthday-present buying, shoe measuring, vaccinations...there are so many little tasks involved in having children," said Becky on reading my extensive list under the heading of childcare. Joel's contribution consisted of three words: "park, zoo, etc."

"Takes a village to raise a child," I said. Joel was right, I was the sort of girl that had to prop my arm on a ruler, my hand was so permanently raised to answer the teacher's questions.

"Joel, anything else to add?"

He looked at his shoes.

"We'll start with childcare."

"Can I just say at this point," I asked, "that childcare is not just looking after children? It means tidying up after them, dealing with household things at the same time."

"Good point, Mary. Can I get on?" She looked down at our contributions. "I'm going to auction these off. Here's your currency." She handed us each a pile of Lego pieces. "You've got 50 of these. I've got 25 key tasks. If you want one, you say so. If you both want it, you buy it with your Lego bits. First off, being rung by the school or Deena when the boys are ill or injured."

Joel put his hands as low as he could.

"Why not make it two points—one of us is the school's contact and one is Deena's?" I suggested.

"Very good, Mary, well done." I was so teacher's pet. "Which one do you want?"

325

"I'll be the school's and Joel can have Deena. You can start by actually saving Deena's number to your phone."

And so it went on, through other kids' birthday parties, listening to reading and accompanying the class on school trips. I could see Becky was good at this, she'd wisely chosen to begin with the most uncontroversial area of our unholy trinity.

"Who knew," she said as we finally thrashed out our respective responsibilities, "that there was so much work involved in bringing up children?"

"Indeed, who knew?" said Joel.

"I knew," I said. "Speaking of which, Becks, have you made any decisions in that area? You know, children, babies, having them?"

"I think so. The issue's in abeyance. Which, given my age and the state of my insides, is in practical terms a decision."

"To not?"

"Yes, to not. I've realized that just because I can, or maybe can't, have children, it doesn't mean I have to. It was all mixed up with how I felt about Cara." Joel gave a pantomime hiss. He didn't know the half of it, about Cara and Mitzi, and about Cara and me. He and Becky would never know. "I think children maybe represented the sort of anti-Cara. Do you know what I mean?"

"Yes, I do." I knew exactly what she meant. "I hope we're not the ones to have put you off."

"Not really. I'm just not sure everyone is supposed to have children," she said.

"I used to think that about Ursula," said Joel.

I was surprised. "Really? You never told me."

"I'm over it. In the end, I'm glad she did have me, it's just that she wasn't exactly child friendly when I was growing up."

"I thought you did everything together."

"Everything she wanted to, yes, but nothing I wanted to. Have you any idea how boring it was being dragged around listening to boring adults and never getting to bed early enough and being given vol-au-vents instead of fish fingers? I hated being hauled out of school for whole terms while she had a sabbatical somewhere."

"But she clearly loves you and being with you."

"More now. I think I have become more interesting at the exact same time as her life has become more boring. You know how history didn't exist until people learned how to write? Ursula feels the same about children. I had no value until I could read. I look at you and the boys and it's so different for them. You're so with them. They're very lucky."

"You're being sarcastic, aren't you?"

"No, of course not. You're a great mother, you know you are."

"I don't do enough arts and crafts with them and teach them math in a fun way and make up journals filled with pressed flowers and coloring-in."

"You read too many parenting books. You sing made-up songs with them and play football like you really want to win."

"I do really want to win, but Rufus is getting better than me."

"It's not what you do, it's that you're really there for them—they take you for granted, but in a good way. I could never bank on Ursula."

"Thanks. I really appreciate that. And you're an amazing father. I know everyone says that, over and over, but it is actually true. Especially since you didn't have your dad around when you were growing up. Or your mother, as it turns out. I think it's a real achievement to be so good at something you never had yourself."

"Even though you think I'm so useless around the house."

"Despite that. Sometimes even because of that. You let them

do the measuring when you bake even though it might ruin the recipe, you spend hours making complicated junk marble runs and space stations, you get all the toys out at once so that they can create strange worlds where Lego, trains and dinosaurs co-exist. OK, you don't tidy them up afterward, but, well, they have a lovely time with you."

"Thanks. It means a lot for you to say that."

We smiled at one another.

"That is so sweet," said Becky as she scrawled another thing on her dossier.

• *M and J to find five things to say thank you to each other for at the end of each day.*

"Five?" I exclaimed. "Every day?"

• *M can get back to working directly on productions, which will sometimes mean a five-day week and J will have to take holiday or work from home to cover missing days.*

"Really?" said Joel. "You want to work as a producer again?"

"Producer-director, ideally," I replied. "I didn't tell you because we weren't really speaking, but I came up with a pitch idea recently and they love it and there's a really good chance that we'll get a proper commission. I don't want anyone else working on it, it's mine."

"Mary, that's fantastic!" Joel hugged me. "I want to hear all about it, you should have told me. You are so clever, nobody's getting anything commissioned at the moment. Bloody hell, you should come and work for me. What's it about? I can't believe it, you are a dark horse, my gorgeous clever girl."

I couldn't wait to show him all my ideas. There's no one whose opinion or enthusiasm I value more. The whole time I'd been struggling with the format on my own, when all the while I had my own personal sounding board. "It will be difficult, Joel, me working full-time, and you're going to have to step up at home, but there's no point in me working if I'm not going to be doing what I find most interesting, and being this production admin slop-cleaner is not it. Gabe's going to start nursery full-time, so it seems like a good time to give it a go. If it doesn't work, then we'll have a rethink and train to become a teacher or psychotherapist or whatever, but I want to give it a try. And I can, with your help."

"Well done, Mary. Brings us neatly onto money," said Becky. "Presumably, you earn less."

"At the moment, yes, I do, but when we met I earned more and when I can work—"

"All money earned to be pooled for household use, buying things for children, paying child minder, etc., and each of you to draw a 'salary' from this pool which is yours to use as you will." She wrote quickly.

"And he needs to do his expenses. Every week, doesn't he?"

"Yes, that sounds valid."

"Every week..."

"And every month, you will be allowed to revise and rethink the whole of this list. In a calm and rational way with some ground rules. No discussion of it in front of the kids or others. No tutting or eye-rolling. No shouting or sulking." She looked from me to Joel as she said that. "And if you can't manage to do what I ask alone, then I will schedule a once-monthly meeting with me to bang your heads together to make sure that you do."

"We will," Joel and I said with one voice.

"And no revising the list between times, and when you do revise it, there's to be no distractions, no listening to the radio or watching TV."

"Or checking your BlackBerry," I added. "Which reminds me..." I think about sex and how we don't have time for it, what with the kids and all, but do have time to check our emails and our storage solution catalogs.

"What?" asked Becky.

"Nothing." I blushed.

Housework took the longest. My initial list had over a hundred suggestions, including some obscure blinders.

"Taking out the rubbish," posited Joel. "Taking special care to make sure all recyclable items are in the green box."

"De-fluffing the tumble-dryer drum," I countered.

"I see your de-fluff thingie and raise you a..." he paused. "A trip to the supermarket."

"Disinfecting the powder-dispenser drawer in the washing machine."

"Oh, for god's sake," said Joel. "You are making these up."

"I'm with Joel on this one," said Becky. "I don't believe anybody disinfects their drawers."

"They do. And a monthly boil wash with vinegar. Wait a minute." I go to the washing machine and pull out the drawer, which is gratifyingly treacly.

"It's like some sort of primordial slime," said Joel. "I feel sick."

"What is that stuff? Does everyone have it?" asked Becky.

"I don't know where it comes from, either. There must be landfill sites crammed with dust and hairballs and the fluff from between people's toes and that brown limescaley stuff in the toilets..."

"Make it stop." Joel was clasping his ears.

And so it went on. And on. I found myself enjoying it as a validation of all that I had been trying to prove to Joel since the day

Rufus was born. Maybe it was the presence of Becky, but he was receptive in a way that he had never been before.

"It can't just be one way," he said, once we'd thrashed out yet another point. "If I'm to raise my standards, then Mary's got to lower hers, too. We should be meeting halfway, right?"

"Not quite halfway," said Becky. "Sixty-forty, I think. But you're right, one way of feeling more satisfied with your house is to care less."

"Quentin Crisp and all that," said Joel.

"You what?"

"He said that after a few years, the dust didn't get any worse."

"You are revolting. Dust is made of human skin."

"If it's yours, it makes me love it even more, my sweet."

Becky was scribbling another point on the list.

• *M to learn to care less about the state of her house and to be more tolerant of occasional drops in standards.*

In the manner of an aging woman changing the lightbulbs in her bathroom to 40 watts, I thought, but they had a point. If I stopped seeing my house through the prism of others' eyes then maybe I could just step over the mess. Perhaps it could even be argued that not tidying was a form of time management and efficiency. If I wiped surfaces down at the end of a weekend instead of after every meal, I'd be saving myself half an hour of superfluous cleaning.

When I say I want to stop seeing my life through the eyes of others, I mean the eyes of Mitzi. For years it was as if I'd been wearing a wristband with the legend "WWMD": what would Mitzi do? And now I know: Mitzi would perform humiliating acts of perversion for her husband alongside consequence-free infidelity with another woman's girlfriend.

* * *

331

It had been there, lurking, all the while, but I was hoping we'd manage to avoid talking about it.

"I'm an idiot," said Becky. "There are four areas of this relationship. Earning, childcare, housework and . . . can anyone tell me what the fourth is?"

"Watching TV?" I suggested.

"Anyone? Joel? Nobody? It's you, you idiots."

"Me?" I said.

"No, you plural: you two. Your relationship. How often do you have sex?"

"You can't ask that. You most certainly can't put it on the list for everyone to see."

"Not often enough," said Joel. He has no embarrassment about sex. He can talk about it like an agony aunt in a women's magazine, full of gynecological detail mixed with revolting phrases like "making love." Early on, I remember we were eating a takeaway when he said, "You know, you taste different when you've eaten a curry." I offered to brush my teeth. "I don't think that's going to make much of a difference," he said, before putting down his fork to test the theory.

"You can't schedule sex," I protested to Becky.

"I'm not going to say you have to do it on Saturday nights."

"Thanks."

"But you do have to do it once a week. Without fail." I had a vision of Becky popping up between us in bed, pointing at her watch and reminding us that six days had passed.

"Joel, you were the one who said this was all becoming too business-like."

"If Becky says we've got to do it, then we've got to do it."

"What happens if I'm not in the mood? We're not in the mood."

"You get yourself in the mood," said Becky. I gave her a skeptical look. "Don't ask me, not exactly my area. I don't know, you give each other a massage, do it outdoors, on the kitchen table…"

"Get drunk."

She ignored me and continued, "Have phone sex during the day, role play, a bit of S & M, wear some sexy underwear."

"If I can get rid of all my vinyl," said Joel, "you can chuck out your nursing bras and get some new ones designed for the non-lactating woman."

"I didn't know you noticed."

"I didn't think the little poppers to let down the cups were for my benefit," he said.

"And you'll need to do more things together as a couple. Without your offspring."

"What, like a weekly date night?" I said.

"You know what Ursula would say to that?" asked Joel, and we said in unison, "Horrid Americanism."

"Us sitting in a restaurant trying to talk about things other than the children and giving up and sitting in silence?" I said. "Sounds like it's really going to help our marriage."

"It won't be that bad," said Joel. "We could do other stuff, go to the cinema, watch a band. We never go to exhibitions anymore."

I remembered the time, before we got married, when we saw an exhibition about representations of the nude throughout history and Joel whispered filth in my ear throughout until I could bear it no longer and we slipped into the toilet reserved for those with wheelchairs or babies needing changing for some brisk but highly satisfying sex. I never used to be able to recall that incident without feeling guilty about anybody who might have had more pressing need of the facilities. But then, after Becky's exhortations about weekly sex, I found myself remembering it with a rippling in my groin and a first surge of optimism. This might work, I thought, this might actually work.

"We could have a book club," I said.

"I'm not going to your loopy book club."

"No, just the two of us. I loved how we used to share books, before we had children. How you used to read out loud to me." We'd lie curled around each other for hours and he'd read out the latest literary hit in his deliciously deep voice, like my own personal audiobook. Then we'd talk or argue about its merits and meanings. I never read anymore.

"Good work, team," said Becky, looking at her watch and making a "T" shape with her hands. "Right, guys, time out."

"Did they teach that at mediation school?" asked Joel.

"Yes, they did, thanks. Ten minutes for tea and reflection, let us adjourn to the kitchen."

Joel started flicking through the color magazines that had come with the weekend papers. He stopped at a spread and started making a two-fingers-down-his-throat gagging gesture.

"What is it?" I asked.

"This," he said, pointing at its pages. "If you're fond of sand dunes and salty air," he read out loud, "you'll love Mitzi Markham's Norfolk retreat, which proves that reclaimed can also be refined."

"Oh my god, is that the article they were doing when we were there? Are there any photos of us?"

"I think we've been edited out."

"Not eco-chic enough, even though she made the boys wear that scratchy organic cotton."

He turned the page. "They're here. It's just you and I that don't cut it."

"Look at them." Our sons had mud streaked across their faces like an old-fashioned game of Cowboys and Indians. "Becky, are they not the most gorgeous children on these pages?"

"Definitely. Mind you, that's not hard. There's something of the Midwich Cuckoos about Mitzi's kids." The four of them stood together in one of the photographs, their white-blonde hair blending into the sand dunes behind them.

"Just listen to this crap," said Joel, as he read from the article. "Visitors to the vast family room are rewarded with panoramic views of the Norfolk skies and a wealth of Mitzi's quirky finds. Blah, blah, blah. The glass atop the coffee table was salvaged from a derelict church that Mitzi stumbled upon while holidaying in the Île de Ré. 'The kids love crawling underneath it and seeing how the glass distorts their faces,' she laughs, relaxed about the wear and tear of life with four boisterous children." Joel rolled his eyes before continuing: "And my husband and I find it perfect for our filthy sex games. Michael just won't shit on glass that doesn't have a charming back story."

"It doesn't say that!" said Becky.

"No, of course not. But it should do."

"What do you mean?"

"You never told her?" said Joel. "Becky, Becky, Becky, prepare to be amazed—this is the best story ever."

And so we told her, with Joel taking the part of both Mitzi with her rubber gloves and Michael, using our kids' table from Ikea to crouch over in a tribute to the event. I did a running commentary, with additional dialogue from Joel. We laughed so much that our stomachs ached and tears ran down our faces. Every time we tried to compose ourselves, Joel would make his Michael "strainy face" and we would collapse once more. I laughed like I was young again.

"I don't think I'll ever be able to look at them," said Becky, finally.

"I don't suppose you'll have to," I said. "I'm not going to see her anymore so I don't see why you will." I had seen her only once since I had made my discovery about who the plumber and the gardener were. It was at book club and all was the same— the fawning attendants, the stylish edibles, her choice conversational nuggets—but I was different. Funnily enough, I had had no problem looking her in the eye after the weekend in Norfolk, and I even managed to forgive her for trying it on with Joel nine years ago, but I couldn't unknow what I had learned about her and Cara. I tried to listen to her business plans about her environmental products or her pride at her children's myriad achievements, but I couldn't, not any longer. She alluded once again to her marital sex life and paid tribute to Michael's glories as a husband. Her life is a lie, but I knew one thing to be true: she would never leave him, whatever happened.

"What?" asked Joel. "You're never going to see her? Not at all?"

I shook my head. I glanced at Becky and chose my words carefully. "She's not a very nice person."

"Finally," said Joel. "What have I been telling you all these years?"

"I never much liked her," said Becky. You don't even know the half of it, I thought, and I'm not going to tell you.

"She is actually very insecure."

Joel snorted. "They said that about Hitler."

"It's true, she had a difficult childhood. Though it's actually irrelevant whether she's nice or not, what matters is that she doesn't make me very nice. I don't want to compare myself to her any longer. And to know her is to compare. She invites it. It's kind of the whole point of her. I can still see Daisy and I don't see enough of our old friends, and I've got to fit in these dates with my husband, and actually there are some really nice parents at school and I could do more for the PTA. There are lots of better things for me to do than see Mitzi. And her attendants. God, if I never have to see Alison again, it will be a better world." They both nodded. "But don't put 'Never see Mitzi again' on the list. Not that I'm going to let them back into my manky kitchen ever again."

Who knew, as Becky would say, that marriage was such hard work, that it would need a business plan, strategies and action points? That it would need daily gratitude, weekly sex and monthly board meetings? That we would sit with our diaries every Sunday evening to work out who was picking up which child to take to football, who could work and get up late, whose hobby took precedence? That it would take a trained mediator, a sort of marital management consultant, to hand out redundancy notices to all the inequality and resentment, and to recruit good will and cooperation?

But there it is, on the fridge, our very own little declaration of co-dependence. An A3 sheet of tiny font, glanced at by visitors before their eyes glaze over with the mind-numbing detail and coded shorthand of it. It nestles beside the invitation to Michael's fiftieth birthday party, to be held in one of those old-fashioned gentleman's clubs. I have turned it down, though I like its embossed thickness amid the term dates and shopping lists. Less showy is the invitation to Jemima's thirty-fifth, that watershed date in a woman's life, now passed. She and Dan spent the evening snogging like teenagers and she confessed to me that they had decided to stop using contraception. He'll probably irritate her in the end, but who cares for now.

- *Joel not to indulge himself in the flattering attentions of young underlings in the office, nor to kiss them (or whatever else may have happened).*
- *Mary not to entertain fantasies about sophisticated brunettes wearing nothing but green silk lingerie and clutching a sex aid.*

No, not really. These two strictures aren't on the fridge for the world and their offspring to see. They're in my heart, though, and on my mind.

Joel and I talked a lot about Kitty and I make snippy comments whenever he stays late in the office. But every time I do so, I feel guilty all over again about Cara and feel a compulsion to tell him, though exactly what I'm not sure. Nothing happened—no, really, it didn't. There is nothing to tell, I say to myself, and although Joel would forgive me—because of Kitty he has no choice, after all—but I'm not so sure that Becky would.

The thing is, I believe Joel when he says that he never fancied her as much as he fancies me. And I know that I will never love anybody like I love him. He has to put up with my irritability as the flipside to that fiery redhead stuff that hooked him in the first place, just as I have had to learn that laid-back charm is not always a good quality. Maybe all relationships are like this—the good can become bad if you let it, it can go either way.

I bumped into Daisy the other day, who had lost a ton of weight since I'd last seen her. I asked her if she'd been working out and got the predictable answer about not being arsed with that. No, she said, but she'd read a book that made her examine her eating habits. The hardest thing about losing all that weight, she told me, was writing a thorough list of all the reasons she over-ate. "It took me weeks," she said. "I was knackered by the end of it." By some alchemy, the mere writing of this document allowed her to shed weight almost effortlessly. I was skeptical, but now I think that Joel and I have done the same. It is as if by writing the list—our affidavit of equal parenting, as Becky dubbed it—we got halfway there. Joel and Becky kept asking me what I had hoped to achieve with The List V1.0 and I never knew the answer, but I do now. I thought that by writing down all our domestic problems, I'd cure them. And perhaps, in the end, I did.

If I'm making it sound easy, then I don't mean to. I still want to kill him, frequently. I still do what he calls "the sigh," tell him that life would be easier as a single parent and say things like "I don't mind you staying out late at all, I'm thrilled to do their bedtime alone for the third night in a row." I still say "I don't have time for this," before realizing that actually I do; despite being busier at work, I do have time for lots of things like sex and courtesy that I always thought I didn't. And he still throws leftover food into the sink and puts saucepans that have had only boiling water in them into the dishwasher.

Daisy's miraculous diet has taught me another tip. When she wants to eat a cake or biscuit, she says, she decides to wait five minutes. When that five minutes are up, she realizes that if she had decided to eat it, it would be finished by now. Somehow this is enough to stop her every time she reaches for the biscuit tin. I'm the same. I force myself not to splurge on criticism but to wait a few moments, by which time I find that gentle recourse to the document on the fridge door usually suffices.

No, it's not easy, this new life, but then it's not hard like the period after I found out about Kitty and that Joel had been tampering with The List. We were so frozen in fear and loneliness that I had begun to feel nostalgic for the aggression and irritation we'd been suffering before.

"You've not once told me I'm hormonal," I say.

"That's because you haven't been," he replies. "Have you forgiven me?"

"Yes, I have. Have you forgiven me?"

"So you see that you've got something that needs forgiving?"

"Of course."

He smiles. "Then you are absolutely forgiven." We kiss, and not just because it tells us to on the fridge door.

*　　　*　　　*

We're walking across a wide open expanse just outside the city. Becky and Ursula have escaped the chaos of their house, the building site, to look after Rufus and Gabriel for the afternoon. Becky, bless her, takes every opportunity to facilitate our reconciliation, seeing us as a test bed for her mediation skills and theories. Joel has replaced his romantic gestures of yore with the far more endearing one of following every point on the new list. This morning's metaphorical bunch of white roses was him giving the boys breakfast and making sure that there was no remnant of it left on the worktops.

"I never knew how blissful it would be to walk at my own pace," I say to him.

"Without a chorus of 'Carry me.'"

"Or 'Are we nearly there?'"

"And 'Walks are so boooring.'"

We carry on without speaking for a few minutes. On walks, there's a joyous equality between silence and conversation. I'm so glad that "date nights" can be date days and that we are doing this rather than gulping down a restaurant meal and preparing a poisonous hangover. I never would have known that going for uninterrupted strolls would be one of the things I most missed when we had children.

Joel reaches out and takes my hand. I feel a jolt. It is more intimate than having sex. Anybody can do that, and we've been sticking to our weekly assignations. To stretch the comparison between the restoration of our marriage and weight loss, I've found that sex and going to the gym are similar in that the hardest thing is getting going, but it's always worth it once you've started.

People don't hold hands unless they are five or they really like each other. You don't hold hands with a one-night stand. Mitzi and Cara don't hold hands.

We walk on and it feels awkward at first. I want to wriggle away and immediately feel like adjusting my coat or scratching my nose. I miss the momentum that my solitary arm-swinging gives me. After a while, though, it feels as if he is propelling me forward and I him, that two arms connected can give you more energy than your own. We swing our arms together as though we have an imaginary child between them. We walk faster and faster until we begin to run down the hill into air that's on the turn of winter.

It feels as though we're hurtling into the future.

Acknowledgments

Arabella Stein has encouraged and guided me in writing this book ever since it was a one-sentence idea. She has reined in both my and Mary's madness; made me laugh; suggested important amendments and encouraged me when I've been disheartened. She is not only my agent, but a brilliant reader and friend.

Thanks too to Ben Fowler, Sandy Violette, Tessa Ingham and everyone else at Abner Stein.

I'm grateful to Carolyn Mays, Francesca Best, and Caryn Karmatz-Rudy for all their excellent editorial changes. Karen Kosztolnyik at Grand Central is a wonderful editor to exchange emails with, and thanks must also go to her colleagues Amanda Englander, Deb Futter, Leah Tracosas, Elly Weisenberg, and Jamie Raab.

Over the years, my children have been cared for and the piles of stuff minimized by Jackie Strawn, Debbie Perera and Renata Zakrocka. Thanks also to parents and teachers at Little Ark and Thornhill Primary School, especially the mothers who have shared their gripes as well as looking after my children. Our families are also on hand with generous offers of help, especially grandmothers Sylvia Hopkinson and Jenny Carruthers.

Thank you, David Barker, my "go-to muso," who created the new-baby playlist.

Acknowledgments

Bini Adams and Francis and Charlotte Hopkinson talked me through TV production and the various roles within it, as well as reading an early draft of the book.

Finally, thank you to William, Celia and Lydia Carruthers for all the ideas unwittingly contributed.